I0672673

Stars In Motion

Kay Hawkins

Starchasers Press

All rights reserved. No part of this book may be reproduced or transmitted in any form or by any means, electronic or mechanical, including photocopying, recording, or by any information storage and retrieval system, without written permission from the author. To contact the author, visit:

https://www.facebook.com/StachasersPress

Names, characters and incidents depicted in this book are products of the author's imagination or are used fictitiously. Any resemblance to actual events, organizations, or persons, living or dead, is entirely coincidental and beyond the intent of the author or the publisher.

Cover art by Leah Keeler

Copyright © 2023 by Kay Hawkins

Published by Starchasers Press

All rights reserved.

First Paperback Edition: 978-1-989548-14-1

To Lorna Toolis
whose inspiration and encouragement meant a lot to me.
and
Luke Maynard
our struggles make chasing stars all that more important.

Contents

Chapter 1

"What do you mean my request to stay another year on Catillion was denied?!"

Skyler slammed his tablet down onto the desk. The dark-haired, cat-eared, gray-uniformed man sitting behind the posting's desk glanced at the cracked tablet on the desk.

"Cadet Therris, I'm sorry to inform you, but I just issue the notices. I don't make the decisions. According to your file this order came from Fleet Admiral Cane. If you want to complain to anyone about this, it's him." The Catillion man typed in a few things on his computer. "He's in his office for the next three days. I would take it up with him. Do you want directions to his office?"

"No, thanks. I know where I'm going." Skyler got up and headed towards the office.

He went past the secretary and barged into Cane's office. "Cane! Why was my extension rejected?"

Cane spoke into his computer screen. "I'm sorry, Admiral Chamberlain. I must go. I have more pressing matters to deal with. We will finish this later." He turned off the computer screen and changed focus to the pouting cadet. "Skyler, you know I care about you and am willing to help you in any way possible, but you can't just barge in here whenever you want. Now please repeat, what is the problem?"

Skyler took a seat and showed Cane his newly cracked tablet. "This, sir, is my problem. I sent in a request to extend my posting on Catillion, and I was rejected. Postings office told me you were the one who put the order in for me to return to Earth. Why, sir?"

"Yes, that is true." Cane picked up the tablet and looked it over. "How did you break this? They're made of two sheets of Diamondium. You can't break that."

Skyler rolled his eyes. "I just slammed it on the table. Maybe it's a defect, I don't know. What I want to know is why am I being sent back to Earth? I have friends and a boyfriend here."

Cane hit a few buttons on the cracked table and opened another e-mail. "Because you have been given a promotion, Cadet. Remember this summer when I asked you if you wanted to stay on as a cadet or graduate early—"

Skyler's eyes widened. "Wait, I have to go back to Earth because I chose not to graduate?"

"If you would let me finish!" Cane shouted. "Skyler, you want to be a captain and you won't settle for anything less. I know you don't want to go back to Earth even though the base has been reopened. But Skyler, you can't keep running. When you first applied to stay on Catillion last year, if I would have known it was to avoid your mother, I would have stopped you. I get that you don't get along with your family, but you can't run from your problems forever."

Skyler rubbed his face. "You know as soon as I go back to Earth my UGF number will be listed on the Earth directory, my mother will get it, and she will start harassing me, asking me to help her take care of the little spawn."

Cane groaned. "You won't have the time. She might get your number, but like I said, you got a promotion, so you won't have the time to see her."

Raising an eyebrow. "What do you mean promotion, sir? I'm a cadet."

"You are, but in a few days, when we get back to Earth you will be my apprentice. You will still be expected to go to your classes, which will be reduced, but when you're not there you're following me around."

Skyler scratched his head in confusion. "But I don't want to be a Fleet Admiral! I want to be a Captain."

"You can still be a Captain, and you can stay as a Captain for your entire life if you want to. But if you don't apprentice with a Fleet Admiral at some point in your career, you will never have the opportunity to become one. I know you don't want to go to war, and with your scores and training you should be graduating.

There's not much more for you to learn in a textbook. So why not spend a year with me?"

Skyler let out a deep breath. "I guess you have a point. It would be fun."

"I know you were explained this when you joined. The only ones who really get the full seven-year education are the ones who picked two divisions to study. You only picked one, so classes are running a bit thin for you."

Skyler brushed his hair back. "Well, I could take the classes over again."

Cane shook his head. "Not with your grades. You're in the advanced category; you have passed everything with flying colors. We only make cadets who barely passed or failed repeat. There is work for you to do but it's light. Unless you chose to be a working cadet, like Michael is doing. Where the pay sucks but you're still learning."

"I get it, Cane. But if I were to become a working cadet in the command division, do you think I really would work good taking orders from somebody else?"

Cane covered his face. "You sound just like your father when you talk like that. Your Dad wanted all the control he could get when it came to work. He wanted to run a ship and the base. But you can't have both, so your dad kept his ship. But for the next year you will be taking orders from me. You will eat when I do. You will sleep when I do. You will not do anything on your own unless I give you permission. I know this will be hard for you, but you will thank me for this one day."

Skyler looked down at his pants. "What about my, um you know, sex life?"

Cane coughed a little into his hand. "Oh, that. Well, from what I have seen it will drop significantly. You will still have some free time, but nowhere near the amount you have now."

"So where will I be staying when I get back to Earth?"

"You will be given a room in the officer's barracks and be on call 24/7. You may not spend much time there. You can also stay at my house and there is a back room in my office that's has a cot. That's where I spend most of my time sleeping. I'll put an extra cot in there for you."

Skyler rubbed his head. "So, my social life going to go out the window and I get to share a room with you. How's my drinking situation going to go?"

Cane pointed to a half-drunk bottle of brandy on his desk. "That may increase, but you're not allowed to be drunk on duty, understand?"

Skyler smirked. "I think I can live with that." He reached out to grab the bottle.

Cane took the bottle away before Skyler could grab it and put it back into the drawer. "Not right now. You must get packing. You have been here a year, I'm sure you have lots of stuff."

Skyler got up out of his seat. "Yes sir, and I have a few last minutes going away gifts to get."

"Go enjoy your last three days."

Skyler saluted Cane and made his way out of the office.

Skyler was strolling down the halls making his way back to his dorm, watching his feet, when he felt the bump of another person. He jerked up. "Oops sorry..." He saw the person was none other than Kax. "Hey Kax, how are you doing?"

With a red face and narrowed eyes, she replied. "I'm not in a good mood Skyler, watch what you say."

He stopped and appeared attentive. "What is the matter?"

She rubbed her forehead and let out a deep breath. "My application to go to Sagitarion for advanced flight training was rejected. Instead, I was sent back to Earth to be a patrol pilot. Damn, that is degrading. I don't want to watch out for attacks I want to be flying Galaxy Class ships."

He placed his arm around her shoulder. "Did they give you a reason?"

She rested her head on Skyler's shoulder. "Admiral Hamilton said because of the incident with Commodore Kreeve, they don't trust sending me to work alone with another male instructor."

"Really?" His face scrunched. "That was the reason they gave you? I mean that's dumb."

"Tell me about it," she said, breaking the hug, "So what's your assignment?"

Skyler's hands shook and he took a deep breath. "Well, I'm going back to Earth...to be Cane's apprentice."

Her eyes bulged. "Wow! You got the job as Cane's apprentice! That's one of the best jobs you can get, lucky bastard." She playfully punched his arm.

He laughed and pushed her back slightly. "I guess I am. I didn't ask for the job, I was just chosen."

"Will you be moving back to the cabin?"

He placed his hands on his chin. "I totally forgot about that. But no, I won't, they're giving me a room in the officers' barracks or I will be staying with Cane. You can have the keys to my car. I won't have much time to use it."

She smiled. "Thanks. Come on, let's go get lunch. I'm sure Michael and Perry are waiting for us."

"I got a better idea. Let's skip lunch with them, go shopping and pick lunch up in the city. We don't have classes today, and I want to get a going-away gift for Perry."

"Oh right, Perry is permanently staying with Dr. Fogg. I'm going to miss him. Okay, let's do that. A day out just as friends."

"Yup, just friends," He placed his arm around her as they walked out of the building.

Skyler opened the door to his room. Stepping inside, his eyes widened when he saw Perry sitting on his bed in the room. "Perry, whatcha doing here? I thought you were living full time in the greenhouse."

Perry looked up from his tablet. "I am, I just had to come get a few things I left behind. Are you staying for another year?"

Skyler closed the door and sat on his own bed putting the paper bag down on the ground. "No, I'm going to be Cane's apprentice so I'm leaving in two days, going back to Earth."

Perry scoffed. "Lucky! I mean, not the going back to Earth but your job that's hard to get. You do realize that there are only three Fleet Admirals, and they only pick an apprentice about once every ten years? They could pick one more often like Davis does but it's not a high demand job. Once you complete the year you get put on the list of who to choose from when the Fleet Admiral dies. And they can choose anyone, cadet, or officer with command training..."

"Stop it Perry, I know." Skyler wiped the sweat off his brow. "You always have these long stories of things I already know."

Perry's legs fidgeted. "Sorry, I'm just excited for you."

Skyler bent down and looked in his shopping bag. "Well, Perry, I thought since I am leaving and don't know when I will see you again, I thought I would get you a few going away gifts."

Perry's face lit up. "You didn't have to. Thank you, so what did you get me?"

Skyler pulled out a small rectangle box. "I have never bought a guy jewelry, but when I saw it, I had to get it for you." He handed it to Perry.

Perry opened the box and his eyes widened. He lifted a small sliver chain and at the end was a large oval. He opened it to see a side pocket covered in glass that was easy to remove. "No way dude you got me a seed locket! And it is sliver! Dude, you are so awesome!"

Skyler hide his blushing face. "No problem. Come on, there are other gifts."

Perry put down the locket on the bed and focused his eyes on Skyler.

Skyler handed him a black bag. "The item in here is for practice."

Perry opened the bag. "You got me a Fleshlight?"

"In case your Squallite girlfriend isn't around and you need something." Skyler winked.

"Ugh, sure, whatever you say." Perry laughed it off.

Skyler then pulled out a little baggy. "And here are some mixed Catillion seeds."

Perry got up off his bed and crossed the room to Skyler. He gave him a hug. "You are sure an awesome friend. I'm going to miss you."

Skyler tussled Perry's hair and wiggled out of the hug. "Ya, I'm going to miss you too. You have been a good friend."

Perry sat next to Skyler. "Hey, we will still have time to video chat. Maybe one day I'll join your crew, Captain."

Skyler put his arm around Perry. "If you do, I'll make you clean the poop deck."

"You know our ships don't have poop decks, that's an old-fashioned thing."

"It's not going to stop me."

Perry laughed and pushed Skyler away. "You sure know how to ruin a good moment, don't you?"

Skyler smirked. "That's what makes me so awesome." He looked at the clock. "Hey Perry, it's getting late. Want to go to the bar and get a few drinks?"

"I really should just get my things and head back."

"Perry, Dr. Fogg knows how important having a social life is. And who knows when we will see each other again? Let's have one more night of fun, okay?"

Perry's lips twisted. "Okay, I guess one last night can't hurt."

Skyler got up off the bed, went over to the closet and started getting dressed. "Oh, hey, call Kax, Kandice and Clyde. We got to make this a night to remember."

Perry smiled and pulled out his phone. "You betcha!"

Chapter 2

Skyler awoke in the morning holding Kandice in his arms. He moved back in confusion, tying to remember the events from last night. As she began to wake up, he remembered. They were all at the bar having a fun night when he made the announcement that he wasn't staying on Catillion another year like he had planned. He was going to have to say goodbye to Perry, Clyde, and Kandice. Clyde and Kandice were shocked by the short notice and she requested that they have a threesome for Skyler's going-away gift.

Last year Skyler came to terms with his bisexuality and asked Kandice to help him find a guy. She had hooked him up with her former lover Clyde. Skyler had been in a relationship before with Kandice but broke off their casual relationship because it made Kax uncomfortable. Clyde was active with both Skyler and Kandice. Kandice had been wanting a threesome with the two guys all summer. Out of respect for Kax, Skyler had always said no. But last night at the bar after his announcement and Kandice's suggestion Kax gave him her blessing. Not that Skyler needed her permission to sleep with whoever he wanted, but after the events of last year he felt it best if Kandice was on a conditional basis.

"Morning, hot stuff," Kandice said, curling into Skyler more.

He kissed her on the head, "Morning, pretty lady."

Skyler felt a thrust from behind him. "You did great last night." Clyde kissed the back of Skyler's shoulder.

Skyler rolled over to face Clyde. The golden blond, muscular, blue-eyed man brushed Skyler's hair back. "I'm going to miss you."

Skyler had grown fond of the blonde Catillion. Even if this relationship was never meant to last, Clyde was the first man he had let himself get close to. "We knew this day would come. I just thought we had more time."

Clyde gave Skyler a charming smile. "It was great while it lasted."

Skyler kissed the muscular large nosed man. He rubbed his shoulders. "I'm really going to miss you."

"Hey, don't worry about it. I'll be here if you ever come back to Catillion. Maybe one day I will visit you on Earth."

Kandice rolled over. "Don't worry, Skyler. I will keep him company for you."

"You two have been so great to me this last year. I really enjoyed my summer with you two." Skyler said.

Kandice began kissing Skyler's neck. "Do you think we have time to go again?"

Just then Kax opened the door. "Sorry to break you guys up, but Skyler is needed in the greenhouse. Also, Sis, I need you to give me a ride up to the house. I got to pack up my things."

Skyler kissed Clyde and Kandice before getting out of the bed. As he was getting dressed, he faced Clyde. "I'm here for a bit more. I will try and see you again before I leave."

At the greenhouse Perry and Dr. Fogg were waiting from Skyler. "What's going on? I thought all this plant stuff was done."

Dr. Fogg handed Skyler a box. "It is. Well sort of. Michael is doing all the paperwork on Earth, and Perry and I are doing all the growing and research. But before you go I need you to deliver this package to Michael."

Skyler examined the box. He remembered Dr. Fogg's past about being a smuggler and delivering poisonous plants to the colonies. "Um, what's in it? Can't you just get Perry to teleport it to Earth? Why do I have to deliver it?"

Dr. Fogg's eyes bulged, and he gripped the box. "Skyler, this is a living plant! You cannot put it through the transporter! You will kill it!"

Perry rushed over and gently took the box from Dr. Fogg. "James, remember Skyler is not like us he doesn't know these things. He meant no harm to the plants."

Dr. Fogg took a deep breath. "You're right, Perry. I'm glad I have you. Skyler, these plants are alive. The transporter cannot properly replicate them on the other side. I could have these sent with a courier, but they are very picky, and given my record, they will tear them apart. So I have Perry here with me to show you that they are not to cause harm to anyone. These are just a new set of seedlings for another of the same plant we have been working with. I want Michael to be able to work with something there on Earth and help grow these there instead of here."

Perry opened the box and showed Skyler the inside. "Skyler, I grew these plants myself. James didn't touch them at all. I will go over the scans with you if you want?"

"No, it's fine. I believe you." Skyler picked up the box and turned towards the door. Perry followed him.

When they left the greenhouse, Skyler turned to Perry. "Perry, you are my friend. I need to know the truth. Are these plants safe?"

Perry nodded. "They are. I was going to make a trip to Earth myself to deliver them, but when I heard you were going to Earth, I suggested you. Skyler, I would not give you anything that could hurt your career or contribute to James's record. You're my best friend."

"Thanks Perry, I trust you."

Perry paused and stared at Skyler for a moment. Then leaned in and gave him a kiss on the lips.

"What was that for? I thought you said you didn't like me that way?" Skyler smirked.

"I don't, but I care about you and this is really important to me, and I'm never going to be able to do what Clyde does for you, but I wanted to kiss you because it was like my going-away gift to you and to show you how much this means to me."

Perry was the first male crush Skyler had ever had. Last year, Skyler told Perry how he felt. Perry could not return Skyler's feelings the same way. They remained good friends but Skyler still had that crush. This kiss told Skyler just how important these plants and their friendship was. Skyler leaned in and kissed Perry one more time. "Thank you, my friend, and I will make sure these plants get there safely."

Chapter 3

Skyler smacked his alarm clock onto the floor, breaking it into a dozen pieces. "Shit, I didn't mean to do that." He rubbed his eyes and checked the time on his tablet. "At least I'm on time. I got to get going." He rolled over and shook Clyde. "Hey Clyde, time to get up."

"Morning already?" He rubbed his eyes and sat up. "I had had an amazing time with you last night. I'm really going to miss you."

He changed into his cadet uniform. "Me too. This summer was great." He put his bag over his shoulder and grabbed the other suitcase. Once Clyde was ready, they headed towards the door.

Kax walked in with her backpack on. "Oh Skyler, Clyde, you're dressed. I guess you're ready to go?"

"You bet we are." Clyde smiled, making his way out of the room.

"Skyler, is that all you are carrying? I thought you owned more than that?"

He locked the door. "I do, but I sent it ahead last night, so it is already on the ship. This is just a few things I didn't want to send ahead." He scanned around. "Hey, where's Perry?"

Kax followed Skyler down the hall. "Perry went ahead. He will say goodbye to you at the shuttle."

"Well then, let's get going." Skyler rushed getting down to the ship. He wanted to say goodbye to his friends, not the academy.

When they got down there, Perry was standing on the platform.

Perry ran up and gave Skyler a hug. "I'm going to miss you man."

Skyler hugged back. "You're so emotional. I'm going to miss you too."

They broke the hug. Skyler noticed the sliver chain around Perry's neck. "You're actually wearing the locket."

Perry picked it up in his fingers. "Yeah, it's a seed locket, of course I'm going to use it. Also, because I'm working with seeds and plants, it is vital to my work. It is one piece of jewelry I can wear while in uniform."

Kax looked at Skyler. "Well at least it is more useful than that thing you have in your ear."

Skyler pointed to the gold ball in his left ear. "What you mean this? It's tradition I should have an earring and your sister said it make me look sexy."

Clyde cut in. "It's traditional and cute on you. I had a wonderful summer with you."

An announcement for boarding came on.

Kax gave Perry a hug. "I'm going to miss and your plants."

"Me too," Perry said, hugging Kax.

Cane came over to the group. "Skyler, I am going to have to get you to follow me."

Skyler frowned. "What do you mean, sir? what did I do?"

"Nothing. But we're not going to Earth. Your apprenticeship started and we must go to Skwoampan and we are on a time crunch. So come with me. I will need you to ride with me in my cabin."

"What about the plants I have for Michael?" Skyler asked.

"Give them to Kax, she's going to Earth." Skyler knelt and took the tray of plants out of his backpack. "Take care of them and I will see you soon."

She took the plants. "Have fun on your adventure."

Skyler's hand shook. "Okay sir, just one last goodbye."

Cane nodded. "Make it quick."

Skyler gave Perry a hug and whispered into his ear. "I will truly miss you."

Perry hugged a little tighter and whispered. "I know." Then broke the hug. He patted Skyler on the back. "Good luck, buddy."

They all gave Skyler a group hug. Clyde patted him in the back. "You have fun, you lucky bastard."

Kax went up to Skyler and surprisingly put her right hand around his neck and gave him a kiss.

His eyes widened and his heart fluttered. He put his hand on her shoulder and deeply kissed her back. When they broke the kiss, he asked, "what was that for?"

She tossed her hair. "Oh, it was just for good luck. Enjoy your apprenticeship."

He turned back as he walked away and waved. "I will."

Cane put his hand on Skyler's back. "Come on, we got to go." He walked with Skyler to the other platform and over to his private cabin. Cane showed his ID to the security guard and walked in.

Skyler handed his ID to the security guard.

The man in the black uniform with the red stripes looked at him.

Before he could say anything, Cane cut in. "He is my new apprentice."

The security guard addressed Cane. "Has he gone through all the necessary security checks?"

Cane shook his head. "No but, I know he is fine."

"Sir it is procedure that we do a full security scan on anyone before they ride in the same cabin with you."

"You can give him a pat down and search his bags once we are boarded, and that is an order. I trust this boy with my life."

The security guard nodded. "As you wish, sir." He then waved Skyler on.

Skyler walked into the cabin. He saw Cane sit in the back of the cabin, setting up paperwork on the round table.

The security guard closed the door of the cabin. He then tapped Skyler on the shoulder before he sat down. "Sorry, sir. I need to do this."

"It's all right, I understand." Skyler stood like a starfish while the security guard patted him down. Skyler looked around the cabin. It had a red shag carpet. The walls were oak in color. There was a half wall that divided the sitting area where Cane was in a maroon lounge seat next to two small round tables. There was a lounging area with a small bar fridge, more maroon loungers, a black leather ottoman and a holo-projector. There was a bathroom in a back room and a bar with a robot server next to it. He also saw a curtained area, and could see through the crack there was a futon.

The security guard finished patting Skyler, and turned back. "You're clear I. have to check your bags now."

Skyler handed the man his backpack and pointed to his suitcase. "There you go. Have fun looking. It's mostly clothes and my uniforms."

The security guard took his backpack. "Thank you for your cooperation. The Fleet Admiral must really trust you." He then got on one knee and emptied the contents of the bag onto the floor.

Skyler made his way over to the seat next to Cane. "So, what are you doing?"

Cane was focusing on his paperwork, and without looking at Skyler he slid over a pile of papers. "Read over that pile and sign it when done."

Skyler looked at the stack of papers. "What are these for?"

Cane didn't lose focus on his own pile of papers. "That's your agreement to be my apprentice, and all the duties you will be required to do. And some insurance forms. It's basically the same set of papers you signed when you joined."

"So where are we going?"

"Skwoampan. It is a swamplike planet and I need you to come with me." Cane said.

Skyler scratched his head. "I have never heard of this planet. Why are we going there?"

"It's not a Federation planet. But remember how told your father left a lot of unfinished business? And remember how I told you that I was going on vacation last year?"

Skyler nodded. "Yes, what does this have to do with me? You got your vacation."

Cane signed. "You're right. I did, and I went to Skwoampan as planned. But it was to finish something your father was meant to finish. Turns out as much as I made the effort to get there, they wanted your Dad. I told them the news and they said it had to be someone with the same DNA. You are his only living relative and son, so I got to get you started on finishing up his work."

"Wait, what? I don't understand. What kind of stuff did he leave behind? Am I really your apprentice, or was that an excuse to kidnap me?"

Cane laughed. "Skyler, I'm not kidnapping you. But this is a way that I can write off that you will be doing Federation work while leaving Federation space."

"Wait I have never left Federation territory in my life. Am I still safe with my passport? what happens to me if I only have Federation citizenship?"

"Nothing. Some places will require us to go through customs check and they check our papers. But this planet is primitive. We will take a shuttle down to the planet and be greeted. We are going to areas that are not protected by the Federation, but I assure you this planet is safe. Stick with mE and don't touch anything and you will be fine." Cane said.

Skyler slouched down on the couch. "So, then what are we going to be doing for the next while? How long is this trip?"

"Twelve hours, which is quicker since we are leaving from Catillion. As for what we are going to do while we wait, you have paperwork to fill out, then you need to read the briefing then start practicing the words for the ceremony."

"What do you mean 'ceremony,' Cane?" Skyler asked. "What am I doing?"

Cane sighed, "This is all in the briefing but I will give you the short of it. Do you remember in your father's journals a story about Skwoampan, the swamp planet?"

Skyler paused, thinking back. "Kinda, I don't think he wrote much about it? It was one of his first contact stories."

"Yes, that is correct. They are a planet full of resources and your father was the one to make first contact with them. We started a trade deal, but they did not want to join the Federation. They wanted to keep their peaceful original ways. The Federation agreed to this. They did not want any of our technology but were willing to share with us, so now we leave them alone while they provide us with some goods. There are a few from their planet who did want to come, with us and we take them with open arms. So why are we going to this place now? It is the anniversary of the first contact. 30 years and we have kept our word. They have a gift for your Dad thanking him, and it must be claimed by him. I thought it could have been anyone on the crew but according to them it must be his DNA. The swamp goo on the planet is alive and they are all connected to it and it always remembers. So, we need to go and claim it, then decide what to do with it."

"Wait, so this thing is just a gift? Why is it so important? Why do we have to claim it? Couldn't my dad have picked it up before he died?" Skyler was confused.

"I'm not sure what the item is, but what I can tell you is that it took all this time to make. It is a powerful item made as a thank you for holding the treaty. If the treaty would have been broken, it would have stopped forming. But the problem is it must be claimed with Therris DNA and it has some kind of life force that will die if not claimed soon. I'm not sure what type of power it has, but the Federation is interested in it. But they know it will be yours and not try to take it. It will be your choice what to do with it."

"Okay Cane, this is all weird to me. I guess I will see how it goes." Skyler replied.

Cane handed Skyler a stack of papers. "Get reading."

Skyler sat down on the couch across from Cane. He placed the papers on the table and went over to the mini fridge. He pulled out a beer.

"What are you doing?" Cane asked.

"Beer helps me think. Can't I have one?"

"You can, but no getting drunk you're not allowed to be drunk on the job."

Skyler cracked open his beer and sat down looking at the stack of papers. "Don't worry. I know my limits."

Chapter 4

Skyler woke up in the morning on the couch rubbing his head. "Ow...where are we?"

Cane tossed Skyler his dress uniform. "We have arrived. You passed out on the couch last night. But we have arrived on the planet and you need to be in your dress uniform."

Skyler stood up. "Wait how come we need to be in dress uniform when we're not on a Federation planet?"

Cane groaned. "Because you are an officer, and you still need to wear it for all formal occasions. Understood?"

Skyler started to get dressed. "Fine, whatever you say, Cane." Skyler stood and rubbed his temples.

Cane reached over and handed Skyler a pill. "Take this. You appear to be in pain from that hangover."

Skyler took the pill. "Ugh, I hate hangover pills. Michael always tries to give these to me."

"If you keep drinking like you do, you will need them. you must keep your brain functioning to the max when on missions. Do you understand?" Cane watched Skyler take the pill. "When we get back to Earth, I will get you a prescription for these."

Skyler followed Cane off the ship. The planet was a giant swamp. The ground was muddy and the air smelled like decay and algae. Skyler quickly plugged his nose.

Cane whacked Skyler's hand down. "Don't do that, it's offensive. Just try not to think of the smell. You will have to get used to it."

Skyler groaned, trying to remember everything that he read last night.

There was a big bog in front of them and out of the bog appeared a green amphibious alien. The creature rose, then stood in front of them wearing its ceremonial clothes. "Ah, Cane, you have arrived. It is nice to see you again." The alien sniffed the air and smiled. "Ah, and you brought the boy. Captain Therris's son is here. Good, just in time. Things were becoming a little overdue."

Skyler stared at the green lobster-eyed alien. He was astonished. This was the first time he had ever seen a living creature like this.

The alien held out his froglike hand, "It is nice to meet you. You must Levi Therris's son."

Skyler stared at the seemingly slimy hand.

Cane elbowed Skyler in the side and whispered to him. "Don't be rude to Lord Ackle."

Skyler took Lord Ackle's hand. "It is nice to meet you. My name is Skyler."

Lord Ackle turned his attention to Cane. "Did you bring the amulet?"

Cane pulled a glowing cylinder amulet out of his pocket and handed it over. Lord Ackle took the amulet and placed it around Skyler's neck. "Come now, only Skyler. Follow me." Lord Ackle turned and began to descend into the swamp.

Skyler looked back at Cane. "I can't..."

Cane waved his hand. "It's not a swamp underneath. You will be fine, just go."

Skyler hesitantly followed lord Ackle into the swamp, worried about his uniform and the smell. As he held his breath and ducked his head into the brackish water, he saw that the swamp was just cover. This planet had an advanced underground city, and below the water he passed through a shield of some kind and into a vast world of breathable air. Skyler's feet found a floor of white stone, and he descended into a white stone building. There were glowing lights coming from the stones themselves that lit up the entire place. There were many other beings walking around. Not all of them were the same race as lord Ackle. Some who were more humanoid and some more like amphibians but all of them having different shades of green and blue skin. Skyler ignored the people and the continued to follow Lord Ackle down the long hallway. When they got to the end of the hallway there was a large grey door. Lord Ackle pulled out a key from his pocket and unlocked the door. The large doors automatically opened, and closed behind them as they entered the large room. The room had a fountain in the center of the room and a large chair behind it. Along the walls there were small deposit boxes.

Lord Ackle took Skyler to the back of the room to one of the deposit boxes. "Therris, this is the box I wish you to open. Could you please use your key?"

"What key?" Skyler responded.

"The one around your neck." Lord Ackle pointed to the cylinder around Skyler's neck.

"Oh, this thing." Skyler took it off and saw a circular opening and placed his cylinder into the hole. The box opened, and Lord Ackle took the contents and handed Skyler a piece of paper and then a small bag of stuff.

Skyler looked at the writing on the paper. He recognized the handwriting but still didn't understand what it was. "Um, why did my dad leave this note?"

"Instructions your father wrote out the words to say, so that he didn't forget." Lord Ackle closed the box. "Come now, and follow me."

Skyler stared at the letter for a moment. The reality of what he was doing was finally starting to hit him. He didn't understand what was going on, but he knew that his father did something very important for these people and that this was something that meant a lot to both sides. Skyler followed Lord Ackle over to the fountain.

Lord Ackle threw the bag into the fountain in the middle of the room. He looked at Skyler. "The words in the letter—please read them out loud."

Skyler with a lack of confidence started to read them out very quietly.

"Louder!" Lord Ackle said.

Skyler read the words "Roker Moker Gooter Sooter." He stopped. The water in the fountain was starting to bubble but that was it.

"Keep going! Repeat them louder and louder with more feeling!" Lord Ackle shouted.

In a panic, Skyler followed the instructions. The water in the fountain bubbled more and more. It began to change colors. Finally when Skyler thought he couldn't take any more, a small brown box came out from the water.

Skyler stopped reading and reached out to grab the box once the water stopped bubbling. He took the box out of the water and stepped back to examine it.

Lord Ackle's eyes were on Skyler.

"What is it?" Skyler asked.

"It's yours. Thank you for helping our world stay a secret," Lord Ackle said.

Skyler stared at the box. He had an uneasy feeling. He was curious to open it. But he could feel a great power coming from it. It didn't feel right to open this box right now. He turned to Lord Ackle. "Should I open it?"

"It is yours to do with as you wish."

Skyler examined the box. "Do you know what is inside?"

"No, I don't."

"Should I open it now?" Skyler asked.

"That would be your choice, not mine. Do whatever you wish. I need to get back to work. When you are ready, you can go out those grey doors and Leon will be off to the side. He is taking care of some diplomatic business. It was nice to see you, Skyler," Lord Ackle said before vanishing.

Skyler stood confused for a moment, unsure what to do with the box. He was given a strange box, and where did Lord Ackle go? *People don't just vanish...or do they?* He thought. His dad used to write about strange occurrences. Maybe it was just one of them. This might be his first taste of the unexplained questions of space. With nowhere to put the box, he held it in his hand and walked out of the room. He closed the grey doors behind him and headed back into the white stone complex, passing into what looked like an underground shopping mall. He checked his pocket. *Damn, I forgot my wallet, it must be on the shuttle. Oh well, I guess I will just have to go find Cane then.* He turned to his right and followed the directions that Lord Ackle had given him.

At a desk in the long hallway, there was a secretary—an amphibian-like humanoid of indeterminate gender. "Leon is just through those doors," the secretary said. "He told me to let you in. He is just finishing up some paperwork."

"Uh, thanks. But how did you know I was looking for Leon?" Skyler, asked making his way to the door.

"Simple, we don't get many of your race here, or people in that uniform. Enjoy your time."

"Ya, uh, thanks." Skyler opened the door. There was a large round purple table in the middle of the room. Cane was sitting across from some other various amphibious aliens. A more humanoid one with green skin was sitting next to Cane quietly. Skyler walked over and took the other seat next to Cane.

"So, I think we have come to a deal here." Cane pointed to the boy beside him. "Groakie will come back with me and join the United Galactic Forces, and we will not pressure you for any more recruits for the next five years unless you contact us."

Skyler looked at Groakie and waved. Groakie remained serious.

The leader on the other side of the table slid over a stone tablet to Cane. Cane took the tablet and with a small chisel like pen etched his name into the stone. Cane passed it to Groakie for him to do the same before sliding it back to the leader.

When the meeting was done Cane turned in his seat to Skyler. "So, Skyler, how did it go?"

Skyler tapped the box on the table. "It went well. I got this box."

Cane stared at the box. "Did you open it?"

Skyler shook his head. "Not yet."

Cane nodded his head and pointed to Groakie. "Skyler, I would like you to meet Groakie. He is our recruit. He will be coming back with us to Earth."

Groakie held out his hand. "It is nice to meet you Skyler."

Skyler was hesitant to take his hand, worried that it might be slimy. But he did and was relieved that it wasn't. "It's nice to meet you too, Groakie."

"Well then, since all our business is done, we should head back," Cane said, packing up his files. "It is a long trip back to Earth."

They all got up and headed towards the shuttle.

Chapter 5

Kax walked down the hall to her class. She entered the control room to report in for duty. She took her tablet over the lady at the control desk.

Michael smiled. "Well then I wish Skyler the best of luck."

A greying haired woman took her tablet and glared. "Cadet Kax Tillion, you have been assigned to patrol pilot." She looked up at Kax. "It's nice to see you again."

Kax's eyes widened when she realized who she was talking to. "Um Mrs. Therris, I thought you retired? And were in the other fleet."

Sandy Roux narrowed her eyes. "It's Commodore Roux now. I'm retired, but because the base is being reopened, they asked me to come back part time to help. I didn't realize I would be working with you."

Kax clenched her fist. She got an uneasy feeling in her stomach. "Well, I'm just a patrol pilot. I can't see how we would be seeing much of each other."

Sandy put the tablet down. "If I wasn't semi-retired, I would be the one working the radar desk, then you would see more. But good thing I'm not. I will just be the one you sign in and sign out with every day, and will double check your daily findings."

Kax frowned. "Aren't you with Judson's fleet? Why would you be around with me? I'm in Cane's fleet."

Sandy let out a disgruntled sigh. "You're a working cadet and a pilot so you are with a mixed group. Some of the people you are working with will be from Davis's fleet and Judson's. I'm not going to hold anything against you while you are working but be warned I don't like you for several reasons, so don't talk to me and everything will be fine. Understood?"

Kax quickly nodded her head. "Yes Mrs. Therris."

Sandy snarled. "Commodore Roux, don't you dare call me Therris."

Kax nervously replied. "I'm sorry. I won't do it again."

Sandy hit a few buttons the tablet and handed it back. "If you want to get on my good side, you could always give me my son's new number."

Kax took the tablet. "I don't think Skyler would appreciate that."

"I thought you would say that. Enjoy your patrol of the garbage dump."

Kax's jaw dropped. "Why did I get that? I'm qualified to do so much more."

Sandy smirked. "Yes, but there is no place for whores here. And besides someone must, shall we say, take out the trash."

Kax held back the urge the slam the table over her head. "I'm not a whore," she said, and made her way to work.

Another Catillion walked up beside her, smiling. "Hey, so Commodore Roux doesn't like you either?"

She looked at the dark ginger Catillion next to her. "What reason does she have to hate you?"

He laughed. "She hates everyone. I don't know why she is back at work."

"I have no idea either, she has a baby at home to watch."

The other Catillion frowned. "She had a kid at her age? I thought she was just gaining weight before her retirement."

Kax laughed. "That would have been better then what did come, out according to Skyler."

He typed in a few things on the screen at her post. "Who's Skyler?"

Kax paused. "Oh, Skyler Therris, that's her other son. He's just a year younger than me."

"Hmm I have worked with her for the past 5 years and she has never mentioned him. But then she didn't brag about being pregnant either. I'm just the guy who works at the control station. I should introduce myself I'm Officer Baily, Rex Baily."

She smiled. "I'm cadet, wait I guess since I'm working, I'm Petty Officer Kax Tillion."

His eyes widened. "Are you by any chance Karmantha Tillion's daughter?"

She smiled. "Did you know her?"

He shook his head. "I'm not that old, I'm only 30. But my dad worked with her back when she was on the *Aquarius,* he was her navigator."

Kax tossed her hair. "Wow, that's so cool. *Aquarius* was one of her first postings."

He looked at the clock. "I would love to keep talking but we have work to do. How about after work we go and get some drinks?"

She smiled. "Ya, that would be great."

He handed her a helmet. "Enjoy your patrol."

She took the helmet. "You know I will," Kax said sarcastically then put her helmet on. She climbed up into the cockpit and got ready to fly.

Michael broke from his meditation in the morning to a message on his tablet. 'Officer Jones, please report to engineering for your new job posting.' Michael played with his hair. *This makes no sense. I have been working with Grey all summer. What has changed?*

Michael made his way down to Engineering.

There was a ten-foot-tall Squallite sitting at the desk. "Name and rank?"

"Officer second class Michael Majerik Jones," he said pridefully.

The dark haired Squallite looked down at Michael. "Your file says you're only six foot five. Are you sure you're a Squallite? You seem a bit short."

Michael frowned. "My dad wasn't a tall one either. I'm sorry I am not taller, sir."

The Squallite looked at him curiously. "Your dad's Sam Rajerik Jones. He is seven feet. I have never seen a Squallite under seven feet tall."

Michael sighed. "Is there a point to all of this, sir? I have been working with Grey all summer. Why am I being transferred?"

"You graduated, and Grey has been transferred. You're an engineer, not doing your cadet stuff anymore," the man said. "The section you have been assigned to doesn't have the bottom controls. It just has the top ones. I'm worried you are not tall enough to work in this area."

Michael frowned. He knew that the reason for this transfer was someone saw he was a Squallite on his file, and wasn't going to let him advance in the inventing department. "Well then, get me a stool."

The man shook his head. "You need to move around too much for that to work. Would you mind taking a seat while I call the higher ups and ask what to do with you?"

Michael groaned. "If that's what it is going to take." He walked over to a nearby seat and sat down. *Damn. I wonder how everyone else's day is going.*

He sat alone in the waiting room for a while watching the minutes on the clock tick. He wondered if they would ever find him a job that wasn't on the front lines.

Two hours had passed when the tall Squallite came over to him. "Good news Officer Jones, we have found you a place of work. I'm not sure if you will like it, but it's the best we can do right now."

His hands shook, *I hope this is good news.*

The man continued. "We're assigning you to the patrol pilot maintenance."

Oh, hey that's where Kax works. He got up and smiled. "Well, it's not the best job but I can do it, thank you sir."

The man shook Michael's hand. "Do good at it and it will be permanent, but right now you are just there temporary."

Michael shrugged. "As long as I'm not on the front lines I'm happy, sir."

The man smiled. "That's the spirit." He patted Michael on the back as he walked away.

Michael made his way over to the aircraft hangar and looked for the patrol station. *There doesn't seem to be spot for maintenance. I'll just go over to the front desk and ask where I am supposed to check in.*

He walked up to the front desk; he noticed the lady sitting at the desk looked familiar.

She looked up at him. "Hello, is there is there anything I can help you with?"

When he said her dark brown eyes, he knew exactly who she was and froze. "I thought you retired?"

She narrowed her eyes. "Do I know you?"

He nodded. "I don't think we have ever been formally introduced but I have heard about you, I am Michael Jones, your son's old roommate. If I have it correct that you are Sandy... Roux?"

She nodded. "Yes, that's me. I didn't realize they were mixing the Squallites with the rest of the people nowadays, but you electric bugs are so pushy. I hope my son put you in your place."

He clenched his fist. "I don't have time to explain to you my relationship with your son. I have a job to do. I have been assigned the mechanic for the patrol craft. Where do I sign in?"

"Skyler is into men now. Or was it more of a dominance thing?" she asked, looking Michael up and down.

He glared at her. "Neither. We do nothing of the sort. Now where do I sign in?"

She got an awful grin on her face. "I'm human and you are a Squallite. It's my word against yours. I want my son's number, or I will report you and say you were harassing me."

Michael rolled his eyes; *I see why Skyler hates her.* He groaned. "You do realize he doesn't want to talk to you, right?"

She glared at him. "I have a 1-year-old at home. I have a babysitter right now watching him. Skyler's help would be greatly welcomed."

Michael knew how much that was the last thing Skyler would ever want to do. "He's not a babysitter. He is..." Michael paused. "He is Cane's apprentice."

Sandy's eyes filled with a boiling rage. She stood up got out from behind her desk and rushed out of there.

"Shit, did I say the wrong thing?" Michael said out loud to himself.

"No, you didn't. I think it was just the right thing," came an old scruffy voice behind him.

Michael jerked around to see a white haired Squallite in an engineering jump-suit. "Excuse me, who are you?"

The man smiled. "I'm the maintenance guy around here and you are my new assistant. The name is Roderick. And I have worked with Sandy since the days of Captain Therris. She is bitter and never changes. I'm glad her son is Cane's apprentice. She can't pull him out of the academy now. Cane has finally won."

Michael frowned. "Cane won? What are you talking about?"

The man smiled. "Once Captain Therris died, Cane took over as Skyler's father figure, she pushed him away, and they have always competed over who is going to raise Skyler, even if Sandy wasn't the best mother. And now he is the Fleet Admiral's apprentice. Nothing can take that away from Skyler. She can bitch and scream all she wants but she has no power."

Chapter 6

While on the shuttle Groakie was sleeping in the back, Cane handed Skyler a tablet and a stack of papers. Skyler was lounging on the couch with his feet up and a beer in his hand. "What are these for?"

Cane looked up for a second. "They have to do with the meeting. We are going to the war and the reopening of the base."

"Okay, I get it." Skyler continued to read his paperwork.

The security officer came over to them. "Fleet Admiral Cane. I would like to inform you I have found nothing suspicious on the boy or in his luggage. With the limited security check I have done, I would like to inform you that I find him not to be a security risk."

Cane lifted his head from his paperwork. "I could've told you that, but thank you Lieutenant. You are now relieved of duty."

The security guard frowned. "Relieved? Sir, I can't leave you here all alone. Who knows what kind of things this boy—or what other dangers are out there if I leave you—"

Cane shot him a look. "You're a fine security guard, but I need some time alone with my apprentice and you can either take the rest of your shift off or wait outside the door if you are so worried. Is that understood?"

The lieutenant nodded. "Yes, sir." He saluted and made his way out of the cabin.

Skyler signed the document and handed it to Cane. "All signed."

Cane took the papers and put them aside. "Thank you, Skyler." He put his paperwork down. "Any word from home yet?"

Skyler cringed. "Do you have to bring up my family?"

Cane scoffed. "Sorry, I know they bother you; I just would like to know when your mother decides to contact you what she will say."

Skyler got up and made his way to mini fridge and pulled out a beer. "I was planning on getting her number blocked if she does call me."

"She might be retired, but you can't block a superior officer's number. Only if they're a lower rank and not while you are a cadet." Cane placed his paperwork in his briefcase. "By the way, you can drink, but no getting drunk on the job."

Skyler downed half of his tall one. "What are you talking about? I have seen you drunk."

Cane got up and made his way over to the bar. "Not on duty. I have a pretty high alcohol tolerance."

"Ya, well, so do I," He finished his can of beer.

"If we're drinking, then, could you get me a glass of brandy?" Cane asked Skyler. "Your alcohol tolerance is nowhere near as high as mine. I have your father to thank for that."

Skyler grabbed another beer out of the fridge and got Cane his brandy. "My dad was a heavy drinker?"

Cane took his glass of brandy and sat in the lounging area. "No, he only drank on special occasions which happened about every week with him. Then he would not stop till the whole crew blacked out. I built up my tolerance because of him." He took a sip from his brandy, "The day I lost my eye, the day your mother broke my heart, the day your dad got married, the day you were conceived, the day you were born, the day I found out about your dad and Karma, the day your father died, when Karma died, when your mother broke my heart again." He downed the rest of his brandy. "So many emotional memories. The list goes on. I think the day your dad died was the worst on all of us. I did my best to be there for you but for the next month I was drunk out of my mind."

Skyler handed Cane a tall one from the fridge. "Here, I think you need to try this."

Cane took a sip. "I'm your mentor. I shouldn't be drinking with you, I should be teaching you how to deal with things without alcohol." He took a larger sip,

"Oh who am I kidding, if I told you not to drink, I would be the biggest hypocrite. Just don't come to work drunk you got to be professional."

Skyler sat down next to Cane, stretching his feet out onto the ottoman. "Why did it bother you when my dad was with Karma? Did you like her too?"

Cane shook his head, "No, just I was still in love with Sandy and was mad he had two women and I still had none."

"Well why didn't you find another? My mother couldn't have been that great."

Cane took a sip of his beer, "If Kax married Michael or Perry, would you find another girl to love?"

"So, you loved my mother, but she never loved you?"

"I thought she did a couple of times. But every time she broke my heart. And I was a very busy man. I didn't have time for a wife or a family. And I really don't have the time now."

Skyler finished his beer. "Did you ever tell my mother how you felt? I sure would have preferred you being my step-father then Charles."

Cane took a big sip of his beer. "No one wanted her to marry Charles and I did tell her how much I loved her, but she never loved me."

Skyler was silent for a moment as he listened to Cane's story.

"I'm sorry. I should have never brought up your family. It's not appropriate for your superior officer to bring up these things." Cane finished his can of beer.

"It's fine you were curious; we have a history. But are you sure my apprentice-ship with you will not be a conflict of interest?" Skyler asked.

"They asked me that when I suggested you and honestly off the record, I'm not 100% sure." Cane rubbed his forehead. "But I know it is the thing for you and you need it now more than ever. It was the only way I could stop you from going into a war you are not ready for. Heck, most cadets aren't ready for it. If I could stop this war I would. Also, this is giving you a boost on your career. Even if you get kicked out you will still be on the list. Well bottom of the list but it is better than nothing."

Skyler grabbed them another set of beers. "Am I at risk of getting kicked out sir?"

Cane took his beer. "Not at this moment, but being my apprentice will keep you out of trouble."

Skyler took a sip of his beer. "Is my record really that bad?"

Cane chuckled and shook his head. "I have seen worse and what you have going for you is normally when you get into trouble you have something greater keeping you out. You should see your dad's record. He was one of the worst in the fleet but somehow, he always got the job done better than expected. I have 100% faith in you and am willing to risk my career on you."

Chapter 7

Skyler rubbed his head as he woke up. He scanned around at his surroundings. He sat up and saw a pile of beer cans all over the ottoman and floor.

"So, you're finally awake, good. We will be landing soon." Cane stepped out of the curtained area. He was already in his gold dress uniform and bright-eyed.

Skyler tried to stand up in his wrinkled cadet uniform, but fell back down in his seat. "Uh, hey Cane, what happened last night?"

Cane sat down next to Skyler and gave him a little purple pill. "Well, we drank and talked for a while. Had dinner, went over your duties and what was going on for the next week."

Skyler took the pill and swallowed it without any water, "Ya, it's starting to come back to me. Wasn't one of my duties not getting drunk?"

Cane laughed. "You can get drunk, just not on duty. I let you slide last night, because your job doesn't start until we land."

Skyler sat there staring at the ceiling for a moment. "Was that a hangover pill you gave me wasn't it?"

"Extra strength. I want you well focused when we get to this meeting. You are going to be my extra set of eyes and ears, you understand that?"

Skyler stood up. "I can do that. But I do function quite well with hangovers, I think that's on my file."

Cane stood up. "It was, and you do. But it is noticeable when you have one. I need you to look clear headed." Cane looked at Skyler's wrinkled uniform. "Did you pack your officer uniform and dress uniform in the suitcase you brought on board?"

Skyler nodded. "Yes, and my backup cadet uniform."

"Well, you will not need your cadet uniforms any more. You are an apprentice, you will just need your officer uniform and dress. You are a working cadet so you will not have any rank stripes."

Skyler went over to his suitcase. "You're wearing your dress uniform right now, is this meeting that important?"

Cane shook his head. "No, but it is formal and as soon as we're out of there we have to rush over to the summer graduation ceremony and I will not have time to change."

Skyler nodded and pulled out his folded dress uniform. "I'll just go get changed right now and grab breakfast." He got up and started making his way to the bathroom to change.

Cane called out. "I will see what we can do about food, but probably once you are done, we will be landed and it will be go, go, go."

Skyler faced Cane. "Okay, I understand, sir. I will do my best."

Skyler came out a few moments later ready to go in his satin forest green uniform.

Cane was going over more paperwork, He got up and inspected Skyler's uniform. "Attention!" He called out.

Skyler stood up straight with his hands behind his back.

Cane walked around Skyler inspecting his uniform. He made his way to the front and swiped his hand on Skyler's shoulder. "You had a piece of lint, besides that you're good to go."

Skyler smiled. "Thank you, sir."

Cane handed Skyler a power bar. "I would have ordered your food, but there is no time to eat. We are about to arrive in ten minutes. Eat the power bar, leave your luggage here. I will have someone send for it. We are running about ten minutes late."

Skyler sat down next to the beer fridge. He went to open it and saw there was a lock. "Um Leon, there is a lock on the beer fridge."

Cane came over and sat down next to Skyler. "Yes, besides we're pretty much out of beer. I had all the alcohol locked away in case you tried to drink some more before we landed."

Skyler struggled to try and open the door. "Well, what am I supposed to drink then?"

Cane got up and went over to the tap and got a glass. He brought it back to Skyler. "You can drink this."

Skyler looked at the clear liquid. "Vodka?" He took a sip. "That is not vodka, it's water."

Cane nodded. "How many times do I have to tell you? You need a clear head. Also, water won't hurt. You need to stay hydrated."

Skyler took a sip of his water. "I have nothing wrong with water. I just was hoping for a morning drink is all."

"You're beginning to sound worse than me. You will be fine, don't you worry about it."

An announcement came on. 'We will be landing in five minutes please collect your belongings. Once we have landed, please be calm and exit in an orderly fashion. I hope you have enjoyed your ride.'

The security guard entered the cabin. "Everything all right in here, Fleet Admiral?"

Cane nodded. "It is. Now you know we will be busy as soon as we get off. Could you please take his two bags to his quarters? I will send you the address right now." Cane hit a few buttons on his tablet and the security officer nodded. "Yes, sir, that is not a problem."

They felt a 'thunk' when ship did land. They waited for the three beeps to tell them the doors would be opening.

Cane and Skyler stood by the door of the cabin and waited for it to open. Cane turned to Skyler. "Now when we walk out that door, I want you to follow and stay as close to me as you can. You might see your friends in passing or a pretty girl. Do not stop to talk to them. You are on duty, no time for goofing off. Is that understood?"

Skyler nodded. "Yes, Fleet Admiral sir."

Cane rolled his eye. "You do not have to be that formal with me. On duty, you will call me Sir. Off duty I don't care what you call me." Cane paused. "Well, if Davis is around do call me Fleet Admiral, make her think I have broken you or something. She really doesn't think I can handle you as an apprentice."

Skyler laughed. "Whatever you say, sir."

The doors opened, and without a second to spare Cane walked out onto the platform and headed towards his hover limo. He was walking so fast that Skyler did his best to keep up.

The limo took them to the back entrance to the main hall. Cane typed in his passcode and a large steel door opened.

Skyler stepped in to see a lovely blue marble floor, red painted walls with crown molding, and a chandelier along the ceiling. A large long oak table dominated the center of the room. "Wow! I had no idea there was a back door to the main hall, let alone this. It is amazing!"

Cane smiled. "Cadets and most officers don't know about this place. This room used to be one of the main dining halls but has been changed, into a large meeting or ceremony room."

"So, if we're late, then where is everybody?"

Cane shook his head. "We aren't using this room. We're using the other room." Cane took him to the left side of the room to a large oak door. He put his hand on the handle. "Now Skyler, when get in here, you be very quiet and do not speak unless you're being addressed, is that understood?"

Skyler nodded his head. "Understood, sir."

Cane opened the door to reveal a similar room but with a smaller oval table and gold trimmed crown molding.

There were six people at the table: the King of England, the Minister of Defense, Fleet Admirals Davis and Judson, the President of Earth, and Admiral Payne. Cane took his seat to the left of the King and Skyler next to him.

The King spoke. "Ah Fleet Admiral Cane so glad you could make it. We heard about the delay and held off the meeting for as long as we could." He shifted his head to the right of Cane, "This must be Cadet Therris your new apprentice. It's nice to meet you."

Skyler tried to keep a serious face. *Oh, boy this is awesome. I get the meet the King and the President all on the same day and the King's talking to me.*

"Fleet Admiral Cane, is there a reason your apprentice isn't speaking?" The King's brows tilted.

Cane lightly nudged Skyler with his elbow and whispered out of the side of his mouth to Skyler. "Speak when you are spoken to."

Skyler was high pitched. "It's nice to you meet you, sir." He covered his mouth, cleared his throat, and this time more calmly said. "I mean Your Highness. Sorry I'm just excited, didn't think I would ever meet the President and the King."

"Your Majesty," Cane whispered sharply.

The King let out a small laugh. "It's quite all right. It's it nice to meet you too."

The President cleared his throat. "I'm overhear if you would like to speak to me, Young Cadet."

Skyler turned his head with a big grin shaking. And busted out with the with thought he had in his mind. "Hello Mr. President, nice to meet you. My brother is going to be President one day too."

The President held back the urge to laugh. "Really? Who is your brother?"

Skyler paused, realizing what he had just said. "His name is Phineas Adam Roux. He's only a year old, but my stepdad is determined to make him President."

The President nodded. "Is your stepdad Senator Charles Roux, by any chance?"

Skyler, realizing what he was saying, nodded more seriously this time. "Yes, sir."

"Well, I think your stepfather has a higher chance of being President before your baby brother."

"Oh, I hope not," Skyler blurted out. He quickly covered his mouth when he realized what he had said.

The whole table busted out in laughter. The president then cleared his throat. "Well, I think that is enough chit chat for now. Let's begin the meeting."

There was a silence that filled the room as the Minister of Defense typed a few things into the table's built-in keyboard and pulled up a hologram map of the Earth. "As we all know, Earth has been hit by numerous attacks in the past three years. Last year we were able to draw the Cass away from Earth and have them focus on the Lunar and Mars cities. The moon has a great deal of weapons on it, but is running low on resources. Mars has nowhere near the weapons it needs to keep on its defenses. Earth is producing all the weapons as fast as it can, which will go up: now that the base is open, we will have more officers around. The Squallites are helping to, those little bugs work quite fast."

Skyler's ears picked up when he hears the word 'bug' and busted out. "They're not bugs. They're closer to rodents than a bug."

All eyes were on Skyler. The Minister of Defense cleared his throat. "Right, sorry, the electric rodents."

Skyler interrupted once again. "Excuse me. I know I'm speaking out of turn, but I think this might be the best time to bring up that if it wasn't for the Squallites we would be losing the war at this point. But fighting is not the answer with the Cass. They have more weapons than we can compete with. But what we need to do is this. They hate Earth because of one reason, something our forefathers did to them. Only the Cass know what it is. If you want to win this war, find an Earth-born Cass, one loyal to Earth, and have them go back to the Cass and find out what we did so long ago to piss them off and find a way to correct it."

Davis spoke up. "Don't you think we've tried that? We have known for years that the Cass hate us, and no one will talk to us. We are screening all Cass. No one will speak up."

Cane spoke up. "I'm sorry about my cadet. This is his first day on the job. He is not up to date with our war efforts."

The King spoke up. "Davis, whom have you been questioning? I was not aware of any interrogations going on. I think this cadet has something." He turned to the Minister of Defense, "I know the Cass don't like us, but didn't know there was a deeper meaning behind it. Yes, they have more weapons than us. But what is the reason they don't like us? What did we do to them?"

The Minister of Defense was silent.

Judson cut in. "Your Majesty, as the oldest one here, I can say that the reason you have more than likely been left in the dark is it was a military mistake, made long before UGF was fully formed. Someone has been covering it up."

The King looked at the Minister of Defense. "Did my father know what the feud with The Cass was?"

The Minister of Defense took a long sigh. "No, Your Majesty, we never mentioned the feud."

The King took a deep breath. "Is there anything new you have to report?"

The Minister shook his head. "I am afraid not Your Majesty. I was just going to give you the update on where our forces stand."

The King calmly replied. "In that case, I will ask you to excuse yourself from the rest of the meeting."

The Minister of Defense put his head down. "As you wish, Your Majesty." He then got up and pushed in his chair and left the room.

The King turned his attention over to Admiral Payne. "You have been awfully quiet. What are your thoughts on what we should do with the war?"

Admiral Payne spoke up. "The boy is right. I didn't know about Davis's interrogations, but we need to find out why the Cass hate us. It is the only way to make progress in this war."

The King shifted to Davis. "I want you to stay behind after the meeting to talk about interrogations."

Davis spoke up. "Your Majesty, if I may interject. After this meeting I, must be at the summer cadet graduation to hand out the diplomas to my fleet."

The King paused. "Okay then, once that is done, I will meet you in your office."

The President looked at the King. "So, Your Majesty, what is our new battle plan for the war?"

The King turned to the Cane. "Looks like it is your turn to speak up."

Cane typed a few things in on the map. "Well, I do know one way we can neutralize the Cass which should help in getting info out of them, or at least get them talking. If you give me a moment, I will show you my plan."

The King nodded. "Please do."

Cane typed in a few things into the keyboard and pulled up his map. "We take what we have from our fleet, the Squallites and Catillions and surround the planet blocking all from entering and leaving. We have all three ships fully loaded, we threaten to destroy them unless they actually talk to us. Take a handful of our ships to fight with their ships elsewhere, leaving their planet defenseless or at least weakened."

The King nodded. "It sounds like a plan. If everyone is in favor of this idea, say aye."

The table all said, "aye."

"Well then, since this meeting is running long, we will continue this meeting at a later date. The meeting is adjourned."

They all got up from their seats. Cane rushed out of the room. "Come on, Skyler, we have to get to the other side of the base now."

Chapter 8

They made it just in time to the ceremony. The cadets were divided up into three groups. One for each fleet.

They were in the middle of the other two fleets on the parade square. The friends and families were sitting in chairs on the pavement. And on the other side of them were some of the faculty. On the stage, there was a set of bleachers where graduating cadets sat.

Skyler sat down in the seat next to Cane. Cane made his way up to the podium and began his speech. "You all dreamed this day would come when you first joined the academy many years ago. Some are here quicker, and some are a little late. Doesn't matter. What matters is you made it to this point. When you get your diploma and rank bands when you come up here, remember one thing: you earned it." He stepped down from the podium and looked over his shoulder. "Could you read the names out? The list is right there."

Skyler nodded. "Yes, sir." He got up out of his seat and stepped up to the podium.

Cane stepped over to the side of the table stacked with the diplomas with names written on the seals.

Skyler began reading out the names. "Albert Albertson, Betty Allen..." One by one as he read their names, they came up on stage and shook Cane's hand as he handed them their certificates.

Finally, he made it to Michael's name and proudly read it out. "Michael Majerik Jones."

Michael walked on stage. Cane was there to greet him. He smiled and looked down at the crowd seeing his father and Kax cheering and taking pictures of him.

He waved his diploma in his hand and smiled. Cane shook Michael's hand and whispered into his ear, "I'm proud of you," and patted him on the back.

"When you have a moment, I need to talk to you." Michael nodded and made his way back to his seat.

When the names were all read out and all the diplomas had been claimed, Cane walked with Skyler off the stage. Cane walked around quickly to catch Michael before he left. He and his Dad were about to leave with Kax. Cane went right behind them and spoke in a stern tone. "Officer Jones!"

Michael stopped dead in his tracks and turned around.

Cane smiled. "You like that new rank, Officer Jones?"

Michael nodded. "Yes, it was just a shock to be called that. Thank you, sir, for such a high rank."

Cane shook his head. "Officer 2nd class isn't that high for a cadet with your experience. Give it a few more months and you will probably get promoted. You aren't that far off. I came by to congratulate you and I wish you all the best. And call me Leon, Blinky or Cane you don't always have to be so formal with me. You have known me personally for almost 5 years now."

Michael smiled. "Your right si...Leon. Thank you for everything and every opportunity you have given me."

"So, Michael, what did you wish to talk to me about?" Cane inquired.

"They have transferred me from inventing with Grey to ship repair. I wanted to make sure that was correct." Michael said.

"You were going to be transferred but not that big of a jump. It might take me some time but I will investigate it for you," Cane answered.

"Thank you, Leon."

Sam smiled. "And thank you for everything, Cane, you have been a great help to me and my son," Sam said.

"Well, Sam, I just want to see you well. And I'm glad you're in good health. Keep up the good work."

Sam looked over at Skyler. "So, you're the new apprentice, good for you and thanks for being such a good friend to Michael."

"Hey, he's not too bad himself. Ya, first day on the job." Skyler turned to Michael. "Did you get the seedlings Perry was sending you?"

"I got them from Kax, thanks," Michael replied. "I need those for the next stage of the project."

"Michael, Skyler is probably going to busy for the next while. I will send you a message on where to pick up the plants. Don't want them wilting." Cane said.

Sam pointed to Skyler's collar. "You're missing your apprentice pin."

Cane cleared his throat. "We have been going since we landed. His pin is in my office. Which is where we are heading to next."

Skyler put on his charm and went over to Kax. "Hey there, cutie. I'm the Fleet Admiral's apprentice, does that impress you?"

Kax playfully batted her eyelashes. "Oh really, well then, that makes so much of a difference."

He moved toward her. "You like a man with power, don't you?"

She blushed. "Oh, a man with power, *that* makes all the difference." She turned her head away and called out, "Leon! Skyler is bothering me again!"

Cane put his hand on Skyler's shoulder and pulled him away. "Skyler, stop bothering Kax."

Skyler put on his big 'not guilty' eyes. "I got a new rank and new job. I thought I would give it a shot."

Cane scoffed. "You have lots to learn about women. Come on, we have more work to be done." He turned to Sam and Michael. "It was nice talking to you, but we've got to go. Michael remembers, look behind you."

Sam held back a laugh. "Thank you we were just off to dinner." He focused on Skyler. "It was nice seeing you again."

Skyler bowed his head. "It was nice seeing you again too."

Cane put his hand on Skyler's upper back and walked with him away.

Skyler looked back over his shoulder at Kax.

She blew him a kiss.

"Knew it," he whispered to himself.

Chapter 9

Finally, Skyler had time to go to his room. He was tired and sore from running around all day. He finally finished his first official day as the Fleet Admiral's apprentice. He had the number and key to his new living quarters in the officer's barracks. As he was walking down the hall looking at his feet, trying not to fall asleep, not paying attention to where he was going, he bumped into someone. He picked up his head up, seeing a very leggy light brown-haired woman. She was wearing a cadet uniform, had fair-sized breasts, a tiny waist and apple bottom. This put a smile on Skyler's face. "Sorry about that, miss. I'm very tired and was not looking where I was going."

She tossed her hair back. "You didn't hurt anything, it's fine. You look a bit young to be in the officer's quarters?"

Skyler pointed to the pin on his collar. "I'm Fleet Admiral Cane's Apprentice."

She moved closer to him. "So, you have a room here all to yourself."

He grinned. "I got my own private suite. How would you like to look at it with me cadet?"

She blushed. "You're cute, but I'm not that kind of girl."

He looked around. "Well, we could go out to dinner first; I do have a car. But if you're not that kind of girl, what is a young cadet doing in the officer's quarters all alone?"

"Dinner sounds nice. But I'm not here alone. My mother is an officer. I was on my way back from visiting her." She moved her finger around his pin. "The names Zarina, what's yours?"

He leaned in close to her ear. "The name's Skyler Therris."

She let out a light giggle. "Let's go get that dinner, Skyler."

He took her to the parking garage and went over to his parking space to find out it was empty. He pulled his tablet out of his pocket and looked for the tracking. He saw that the car was at the cabin. "Dammit," he said, slapping his forehead.

Zarina lowered her brow. "What's the issue?"

He pointed to the empty space. "Kax has the car. I can't take you to the city to go out for dinner."

"Is Kax your girlfriend?" She frowned.

Skyler shook his head. "I wish she was. But no such luck. I gave her my car because Cane said he would be keeping me busy all year. I figured I wouldn't need it."

She nodded and smiled. "You look pretty tired. You sure you want to go out to dinner?"

Skyler stomach grumbled. "I'm dead tired, and I'm now getting hungry. You're so pretty I want to impress you…"

She put her finger on his lips. "Shh, you're cute and seem like a nice guy who is just too tired to drive. Let's go back to your room and order take out from the bar. Officers can do that."

Skyler was at a loss for words. "Wow, you must like me or something."

She gave him a kiss on the cheek. "Or something. Come on, let's get back to the room so you can rest. On the way, tell me what you want to eat?"

Back in the room she helped Skyler out of his uniform and into bed. She called up on her phone and ordered take out. Well before the food arrived Skyler was fast asleep.

It was still dark when he awoke, and turned his head to the side to see Zarina ironing his uniform. He jerked up and said. "You're Zarina, that girl from last night. What are you doing here?" He paused, "I mean, what are you doing to my uniform?"

She took his jacket off the ironing board and held it up. "I'm ironing your uniform, so it is not wrinkled. You almost fell asleep in it, if it wasn't for me."

He rubbed his head. Looking around the room he saw the food on the desk, "So why did you stay? You could have left. Did we sleep together?"

She laughed and started ironing his pants. "We shared a bed because you have a double, but no, you fell asleep before the food showed up. Your pizza is sitting on the desk, I didn't touch it. I stayed because you looked like you needed some help, and you seemed very kind."

Skyler smiled and got up. He headed towards the food. He looked out the window. "Hey, what time is it?"

She looked at her watch. "4 a.m., you have time to eat your food and get dressed before Cane calls you into work."

Skyler picked up the small pizza and sat back on the bed and opened the box. "You're awesome, you know that? Is there a way I can thank you or repay you for being this awesome?"

She put the iron down and went over and kissed Skyler's pizza-covered face. "You could take me on a date when you have the time."

Skyler grinned. "I can do that." He moved the pizza off his lap. "Well, we have eaten, slept together and you're doing my ironing, I think the only thing to make this a full date is to have sex."

She laughed. "Temping. You're are a cuddler and I do like that."

Skyler's eyes widened. "Cuddler, how do you know that?"

She played with the curls on his head. "I because I slept next to you and you kept holding me cuddling. Poking me and talking in your sleep."

Skyler covered his face. "Did I really do all of that?"

She moved his hand aside and gave him a kiss on the cheek. "Don't worry about it. I think it's cute and I love to cuddle."

Skyler grinned. "Well, if you want, I have time for a quickie. We can cuddle till I have to get ready."

She kissed him on the lips. "Not right now. But we can tonight when you get off work. If you want to see me again?"

"I do want to see you again. I would like to get to know you too." He frowned. "Are you picking me up?"

She laughed and kissed him again. "Only if you want me to."

Skyler paused for a moment. "I can't see how a date or two would hurt. You got me food and did my laundry, why again? Sure, I will go out with you, just so you know I'm a very busy guy now."

She grabbed a slice of his pizza. "I have no issue with that, I'm going to be busy too. I'm a cadet. But when I have time, I'll stop by your room. As for the why I stayed, some men just need a woman's touch. And by the looks of it last night, you could have used someone."

He finished his slice of pizza. "Well, I'm very thankful you helped me out there." He grabbed another slice. "This has got to be the oddest way I have ever gotten a girlfriend."

She giggled and sat down next to him. "I have been in the Forces for 5 years now. My dad is a very high rank and my mom raised me, then joined late. I know that if you see someone in this place and you think they're cute grab them because you blink, and you will never see them again, especially during a war."

Skyler put his piece of pizza down. "You know, I never thought of it like that. 5 years, you say? We're the same age. Also, I don't really do the girlfriend thing. How come I haven't seen you before?"

She played with the curls around Skyler's ears. "I'm from Earth but my mom has been stationed on Mars colony for the past 8 years and we just moved back over the summer. I'm in command division like you. But my second division is security. I don't really care for command that much. Being a Captain is not for me, I'd rather protect my man."

He smiled and turned his head away. "Your fingers are tickling me. And that's cool, I've never been to Mars yet. I have been to Squall and Catillion but not Mars."

"Well maybe if Cane gives you some time off this year, we can jump over there one weekend, It's only a two-hour ride away."

Skyler's eyes widened. "Two hours? Wow, how come I have never been? That's almost what it takes me to get to my Mom's place. But that's by car."

"Is your Mom an officer?"

Skyler cringed. "Ya, she's in Thoms...I mean Judson's fleet, and in the in the ground crew division she works with the launching bays. She used to just be a science officer till I was born."

"Nice, my mom is in medical and my dad went with command."

The alarm went on Skyler's tablet. He jumped up. "Crap! I got to get ready, almost time to go."

She got up and handed him his pants then jacket. "What time do you get off?"

Skyler looked at the time on his tablet while he zipped up his jacket. "I'm supposed to be done around 7, but anything could make us run later. If you want send me a text when you're out and I will tell you how much longer I will be."

She pulled out her tablet. "I can't find you in the directory, what's your ID number?"

He combed his hair. "That won't help, I'm under the Catillion registry. But the number is 5689, if you want you can walk with me to Cane's office?"

She smiled and took his hand. "I would be glad to."

He walked with her to Cane's office. He looked at the time on his tablet. "I got five minutes before I need to walk in that door. Want a quickie?"

She laughed and kissed him against the wall. He placed one hand on her waist and the other on her head. He kissed her deeply back.

Cane opened the door and coughed into his hand.

Skyler broke the kiss. "Hey, Cane, I had five minutes to spare so..."

"Skyler, get into my office now." Cane held the door open for him.

Zarina and Skyler waved goodbye to each other. He entered the office.

Cane closed the door and looked sternly at Skyler. "Well, it appears like you had a good night."

Skyler scratched his head. "Well, kind of, I mean we didn't do anything I swear. We met in the hallway on my way to bed and she bought me dinner, and she ironed my uniform."

Cane sat down at his desk. "Did she tell you who her father is?"

Skyler shook his head. "Just that he is a high-ranking officer. Is something wrong? Kissing is as far as it went."

Cane sighed. "Her father used to be an officer and the Minister of Defense. Well soon to be former Minister; there is a new election happening to appoint a new one because of you."

Skyler got an awkward feeling in his gut. "Does she know who I am? That would make a lot of sense."

Cane frowned. "What do you mean? Of course, she knows who you are, she saw you leave with me after the meeting, she was there and I'm pretty sure her dad grumbled to her."

Skyler covered his face. "And here I thought she liked me. Damn, I was a fool. Well, good thing is I didn't sleep with her. She stayed the night in my room, but she chose to stay I was asleep then."

"Fine, but make this the last time you see her. She could have ulterior motives."

Skyler looked down at his feet. "I guess I'm single again."

"I'm sorry, but I'm just worried about you. That's all. Also, watch out, it's fine to brag but lots of women will want you now that you are my apprentice. Not because of the title but because one day you could be the Fleet Admiral and well, who wouldn't want to be the wife of a Fleet Admiral."

"My mother," Skyler blurted out.

Cane's jaw dropped. "Why would you say something like that, after all I have done for you?"

Skyler shook his head. "I'm sorry, I'm just a bit upset. I liked Zarina. And you're going on like being a Fleet Admiral is like being made of gold, but you're single and you couldn't get my mother. And well, I don't want to be Fleet Admiral. I only want to be a captain."

Cane let out a sigh. "I'll let that one slide. Really, I just got too busy. I spent too much time on your mother and by the time I realized it I got the promotion. I gave her a chance to stop me."

Skyler sighed. "Well, it's a good thing I don't plan to ever get married."

Cane looked confused. "What do you mean, I thought you wanted to marry Kax and have kids with her?"

Skyler shook his head. "Well, if she wants to marry me I will. I would give her all the kids she wanted. But anyone else, no. Being a captain and having a wife is too hard. Kax is perfect, she's a pilot and will follow me around. With anyone else, I might never see my wife…"

"And there aren't many women pilots, and they know how you like to take care of your ship." Cane finished Skyler's speech.

Skyler looked confused. "How did you know what I was going to say, sir?"

Cane laughed. "That's the same speech your dad gave me after he met Karma. She was the woman who woke him up and changed his opinions on a lot of things. I hope you change your mind on the marriage thing. Your dad would have wanted grandkids."

Skyler shook his head. "I don't think I'm the type to get married. And kids, naw, not my thing. I want to be a single Captain who is married to my ship and is seeing a different girl every night on the side."

"Don't marry your ship, I get it. You don't want to get married or have kids but get a girlfriend or a companion, someone to keep you company. I've done it alone and it gets lonely."

"I'll think about it. Until then, what is our assignment today?"

Cane let out a deep sigh. "Background checks on all the new cadets. Because the base just reopened, we are a bit behind on accepting the new cadets. They will start next week. So, we got to get as much as we can get done today before we get called to another issue. Today will be all the people who want to be in my fleet. If we have time, we can go through the ones who were rejected for the other fleets. You don't know what I'm looking for, so I just want you to go through them. If they have a criminal record such as felonies hit reject, misdemeanor let them through. And divide them up into categories of what division they want to join, or if they scored higher on their test for another division put them in there. I will be on my computer making the final decision." He reached into his drawer and pulled out a blue tablet. "Use this to go through the files."

Skyler took the tablet. "What if they failed their entrance exam?"

"Then hit reject. It's a basic test, it's mostly just an aptitude test so it is very hard to fail."

Chapter 10

Skyler was working hard at reading all the files. His head was beginning to hurt. "Leon, I had no idea so many people wanted to join the Forces. Do you ever get through this entire list?"

Cane nodded. "I have been doing this job for ten years now. Every year the list seems to get longer and longer. We will manage to get through it, don't you worry, and not all these people are from Earth. If you notice on the files, some are from other planets and colonies so not all will be placed here, which helps when finding room for all of them. Good thing I just have to make sure the Academy they want to enter has the room."

Skyler smiled. "Am I allowed to collect any of these girls' phone numbers?"

Cane shook his head. "No, you just make sure they fit the criteria."

"Damn, a lot of these girls are hot!"

Just then the door made a large crashing noise as Sandy barged in. "Give me back my son, you one-eyed, cocksucking pervert!"

Cane jerked up from his desk. "I have never sucked a dick in my life. Don't go spreading lies about me you cold hearted bitch, you're so cold I got frostbite on my dick. Why the fuck are you here?"

She grabbed Skyler's arm and pulled him up. "From this day forward, he is not your apprentice and he is not in the Forces. He is coming home with me!"

Cane grabbed Skyler's other arm. "He can't. He has signed the paperwork. He is my apprentice. He can no longer be relieved from duty."

She took a deep breath and gave Cane a cold dead stare straight into the eyes. "You bastard, I told you to stay away from my son and all you have done since he turned 18 is force your ways on him. He was going to be a politician and marry a princess but no, you want to send him to his death like you did with his father, just so you could have your way with me."

Skyler scrunched his face. "What would give you that idea?"

Cane put his hand up. "Skyler, don't speak. This is between your mother and me." He looked dead into her eyes. "Skyler came to me when he was 18, I had nothing to do with it. If you had paid attention to anything, he had said for the past 18 years you would know that he wanted to join the Forces on his own. I never wanted Levi to die, I wish it was me who died that day, but he insisted I go. The Cass killed him, not me; he died a hero, he saved every one of his crew. If I remember correctly, you didn't wait 24 hours for your husband to be dead before you jumped my bones. Everything you see here today is your fault, not mine! I stayed away from Skyler when you married Charles, a man who I might add beat your son. I never laid a hand on the boy. If you're unhappy, you only have yourself to blame!" He let go of Skyler, and sat back down returning to work.

Sandy snarled at Cane and pulled Skyler's arm. "Come on, son, let's go home. You must see Phineas. He has grown so big."

Skyler pulled back. "No, mother, I'm not going with you. I want to be here, and I love it here. I don't want to have anything to do with Phineas or Charles. They're your family, not mine."

A tear came to her eyes. "Skyler, what are you saying? Please come home with me. I'm sorry I was a bad mother, I will make it up to you. Just please come home. Charles is a senator, he is rarely home; I'll keep him away from you."

Skyler shook his head. "No mother, it's over don't contact me, I made my choice."

She let go of his arm. "In that case don't come home, Skyler, there will be no one waiting for you." She looked at Cane one last time. "Well, you won. I'm just glad I have another son. That one you can't steal." She stormed out of the office with tears running down her face.

Cane gave it a moment of silence before he pulled a bottle of sherry out of his desk, he poured Skyler a glass. "I'm sorry."

Skyler took his glass. "I should be the one saying sorry to you, my mother shouldn't have said those things..."

Cane raised his hand. "Skyler, I do not want to talk about her or the past right now. I love you like a son and nothing can change that."

Skyler finished his glass. "Do you want me to leave?"

Cane shook his head. "It's better if you just stay right now." He took a moment to rest and poured another glass for himself. "Come on Skyler, let's get back to work."

Skyler picked up the blue tablet and went back to checking the applications.

There wasn't much talking after that.

9 o'clock came and Skyler finally got off work. He made his way to his room. Standing outside the door was Zarina.

"Hey cutie, you got off work late. Or is this considered early?" she said, twirling a strand of her hair around her finger.

He unlocked the door. "Before I let you in here, I need to ask you a few questions."

"I'll put out if that's what you want to know." She batted her eyelashes.

He shook his head. "That's not it. Who is your father?"

She frowned. "Terry Vorkovich. He is the Minister of Defense."

He nodded. "Then why are you here? They're calling for his resignation. I exposed your father was hiding things from the King. I might have put him out of a job."

She looked right into his eyes. "I don't care about that. My Dad has a reason to retire. I saw you thought you were cute and used my Dad's computer to do a background check on you. I thought you were Cane's son for a the most part till I realized you Captain Therris's, which is more impressive." She brushed his hair back giving him a kiss on the lips. "I think you're cute and you seem like a great guy. Why not give me a chance?"

He played with her hair and held her close. "You know, with the rotten day I have had, even if you were a spy trying to ruin me, I wouldn't care. I just need someone by my side. Do you understand?"

She kissed him deeply on the lips. "I know exactly what you mean."

He opened the door. "Well then, my room awaits us." He sat down on the bed, taking his uniform off.

She looked at him. "Am I missing something? You don't seem to be on your A game today."

He laid on his back. "I had a real rotten day and don't really feel like trying. I am sorry, if you want to go you can."

She took off her uniform and laid in the bed next to him. "I think you need a little TLC. You just lay there, and I'll do the work?"

He laughed, covering his face. "If you want to, then go for it. I'm not going to stop you. But don't lead me on."

She moved on top of him. Leaning down, she kissed him. "Cutie, you need to relax and let me comfort you."

He kissed her, placing his hands on her breasts.

She kissed his neck, working her way down his chest, licking his nipples with her tongue.

He moaned, running his fingers through her hair.

She kept kissing her way down. Unzipping and pulling down his pants, she was taken back. "Wow, you're bigger than I thought."

He grinned. "It's genetic, it's not too big for you, is it?"

She licked her lips. "Nope, it's just the size I like." She put her mouth around it, and he began to moan.

His head rolled back in pleasure. "I'm guessing this isn't your first time."

She picked her head up. "No talking, I'm concentrating. You just relax, you're very tense." She went back to her job and massaged his pelvis.

He moaned and groaned. "Oh baby, harder. I'm getting close." He grabbed her hair and tugged it gently, then jerked his pelvis.

She picked her head up and licked her lips. "Mmm, you were really tense."

Skyler sat up and kissed her on the lips. "Oh babe, that was great." He kissed her neck. "Thank you. Want me to return the favor?"

She smiled. "Only if you're man enough to take me."

He grabbed her shoulders and tossed her down on the bed. "Oh baby, I'm man enough!" he unhooked her bra and pulled down her nylons with his teeth.

She screamed. "Oh Skyler!" as he went down between her legs.

Chapter 11

Morning came. Skyler awoke, holding Zarina in his arms. He kissed her on the neck and whispered in her ear. "Good morning."

She rolled over to face him. "Good morning, cutie."

He laughed. "After last night, you are still calling me cutie?"

She played with the curls in his hair. "It's because you're cute." She booped his nose. "But if you prefer, I could call you stud or Captain Sexy."

He blushed. "Captain will do just fine." He kissed her on the forehead. "Just a thought, you're not going to tell Mommy or Daddy about what we did, are you?"

She laughed. "No, I wouldn't do that to you. They still think I'm a virgin. That ship sailed a long time ago."

Skyler laughed. "Well, my Mom knows now. But I lost my virginity when I was 14."

Her eyes widened. "14, wow. You were just a boy. I was the same age, but I had boobs, and it was with an older guy."

He squeezed her large breasts. "So, you would believe me if I was 14, had boobs, and slept with an older man?"

She laughed. "I didn't say I didn't believe you. Just that you were young. I thought I was so mature at that age. So, who was it, a teacher?"

Skyler shook his head. "Never slept with my teachers, one did hit on me but that was when I was 17. Naw, the girl I lost it to was another 14-year-old virgin. She came up to me and said, 'I think you're cute, I'm not going to be a virgin forever. Want to have sex?' And the rest is history. We did it on my old cot next to the window in the attic under the stars. Since then, girls have always just thrown themselves at me."

"That's much nicer than my story. I was developing early and had a high sex drive, didn't understand a lot of things, and one of my brother's friends who was 19 came by and seduced me. We did it a few times till my brother found out and beat him up. He didn't tell Mom or Dad."

Skyler looked around. "You're not going to have your brother beat me up, are you?"

She laughed. "I'm an adult now he doesn't care unless you hurt me."

Skyler grinned. "Well then, I'm safe. Just so you know, I have never hurt a woman intentionally."

She kissed him on the lips. "So, do you want to be my boyfriend?"

Skyler stroked her cheek. "I thought I was because of what you said yesterday?"

She started playing with the hairs on his chest. "Okay, but is it fine if we're not exclusive?"

He frowned. "What? Why? I mean I like women just as much as the next guy, but I'm not looking to cheat on you. I don't cheat."

She shook her head. "I don't mean it like that. We both have busy careers and things going on. What if you're gone away for a month and I want sex? Could I find a partner or are you saying I must wait for you? Or vice versa?"

Skyler nodded. "Okay, I can understand that. I have been in open relationships before, but they were more casual encounters."

She rolled over on top of him. "Can we stop talking for a moment?"

He kissed her passionately on the lips. He kissed her neck.

She giggled at the feeling of his soft touch.

His phone rang suddenly on the desk next to bed. She picked up the phone and answered it. "Hello, Skyler's busy right now. Can I take a message?"

A stern raised voice blared though the phone. "It's Fleet Admiral Cane. put Skyler Therris on the phone, now."

She moaned and tapped Skyler on the head. "Skyler, phone. It's Cane."

He picked his head up and grabbed the phone. "Hey, Cane, what's up?"

"It's 6 a.m., Skyler. You're late. Get your ass down here now!"

Skyler looked over at the clock and his eyes widened. "Sorry sir, I will be there in ten." He jumped out of bed and put his uniform on.

Zarina sat up in bed. "I'm sorry. I didn't mean to make you late. Will I see you tonight?"

Skyler zipped up his jacket. "I don't know. Send me a message. If I get off early and have a good day I might want to go to the bar. But you could join me. If it was like yesterday, I could meet you here."

He ran a comb through his hair. "Lock up when you leave." He kissed her on the lips and ran out of the room.

He made his way to Cane's office.

Cane was sitting in the office, tapping his watch. "You're late. What is your excuse?"

Skyler's hands shook and he looked at Cane and snickered. "Well sir, I woke up nice and early and got in the middle of something that kind of got me distracted."

Cane covered his face. "Please tell me that the girl you were with wasn't Zarina."

Skyler rubbed his neck. "Well, I talked to her about what you said and well she really likes me for me. She thought I was your son till she ran a background check on me."

Cane stopped him right there. "I warned you, don't do it. She is just using you."

Skyler frowned. "Cane, I have used women for information before, I know the tricks. She seems legit. If you just talked to her, you would know what I'm saying is true."

Cane let out a deep sigh. "Fine, you're not going to listen to me, so go ahead, date her, but if she screws up your career don't ask me to fix it."

Skyler took a seat at the desk. He put his head down. "Last night I was so upset it didn't matter if she was going cut my chest open. I needed to be with someone, and she was there. I don't know if you will understand sir, but last night, I needed her."

Cane let out a deep sigh. "No, I understand exactly. We have all been in that stage at some point in our lives." The room went silent for a moment. "Well then, enough of that. Let's get back to work. We need to keep going through the list of applications and then start placing them."

Skyler picked up the blue tablet off the desk. "Do you think it will be an early day today?"

Cane shook his head. "There is never an early day, just days when you get off before you need get back to work."

Kax hopped out of the cockpit of her fighter. She saw Michael working on another fighter. She went over to him. "It's nice to see you get down and dirty for once."

He lifted his head from under the fighter. "I would like to see you go down on one of these things." He slapped his forehead, "I didn't mean it like that."

She laughed. "I get it. Um, the reason I'm here is I'm having a problem with my signals they're not lighting up at the right times. I was able to get through patrol with it today because that's how I discovered it, but I had first shift, so no one else was flying around."

Michael got up. He grabbed a rag and cleaned his face and hands. "I'll take a look at it and see what I can do."

She followed him to the shuttle. "Hey, do you know what happened with Skyler and his Mom yesterday? She hasn't said a thing. I thought I was going to walk into work, and she'd be calling me names worse than whore or tramp, but instead she was silent and handed me my assignment."

Michael opened a side panel on the fighter. "No idea, but he didn't call me and complain, and I didn't see him at the bar so maybe she is finally listening to him."

Kax scoffed. "That'll be the day. We can find out tonight, he invited us out for drinks whenever he gets off work."

Michael took an electronic screwdriver and played around with a few wires. "Going to the bar would be great. I wonder what kind of job Skyler is doing." He connected a few wires. "Could you please get in and test your signal now?"

"No problem," She climbed up into the cockpit, she turned on her fighter and tried the signal. "The green light is blinking now."

Michael rubbed his chin then tried changing a few cords. "Now try it."

She turned her signal back on. "It works! Thanks Michael."

He put the cover back on the side of the fighter. "No problem, that's my job."

Kax got out of the fighter and gave Michael a hug. "Thanks, just wondering how much you're getting paid for this job?"

Michael shifted his eyes around. "Less than what you are getting paid as a working cadet. But this money goes to help my Dad out with bills. His pay has been less the last couple of years with his injuries. He took out a few loans." He paused for a moment, "Hey, can I move back into the cabin with you? I'm in the officer dorms and for Squallites they suck, and they charge us rent."

Kax's eyes widened. "They reduce your pay and still charge you rent? That's horrible. Yes, you can move in, I thought you wanted to be in the barracks."

"I wanted my own place," Michael said. "But it's not fair that they take the rent out of our pay. At least food here is still free."

"You know if you're having money problems you can always ask Skyler. I'm sure he will give you whatever you need."

Michael shook his head. "I'm not going to ask him for money, it's not right. My Dad and I have the money to pay for our place, it's just we need to be tight with the money. And try to get out of debt at the same time."

Kax nodded her head. "Ya, I understand. Hey tonight at the bar do you think Skyler would mind if I brought a friend?"

Michael raised an eyebrow. "You know he would. I mean, he wouldn't mind if she was a girl but a guy, he is going to be jealous."

Kax nodded. "Well, see, there is this guy I like but he doesn't know that yet, I think he likes me and I thought maybe if we invite him out for drinks we could all get to know him and see what he is like outside of work."

"Outside of work? Are you talking about Rex? He's what, ten years older than you?"

Kax shrugged. "Something like that. He seems nice and mature."

Michael bit his lip. "I'm not going to judge you, but you know how Skyler is going to react."

Rex walked up to Kax. "Hey, is this guy bothering you?"

Kax laughed off the rude comment. "No, this is my friend Michael. He was fixing my ship and we stopped to chat."

Rex narrowed his eyes at Michael. "Friend, you say." He held out his hand, "It's nice to meet you, Michael. I'm Rex Bailey."

Michael took his hand. "Nice to meet you too. But I need to return to work." He turned to Kax. "See you tonight."

She waved to him as he left.

Rex shifted his eyes to Kax. "What did he mean, tonight? I thought you said he was just a friend?"

"He is. Me and him are going to the bar tonight with another friend." She played with her hair. "I was going to ask you if you would like to join us."

Rex moved in closer. "I think that would be a great idea."

Later that night when Kax got off work, she waited for Michael and Rex outside of the hangar. She sent a message to Skyler hoping he would be joining them.

Michael and Rex walked out of the hangar together. Rex went over to Kax. "Hey, sorry to make you wait, but you know I had to sign out."

Kax tossed her hair. "It wasn't that long of a wait. I would have stayed inside but I didn't want to be anywhere near Commodore Roux."

Michael took a comb out of his pocket fixing his hair. "I saw her on my way out. I'm lucky she didn't say anything to me."

Rex looked confused. "I know Commodore Roux is a bitch, but you guys seem to hate her for more personal reasons, why is that?"

Kax turned her head and coughed. "It's kind of complicated but the easiest way to explain it...you know the friend I said we were meeting up with at the bar?"

Rex narrowed his eyes. "Yeah?"

Kax hesitantly replied. "Well, that's her son."

Rex put his head back. "Oh, I get it. You used to date her son."

Kax choked. "What? No! Why would you think that? Skyler is just a friend."

Michael cut in. "Skyler was my roommate and now a friend. He does like Kax but, well, she has no interest in him that way, so friends."

Rex nodded his head. "Okay I think this is all starting to make sense."

Michael shrugged. "If you want to know more, you can ask Skyler yourself."

Kax's tablet pinged. She checked the notification. "Skyler says he is on his way to the bar now. And he is bringing his girlfriend."

Michael frowned. "Girlfriend? He doesn't do girlfriends. And we have only been back for three days. How did he get one so quickly?"

Kax shrugged. "I don't know, he's Skyler. Come on, let's go to the pub."

They all made their way across the courtyard and to the old campus bar. They walked into the door. Kax saw from a distance, Skyler face sucking some girl in one of the booths off to the side.

"Well, I guess that's his new girlfriend," Michael said.

Kax rolled her eyes. "Come on, we need to stop them before they reproduce right in the booth."

They went over. Skyler broke the kiss with Zarina. He looked up at the gang. "Hey guys, I would like you to meet my new girlfriend, Zarina."

Zarina held out her hand. "Nice to meet you, everyone. Skyler has told me so much about you."

Kax shook her hand before sitting down. "Nice to meet you too, I'm Kax."

Rex shook her hand next before sliding in. "I'm Rex."

Michael shook her hand before moving in next to Rex. "And I'm Michael."

Skyler turned his attention to Rex. "So Rex, who are you? I have not met you before."

Rex put his arm around Kax. "I'm Kax's control pilot. She invited me out tonight."

Skyler shot Kax a look. "Oh, I see."

"Um, Kax and Michael told me to ask you why your mother is such a bitch?"

Skyler's eyes nearly popped out of his skull. "Don't bring up my mother." He shot a nasty look at Michael and Kax. "Why were you two talking about my mother?"

Kax spoke up. "We haven't seen you, so we haven't gotten a chance to tell you. Me and Michael are working in the control center with your mother. Rex has been working with her for the past few years. No one likes her there."

Skyler picked up his beer off the table and took a big sip. "That makes a lot of sense, especially the visit I got from her yesterday. But I thought my mother was retired. Why is she back?"

"Because the base is reopened they need as much staff as they can get. So, they asked your mother to come back part time, she has a desk job. She monitors the sign-ins for the patrol pilots," Kax explained.

Skyler looked over at Michael. "I thought you were going to be in engineering or something? What are you doing with the pilots?"

Michael let out a deep sigh. "Turns out I'm too short so they found me a job as the assistant fighter repair guy. And remember back in first year when I called you racist?"

"Back when I called you an electric bug?" Skyler laughed.

Michael kicked Skyler under the table. "Yeah, that attitude. Well, I apologize, your mother is so much worse. I see where you got it from. But at least you're learning."

Skyler flinched. "Dude, I was joking. You know that, right?"

Michael laughed. "You know, you're the only one I will tolerate that kind of attitude from."

The waitress came over to the table. "What can I get all of you?"

Skyler pointed to the gang one by one. "He will have a Squallite soda, she will have a Catillion Sunrise, my girl will have sex on the beach, and I will have a beer." He turned and looked at Rex, "And what do you drink?"

Rex spoke up. "I'll have a Catillion draft, thank you."

The waitress wrote down all their orders. "Okay, I will be back in a few with your drinks." She picked up Skyler and Zarina's empty glasses and walked off.

Michael spoke up. "So, Skyler, what's up with the girl? I thought you didn't do girlfriends?"

Skyler grinned and placed his arm around Zarina. "Well, she found me. I don't normally have girlfriends, but with the way my schedule is, why not try it? I was lucky I got off on time today. But Cane says we're going to get busier soon and I won't have much of a personal life, and Zarina likes me and is willing to put up with it. So why not just have one? You know, try it out." He looked over at Kax. "So, what's going on with you and Rex?"

Kax's hand shook. "Well, you know we work together, and I think he is a cool guy. I thought I would bring him along to hang with us."

Skyler shook his head. "That's not what I mean, and you know it." He leaned on the table and stared down her and Rex. "I don't know when I will see you again, so I want to know. Is he your boyfriend or going to be?"

Kax's heart was racing, and her palms were sweaty. She looked over at Rex for some sort of sign to tell her what she should say next. She looked back at Skyler. "Well, I was hoping if Rex wanted to, he could be my boyfriend."

Rex put his hand on Kax's leg. "Hey, you're cute. I wouldn't mind going on a couple of dates with you."

Kax put her hand on Rex's. "You don't mind I'm younger?"

Rex grinned. "I don't normally go for younger girls, but you seem nice enough."

Skyler rolled his eyes. "You really are into older men. How old is this one?"

She looked at Rex. "How old are you?"

"38, you're still a cadet so you're 22?"

"She's 23, and that would make you 15 years older than her." Skyler pointed out. "Which is much younger than your last boyfriend, might I add."

The waitress came over with their drinks.

Kax glared at Skyler. "Ya, well, he was a jerk. Can we not talk about him?"

Rex looked over at Kax. "You don't have to tell me anything about your relationship, but how old was he?"

Kax groaned. "He was 62."

Rex's eyes widened. "Wow, talk about a cradle robber."

Kax took a sip of her drink, shooting Rex a look.

"So, Michael, did those plants make it to Earth?" Skyler asked.

"Yes, they did. I sent Perry a thank you message, and let us hope they are what I need to get out of my maintenance job." Michael looked towards Zarina. "So, Zarina, where are you from?"

She finished her sip. "I'm from Earth. But because of my dad's job we were posted around a lot, so I grew up on many different planets. This is my first year at the Earth academy. My dad has been working on Earth the last few years, but my mom had her posting to Mars when I was 17 and decided to join the academy there. My brother was doing his training here, but this is the first year he is not on Earth. He is a medical science officer and is in his last year, so they assigned him to Taurton Station because of his knowledge. Were you raised on Squall?"

Michael shook his head. "Nope, only went there to visit. I bet you know a lot about the stars. Skyler loves the stars."

She turned her attention to Skyler. "Really, I knew you wanted to be a captain, but you love the stars too?"

Skyler smirked. "Well, the stars are one thing no one can take away from me. But what Captain doesn't love the stars?"

"Lots, most people want to be a Captain so they don't have to take orders and can boss their crew around, but you really want to be one because you want to travel the stars, that's so rare to see nowadays."

Skyler held up his beer. "I want to take a ship and go for a joyride, exploring different cultures and discovering new places."

She snuggled up close to him, placing her hand on his leg. "I love true explorers."

He took a sip of his beer and looked deep into her eyes. "Well, then, how about we go back to my room, and explore the strange, new worlds under the sheets?"

"Mmm." She leaned closer and rubbed his leg. She moved her hand higher. She then pulled away. "Um, Skyler do you have a vibrator in your pocket?"

Skyler shifted and pulled his phone out of his pocket, and he looked at the message on the screen. "Sorry, babe that's Cane. I gotta get back to work." He kissed her on the lips. He finished his beer and got up. "See you later, guys." He pulled a couple of large bills out of his pocket. "Your drinks are on me. Keep drinking, order food, whatever. It's paid."

Kax took the money off the table. "Wish you the best."

Chapter 12

Skyler rushed into Cane's office. Cane was sitting there with a small suitcase packed sitting next to his desk. He looked around. "I came as soon as I could, sir. What's up?"

Cane finished typing a few things into his computer, then looked up at Skyler. "We have contacted the Cass and have agreed to try and negotiate peace. The meeting will be held tomorrow morning on Taurton Station. You need to pack a bag ASAP. We leave in 45 minutes."

Skyler pulled out his tablet. "How long are we going to be there?"

"Who knows could be one day, it could be two weeks. You can replicate and buy clothes there; it is just your uniforms you will be needing."

Skyler typed in a few things on his tablet. "Okay, I have sent Zarina a message. She has a key to my room, she can pack for me."

"You have known her for three days and she has a key to your room? What about your valuables?" Cane asked.

"Everything moved to the base storage center. I haven't had time to unpack. I just have clothes in my room, sir. I wouldn't normally give her a key, but I must go before she goes to school and she can't wait in the hall for me to get off work. It just made sense to give her a key."

Cane rubbed his forehead. "If you know what you're doing. There is no crime in giving her your key, but she should be careful when she is in your room after hours. That's still an offence."

Skyler nodded. "I know, sir. But her Mom is on the same floor as me so if she is not in my room she's there. I have no control over what rules she wants to break."

Cane typed in something on his computer. "Her mother is back in town? I didn't realize that. I thought she was still on Mars. Well, that is good news. I might need her for something."

Skyler frowned. "I thought you knew of everyone who was on base?"

Cane shook his head. "Normally I do, but Officer Vorkovich is with Davis's fleet, I don't know who the other Fleet Admirals choose to have brought to the base. Like how I didn't know that your mother was back. She is in Judson's. His choice, not mine."

"Ya, I just got back from talking about her with Kax and Michael, she's really driving them nuts at work."

Cane typed in a few more things on his computer. "I feel sorry for Kax. Damn, who transferred Michael?" He got up from his desk and turned his computer off. "I will have to deal with that when we get back. Till then they will have to deal with it."

Skyler followed Cane out of the room. He checked his messages one last time.

Cane looked over at Skyler. "Where is Zarina bringing your stuff?"

"She's taking it to the loading bay and she will meet us there."

Cane rushed down the hall. "She better bring it quickly; you can't replicate a uniform."

They got to the docking bay and Zarina was standing there with a small suitcase.

Skyler went over to her and gave her a big hug and a kiss. "Thanks for coming."

She kissed him back. "How long you going to be gone for?"

Skyler shrugged. "No idea, it could be a day, two weeks or longer. The meeting is tomorrow but we're there until a deal is reached."

She nodded. "My dad's in the car next to you. I haven't told him about you yet. He has been so busy."

He laughed. "It's okay, I won't mention it to him."

Cane cleared his throat.

Skyler grabbed his suitcase and gave Zarina one last kiss. "I got to go. I will send you a message when I'm back." He waved goodbye and walked into the cabin with Cane.

The doors closed behind them.

Skyler let out a yawn.

Cane shook his head. "No sleeping, you need to be briefed about tomorrow's meeting. The Governor-General just sent me a message while you were saying goodbye that when the ship takes off, our cabin is number 5 and we are to talk about plans for tomorrow."

Skyler yawned again. "Can't we do that in the morning over breakfast?"

Cane shook his head. "The talks are at breakfast." He pulled out a power bar out of his suitcase. "Here, eat this. It will give you energy. I have a few more, we will need them on this trip."

Skyler took a bite out of his power bar and sat down. He rubbed his neck and put his feet on the ottoman.

"No feet on the furniture!" Cane snapped.

Skyler took his feet off. "Sorry Cane, I was just trying to relax."

Cane sat down next to Skyler and brushed his curls out of his face. "You know, when you were on the platform with Zarina, you really did remind me of your father there."

Skyler smirked. "Really? How did I do that?"

"Your father was a lady's man. Not as active as you, but he always had a girl on his arm. But we went on dangerous missions, some long and some short. When he had time off, he would find a girlfriend and then before we left, give her the choice if she wanted to wait for him or not. A few waited but a lot didn't, because they were officers too and were probably not going to be there when he got back. But he was a heartbreaker. There were a few missions he had to break up with them because we would be gone for most of the year."

Skyler nodded. "It makes sense. Me and Zarina have agreed to not be exclusive because of that. Now that we're far apart, if I found a girl where we are going, I could be with her."

Canes eyes widened. "You can't wait two weeks?"

Skyler shook his head, trying not to laugh. "I'm not planning, just saying it could happen. Two weeks is a long time for me, though."

Cane shook his head. "Wait till you get older. Two weeks is nothing. Try 7 years."

Skyler's eyes popped. "Seven? How does that happen? Did my mother really break your heart that bad?"

Cane let out a deep sigh. "Yes, she did but that was 11 years ago. There was one more girl after her. I wanted a family. I found a lady and tried to juggle my career and date her. There was no time for a wedding. But it was in the plans. She got pregnant, and it was all looking good. Then she had a miscarriage. I realized I was too busy with my job and that was the end. I did it once or twice with professionals, but that's it. Not that I had a high sex drive before that."

Skyler looked at Cane as he spoke. "I'm so sorry, that sucks. I didn't know."

Cane shook his head. "Not something I talk about. She got married to another guy about a year later. But I don't have a good love life. I like to just look forward and pay attention to my career. You're the closest I ever had to a son you know, that, right?"

Skyler nodded his head. "I assumed that, and I'm glad to have you in my life."

The ship began to take off.

Cane got up and went over to the bar and poured himself a glass of sherry. "Want one? we have a meeting in a few moments."

"Can't hurt. I already have two beers in me."

"You have had enough time, you can have some more." Cane poured the drinks and brought Skyler's over to him. He sat down, taking a sip.

Skyler's eyes became heavy.

Cane hit Skyler in the arm. "Stay awake. They're going to call us for the meeting anytime."

He fixed his posture and finished his drink. "I'm awake, don't worry."

Cane sat there drinking his drink, watching Skyler struggle to keep his eyes open. He started to hum a tune.

Skyler's eyes widened when he heard the noise, he watched Cane hum. "What is that song you are humming?"

Cane stopped and rubbed his head, "It's nothing. Don't worry about it. I will stop."

"Don't stop, tell me about it. I know that song, I haven't heard it in years. What is it?"

Cane took the last sip of his drink as the announcement came on.

'Calling all council members to cabin five for a meeting.'

Skyler followed Cane as they made their way to the cabin. "Leon, tell me what song that was?"

Cane shook his head. "Now is not the time. Drop it, we will talk about it later."

Chapter 13

The meeting building was like a basic hangar, but the distant walls were cobalt blue. Skyler looked up as he entered and saw a glass ceiling. Because they were in space, he could see the stars above. He tried to keep up with Cane and take in the beauty of the new place. They rushed past the promenade. There were food stands and a shop. So many aliens were going about their daily marketing business.

Skyler caught up to Cane. "So, this is it, Star base 56. Why are the walls blue and not grey?"

"The walls are blue because all star bases have different colors. Well, most try to be unique. They may have the same set up inside so they try to keep different colors so you can tell them apart."

They went down a long hallway that was practically deserted. There was a key code on the door and Cane typed in his code.

The meeting room had the same blue walls and an oak table in the center. The Governor-General, Minister of Defense, and Fleet Admirals Davis and Judson were already there.

Skyler checked the clock; they were still on time. Cane took his seat next to Judson. Skyler sat next to Cane and the Minister of Defense.

Skyler looked around the table, leaned over and whispered into Cane's ear. "Where is the Cass leader?"

"High Emperor Fraxil will be here any time now. It's our job to be here before. Do you understand?"

"Yes sir." Skyler sat straight up. He got a message on his tablet and pulled it up quickly. He smiled when he saw it.

"Is that a picture of my daughter?" The Minister of Defense said, looking over Skyler's shoulder.

Skyler's face went white and he quickly turned off his tablet. "Um, what if it was?"

He shot Skyler a dirty look. "What is she doing sending you photos?"

Skyler's palms got sweaty. "Um sir, this isn't the place or time to talk about it. After the meeting I will be glad to tell you."

Before more words could be said, the door opened and in walked two large armored Cass bodyguards escorting a long-horned Cass. His teeth were pointed and sharp. He head was crowned with a thick set of horns that covered half of his head, with golden eyes and dark tanned skin. He sat down on at the head of the table. Just the look of him sent chills down Skyler's spine. His horns were golden in color and shone in the light, like a natural crown of thorns. He placed his long bonelike hands on the table. "Wells then," He hissed, "Sshalls we begins the meetings?"

Cane put his trembling hands under the desk. Skyler knew right then this emperor was more than he seemed, he had powers and was older than time itself. *If only I could take a picture. No one has seen this guy in years. I bet if I showed a picture of him to Michael, he would tell me more about the feud.*

The Governor-General spoke up. "Yes, everyone is here so let's begin this meeting," She lifted her tablet. "Okay, first issue—"

The High Emperor lifted his hand. "Excusess me buts I'm thes guest ofs honor. Is think Is sshould haves the rights to picks the orders and whichs topicss wes talk abouts."

The Governor-General cleared her throat. "If that is what you want then that is okay."

He placed his hand down, his eyes like laser beams staring everyone down at the table. "Firsts issue Is want thes remainss ofs my peoples returned tos their homeworld ats your costs and nos matter hows old thes corpses ares."

The Governor-General spoke. "There are many Cass who have lived their entire lives on Earth. I don't think they would want to be returned to their homeworld. Any Cass has the choice when they die where to have their body sent."

The High Emperor snarled. "Ands you humanss charge thems to burrys their deads. You peoples have nos respect fors the deads. No Cass would wants to bes buried ons Earth ors any others planet."

Cane spoke up. "If you would stop bombing areas where Cass live, then you will have fewer dead bodies to worry about."

The High Emperor peered over at Cane. "Does yours sscar sstills hurt? Dos you sstills get thes visionss ins your missings eye? Ors sshould Is ssay takens? It's been a long time since I have seen you."

Cane rubbed his eye patch. "It has been a very long time since we have last seen each other, but this is not the time to talk about that. We are here to talk peace."

"Wells, with your blockade ofs my planet, it iss hard not to ats least discuss terms, buts you humans needs to change yours ways ifs you ever want us to sstop."

Skyler knew there was more to what the High Emperor was saying. It was almost like they were speaking two different languages. He pulled out his phone and under the table texted Michael, hoping he would spill the information or connect him to someone who could help.

Cane looked down at Skyler, nudged him and whispered. "Put the phone away."

Skyler shook his head. "It's important, trust me."

Cane looked back at the High Emperor.

The Governor-General continued. "All the Cass bodies that have been buried on Earth or other Federation planets will be dug up and sent home free of charge to their families."

The High Emperor licked his lips. "Very good. Now I have more demands that need to be met."

Skyler cut him off. "Damnrok."

The High Emperor stopped. All the tables' eyes were on Skyler.

Davis spoke up. "What are you doing? this a very important meeting and you're playing on your phone and making random noises. Do you have no respect?"

Skyler turned his focus just on the emperor. "Damnrok. The Squallites said they are willing to enact the Treaty of Damnrok if you put a standstill to this war."

The High Emperor gave a smug smile. "I don't knows who yours contact is, but tells them. I will calls my mens offs if they enacts Damnrok. But theys must do it first."

The Governor-General looked over at Skyler. "What is this Damnrok?"

Skyler looked down at the rest of the message. "Um, it is something to do with a blessing and trees and bodies…"

"With the return of our bodies to our planet they have promised to bless the bodies, plant a tree in their honor." He stood up, "The war is still on until this is done. When I see some progress, I will consider calling off the war. I give you 2 weeks from today to discuss more." He got up and left the room with his bodyguards.

The Governor-General turned to Skyler. "Please hand me your phone."

Without hesitation Skyler handed her his phone.

She looked it over. "I'm going to have to take this in for evidence. For now, please inform your contact about the update."

"I understand."

She stood up. "I guess the meeting is dismissed. Please stay on the station till further notice."

They all got up and made their way out of the room. Cane grabbed Skyler's arm and pulled him aside. "Okay, kid, I need answers. What was that?"

Skyler smiled. "Well, you know how I said the Squallites know something we don't about this war? Well, it started off innocent. I took a picture of the emperor and sent it to Michael. He is the creepiest Cass I have ever seen. Thinking that would scare Michael into telling me something. It did, and he contacted his contacts and the high elder said the Damnrok thing."

Cane slapped his forehead. "You can't take a photo of the Emperor, he could have you killed for that. Only certain times we're allowed to photograph him. Let's hope he doesn't find out about that; I can't save you if he tries to kill you. Besides that, I think you did good for now. We have to wait two weeks to see how this pans out."

"So, what are we doing now?"

Cane looked at his tablet. "We have been put in a suite together for the wait. I have a computer there so I can get my office work done, can't do all my work but we can get some. So, we may have a bit of free time, more than we do on Earth."

Skyler got a grin across his face. An awfully large grin. "Well then, on the way in I saw a sign for a brothel here on the station. I don't normally pay but you have a 7-year itch and we're pressed for time. Want to go for a poke before returning to work?"

Cane frowned. "Is sex all you think about? It's been so long for me I don't think I need it."

"Are you nervous about paying for a girl? We could find some girls at the bar, but that might take longer."

Cane looked at his tablet one more time. "Maybe you are right. Okay, let's go, I think I'm overdue."

Chapter 14

They got to the outside of the brothel. Skyler went to walk into the building. Cane grabbed his shoulder and pulled him back. "Maybe we should think about this first. You have a girlfriend, and this is clearly unprofessional for me."

Skyler turned around. "Leon, we have the rest of the day off so let's get off. Lots of businessmen come here. Your secret is safe here. Zarina doesn't care, and I'm nowhere near her. I think this will help you get the edge off. You know how tense I am if I don't have sex."

Cane rubbed his forehead. "Skyler, this isn't right. You can go 2 weeks without sex."

Skyler rolled his eyes and pulled out his phone. "Hey sexy, we're going to be stuck here for about two weeks. Ya, I know, I will miss you too. Look, I am trying to convince Cane to go in with me to the brothel and he doesn't think you will approve. Could you talk to him for me? He hasn't had sex in 7 years I think he needs to get off." He handed the phone to Cane.

Cane took the phone. "Hello, Zarina, nice to talk to you."

"Hey Cane, it's nice to talk to you too. Skyler is fine to go to the brothel. If I was there, I would get him off myself, but I can't be there. He needs to relax. As for you I can't say. It can't hurt to try. You could consider it a bonding moment, like a father taking his son to lose his virginity."

Cane raised his eyebrow. "I never would have thought of it like that. Does your dad know what you're like?"

She laughed. "Only my brother."

"Well, it was nice talking to you Zarina, we will see you when we get back." He hung up the phone and handed it back to Skyler. "Well then, it looks like we're going in."

Skyler cheered. "Yes, let's have some fun!"

They walked into the brothel. Skyler went up to the front desk, "Two girls please, one for me and one for my friend."

The lady looked Skyler and Cane over. "Leon, long time no see."

Cane's eye widened when he saw the madam at the front desk. She was an aging woman with long blonde curly hair, lots of makeup and jewelry to distract from her age.

He went up to the front. "Suzina, long time. I didn't think you would still be working here."

She tossed her hair back. "When you last saw me, I was just starting out here, now I'm the madam and I see you are a Fleet Admiral, not an officer, and have a son. Times do change."

He grinned. "Skyler isn't my son, he is my apprentice. His father was Captain Therris." The man you were nervous about being first officer to, if I remember." She smiled.

He looked her over. "I'm guessing, though, if you're the madam you don't take clients anymore?"

She looked at Skyler. "He looks like his father. I have followed your career in the papers. I don't service clients anymore, but for you I'm willing to make an exception."

Skyler spoke up. "What about me?"

She whistled and three girls came out. A brunette human, a green-skinned lizard girl and a purple-skinned redhead came out.

He locked eyes with the purple girl. "I'll take her."

She came over and took his hand and took him to a private room.

Suzina took Cane's hand and walked with him into the back. It was a small room. Cobalt walls, low lights, and a queen-sized bed in the center.

Cane looked around. "I must warn you I'm a bit rusty. I haven't done it in 7 years."

She took off her top and brushed his hair out of his eye. "I don't do this often anymore. But I will tell you this, you never forget how to please a woman."

He kissed her on the lips.

She unzipped his jacket, revealing his chest, covered in large scars. She ran her hand up and down his scars. "You really have changed."

He picked her head up. "I got more on the inside."

She stroked his cheek. "I'm sorry."

He kissed her and took her to the bed. "Don't be. A lot of them I would not trade. Others are close to my heart."

She rolled on top of him and undid his pants. "You're too tense and locked up, don't hold back. Let go."

Skyler walked with the girl to the front desk. "How much do I owe you?"

She typed a few things into the computer. "$150 plus tip."

Skyler pulled out his wallet.

Cane came walking out with a smile on his face. "Put your wallet away, this is my treat." He pulled out his wallet and handed his card to the girl.

Skyler looked over at Cane. "You're in a good mood."

Cane looked over at Suzina. "A girl like that will do that to you. I trust you had fun?"

Skyler grinned. "You can bet I did."

The girl handed him his card back.

Suzina put her hand on Cane's face and kissed his lips. "You're here for two weeks. I hope you come back. I also make house calls."

Cane grinned. He kissed her back. "I'll be back."

He waved goodbye as they left the brothel and returned to the main complex. Making their way to their room, they passed the Minister of Defense.

"Therris, Cane," called the minister. "Over here. I want to speak to you."

They made their way over.

Cane spoke up. "Terry, what's up?"

Terry looked at Skyler. "During the meeting, I noticed you had a picture of my daughter Zarina on your phone."

Skyler's belly filled with butterflies. He and Zarina hadn't talked that much about telling her parents, just that he was supposed to wait. She wasn't closely related in jobs so he couldn't use that excuse. It was all or nothing, he was going to have to tell the truth. "Well sir, me and Zarina have just recently started—"

"Working on an assignment together," Cane cut in. "Skyler still needs to keep his studies up and your daughter had good knowledge of other bases and how they operate so I have teamed them up as his tutor on slow days."

The Minister of Defense nodded. "Good, I hope you two get along. She is a good girl, don't tarnish her reputation."

Cane put his hand on Skyler's shoulder. "Well, if that is all, then I think we will be going. It's been a long week and I think we all could use a little rest."

The Minister of Defense nodded. "I agree, enjoy your rest."

They made it to their quarters. Skyler looked around and saw the cobalt blue room. Simple decorations with plants and a few pictures on the wall. The main room was divided by half walls with the sitting area, kitchenette, and dining area. A small apartment. There were two rooms on either side of the room.

Skyler walked to the back of the place and opened one door. He looked in at the cobalt room. There were two end tables with lamps, a double bed and a standard bathroom to the side. He saw the green suitcase on the bed. "Looks like this is my room. They put my suitcase in here."

Cane walked over to his room. "That's fine, the rooms are the same. But it's getting late, so change into your off-duty uniform. And I'm going to take a nap. Do whatever you want."

Skyler started to undress. "Want me to order some food for us? I'm hungry and you will be when you wake up."

Cane was already in his pajamas and was getting into bed. "Sure, I saw there is a nice Pisces restaurant, order me something from there."

Skyler called over to Cane. "Hey, um, why did you lie to Terry out there for me?"

"I know he is very protective of his daughter and you two have just started your relationship and she isn't keen on telling him yet. Give it a month or two before you start bragging."

Skyler changed into his off-duty uniform. He put his dress uniform away in the closet. He laid down on the bed. He picked up his tablet and looked for the Pisces's menu on his tablet. His stomach rumbled as he looked for something to eat. He placed his order. While waiting for the food to show up he picked up his tablet and video called Zarina.

Zarina answered on her tablet, wearing a nighty. "Hey, Skyler, how are you doing?"

He looked at the background. "Are you in my room?"

She tossed her hair. "Oh yeah, my roommate, she has a guy over and they're too noisy so I figured you're not using your room. I could stay here. Is that okay?"

Skyler nodded. "Ya, that's fine. I got nothing of value in the room, just some clothes I haven't unpacked. What time is it there?"

She looked at the clock. "1 a.m. I was sleeping. But it's okay, I like talking to you."

"Ya it is only about 5 p.m. here, Cane is taking a nap and I'm waiting for food. Ordered Pisces takeout. I ran into your Dad and he saw the photo of you on my phone."

Her eyes widened. "What did you tell him?"

"Cane told him that you're tutoring me in how the other bases operate. So, your Dad is okay with us working together."

"Well, that's good. "How was the brothel? What did she look like?"

Skyler blushed. "You're not going to get mad at me, are you? This isn't a trap?"

She shook her head. "I told you to go. I want to know what she was like."

Skyler grinned. "She had purple skin, red hair and a forked tongue that felt amazing."

"You slept with a Bellatrixian? Wow they're uncommon in your part of space. If I ever decided to sleep with a woman, I would pick a Bellatrixian."

Skyler shook his head. "If you want to take time off and come out here and try her out, I'm sure Cane could get her to do a couple. He's old friends with the madam."

She laughed. "I'll think of it. It is only a few hours to get there. I might come up this weekend. Can't have you wasting all your money on her."

Skyler grinned. "Anything you want you can have. I do miss you."

She pulled down her top revealing her breasts. "Want to have a bit of fun over the video?"

Skyler propped up his tablet, got up and closed the door. He undid his pants. "When you're ready, baby."

She propped up her tablet and lifted her nighty.

"Oh, baby, I love you for this. I wish I could touch you."

She rubbed her inner thigh. "I wish you were here too."

Chapter 15

Cane woke up and saw Skyler at the table eating. The table was covered in takeout containers. He took a seat across from Skyler. "How much did you order?"

Skyler smiled. "Well, I was hungry, and I didn't know how much you would eat. Any leftovers we can eat later."

Cane looked in the containers. "Did you order everything on their menu?" He kept searching through the boxes. "Oh, you didn't, you got purple Echinozoa balls. These are my favorite." He looked in the bag for a pair of chopsticks.

Skyler was still smiling. "I ordered what they had. I'm glad you like them."

Cane lifted his head up from his plate. "You seem happy, what happened when I was asleep?"

Skyler grinned. "I can't lie. I had a really good conversation with Zarina. She might come and visit me this weekend."

Cane shook his head. "I should have guessed. I think it is nice she wants to come out and see you but just reminding you, this is not a vacation. Tomorrow we are back to work. Admiral Taylor is taking over my duties on Earth, but there is still lots of work I can get done on the computers here."

Skyler finished his plate of food. "I get that. But there are lots of things for her to do here. It's not that long of a trip if and she doesn't like it, she can go back. Also, there might be a threesome."

Cane pushed his chair back. "I'm not doing that, she is your girl and I have, no, just no!"

Skyler shuddered. "Ew, no, the Bellatrixian girl at the brothel. She isn't really into girls but would love to try one on them out."

Cane let out a huge sigh of relief. "Oh, thank you. Yeah, that's fine as long as it's not me."

Skyler grabbed some of the ostation crab noodles and put them on his plate. "That and her brother is going to be passing through. She must contact him for more details. If she is not here, she still wants me to meet him."

"He isn't going to kill you, is he? You know, for touching his sister?"

Skyler shook his head. "No, she wants to tell him first, he knows her better than anyone."

"I understand you now." He looked at his watch. "It's getting late. Have you slept yet? If not, I would recommend getting some sleep now. We need to be up at 6 a.m. They set me up a temporary office, where I can continue my work."

Skyler nodded. "Ya, I will be going to bed after I'm finished my food."

Chapter 16

Thursday night, Skyler was awoken by a call on his phone. He rubbed his eyes and answered his phone. "Captain Therris speaking."

A soft voice replied. "Hey Skyler, I just thought I would let you know I got the day off so I will be heading out in about 1 hour to catch the ship to see you."

Skyler grinned. "So, when I get up you will have landed. Sounds good to me. I can go pick you up, but I still must work all day, so you will have to entertain yourself."

"I'm fine with that. I can't wait to see you." She paused. "By the way, my brother is going to be passing through Sunday morning and will be there for a meeting with the medical board. But once he is done, he can have a late lunch with us."

Skyler brushed his hair back. "That sounds great. But what about your dad? Will he be at lunch? I bet he will want to see you and your brother too."

She paused. "My Dad and brother don't get along that much. So, my brother is going to meet him later in the day."

A loud voice blared in the background. 'Boarding call for all passengers heading to Star Base 56.'

"I got to go now, sweetie. See you in a few hours."

He rubbed his face. "See you in a few hours, sexy."

He got some more sleep and woke up at 5 a.m. He had one hour before he had to be at work with Cane. He got dressed in his off-duty uniform and headed down to the loading bay. When he got there, the ship had just landed. He waited outside the doors.

Two hands came up from behind him and put his hands over his eyes. "Guess who."

He grinned and turned around. "Oh, Zarina, I'm so happy to see you." He picked her up and kissed her on the lips.

She smiled back and hugged him. "I missed you too, sweetie."

He put her down, placing his arm around her and walking with his arm around her. "I don't have much time before I start work." He looked at his tablet, "I got about half an hour before I need to be there."

She pouted. "You mean we don't have time for a quickie?"

Skyler grinned. "I wish we had time, but you know I like to take my time."

She kissed him on the cheek. "That's okay, I can wait for you to get off work. I will just go shopping. I might go see my Dad and tell him I'm 'tutoring you.'"

He kissed her again. "You can do that. But hey, tomorrow I'm just on call. So we will have lots of time to have fun."

They made it back to the room. She pinned him against the outside of the door. "Maybe today I will buy a sexy outfit or something?"

He grinned. "Do it. I would love to see you in something sexy."

They started making out in the hallway when Cane opened the door.

He coughed. "You two better do that inside if you don't want your father to find out, Zarina."

Skyler and Zarina broke their kiss and entered the room.

Cane held out his arms and gave Zarina a hug. "It's nice to see you again."

She hugged him tight. "It's nice to see you too, Leon."

Skyler frowned. "I didn't know you two were so close?"

Zarina pulled away from the hug. "Because of my Dad's job he has worked close to Leon all these years."

Cane ruffled her hair. "I have known her since she was just a kid. It's no question you two would have crossed paths when you were older." Cane patted Skyler on the shoulder. "But you, Cadet, need to get changed. We're leaving for work in ten minutes."

"Yes, sir." Skyler went into his bedroom and got dressed. He came out a few moments later.

Cane had just finished showing Zarina the kitchen. He looked over at Skyler. "Good, you're ready to go. Let's get going."

Chapter 17

Skyler awoke to the soft touch of the woman in his bed. He rolled over and cuddled her. "Morning, sexy." He kissed her neck.

She moaned and held his arm close to her. "I love it when you hold me like this."

"I love having someone to hold." He kissed her neck.

"So, you have the entire day off?"

He nibbled on her ear. "On call, but that might as well mean that I have the day off."

She rolled over and kissed him deeply on the lips. "Well then, let's stay in bed all morning."

"Sounds good to me."

At noon, Skyler's stomach began to rumble. He kissed Zarina's neck. "Hey sweetie, I'm getting hungry. I think it's time we got out and got some food."

She kissed him on the lips. "I think you're right. Have you ever had Sumacinite food?"

"No, I grew up on meatloaf and standard Earth foods. Well, my mom did enjoy Ypanzoin, which is like a curry pizza. And Charles likes imported moon cheese. My experience with foreign foods is only recent."

"Well you will like Sumacinite food is like a berry curry. Very bitter. I love eating it on ice cream, but they find that offensive so we will order some in takeout, you got to try it."

Skyler laughed, making his way out of bed. "I will try it. I like food and I have been finding out there is more to the world than just Mom's meatloaf and casseroles." He started putting on his off-duty uniform.

She looked at him. "Why are you always wearing your off-duty uniform?" She got up and started dressing herself.

"Because I'm on call, it's not like this uniform is much different. I would just have to throw my jacket on. And I can still go to work in it." He put on his pants and black tank top and combed his hair. "Well, I guess it is time to get going."

They walked out into the living room. Cane was sitting on the couch in his off-duty uniform with a gold hoodie on.

Skyler looked at the hoodie. "Never seen that before. Where did you get the jacket?"

"There are many variations of the off-duty uniform you can buy. So, you don't have to wear the same one each day. I'm in my 60s. I'm not walking around looking like you."

Skyler looked down at his revealing ensemble. "Well where do I go to buy these elective uniforms?"

Cane looked at his tablet. "There is a surplus store on the second level. You should be able to get some. Let them know you are a command cadet, don't tell them you're a captain."

Skyler grinned and crossed his fingers. "I won't."

Zarina spoke up. "Well, we will see you tonight Leon, we're going to paint the town."

"Spaceport. Paint the spaceport. It's not a town." Skyler corrected. "But it doesn't matter, I'm hungry."

"You two are going out to eat? The food in the fridge is going to go bad."

Skyler sighed. "There is not much left. I thought it was all gone."

"Well then, enjoy your day out. Don't get into trouble." Cane said.

Zarina grinned. "No promises."

They kissed and walked out the door.

They began making out in the hall. One of the other doors opened in the halls. They stood standing not touching. A blue scaly alien came out of the room with a curvaceous figure.

Skyler was checking her out.

Zarina hit him in the arm. "Hey, I'm right here."

Skyler grinned. "What? I can't admire a sexy lady when I see one?"

"You can, just not in front of me, I won't check out other men or women in front of you."

He put his hand on her lower back. "Hey, you can hit on other women in front of me, I won't mind."

She laughed, leaned over, and gave him a kiss on his cheek. "I'll keep that in mind, sexy."

They made their way onto the promenade. There was a large holographic map in the middle of the entrance that told them where they were.

Skyler looked at the map. "Okay so the Sumacinite food place is on the second floor right near the surplus store. But the brothel is on the main floor where we are now, if you want to try it out."

She grinned. "We will see." She pointed to a few other stores on the first and second levels. "There seems to be a lot of places for shopping here. We should check them all out."

He pulled out his fat wallet. "Shopping is no issue for me."

They made their way over to the surplus store Skyler noticed so many different types of Aliens walking around the station there were many more than there were on the Earth base. But he noticed there was a lot more Cassiopeians than any other species on the base. "Hey Zarina, is this base near Cass space or something?"

She shook her head. "No, why would you ask a thing like that?"

Skyler pointed to the mall around them. "Because there are so many of them here."

Zarina paused and looked at the Cass for a moment. "Some look like civilians but the ones in the black armor, those are security. I wonder if this has something to do with the peace talks. Who do you think is here?"

Skyler paused for a moment to think. "You don't think the High Emperor would be here in person, do you?"

"Sweetie, there is so much security here they would blast you before you even thought of doing something to the Cass." She blushed and winked at one of the guards.

Skyler's hand shook nervously. "Great to know."

Inside the surplus store, on the walls, there was gear and uniforms from all ages of the military. Taken in by the place, he was grinning like a schoolboy when he got to the back of the room. He walked right up to the counter.

A young man was there in a tight old green military top, black slick hair, chiseled jaw and strong muscles. In a light Russian accent, he said. "Hello, I'm Dimitri, I see you are a member of the United Galactic Forces, how can I help you?"

Skyler grinned. "Right now, I'm just looking for my off-duty electives. Leon... I mean Fleet Admiral Cane told me there were different options besides what I'm wearing."

Dimitri smiled. "I can see how wearing the same thing can get you down each day. Follow me." He took him to the far wall and pulled a green leather jacket off the wall. He handed it to Skyler. "This seems to be your style."

Skyler's face lit up when he saw the jacket. "I love it!"

Dimitri smiled. "I thought you would like it. It can be worn by cadets and officers, weatherproof, and if you have a bike this would look awesome."

Skyler tried the jacket on. "I love it! I don't have a bike though; my friend does, he is in engineering. Do you have a blue one?"

"Let me look in the back. We don't have many electives for engineering." He went into the back while Skyler was checking himself out in the mirror.

Zarina put her arms around him. "You look really sexy in it, stud."

He grinned. "Do you want me to get you one?"

She shook her head. "No, I own most of the electives, you can buy me something else after."

The guy came out of the back with an older blue leather jacket. "Found one, it's the only one. I think they stopped making these several years ago. Do you think it is your friend's size?"

Skyler looked at the tag, remembering back to the last leather jacket he bought Michael back in their first year in the Academy. "I think that's his size, if not I will find someone who will fit it."

Dimitri frowned. "It's a 500-dollar jacket. Are you sure you don't want to call your friend and find out first?"

Skyler shook his head. "It's your only one, I want this to be a surprise to him."

Dimitri nodded. "I understand. I think they discontinued these when they allowed Squallites in the forces." He paused for a moment. "Is your friend a Squallite?"

Skyler nodded. "Yup, but he is a short one so I can't see him having a problem with the length."

"How short?"

"6'5" but his dad is 7 feet, they're short ones."

"Ya, this was one of the smaller jackets, I think that's why it wasn't issued, odd size." He examined the jacket. "Ya, it will probably fit. Anything else I can help you find?"

"Well, are there any other elective uniforms I can buy? I have money, that's not an issue, just dressing the same when I'm off duty is the issue. Also, I know I'm a cadet, but do you have anything a captain might wear? Once I graduate, I will be a captain, so might as well stock up now. Also, for women I got a friend who is a pilot and should pick something up for her, I know her size."

Zarina frowned. "You're buying Kax clothes?"

Skyler turned his head to cover his red face.

Dimitri went into the back.

"We've gone shopping a few times together. It's when I really get to spend quality time with her. She hasn't said yes to dating me yet, so this is as close as I get. I bought her a house." He slapped his forehead. *Why did I just say that?*

"Wow, I did not know you had it so bad for this girl. Why does she keep saying no to you if you're so wonderful?"

"She says I need to grow up, and she likes old guys. You met her."

"Yeah, I did, but are you sure her boyfriend won't be mad with you buying her gifts?" Zarina asked.

Skyler shrugged. "Why should I care? I can take him."

Zarina leaned in and gave Skyler a big kiss on the lips. "You owe me big time."

Dimitri came back out with a pile of clothing. "Well, soon-to-be Captain, here are your clothing options."

He looked through the clothes. He saw a few different t-shirts, hoodies, winter, and summer jackets all green like his uniform. Skyler looked up. "Why are there so many elective uniforms that we are not told about?"

"Well, you will be told about them, but you're a cadet from Earth unless you are going to an ice planet or a desert, they figure that your cadet uniform will help you survive all harsh weather. They just don't want to issue you anything you won't need. Some of these they don't make anymore, but have not been discontinued."

"Makes sense. I'm a guy who loves clothes, but I never get to wear them all because I'm always wearing my uniform. Usually when I go to the bar is when I get to try my clothes out. But being the Fleet Admiral's apprentice, I'm going to be always on call."

"Then that leather jacket will get you far. You ready to check out?"

He looked at Zarina one more time. "You sure you don't want anything?"

She shook her head. "I'm good. You can buy me something at a different store."

Skyler grinned. "Anything you want, sweetie."

Dimitri had finished running up the clothes and a total price was on a display above the cash register. "How will you be paying?"

Skyler pulled out his card. "Bank card. It's from Earth, is that okay?"

He looked at Skyler's card. "I will run it and check; I haven't seen that kind in a while. Most people who shop here use their UGF card and spend their credits."

Skyler looked in his wallet and pulled out a sliver-colored card. "You mean this one?"

"That's the card. Would you prefer to pay with that?"

Skyler handed it to him. "I'm still a cadet so I'm not too sure how much is on there."

He took the card and swiped it. "You're an officer, that's all you need. For buying supplies and UGF products they usually cover the amount. What happens is the accountants will look over the charge and then say these ones are covered and these ones aren't. The times that aren't, they will just deduct from your available balance. But most of this should be covered. The gifts you bought will probably be the only thing you get charged for."

Skyler shrugged. "I had no idea; I think they told me about this when I joined the Forces, but I have not used this card since."

Dimitri handed him back his cards. "Well, you know what, I would start using it more. You're on an away mission and they should cover most of this stuff and if not, you're just using the money you have earned. Also, you can go negative on the balance so then you pay back by working or in real cash. But if you're the Fleet Admiral's apprentice you shouldn't have a problem paying it back during your career." He placed all the clothes into bags for Skyler.

Skyler took the bags. "Thanks for your advice, I wish I would have known sooner. I have been spending my own money."

Dimitri smiled. "Well, you know now. Enjoy your new clothes."

"Thanks for everything, see you around." Skyler waved to him as he walked out with two large paper bags of clothes. They stood outside of the store. "So, where do you want to go now?"

"Right now, I want to go eat, then we will talk about shopping. I wanted to do more shopping before, but my stomach is getting the better of me."

Skyler grinned. "Then to the food court we go. Just promise me the item you want me to buy you later is not a ring. There is only one girl I bought that for."

Her eyes widened. "You bought Kax a ring and you're not even dating? What on Earth possessed you to do that?"

As they made their way to the food court, Skyler noticed there was a large population of Cassiopeians in this area too. *Huh, they're here too.* He returned focus to Zarina. "There was this other girl I was seeing at the time, and she told me if I'm really in love with Kax I should show her I'm serious. So, I went out and bought her a ring."

Zarina rubbed her face. "Sweetie, I don't know what type of girl she was, but you never do that if the girls are not interested. Please tell me you didn't propose?"

He took a seat on one of the glass booths in the food court and put his bags down, "I never got to show her the ring, but I did try to propose and she laughed in my face."

She leaned over to Skyler and held his face in her hands. She kissed him on the lips. "I'm sorry, sweetheart, but that's not how you get a girl."

He slouched down in his seat. "Well, I have tried everything else I normally do. But she doesn't want me."

Zarina giggled. "It's funny we're together and I'm giving you advice on how to win another girl's heart. You owe me big time. But I like you a lot, so I will do you a favor because even if we don't last you need to be a little smoother, and not mister one-night stand. Bad girls like that, and this Kax sounds like she's a good girl who already knows your tricks."

Skyler grinned. "You're awesome, you know that? So, which one of these places is the Sumacinite place?"

She got up from the booth. "Do you trust me to pick out some food you will like? Or do you want to pick from the menu yourself?"

"You can pick out my food. I trust you. Anything on ice cream tastes great."

"Yeah, I wanted to wait till we went back to the room to eat it, but I'm too hungry so who cares if they don't like it."

He leaned over and whispered in her ear. "If I like it enough, we can order more for later and I will eat it off you."

She blushed and gave him a kiss on the lips. "Oh, trust me, you will like this."

Skyler grinned. "Don't keep me waiting."

A few minutes later, she came back with two large trays of food.

Skyler took one of the trays out of her hands and placed it on the table. He looked at the feast of food. There was a bowl of stir-fry red sauce pasta, a small bowl of something that looked like red raisins, a large banana split and some bread like sticks with a red spice all over them. "Wow you bought a lot, I'm not sure we can eat it all."

She took her seat across from him. "I got a few take-out containers just in case. This kind of food keeps well. But we're going to eat the sundae first."

Skyler watched her take the red raisins and pour the bowl onto the split.

She took the spoon and scooped a spoonful of ice cream and seductively placed it in her mouth. She then took another spoonful and pointed it towards Skyler. "Your turn."

He gently smiled. "Okay then, let's try this." He opened his mouth and received the spoon. He moaned at the sweet, bitterly, and slightly salty taste. It was nothing he had tasted before. "Mmm, that's good, I can't describe it, but it is like sweet and salty popcorn, but creamy with a bit of a spicy aftertaste."

She grinned. "I told you it was awesome!"

Skyler nodded his head excitely. "It is, I love this. I'm glad you introduced me to this."

She handed him his own spoon. "I'm so glad you like it. Now dig in."

They took turns feeding each other and licking the remains off each other's lips.

When the split was done Zarina grabbed one of the bread sticks. "You still hungry?"

He rubbed his belly. "That was huge, it filled me up. I'm good, just pack up the rest of the stuff unless you want to keep eating."

She munched on the bread stick in her hand. "Naw I'm good. I think that split was a little too big for us. But we can eat the rest tonight. Come on, let's go shopping."

Skyler groaned in his seat. "Ya give me a minute, that's the most ice cream I've had in a long time."

She handed two full take-out containers to Skyler. "No problem, but could you put these in your bags, so we have some way to carry them?"

"Sure," He took the containers and placed them in the bag. He shifted around in his seat, "Okay I'm ready to go."

They both got up and made their way back to the promenade. Skyler looked at the stores. "So where do you want to go?"

She took his free hand. "Come with me and I will show you."

Skyler followed her lead. He looked at the sign of the store. It was a pink neon sign that read, *'Secret Lace.'* "You're taking me to a lingerie store? I'm going to enjoy this."

She turned around and kissed him on the lips. "Your budget is endless, right?"

He grinned. "As long as I get to see you in it, I will buy you whatever you want."

"What if I wanted a strap on?"

He shifted uncomfortably. "Are you into that?"

She giggled. "I just wanted to see your reaction. Let's go have some fun."

He followed her in.

She immediately knew where she wanted to look. She was looking at a lacy pink bra set.

Skyler went up right behind her. "You should try it on. I'm certain you would look good in that one."

She hit a few buttons on the keyboard, and the outfit on the mannequin changed. "What about this one?"

He kissed her neck. "If you keep showing me these, we're going to have to go back to the room sooner."

She twisted her neck and kissed him back. "Come on, be serious."

He thrusted his hips against her. "I'm being serious."

"Okay then, I'll make this quick. I already have an idea of what I like."

He let go of her and turned around. He saw a red-haired Catillion with black ears who was also browsing in the store.

"That set in purple would look great on you," he said, typing in a few buttons on the keyboard.

The girl turned around with her brown eyes wide. "What do you think you're doing?"

He saw the shock in her eyes. Her hands were shaking. "I'm sorry your hair reminded me of an old girlfriend and I know she looks dashing in purple. I wasn't trying to be a pervert."

She shifted away from him. "Thank you for your input but I know how to buy my own bras."

He scratched his head. "Right, sorry I'll leave you alone."

"SKYLER!" Zarina called him from the other side of the store.

He made his way over to the check out. "You're done already?"

She nodded. "I picked out the styles and colors I wanted. They are replicating them for me. I just need your card to pay for them all."

He kissed her neck. "Sounds good to me." He pulled out his wallet and handed his card to the cashier. "I thought you had your own money?"

"You owe me, remember? And plus, these are for you."

He put his arm around her waist. "I was just teasing you."

The cashier handed Skyler back his card. "Your card, sir."

He took it and placed it back in his wallet. "Thank you."

The cashier handed a neon pink bag to Zarina. "Enjoy."

Zarina grinned. "We will."

They left the store. Skyler turned to Zarina. "So, are we heading back to the room?"

Zarina shook her head. "One more stop. Then we can go back."

Skyler gave her a deeply passionate kiss. "Make it quick, I don't know how long I can last."

She ran her fingers through his hair, activating his curls. "You look cuter with curly hair."

He quickly brushed his hair with his hand trying to straighten them. "I don't like them. I wish my hair was straight and my nose was bigger."

She narrowed her eyes at him. "Well, the nose can be fixed with surgery but what does that..." Her mouth opened. "You want to look more like your dad and less like, I guess your mother?"

"Don't say that again!" He clenched his fists, "Yes, I have my mother's nose and the curls come from her side too. Everything else I get from my Dad. Well, he had more muscle mass, but I think that will come with age."

She kissed him on the lips. "You're handsome and sexy just the way you are, don't go changing."

"Where is this store you want to go to?"

She took his hand and guided him to a flashy jewelry store.

He froze when he saw the shining diamonds from the hallway. He pulled his hand away. "No way, I will buy you anything else, but we just met. I'm not buying you an engagement ring."

She turned around and burst into laughter. "Wow, your ego is so high you think that knowing you just an over a week that I want to marry you?"

He narrowed his eyes. "What other reason would a woman take her boyfriend to a jewelry store?"

She smirked. "They sell more than just rings; I was thinking of something like a bracelet or necklace."

That wouldn't be too bad. It is a little soon to buy her jewelry, but she is rich, maybe this is what she is used to. He pondered the idea, "I'll buy you a necklace, just don't make it too pricey."

She kissed him on the cheek. "You can pick it out for me if you would like? I just want a permanent gift from you."

He shrugged. "Well in that case, I can't say no."

They walked into the store. She walked over to the display of all the necklaces.

He looked at them, seeing ones of gold, silver, rose and many other colors of other worlds' precious metals.

The sales lady came over. "Can I help you find anything today?"

"Ya, I want to get a necklace for my girlfriend, one not too pricey but something nice. We have only recently started dating and we're not serious. But it can't be too cheap; we both have reputations to uphold."

The lady nodded. "Well in that case, what planet are you looking for?"

"We're both from Earth but we're on the station so is there anything from this area of space?"

Zarina turned her head. "I wasn't born on Earth. My parents are from Earth, but I was born on Neptune and my dad traveled around a lot."

"I was raised on Earth, but I was born in space."

The saleslady pulled something out of the drawer. She displayed a green shining teardrop stone on a silver chain. "It is a little bit more than you may be willing to pay, but this gem is made from a piece of Logantonite. It is a stone only found in certain meteors in space. It's the only place this is formed."

His eyes widened. "Did you say Logan?"

"No, I said Logantonite." She shot him a frown.

"My middle name is Logan and I was born in space. My mom always said I was named after her father, but now I wonder."

Zarina picked up the necklace and held it up to Skyler's face. "Well, the color does match your eyes."

"We'll take it. I can't think of a better memento of our time together. I don't care about the price, I have the money." He handed the lady his card. He picked up the necklace and put it around Zarina's neck. "It looks lovely on you."

"I will always think of you with this necklace. So, Logan is your middle name? That's got a nice ring to it, Skyler Logan Therris."

He grinned proudly. "That's the name my dad gave me. He named me Skyler because I was born in the stars and I'm of the sky. That's one way I know it is my destiny."

She turned around and kissed him on the lips. "Your dad really did care about you, didn't he?"

Skyler nodded. "Yes, and I miss him every day."

The lady came back and handed Skyler his card. "Payment went through, congratulations, Mr. Therris."

He took the card. "Thank you, this was an excellent choice."

Chapter 18

Skyler stepped out of the bedroom. He was wearing his new green tank top. He went over to the fridge and pulled out some left-over stir-fry and a fork. He walked over to the living room and sat down on the couch.

Cane was reading over some paperwork. He didn't lift his head. "I see you found the surplus store. And you shouldn't eat on the couch; there is a kitchen table for that."

Skyler ate some of his food. "It's not my couch, and I won't spill it."

Cane put down his papers. "But you have to clean up the mess."

Skyler put his bowl down on the coffee table. "So, I was thinking of calling my mother to ask her a question, but you might know the answer."

Cane looked up at Skyler. "Well, I saw your dad more than your mother ever did, so I should know."

"Who was I named after?"

Cane took a moment. "Your dad named you Skyler because you were born of the sky. Your mother wanted to name you Ryan. You're not named after anyone specific. He gave you your own identity."

"I know about my first name he always told me that, but what about my middle name, Logan?" Skyler said.

Cane paused and rubbed his chin. "I'm not sure. He seemed to have it planned. He never talked about the details. I knew your Dad so well that you would have been named Skyler if you were born on Earth, or a girl, he just would have switched the E to an A."

"Well, my mother always said that I was named after her father but I was at the jewelry store today and the lady showed us a stone Logantonite, it was green and it made me think of Logan and it is only formed in space."

Cane put his head down and let out a deep laugh. "Wow I never caught that before. I would not doubt if that what your dad thought of. Your grandfather might have been named Logan, I never met him, he was dead long before I came along. He died when your mother was 16 your uncle took care of her until she was an adult."

"I have heard a bit of the story, but my mother doesn't talk too much about the past."

"If you want to know for sure, call your mother and find out. You can use my phone since I know you don't want her to have your number." Cane pulled his phone out of his pocket, leaned over, and handed it to Skyler.

Skyler took the phone. "You think Zarina is still asleep? I don't want her to hear this conversation."

Cane laughed. "After the noises I heard coming from that room, she will be asleep for a long time."

Skyler blushed. "We were that loud?"

"She was, I didn't hear you. Now call your mother."

Skyler typed in his mother's phone number. "But what if it is too late to call?"

"She has a newborn and she really wants you to contact her. I think she won't care about what time you call."

His hand trembled, as he tried to hit the call button. "Maybe my uncle will know, I can call him."

Cane reached over and hit the call button. "I know more about you than your uncle Justin, now talk to your mother."

Skyler's heart pounded as the phone rang. He wanted to hang up, he didn't want to talk to her. *Is this really that important?* Before he could hang up and throw the phone someone picked up.

"Leon, what are you doing calling me this late? Skyler better be okay, because if something happened to my boy, I will personally kill you!" A shrieking woman's voice blasted through the phone.

"Mom, it's me, Skyler. I'm using Cane's phone."

She let out a sigh of relief. "Oh, baby, thank you for calling. Have you quit the academy? Are you coming home soon?"

Skyler clenched his fist. "No, Mother, I have not. I called to ask you a question."

She groaned. "If it's about your father, ask Leon, he knows more than me."

"It's sort of about Dad, but Cane doesn't know. I want to know about my middle name, Logan."

"What about it?"

"Who picked it and who or what was I named after?"

"Your grandfather, my father, his name was Logan Munroe. Why do you ask? I have told you this before."

"Mom, do you know what Logantonite is?"

There was a long pause. "That son of a bitch! He could never let me have anything. It was always about him. That rat bastard, he made me think he wanted to name you after my father when he just wanted to name you after a stupid rock!" She screeched through the phone.

He held it back from his ear. "Mother, calm down, okay? Dad's gone, you can't stay mad at him."

She took a deep breath. "You're right, son, he just took you from me. I wanted a baby too, but no, everything about you had to be just like him. He had to have it his way. Is there anything else you would like to ask me about?"

Skyler shook his head. "No, that was it."

"How are you doing by the way? I'm just curious? Are you staying out of trouble?"

He sighed. "I'm doing fine, mother, and yes, Cane is keeping a close eye on me. I'm not allowed to get into trouble."

Skyler could hear a baby crying in the background. "Skyler, I would love to talk more, but your brother is crying, I got to take care of him. Thank you for calling, please call anytime."

"Nice talking to you to mother, goodbye." He hung up the phone and handed it back to Cane. He leaned back on the couch and covered his face. "That was the best conversation I have had with her in years, and I still want a beer."

"Watch your beer limit. We might be called in tonight. No more than three, okay?"

Skyler got up and went to the fridge and pulled two beers. "Three is such a low number."

"It's low for a reason. How long is Zarina going to be here?" Cane placed down a set of papers to pick up another.

"She leaves tomorrow, she has to get back to class, but she is going to be here in the morning, then have lunch with her brother and dinner with her father before she leaves." He walked back into the sitting area and sat in the chair next to Cane.

"Good, because things are going to get a lot busier for us. There are some associates coming here for meetings. They realize that I can't leave so they will be coming here. I would read over the papers on the table; they're your briefings."

Skyler took a sip of his beer and picked up a stack of papers. "Why do you have so much paperwork? I thought they didn't use paper that much anymore?"

"Because they're top-secret documents. Digital devices can be easily hacked, so to stop that, they only print out the copies they will need and send them to those who need them. They are on heat-sensitive paper, so that even if they get lost a short time later, all the words will fade. Good thing is the paper can be reused if it is not too damaged."

Skyler finished his beer. "So, my other question is: this Starbase, is it UGF or was it built by a private company?"

"It's UGF. But it is a public Starbase. But if you wanted to live here in the future, you could with your UGF citizenship, and all the stores will give you your Forces discount. That's one reason there are a lot of shuttles coming and going here all the time, because it is run by the Forces, we can use any of the meeting rooms at any time. Lots of civilians who live and work on the station, but UGF comes first."

"Interesting. I haven't been on too many space stations, so I don't really know how they work." Skyler finished his beer and opened the second one.

"This year you will be on a lot of them. They're very good meeting points for us. Now enough chit-chat."

Chapter 19

Zarina awoke in Skyler's arms. She shifted around, trying not to wake Skyler. She moved his arm over and got up out of the bed. She picked up her stocking off the floor. As she started to get dressed, she watched the peacefully sleeping Skyler. His face was free from worry and pain. She was nearly dressed when Skyler's body shifted. Still asleep, he grabbed for a pillow and hugged it. He spoke in his sleep, "Mommy, no!" A tear came to his eye, he grabbed the pillow tighter, then started kicking and tossing. She stopped getting dressed and observed Skyler for a moment. Then she went over and placed her hand on his shoulder and whispered into his ear. "I'm here, Skyler, everything will be all right."

Skyler stopped twitching and opened his eyes. "Zarina, what's going on?"

"You were having a bad dream." She gave him a sympathetic smile.

He brushed his hair back. "Was I? Sorry, I didn't wake you, did I?"

She shook her head and gave him a kiss on the check. "No, you didn't, I got up just before."

He sat up in the bed. "You're leaving so soon?"

She sat down on the bed. "I got to meet my brother for noon, but I have a bit of time."

Skyler turned his head to the clock that read 7 a.m. and sighed. "We never got to go for that threesome."

She smiled and got on the bed and crawled over to him. "You only think about sex, don't you?"

He brushed her hair out of her face. "I think about other things. But I know that was something you wanted to do when you were here."

She kissed him on the lips. "Well, there is always next weekend. You are here for two weeks?" She paused. "Call and see if you can book her this early in the morning."

Skyler leaned over and picked up his communicator.

Zarina put on her top and went out into the hall to the living room.

Cane was sitting there doing paperwork again. "Morning Zarina, sleep well I assume?"

She went over and sat next to Cane. "I have a question: does Skyler always have nightmares?"

Cane picked his head up from his paperwork. "I haven't really watched him sleep. But I remember he used to have them a lot when he was a child. I bought him a stuffed teddy bear to help him. I have no idea what happened to that."

"Wait, I'm confused. His father died, how come you knew him as a kid?"

"I was his father's first officer and his unofficial step-father. I lived with his mother for a few years. But that was before she married Senator Roux."

Her eyes widened, "Wait Senator Roux? So, Skyler is related to the legendary Captain Therris, a Fleet Admiral, and a Senator? Anyone else I'm missing? He is going to go far."

Cane chuckled. "His uncle is married to Lady Melanie, the Duchess of Copthorne. So, as you can see, he comes from a long line of influential people, much like yourself."

She let out a long sigh.

Skyler came out of the room dressed. "Zarina, we got to go. I was able to make a booking for the morning. We have her for the hour if that's okay."

Zarina picked up her head. "Sounds good, thanks for making this happen." She got up off the couch and followed Skyler out.

Skyler gave Zarina a passionate kiss. "Thank you, that was amazing. I hope you enjoyed yourself?"

She nodded. "It was a great experience and I enjoyed it more than I thought I would. And I wouldn't mind doing it again."

He kissed her one more time. "I'm glad you had a good time." He let out a sigh, "When will I see you again?"

She brushed back his hair and stared into his bright green eyes. "Maybe next weekend if you're still here. If not, next time you're on Earth I will be waiting for you."

"Well, I'm very happy you came out here. I look forward to seeing you again. You have a key to my place, you can stay there anytime you want, just don't bring anyone else into the room."

She kissed him on the lips one more time. "I got to go have lunch with my brother now. Enjoy your paperwork."

They waved goodbye and she went into the restaurant.

She typed in a name on the holographic screen and a map with the tables showed up. She walked to the back and found the table her brother was at. She saw him reading something on his tablet. "What are you reading, bro?" She sat down.

"Medical files. Turns out I will be here for a few more days. A Zingiber has gotten sick and since I'm an expert on Zingibers they asked me to stay." He picked his head up from his tablet.

"You agreed to stay, even though you know Dad is on the station for the next week?" She pulled out her tablet and began reading the menu.

"And you came to this station to see your boyfriend knowing Dad was here?" He narrowed his eyes. "People's lives are more important than my personal feelings towards our father."

"How did you know I had a boyfriend?"

He laughed. "Why else would you come all the way out here on a weekend? This is a nice Starbase but there are nicer ones if you wanted to go shopping."

A green light lit up on the wall next to them. He reached over and opened the small door and pulled out a bowl of ginger squash noodles.

"I told Dad that me and Skyler are working on a project together."

"Skyler? I thought you were dating a guy; you're now dating women?" He put his tablet away.

"Skyler with an ER, not AR. He is Captain Therris's son." She placed her order on the tablet.

"The one who is the Fleet Admiral's Apprentice? Yes, I found out from Dad and did a background check on him. He doesn't seem your type, he seems like the kind of guy Dad would want you with."

"That's true and it bothers me. I wanted to seduce and humiliate him to make him pay for ending Dad's career. But after the first day, I realized he isn't just another rich privileged brat. He honest and a sweet guy." The green light lit up again. And she pulled out her plate of crispy Chicklop Strips.

"Well, you know. You know he has a reputation, right, for being well known with the ladies?" Her brother began to eat his food.

"I know, that's why I knew my plan would be easy." She paused and looked at her food. "I thought it would be easy."

"A week and you have fallen for him already?"

"No, but I think we might need each other right now. There's something about him."

Yurey slurped his noodles. "Well, if this does bloom into something else you found a good choice."

Chapter 20

Skyler groaned and threw his head back as he walked out of the meeting with Cane. "How many more meetings are we going to go through? There are so many, day in and day out."

Cane patted Skyler on the back. "You're lucky they are letting us break for lunch and supper. I told you, this wasn't going to be easy."

Skyler turned his head to look at Cane. "There is no time to sleep or do anything. It's not fair."

Cane walked with Skyler to the food court. "Now do you understand why I couldn't have a family? Why I haven't had time for a relationship? I have been doing this for ten years and the last five, there has been an impending war which has made my job that much harder."

Skyler looked at the holographic menus on the table. "Eating so much take out, I think I have tried just about everything on here."

Cane pressed a few buttons. "I ordered you an Alterian wrap. We don't have much time to eat if we want to get a good night's sleep, we have the big meeting in the morning and soon we get to go home."

"Ya, then I get to do your job and schoolwork." Skyler placed his head down on the table. "I'm so tired of all of this."

Cane chuckled. "No schoolwork, only this, and you will get used to it. And you will be glad about this: Michael is going to be flying out tomorrow for the meeting. We also have one of the Squallite high elders. Maybe we can finally put an end to this war."

A husky voice came from behind Skyler. "Excuse me Fleet Admiral Cane, but could I have a word with your apprentice?"

"Ah, Dr. Yurey Vorkovich, long time no see. You can certainly have a few moments with my apprentice."

Skyler picked up his head and checked over his shoulder. He saw a tall muscular man with a chiseled face and light brown hair. "I'm sorry, but do I know you?"

"We have a mutual friend, Zarina. I'm her brother."

Skyler's heart sank and he slowly got up. "Look I didn't hurt your sister—"

He held up his hand. "You're fine, I just would like to talk to you in private."

Skyler followed Yurey to the edge of the food court where they had some privacy.

"I would've talked to you sooner, but we have both been busy. This is my last day on the station and when I saw you, I knew it was my best chance to catch you. I just want to talk about you and my sister."

Skyler's palms were sweaty, and his eyes were wide. "You're not going to punch me out like the first guy, are you?"

He paused for a second, raising a brow. "Cory? She told you about him? No, he was an asshole who was molesting my sister, from what she has told me you're not doing that."

"She didn't tell me that detail, just that you were very protective of her."

He nodded his head. "I care about my little sister, she is the only family I have. I had a falling out with my parents when I told them I wanted to be a doctor and not a diplomat." He paused. "I know what my sister is like, and for some reason she seems to be really taken by you and you're not her regular type. I just want you to know: Be careful, don't take advantage of her and if you break her heart, I will break you."

Skyler snarkily replied. "But what if she breaks my heart?"

He narrowed his eyes. "Then I will buy you a beer."

Chapter 21

Michael stood on the platform with his bag in hand. This was the first time he had ever been to Taurton Station. It was a place he had always wondered about since he was a child. He remembered back when he was a child and his father left him for a summer on Squall to be with his aunt and uncle while he worked on building one of the new levels. He stood there in awe of this large structure. The grey steel building looked no more impressive than any other station. He was kind of disappointed that they kept the same design as all the others. As he walked off the platform, he heard his name being called out.

"MICHAEL! Michael, over here!!"

Michael turned his head and saw Skyler waving to him in the distance. He calmly approached his anxious friend. "What are you doing here?"

Skyler raised an eyebrow. "What do you think? The same thing as you are doing. You're here for the meeting."

Michael narrowed his eyes. "I know that, but I meant, what are you doing at the loading dock here?"

Skyler pointed towards Cane. "Well, we're sort of pressed for time so Cane thought it would just be best to meet you here now and go straight to the preliminary meeting instead of waiting for you to get settled in."

Michael shrugged. "So, Cane sent you alone?"

Skyler spun around. "No Cane's back there." He scratched his head. "I guess I was just too excited to see you. How is work? How is Kax doing?"

Michael let out a long sigh. "Right now, if you make me work all weekend and don't let me get any sleep, that will still be better than my job. Your mother is horrible. Kind of makes me want to ask for the transfer far, far away."

"Sandy can be like that," Cane said, walking over, "but you won't need to worry about her soon. She is only temporary, and we are getting a transfer from Station 8 to take her place so she can go back into retirement."

Michael just stared at Cane. "Really well the whole department will be glad to hear that. I think Rex is the only one who can handle her."

Cane reached his hand out. "If you will, Michael, hand me your bag and I will hand it to someone to take it to your room. You will not be needing it, and I'm glad you got the memo to wear your dress uniform. It will be needed. Now if you will, boys, follow me."

Michael handed his bag to Cane and followed him down the long platform. When they got back into the main hall, Cane handed the bag to a dark green skinned alien in a black and red security uniform. Then they continued their way.

Skyler leaned over and whispered to Michael, "so, what is the deal with Kax and Rex?"

Michael opened his mouth to respond when Cane butted in. "This is not the time to talk about personal lives. We need to stay focused on the negotiations. There will be time for gossip later."

Michael followed Cane with Skyler and passed the promenade to red elevators in the back of the building. Cane inserted a key and the elevator took them to the 3rd level. They stepped out into a round meeting room. They were the first ones there.

Michael frowned. "Where is everyone?"

Cane took his seat near the front. "We're early because I want to talk to you about what you plan to say before Therris decides to throw one of his curveballs again. That is always why we are having the meetings here. It blocks all electronic signals, so no devices can be used in the room. We don't want to risk the High Emperor finding out that Skyler took a photo of him during the last meeting. This discussion needs to be 100% serious and legit. So please Officer Jones, speak."

Michael took in a deep breath. "Well, when I got the photo from Skyler, I sent it right to the High Elders. They knew that if the Emperor was showing his face again that this war was serious and they are now willing to enact Damnrok."

Cane cut in. "Yes, I heard about that. What exactly is that?"

"Damnrok is a way of saying we will cease fire and answer to their demands until they are fulfilled."

"Are you talking about surrender!?" Skyler blurted out.

Michael shook his head. "No, it is a temporary thing. They are going to war with us for some reason, so we agree to enact Damnrok so then they tell us their demands and we agree to cease fire and we have fulfilled their deal. We can still build armies and be prepared to attack but we need to listen to their demands and try our best to work this out."

Cane leaned forward and rubbed his chin. "Why after all this time are they agreeing to make a compromise and negotiate? They could have done this five years ago."

"Because they have just proved to us that the Cass are not just fighting for honor, they are fighting for a reason. They are not trying to conquer, they just want something—"

"What do they want, Michael?" Cane's glare pierced Michael's eyes.

Michael shrugged. "I don't know. There are things that all Squallites are told that stay with us and things that are only for the high elders. I do not know what the Cass want, but everything is on the table. I can only tell you what I know."

Cane backed off. "That is understandable, and I do want you to know, Michael, that you will be rewarded for your information." Cane hit a few buttons on his tablet and brought up the document. He slid it across the table to Michael.

Michael read over the document. "You're promoting me and making me a mechanic? Sir, I already am one."

Cane took back the tablet and zoomed in on a part of the letter. "No, you are an assistant maintenance man. This will give you the job to work on ships, or just one ship, in repairs so no going to the front. Also, that promotion might be small, but you will be paid full wages, not the Squallite wage."

Wow full wage, that would be nice. I could help my Dad out a lot with that money. "Thank you, sir, I am pleased to be of service to you."

Cane checked at the time on his tablet. "Enough of this talk, the meeting is now about to start."

Just as the three of them turned to face the center of the circle of tables, the doors opened and the King and Squallite's most senior Elder came walking in.

The High Elder took his seat next to Michael. He turned his head over to Michael. "I hope you know what you are doing, Majerik."

"I have just relayed long overdue messages, Your Highness." Michael stayed calm.

Soon more and more people entered the room until all the tables were full. Once they were all settled, another figure entered from the side of the room. He was 8 feet tall, with a crown of thorns growing from his head. he was followed by two security guards. He walked in with his long brown robes and took his seat at the head of the table. He placed his long branchlike hands on the table. He turned his head towards the king and opened his mouth, revealing his fangs.

"Greetings, King Albert," said the long-horned Cass with thick cracked bark-like skin said.

"And same to you, High Emperor. I have the Squallites' High Elder here with me today so we can negotiate the terms of Damnrok."

The Emperor faced the direction of the High Elder. "Rhettoc, it's been a long time. Nice to see you again."

The High Elder kept a serious face. "I do not appreciate meeting under these circumstances, but it is nice to see you again."

The High Emperor narrowed his eyes. "So, you really want to enact Damnrok."

The Elder nodded. "That was the agreement if we ever saw each other again."

The Cass smiled a wicked grin, revealing his fangs. "Well thens heres is a list of mys demands. One: all the Cass buried on other Federation planets bodiess musts bes returns to Cassiopeia for delivery for their proper burial."

The leaders looked around the table and they all nodded their heads in agreement.

"I cannot see a problem with that," Fleet Admiral Cane said. "Is that your only request?"

The Cassiopeian Emperor raised his hand, gesturing, pointing his long pointed finger up. "One mores thing, respects for ours dead. Any mistreatments that comess to them, those whos do wrong to thems will bes handed overs to uss for theirs punishment."

The decision for this was decided less quickly, but it was Fleet Admiral Cane who cast the first vote in agreement. Once all the votes agreed with the terms of the Cassieopeian Emperor, the meeting was adjourned.

Chapter 22

The meeting was over. Skyler unzipped his jacket and lay across the couch in his and Cane's room. "I hate all these peace talks."

Cane grabbed two bottles of beer out of the fridge. He walked over and handed one to Skyler. "They will be all over soon. We now know what the Cass want, and it is just a matter of figuring out how to do it and signing an actual treaty."

There was a knock at the door. Cane got up and answered it. Michael was standing there with a bag in one hand and a key in the other. "My key didn't work for my room. I tried to call for maintenance, but no one is responding. Not even the robots."

Cane stepped back from the door. "Come in, Michael. I will try and call maintenance for you. There is beer and food in the fridge. Help yourself. If worse comes to worse, you can crash on the couch."

Michael stepped into the room and put his bag down next to the coffee table and sat down in the living room chair next to Skyler. "Thank you, sir. I'm good for now."

Cane went off to his room to make the call.

Skyler rubbed his temples. "How have you been doing?"

Michael crossed his legs and sat back in the chair. "I have been doing all right. Your mother is a pain to work with, but Kax and I are managing."

"I miss hanging out with you." He paused and sat up a little bit. "Well really, I miss having free time. This job has so much paperwork I can't stand it."

"Well then, why did you apply?"

He leaned forward and grabbed his beer. "I didn't. Well, I sort of did. Cane asked me a few questions and I signed something, but I didn't realize that this is what I was signing up for."

"Well, your job is an honor not many people get, so enjoy it. It's something no Squallite has ever done."

Skyler took a sip of his beer. "I'm not sure if that's a bad thing."

"Are you still seeing Zarina?"

"Yup, she is great and keeping an eye on my stuff on Earth."

Michael's eyes widened, "You are letting her watch your Dad's top-secret files? Are you crazy? You just met her."

Skyler chuckled, "No. Those files are locked away in storage. It's mostly clothes that are in my room. I have not been there much since the school year started."

"Well, that is good then," Michael looked down on the coffee table. "There is one thing I'm not supposed to tell you, but I think you should know. Kax misses you."

Skyler smiled, "I figured as much. I miss her too. I would call her, but I didn't want her to think I was bothering her. But you can tell her to call me when she has time, I would enjoy hearing from her."

"I will let her know."

Cane came out of his room with a grim look on his face. "I'm sorry, Michael, you're going to have to stay on our couch. There was a plumbing problem in your room, and they have sealed it off until it can be fixed."

He calmly replied. "And let me guess they are not going to give me a replacement room because they are all booked or under repair?"

Cane raised an eyebrow, "Yes, how did you know?"

Michael brushed back his light brown hair to reveal his pointless ears. "It's not the first time I have heard these excuses."

Skyler's eyes bulged. "WHAT!? Are you saying they aren't giving you a room because of racism?"

Cane narrowed his eyes. "I don't doubt what you are saying Michael, but this is a Federation station they aren't allowed to deny you a room. If you want, I will put in a complaint for you."

Michael waved his hand. "No, do not bother, they did not say it was because of my race they said it was a plumbing problem that is how they get away with it. I bet if we broke into that room, we would find out that there is no plumbing problem at all." He said with a negative tone.

Cane sat down on the chair opposite to Michael. "I know Earth citizens are not that friendly to Squallites. But in the Forces, we are all one people, no one is to be put above the other..."

Michael tugged on his uniform and shot Cane a stern look. "Then what is this? If the

Forces are all about equality why am I forced to wear a blue uniform. It is a racist restriction. I am an engineer. A Cass who serves in the Forces has no restrictions and we have gone to war with them many times."

Cane let out a deep sigh. "I know what you are saying, Michael, and I'm sorry. The Forces are run by people of Earth, and they put the restrictions on, not me. I don't make the rules."

Skyler raised his hand. "Wait, Cane you're the head of the Forces, why don't you have a say in the rules?"

Cane sighed. "The King, the President and other world leaders make the rules, not just one person. If we wanted to change our policies I could go to the King and ask him and if he felt there was a big enough concern, he would have a meeting with the other leaders and they would take it to their counsellors and take it to a vote. The Forces might be run by the monarchy, but no one person controls the rules." He turned his gaze towards Skyler. "Charles would be a good person to talk to about your concerns about the Squallite rights."

Skyler busted out in a loud roar of laughter. "Ya if me or Michael told him that we wanted rights for Squallites, he would work on making them have less rights. I'm not sure what his real opinion is, but I do know he has even less opinion of me."

"I know what Charles is like, but my point was it would do you better to go to someone like him and ask for change than it would be to go to me. I see everyone as equal. I judge by abilities and make sure everyone is provided their rights." He turned to face Michael. "And you being provided a room to sleep in for the night is part of your basic rights. If you really feel that you are a victim of racism, I can go and argue with them right now. Because even if they aren't lying, they need to provide you a room."

Michael shook his head, "Do not bother, I am only here for two days, the couch will be fine."

Cane pursed his lips at Michael's response.

Chapter 23

The peace talks began early the next morning. Skyler's head throbbed from the lack of sleep. He hoped this would be the last day and he could go home to his bed and sleep. He missed his friends and he missed his girl-friend.

He sat down in his chair and once again everyone arrived, and the meeting began.

The High Emperor gave a piercing glare through the screen. "Sso will mys demandss be mades?"

The President narrowed his eyes. "Well sir, what you have requested will cost tons of money..."

The Cass bared his teeth, "sso thens what iss yours answers?!" He hissed angrily.

The King spoke up. His hand trembling from seeing the Cass's full dark war smile. "We will do it. We will dig up and return all the bodies of Cass that have fallen on Federation planets and return them to Cassiopeia for their proper burial."

The Cass Emperor grinned.

"We will do this for you," the King said, "and you will stop the war and make peace with Earth and the Federation."

The Emperor paused, "We weres never ats war withs the Federations, jusst Earth. Buts you has a deals, but thes war iss nots over. No peaces treaty wills be ssigned untils you holds up yours end ofs the bargains. Iss that understsstoods?"

Skyler leaned over to Cane, "So what, we have to do all the work and then hope they agree to peace."

Cane gave Skyler a little jab. "It's all we can do for now."

Skyler shook his head, "There is more going on here."

The emperor hissed and looked at Skyler through the view screen. "Rudes humans sstops the talkingss."

Skyler got a good, clear look into the Emperor's deep brown eyes. He had never seen a Cass this old and this close to him before. It might have just been through a screen and he was thousands of miles away, but Skyler saw something he didn't think was possible. He saw right through him, deep into the eyes, to the back of the Cass's mind. He saw visions and flashes of memories he couldn't quite work out the meaning to in the Cass's eyes. Scenes of wars, fires, and betrayal. He leaned back in his seat and nodded. "Sorry, Your Highness, I will keep my mouth shut."

The Emperor turned back to face the King. "I expects to ssees thosse bodiess sstarting to bes returned bys the ends of thes month, iss thats clear?"

The King nodded. "It is, and thank you, your highness."

The meeting was adjourned. Cane had gone to talk to some of the other leaders before they left the room. Skyler, who followed him like a shadow, tapped Cane on the shoulder. "Cane, I need to talk to you."

Cane was talking to the President. He shifted to Skyler. "Go talk to Jones or someone, I'm busy right now."

Skyler frowned. "It's important."

Cane sighed, "Therris, I'm going to see you in the room soon. It can wait until then."

Skyler clenched his fists. He turned and walked away to go and see Michael.

Michael was talking to the Squallite High Elder.

Skyler tapped Michael on the shoulder, "Michael, I need to talk to you right now."

The High Elder looked down at Skyler. "Apprentice Therris, can't you see that Majerik is busy right now?"

"I know that, sir, but it is about the Cass. The Emperor showed me something."

The High Elder narrowed his eyes at Skyler. "What do you mean, showed you something?"

"In his eyes. When he looked at me, they went clear and were like little TV screens into his mind."

"He showed you that, did he?" The High Elder rubbed his chin, intrigued. "Please tell me what you saw in these visions."

"It was a war. An old war, there was a fire and people were dying, and something about a pod being transported through space and stopped. Did anyone else see them?"

The High Elder smiled contently. "No one else sees those types of messages. The Emperor chooses who gets to see them and when. That memory is a very sacred one. Remember it well, and don't forget it." He bowed his head, "Sorry to leave you boys, but I now must be on my way. Majerik, it was nice to see you again."

Michael bowed to the High Elder as he left. He then grabbed Skyler's arm and pulled him out of the room.

Skyler struggled to get away. "What are you doing?"

Michael continued to drag him towards the elevators. "Do you know what you saw?"

He shook his head. "No, that's why I came to you. Could you let me go?"

Michael ungripped Skyler's arm. "Yes, but you have to follow me back to the room where it is safe."

Skyler nodded. They got to the room and Michael crawled around the room.

"What are you doing? That's not how you play hide and seek."

Michael stood up. "I had to make sure the room wasn't bugged."

"Why would it be bugged?"

Michael sighed and slumped down on the couch. "Because what you saw is the story of the Worm Orb and this whole origin of the war."

Skyler frowned and sat next to Michael. "Wait, you know why the Cass wanted to go to war with us all along?"

Michael shook his head. "No, at least not the details, but after this past week I am pretty sure I know it now. But you cannot tell anyone. It is top secret in respect for the Cass and you know they're the last people you want to make upset."

Skyler nodded his head and listened to Michael's words.

"Tell me about what you saw."

Skyler took a deep breath. "I saw bits and pieces, so I'm not sure I got it all. But there was war on this desert planet and the Cass were winning, and near the end this very decorated guy got killed. Then they transported his body back in a fancy pod. They couldn't take the route home and were running low on fuel. Then one of the Squallite elders let them land and pass. Your people helped them repair their ship. They returned home and buried the body deep in the ground. And a little while later a package with the Worm Orb was sent to the Squallites as a thank you."

The room was silent for a moment.

Michael spoke up. "This war is worse than we thought. I always knew the part of the story about my people helping the Cass, but not why and how. Now with what is going on Damnrok makes all too much sense."

Skyler paused, "So what half of the story do you know?"

"What I know is that years ago the Cass needed help returning the body of the Emperor's brother, and Earth was new into space and wouldn't let anyone fly through their space. So, they denied the Cass a quick way home. So, they asked us, and Squallites, being peaceful, helped them. Therefore, the Cass like us so much. It has nothing to do with the fact our ancestors shared similar DNA, if anything that stops them from liking us more."

"So why are they so concerned about their bodies being returned? I get the emperor's brother but why the rest of them?"

Michael shrugged, "All I know is that we were nice to them, so they like us, and the humans were mean, so they do not like you."

Skyler rolled his eyes, "There just must be more to the story. But at least we know the important part of the info, I think."

"I am just hoping we can get this war over. I see no point in this."

Cane entered the room. "Why did you two take off from the meeting? Just because it was over doesn't mean that you can leave, there might have been another meeting, or we were being sent somewhere else."

Skyler opened his mouth to speak.

Michael covered Skyler's mouth. "Sorry sir, it was a Squallite thing I had to discuss things with Skyler in private."

Cane narrowed his eyes, "This time it was okay, but next time make sure you notify me that you are leaving." Cane pulled three thick electronic cards out of his pocket. "Speaking of leaving, I have our tickets. We leave in two hours. Pack your things."

Skyler's eyes lit up. He enjoyed the space station but when all you had time to do was paperwork and order take-out, things started to get repetitive and boring. "So, we're all going back to Earth?"

Cane walked over and handed Skyler and Michael their passes. "See for yourself. Skyler."

Skyler read his. The illuminated lights flashed all the info for a one-way ticket to Earth. "How long are we going to be on Earth?"

Cane headed towards his room. "Michael is staying on Earth, he has school. You and I are only going to be there for two days then we must head to Sagitarion for their new building opening."

Skyler groaned. "Is this job nothing but travel?"

Cane opened the door to his room. "In November we have a month where we will be on base and in December, we will travel a bit, but just around Earth. Now get packing, we don't have a lot of time. We got to get out of here."

Chapter 24

Skyler sat next to Michael in the Fleet Admiral's cabin. Cane made the exception this time for Michael to sit with them. It was late in the cabin and Cane was already resting. Skyler and Michael lay across from each other on the lounger.

Skyler reached into his bag and pulled out a blue leather jacket. "Oh, hey Michael, I almost forgot, I bought this for you. It was the only one the surplus had; they are still allowed to be worn, just no longer issued. It's a Small, but I know how slim you are."

Michael took the jacket from Skyler and tried it on. It was a perfect fit. "You have a good eye. I like it, but you did not have to get it for me."

"I wanted you to know that you're my best friend, it is rare, why not?"

Michael gave a subtle smile. "Thanks, I will treasure it always. But it is time for bed. We will be back on Earth in a couple of hours."

"Agreed. See you in the morning." Skyler reached over and turned off the light.

When they got back on Earth, Zarina was there waiting for Skyler on the platform. She hugged and kissed him. Skyler was very surprised to see her but wasn't the least bit unhappy. "Zarina, who told you I was coming back to Earth today?"

Michael cleared his throat, "I told her. Before we left, I sent her a message. I knew you would want to see her."

Skyler investigated Zarina's shining green eyes. "I'm so happy to see you."

She kissed him on the lips. "I'm happy to see you too."

Cane coughed. "Skyler, we have work to do. You will have tomorrow to see your girlfriend. Right now we have to file the paperwork to say we're back on Earth base and see if any messages were left for us."

Skyler gave Zarina large puppy dog eyes. "I'll see you later, beautiful."

She blew him a kiss as he followed Cane.

Skyler went with Cane to his office.

Cane took his overnight bag and placed it on the floor next to the desk. He typed in a few things on his computer. "Well, there aren't as many messages as I thought."

Skyler stood there with puppy dog eyes hoping Cane would let him off early.

Cane sighed. "I know you miss your girlfriend, and I know we have lots of paperwork to get caught up on." He paused. Cane then pulled up a document on his tablet. "Just sign this saying you arrived back on Earth with me and you can go and see your girlfriend."

Skyler smiled as he grabbed the tablet and quickly signed. "Thank you, Cane, you're awesome!"

"I did you a favor this once, don't spend all your time with her I expect you back in my office for noon."

Skyler saluted Cane. "Yes sir."

He then quickly took off and went to his room. He entered the room and saw Zarina laying there on the bed in a cute pink nighty. Skyler had a big smile on his face. "Do you always sleep like that?"

She got up off the bed and slowly walked over to Skyler. She rubbed her hand on the inside of his leg and placed the other around his neck. "Only when I expect to see a man who is happy to see me."

Skyler grinned. "Happy doesn't even begin to describe it." He kissed her passionately on the lips and took her over to the bed. "Cane gave me the night off to spend with you."

She smiled. "Well then, I'm going to have to thank Cane." She kissed down his neck and unzipped his uniform.

"We can send him cookies or something."

Chapter 25

Kax groaned as she put her uniform on, getting ready to go back to work.

"You could always ask for a transfer, you know that, right?" Rex said from his bed.

She rubbed her forehead. *What am I doing?* She had spent the night with Rex in his room. Over the past couple of weeks with Skyler being gone and work being stressful, Rex was the only thing keeping her sane and calming her down. As much as he was the same race as her, it felt odd that she was with him.

He got up out of the bed and kissed her neck. "Call in sick. I will too, and we can spend all day together." He tapped her butt.

She shifted away from him. "No, we have to go to work, that's our job. We can—" She noticed her communicator flashing and quickly checked the message. It was from Michael telling her Skyler was back in town. A big smile crossed her face as she read the text.

Rex narrowed his eyes. "Who is that text from?"

She looked up and put her phone away. "Michael. Skyler just got back into town last night."

Rex glared. "So, I guess you're going to be seeing him tonight instead?"

Kax frowned. "It's nothing like that. You know Skyler is just a friend."

"A friend who is madly in love with you, and you're going to break our plans to see him."

She stepped back. "I never said that. He might even be too busy to see me-"

Rex moved closer and placed his hand on Kax's mouth. "Don't say another word. I know what he is like. He wants you, Kax, and he doesn't want me around.

So, I will let you see him tonight if you call in sick and spend the day with me."
He put his hand down.

Worry grew in Kax's eyes. She didn't want to miss work, but if she said no, she
didn't know what was going to happen. She sighed. "All right, I will call in sick."

Rex smiled and kissed Kax on the cheek. He slapped her on the ass. "Now get
on the bed."

Skyler was up around 8 a.m. He looked at the clock with his tired eyes and
whacked it. "Mmhm..." He groaned and buried his face into a pillow.

Zarina kissed the back of his neck. "When do you have to be at work?"

He muffled some words into his pillow.

"What was that?" She asked as she rubbed his smooth clean back.

He picked his head up a little, "Noon, but I wanted to stop by the hangar and
see how Kax is doing."

She rolled him over. "Well then, you should get up."

He leaned over and kissed her lips. "What about you? Don't you need me to
take care of you?" He asked with a large hungry grin.

She kissed him back. "Well, that should go without question." She rubbed her
fingers through his light blonde chest hairs.

He rolled on top of her and kissed her neck. "Well then, let's get started on the
day."

Skyler went down to the hangar to check in on Kax and Michael. He saw his mother looking down at her desk. *Damn, I forgot that my mother is on the desk. How do I get in?* He stood off to the side so she wouldn't see him and rubbed his chin trying to come up with a plan. He snapped his fingers. "Got it!" He said and pulled out his communicator and texted Michael to tell him to bring Kax out.

Michael came out a few moments later by himself.

Skyler frowned, "Where is Kax? I said to bring her."

Michael shrugged. "She and Rex both called in sick. So Kax is probably in her room. What are you doing here? I thought you had a full schedule?"

Skyler was disappointed and worried about Kax. "Cane gave me half the day off, so I thought I would stop by and say hi. But I forgot my mother works at the check-in desk."

Michael nodded, "Well then it was nice seeing you, but I do have to go back to work."

Skyler nodded back. "I'll see you tonight, then. I have a few hours off because the next day is busy before I leave."

"Sounds like a good plan. I will see you at the bar later."

Skyler had some time. He had to go back to Cane's, so he decided to check on Kax. He went past the girls' dorm and knocked on Kax's door. The door opened and a younger Asian girl answered.

"Hello, can I help you?" she asked as she looked up at him with big eyes.

Skyler was puzzled. "Is Kax here, by any chance?"

The girl shook her head, "No, she is at her boyfriend Rex's room he is in Hall E. Do you want me to tell her you stopped by?"

"Sure, just tell her Skyler says hi." He turned around and went to go check Rex's room just out of curiosity. He got to Rex's. He didn't knock, but he could feel vibrations on the door and heard purring. He was tempted to knock on the door or check to see if it was locked and ruin all their fun, but he didn't. He knew how many times Kax knew he was with other women and never interrupted him. He just let out a sigh and pursed his lips. Part of him was sad, but the other part was glad that she was happy and having fun. He turned himself around and started on his way to Cane's office. It was time for him to go back to work.

Chapter 26

At nightfall, Kax was finished her day with Rex and was making her way to the bar. She had gotten a text from Michael saying to meet him and Skyler there later. She was in her uniform and walked into the bar. She checked their usual table, but there was a different crowd there. She scanned around until she saw Michael waving her over. He was sitting alone. She went over to the booth and sat across from him. "Where is Skyler?"

Michael shrugged. "I have no idea. He said to meet him here, and he hasn't shown up."

Kax sighed. "I think I know why he is not here."

Michael raised an eyebrow. "Oh? what is going on?"

"I wasn't sick today. Rex convinced me to call in sick and we spent the day in his room. I think Skyler might have stopped by, and, well..." Her speech trailed off as she looked down at the table.

Michael shook his head. "This is Skyler. He has dealt with your other boyfriends before. I'm certain Cane is just keeping him late."

A moment later Skyler came into the bar huffing and puffing. Kax picked up her head when she saw him. He came over and sat next to Michael. "Hey, sorry I'm late. Cane wanted to finish briefing me on tomorrow night. Man, being a Fleet Admiral is hard work. I don't think he has gotten a full night's rest in years."

Michael laughed. "When have you ever gotten a lot of sleep?"

"My sleep pattern is by choice. His isn't, and that's what is hard. You sometimes never know when you're going to be done. But I did ask him for a little bit of time to see you guys."

Kax smiled and a sharp pain of guilt pierced through her chest. She liked Rex, but when she thought of Skyler or was near him, it made her feel like she was doing something dirty and wrong. "Sorry I missed you earlier today."

Skyler smiled. "Don't feel bad. I have more time to see you now then I would then."

The waitress came over with some drinks. She took Michael's empty glass away.

Kax frowned. "I didn't order anything."

"Ya, I know, I just ordered for us. I know what you guys like, and I figured if you don't drink them, I would."

Michael scoffed. "The day I see you drink my drink, I will pay your tab for the month."

Skyler laughed. "Just because you like to drink girly drinks doesn't mean I won't enjoy it. It's still alcohol after all."

There it is, Kax smiled, *The old banter and chemistry they always had. Oh boy, did I miss that.* Her feelings of guilt started to pass, and she began to enjoy herself once again.

"So Kax, what is it like being a patrol pilot?"

She looked down at her drink.

"The job is fine, it is just your mother that ruins it."

Skyler groaned, "Ya, I know what you mean. I'm sorry. If you want, I could talk to her since she is still bothering you."

Skyler is willing to talk to his mother for me? Maybe he really does care. She looked up. "You don't have to, you're busy, you don't have the time."

Michael narrowed his eyes. "I think talking to your mother would be a good thing. You would think that with how many years in the service she's had, she would know to keep her personal feelings behind her."

Skyler took a sip of his beer. "Ya right, have you noticed that's one thing my parents had in common?"

Michael laughed. "Now that is funny."

Chapter 27

Early in the morning Skyler laid in his cot in the small back room of Cane's office. They had a long night of paperwork and briefings. Cane had also wanted to get caught up so there was no more free time. Skyler looked at his watch and noticed it was one hour before Cane would be normally waking up. Skyler got dressed and went into the office to have a bit more privacy. *I know she said never to call her again, but I'm doing this for Kax.* He picked up his communicator and let out a deep sigh. *I sure wish I had a beer right now. Well, here goes nothing.* He used his phone and called his m o t h - er.

"Who's calling me at this hour? You do realize that I have a baby to take care of?"

Skyler groaned. "Hello mother, it's nice to hear your voice again."

Her tone picked up. "Oh, Skyler, that's your number. Wow it is nice to talk to you again."

"Yes, this is my number I got while on Catillion. I was expecting to be posted there for a few years, but they sent me back to Earth." It wasn't the whole truth, but it was the story he was going to tell his mother. "Look, Mom, I have a favor to ask you."

She was silent for a moment. "Well, as much as I would do anything for you, I want you to do something for me."

Skyler grabbed his hair. "Mom, you already know I can't quit the forces."

"It's not that. I want you when you get your holidays or even just a couple of days off to come and spend them at home with me, Charles, and your little brother."

Memories of the past abuse and suffering in that house came flooding back. "I will have dinner, but I will not stay there for the night."

She sighed. "What is your request?"

"Stop harassing Kax and Michael at work, they have done nothing to you."

"Kax is the daughter of the whore that ruined my marriage, and Michael is a filthy electric bug."

"So what? After work, think those things, but during work leave them alone."

"Three days at the house and I will try to be 'nicer' to them," she said in a mocking tone.

"Two days and one night, that's it. No more," he said with a stern voice.

She was silent for a moment. "You sound like your father with that tone of voice. Two days it is, and don't talk to me like that again. Keep me posted on when you plan to visit." She hung up the phone.

Skyler's eyes widened at her last statement.

"She's right, if you are wondering. When you talk like that, you sound just like him." Cane stepped into his office in full uniform.

Skyler put his communicator away and faced Cane. "You heard the conversation? I didn't mean to wake you."

Cane shook his head. "You didn't wake me, I never sleep well. I haven't had a good night's sleep since this eye was taken from me. I'm glad you called your mother. But if your friends were having a problem with her, they should have come to me. I could have dealt with it."

"I don't know why they didn't, sir."

"I can think of a few reasons, cadet." Cane peered at the clock on his arm band. "Time for you to get that assignment finished. We have to get going to Sagitarion. I told you before, they are opening a new building and we need to be the ones to open it. We need to make sure all the inspections have been done, make sure it is solid and construction was done right, and then go to the ribbon cutting ceremony."

"And then where will be going?"

Cane pulled up his schedule. "Three days on Sag, and then we have a week on Earth and then we have to go to the moon. But no more travel after that."

Skyler's eyes were bright. "We're going to go to the Moon!"

Cane frowned. "Haven't you been to the moon before? I remember a time after you were born when your father was stationed on the moon for a month."

Skyler shook his head. "Nope, I have never been to the moon, always wanted to go though. Remember, my Mom wouldn't let me go on any missions with my Dad."

Cane nodded and sat down at his desk. "Right, but you did go on one. Well, two. You were born on one of them. Do you remember which one it was?"

Skyler had to think. "The one with the market, staffed by purple and blue traders."

Cane's eye widened. "That was the one when I was having surgery. I remember now. That was a dangerous mission; no wonder your mother didn't want you back in space. Okay, and she never took you any other time?"

Skyler shook his head. "Not until I got to the Academy. I have traveled around Earth with my uncle, but that's about it."

"I bet you have seen some interesting places thanks to him." Cane looked at the clock on the computer. "Well, enough chit-chat, it is time to open the office up for work. You sit off to the side and get that homework done and I will do the rest of the work. Understood?"

Skyler nodded. "Yes, sir." His communicator then beeped. He reached for it in his pocket and Cane took it away.

"When you are working, this goes off. The only calls you need to worry about are the ones I get. You are my shadow, remember?"

"Yes sir."

Cane took the communicator and put it in the top drawer. "I will give it back to you later."

They arrived on Sagitarion two hours sooner than planned. Skyler was amazed by the sights. He was impressed by the orange and green sun. The ground was covered in a fine red sand. The roads were made of blue cobblestone. The buildings were all a triangular pointed shape. He was caught off guard with all the A-frame buildings.

"This is an odd place. I'm kind of glad I didn't get posted here."

Cane laughed. "You haven't seen nothing yet. Buildings and people will get a lot less, human as you explore more of space."

They walked along the streets of the odd city. Lots of different aliens from around the galaxy were there. As they got closer to the base, the buildings looked the same as the ones on Earth. They walked up to a short brick building.

Skyler touched the side of the building. "These are real bricks, why did they make this building out of brick when all the other buildings on this plant seem to be wood-based?"

"It was done in honor of the Federation," said a loud booming voice from behind Skyler. "When the Sage joined the United Galactic Forces to show our loyalty, we had all these bricks shipped and used it as the main hall."

Skyler turned around. "Oh my gosh, you're a centaur!"

The man frowned and turned to the side. "I am not a centaur! I am a Sagitarian. If you will notice, I have six legs, not four."

"Chiron, long time no see! It's good to see you again." Cane gave his old friend a hug and pat on the back. "Ignore this little cadet, he doesn't know what he is saying." He reached over and tousled Skyler's hair.

Skyler raised an eyebrow. *Why is Cane acting so unprofessional?* He tried to fix his hair with his hands, straightening out the curls.

"So, let me guess, that's Captain Therris's son, isn't it?"

Cane pulled Skyler closer and placed his arm around him. "His one and only. He is now 23 and my apprentice."

Chiron held out his hand. "I was wondering if I would ever get to meet you."

Skyler shook his hand with a puzzled look. "Besides the Forces, how do you know my Dad and Cane?"

Chiron stepped closer to the wall off the building and touched it. "They were one of the crew who delivered and helped build this building about 30 years ago. One reason I requested Cane to come back. We are not just opening a new building, it is the 30th anniversary of our union with the Federation."

"That's one of the reasons I insisted on bringing you Skyler," Cane added.

Skyler shrugged. "I kind of figured that. By why didn't you invite Kax?"

Chiron raised an eyebrow, "Who is this Kax?"

"Karmantha Tillion's daughter. I don't know if you ever met her. She was our pilot near the end," Cane responded.

"When did Karma become the pilot for my Dad's ship?"

Cane put his hand on Skyler's shoulder. "After you were born. Now come on, we have work to do."

They all made their way into the hall. The hall was painted with pictures of many other Chiron fighting in large battles. Skyler stopped to admire the walls. He saw on one side the Chiron and on the other a race of three-legged, hoofed creatures. "What are these?" He pointed to the wall.

Chiron came over. "Those were the Lotrians, we killed most of them off years ago in the war you see in the picture." He took a few steps back. "I'm right there in the painting. I was just a young 30-year-old back then. Still getting used to my training armor."

"Now you're 500 and a master at wearing advanced armor." Cane walked over to admire the painting.

Skyler's eyes widened. "You're 500 years old?"

Chiron laughed. "563 to be exact. We Chiron live very long lives. I have about 200 years left in me if I take it easy."

"Men like us never take it easy."

"No they don't, so I will be lucky to make it to 600." He paused for a moment. "Well then, let's get to work and don't worry, kid Therris. I will make sure you have lots of time to learn and see more of our people's history."

"It's Skyler by the way, not kid."

"My apologies, Skyler Therris. Now come along." They all made their way further into the grand hall.

There were more paintings of Sagitarians fighting in many battles. "You guys sure love to fight a lot," Skyler thought out loud.

Chiron laughed. "Yes we do, but most of the time it is peaceful combat. We were always peaceful and only a couple of times did we have to go to war for the purpose of killing."

Cane let Chiron lead the way as he spoke to Skyler. "Skyler, when you were in school did you ever take alien etiquette class?"

Skyler shook his head, "No sir, my school was too small and my second one never put it on my classes."

"We are going to have to fix that. I will add it to your classes and teach you some of it. you're going to need it this year. Until then, keep your thoughts to yourself when addressing the natives of any planets."

Skyler nodded his head and followed the two into the back office. The office in the back of the main hall walls were covered in a dark mahogany wood with pillars thicker than any tree Skyler had ever seen. Curious, Skyler put his arms around the pillar and his fingers could barely touch.

Chiron laughed. "Thank you for your love of nature. That tree doesn't usually get that kind of attention."

Skyler put his hands to his side, "Sorry sir. I have just never seen this much wood in one spot before. I have seen trees but not this thick. Is it really a tree?"

Chiron nodded, "Yes, it is. We polished the bottom of it but the top of it grows out of the top of the building. We have a few of these pillars around. I'm guessing Earth doesn't have many trees?"

Cane shook his head, "We have trees, but not big ones anymore. I was a child when the last of the large trees were cut down. You should really visit Earth sometime."

Chiron tapped his back legs. "It is a bit hard for me. I have known a few of us have gone to Earth but it is difficult. It is better for when the tripods go."

Skyler frowned, "I thought you said all the Lotrians were dead?"

"We wiped most of them out, but they are far from being extinct. And we have a few who are members of the Forces. You don't get off Earth base much, do you?"

Skyler shook his head. "I have been to Squall, Catillion and Taurton Station."

"Makes sense for bipedal planets. You have seen nothing yet, kid."

Skyler frowned, "I am not a kid."

"Sorry, Kid is what we call our younglings, and you're not 30 yet so here we still call them kid."

"Understood, sir."

"So, are we going to get any work done at all today, or are you going to just chit-chat?" Cane asked, taking a seat on the cushion on the floor.

Chiron smiled. "I'm sorry my race is a little more laid back. but I am very interested in getting to know kid Therris here. I knew his dad so well it is so nice to see his spirit lives on."

"I know what you mean and there will be time to do that later. Right now, I need to check the inspection files for the new building. Is it in use already?"

Chiron shook his head. "No, it is not. We are waiting for the ceremony to open it up."

"Good. From what I have heard, the official auditor has not been here to investigate yet."

"That is correct. Because I requested you to open it, they said you could do that job as well."

Cane rubbed his temples and groaned. "Are you kidding me? I hate that job. You know how much of a memory you need for that? I'm getting too old for this." He turned to Skyler, "You better have a good memory, it's going to be needed."

Skyler frowned. "Isn't an auditor who you call to fix your taxes?"

Chiron laughed. "They do more than that. The type of auditor we need for this job needs to check the entire building, look at every file to make sure it is correct, and then write notes on everything in the construction and condition of the building. Then write it all out into a report. The reason for this is so if anything goes wrong, we can pinpoint if it was in the construction or sabotage."

"But all you will be doing, Skyler, is using your memory. I will know if the items are correct or not, you just keep note of everything." Cane added.

"Well then this is going to be fun," Skyler pointed out.

Chiron handed Cane an electronic clipboard. "All I need from you right now, Cane, is your signature that you have arrived and that you and your apprentice are going to be the official auditors."

Cane sighed. "I really wish they would have sent one of the lesser admirals to do this. Just because I can doesn't mean I always have to." He signed the clipboard and then handed it to Skyler for his signature.

Skyler signed and handed it back to Chiron.

Chiron took it and filed it in his desk. He typed a few things on his computer and then turned it off. "Well now, that's done. The day is almost over. Why don't we head over to the officer's club and enjoy a few rounds and get caught up?"

Cane looked at his arm band and saw the time. "Time change, I forgot. I was thinking we were going to get a whole day's worth of work done. It's morning on Earth."

"Well, you could start your auditing tonight if you wish. I could leave you the keys."

Skyler gave Cane his puppy dog eyes, "Please Cane, can we go to the bar? I really want to try the local beer."

Chiron laughed, "He is just like his Dad, loves to drink."

Cane frowned. "That's one trait I wish he didn't get." He turned to Skyler. "I would not recommend the local brew, it is much stronger than the stuff on Earth."

Skyler grinned and stood up. "I know how to handle my alcohol."

Cane frowned.

Chiron laughed. "I think the kid's mind has been made up."

Cane rubbed the bridge of his nose. "I guess there is no point in arguing. Let's go to the pub."

Skyler tried to get adjusted to the cushions on the floor in place of chairs. Chiron came over with Cane and had three drinks.

Chiron handed Skyler a small glass beer mug, "Old Blinky here says he is worried you can't hold your alcohol because ours is a lot stronger. So, I convinced him to let you try a little pint. Your father was the only one who was ever able to drink me under the table."

Skyler took the half pint and downed it in one gulp. His head spun.

Chiron sat down and watched Skyler regain his thoughts. "If that doesn't make you blind, I think you will be okay."

Skyler shook his head and rubbed his temple. "That's a strong taste, but I can still see and I'm not feeling a buzz."

Chiron laughed and waved to the bartender to bring more drinks. "You're a worthy opponent."

Cane rubbed his face, "I hope you know what you're getting into."

Skyler laughed, "I have been in drinking contests before, Cane."

"Not ones that will kill you."

Skyler and Chiron were half a dozen shots in. Skyler's hand was just beginning to shake and Chiron's head was getting dizzy. The time between the drinks was getting further and further apart. Skyler was still going strong.

Cane was on Skyler's side, making sure that he wasn't going to get to sick.

A few times Skyler pretended like he was going to throw up. But it was just his way of egging Chiron on. His head was getting woozy, but he knew he had to win. There was no other choice in his mind. If his father beat this guy, then so should he. He had never seen his father drink when he was younger, but if his father drank anything like him, then Skyler knew he could win. The liquor was sweet with an undertone of a sour apple taste.

The whole bar was standing around them cheering them on and placing bets. They were now up to a dozen shots. Skyler was not going to stop, this was his thing. The rounds kept coming. By the time they hit fifteen Skyler's head started to get woozy. The effect of the alcohol started to get to him. His vision began to go. But he could see that Chiron was in worse condition. He could barely hold his shot. Skyler may not be able to see, but as long as someone put the drink into his hand, he could drink.

Cane patted Skyler on the back, "You can stop anytime you want. You don't have to continue."

Skyler gave a crooked smile. "I hope bet on me you dis." He slurred his speech.

As Chiron picked up the next shot, as it hit his lips his head hit the table, spilling almost all the drinks. Skyler smiled, still sitting up tall. He had his last shot in his hand and quickly drank it down. He tried to remember his number, but had lost count as his head became too dizzy, and he would have fallen over but Cane picked him up.

"Come on Skyler, is it time to go home." Cane helped Skyler up and carried him out of the bar. Cane quietly collected a handful of money from the booker and made his way out.

Cane carried Skyler to a small A-frame house. Skyler rubber his head. "Eyes gone, going where?"

"Don't speak until we get in, I have to treat you before you get poisoned."

Cane carried Skyler to the bathroom and held him over the toilet. "Can you throw up?"

Skyler wanted to keep falling over. Cane shook his head and reached into his pocket and pulled out a tiny black pill. He opened Skyler's mouth and placed it under his tongue and held his head right into the toilet. Within a few seconds Skyler started to throw up. When Skyler was able to hold himself over the toilet, Cane sat on the floor to the side. "You're such a fool, Skyler. You could have killed yourself." Cane looked at the cupboard above the sink to find something like a cup. There was a small soap dish that was clean, no soap residue. Cane turned on the tap and filled it up with some water. He handed the dish to Skyler, making him drink. "You got to get this stuff out of your system and replace it with water." Almost two hours later, Skyler had finally stopped throwing up.

He lay on the bathroom floor. His vision had returned. He rubbed his head. "How did I get here?"

Cane was nearly falling asleep as well. "I will tell you when you wake up. Come on, I will take you to your room." Cane stood up and held out his hand to Skyler. He carried him to the room. He placed Skyler on the bed. "You better be ready for work in the morning."

Skyler moaned and rolled over onto his side and went right to sleep.

Chapter 28

Skyler awoke in the morning with a headache. He opened his eyes and saw Cane sitting on the coffee table next to the couch. He frowned. "What happened last night?"

Cane handed Skyler a glass of water, "You almost died. You're so stupid sometimes."

Skyler drank the glass of water. "That drinking contest really happened?"

Cane took the empty glass from Skyler and handed him a bowl of fruit. "Yes, and do you realize how strong that alcohol is? If I wasn't there to get most of it out of your system you would have died."

Skyler laughed and ignored the fork, and started eating the fruit with his fingers. "Did I win?"

Cane pulled out a large wad of money. "Not to encourage you, but I did bet you would beat your Dad's record and, well, you have quite a large chunk of change now. I'm not stupid, I know when to place a bet."

Skyler saw the large amount of paper money that was all in Sagitarian currency. "They couldn't pay in Federation credits?"

"No, because we are a civilian bar, but I will get this converted and put this away for you for after you graduate."

Skyler picked at the fruit. "What about Chiron, is he alive?"

"He is fine. The beer here is not toxic to the Sagitarians they just can only handle so much but not die. To humans it is toxic. Your Dad almost died as well, but he only made it to 37 shots. I can't say I'm not impressed. How have you built up that much of an alcohol tolerance at your age?"

Skyler brushed his hair back and grinned. "I have been drinking since I was 13, and heavy drinking since I was 16."

Cane frowned. "Life at home was that bad?"

Skyler finished his mouth full of fruit. "Yup, it started with stealing Charles's beers but then it was going to teen parties. I also know what alcohols will make me drunk and which just get me a small buzz. When my family calls, I'm trying to get drunk."

Cane covered his face. His mouth curved down and his eyes filled with sadness. "You're 23, you're too young for all of this. I wish I was there for you growing up. Oh, Skyler, you know what damage you are doing to your body?"

He finished the bowl of fruit. "Leon, I'm fine. I don't need to drink to survive and I know my limits."

Cane let out a deep sigh and regained himself. "It's almost noon, how are you feeling?"

Skyler rubbed his head. "I have a bit of a hangover, but I can still work." He handed back his empty fruit bowl.

"Good, we need to get going."

Skyler saw Chiron sitting at his desk with a bandage around his head. "What's with the bandage, are you all right?"

Chiron laughed. "It's a treatment for a hangover. I'm surprised to see you alive. I'm very impressed and here I thought I had gotten better."

"40 shots of any alcohol is a great achievement." He took a seat on the pillow.

Cane cleared his throat. "Can we have the paperwork to start the audit? I would like to get this done as soon as possible."

"Always about work with you, Cane." He handed him a stack of papers. "These are all the papers that need to be signed with your approval. Any comments you have can be written on the back. I also recommend you have Therris follow with his tablet and write the report if you really want to get this done quickly."

"I know how to do an audit, and I have a schedule to keep."

"Always about work with your old friend."

"You're an admiral. You know what it means to be late on assignment," Cane said, taking his stack of papers.

"And you know what it is like to be a Sagitarian, we are more laid back here."

"Your race is lazy and disorganized."

Chiron laughed. "We're just laid-back. I really did miss our talks, Cane. See you at the bar again tonight."

"As long as you don't try to kill my cadet again."

"I think this kid can take care of himself."

Skyler followed Cane through the halls, making notes when Cane said to. "So, what's the story between you two?"

Cane stopped in his tracks. "Chiron was trying to get more resources to help the other Sagitarians because their planet was becoming a desert. Your father was sent on a survey mission of this area. We landed and of course he offered to help, and the Forces does help people without joining in order to maintain peace. But it's not a long-term thing, and sometimes resources are sold. When we got here, he realized a bigger issue and that a new irrigation system was not going to be what this planet needed. It needed more, and was going to need a lot more for a long time. So, what he did was he made me do an audit on everything that would be needed. Once the list was made, he showed Chiron and offered him a contract to join the Forces. Chiron said no, and that they were fine. Your father would not take no for an answer. He rarely did. Your father was stubborn, and when he saw something he wanted he often got it. Your father challenged Chiron to a drinking contest."

"So Sagitarion was won in a drinking contest?"

Cane pondered, "That's one way of putting it. He won the contest and got sick very badly sick. Chiron thought it was funny because the alcohol is poisonous to humans, and he figured he would win. But your Dad was not that stupid. He was able to heal and prove he was stronger and beat Chiron at his own game. Chiron agreed to join but on his own terms. The Sagitarians make a lot of resources and materials for us but they don't go to space much. We also took the Lotrians off their hands by enlisting the remaining numbers to the forces. There are no more than 200 left."

"Why do the Sagitarions hate the tripods so much?"

"I don't think it is about hate, more of the need for combat and power. Ask Chiron about it. Any opinion I give you on the subject will be very biased." Cane turned over another page. "Now let's get back to work."

Chapter 29

After their work was done, Skyler, Cane and Chiron made their way to the bar. Skyler checked his tablet for messages. "Oh hey, there is one from Zarina."

Chiron peered over at Cane. "Who's Zarina?"

"His girlfriend," Cane whispered.

Skyler stepped out of the bar and called Zarina. "Hey, ZZ," he said, "how is my girl doing?"

"Tired. You know it is like 1 a.m. here?" She sounded groggy on the phone.

"I'm sorry, it is only 9 p.m. here, I'm not going to disturb your roommate, am I?"

"I have moved into your room for more privacy, if that bothers you, I will move back to mine when you get back?"

Skyler shook his head. "Keep it, I don't think I will be using it much. Just promise you won't bring anyone else back with you."

"Deal," She said. "How's your hand doing?"

"Not as good as yours."

She laughed, "You're sweet. When are you expected back on Earth?"

Skyler shrugged. "Not sure. Now we have to do some auditing while we're here, and that could take longer. The opening ceremony has already been pushed back two days. At this point I'm not sure we will be making it to the moon."

"The moon!" Her voice picked up. "Oh honey, if you go to the moon, I will skip school to see you."

He frowned. "What is so special about the moon?"

"On the moon there is a zero-G club, it is for adults if you get what I mean, and they have rooms to have sex in zero-G, it is amazing because there are one-way mirrors and so you can see the moon and space while you do it."

"Well, now, you have gotten me all excited thinking about that. I would love to go." He adjusted his pants.

Cane called behind him, "Come on out, drinks are here."

"I heard Cane, I will talk to you later, sexy." She hung up the phone.

Skyler walked into the bar with a large smile on his face.

Chiron handed Skyler a drink. "Don't worry, it's a human beer. Cane has banned me from giving you anymore Sagitarian beer."

Skyler took the beer. "As long as you are paying, I don't care what I'm drinking. But what I do care about is why you hate the Lotrians so much?"

Chiron grabbed Skyler's arm and pulled him down onto the cushion, "Don't you say their name out like that."

Skyler shifted his eyes, "Why not?"

Chiron rolled his eyes, "They're our enemy, we don't like them. I'll tell you about them in a less public setting."

Skyler nodded his head and quickly finished his drink. "I'll go and get us another round." He got up from the table and went to the bar.

A female Sagitarion came up to him at the bar. "Hey, cutie. In town for long?"

Skyler looked at her and smiled. "Only a couple of days, but I think I could make time for you."

She blushed and moved in closer. She tossed her long brown hair back and then held out her hand. "Grettle is the name."

He shook her hand. "Would you like me to buy your drink?"

She took his hand. "No, I would like to take you somewhere."

He grinned. "Well in that case, lead the way."

He was led out of the bar. When they got to the door he stopped and said, "Wait, shouldn't I tell Cane and Chiron where I am going?"

"No need, we will be back before they notice you're gone." She continued to guide him.

He grinned, "So it is just a quickie you want, I can do that."

She smiled. "I have never been with a human before. I want to try it is all." She took him to what appeared to be a stable out back.

"What is this place? I thought you weren't horses?"

"This might look like an Earth stable, but it's not, this is just how our brothels are set up. come on now, I see an empty stall."

"You really are eager." He couldn't stop grinning. "I don't mind you being eager, it's just something I don't see often, and I like it." He got into the stall with her, "Okay, so how do I do this? Do you want me to play with you for a bit? You're a bit long for me to touch your front and your back at the same time."

She laughed. "There is a stool back there, use it to get behind me. We aren't big on the foreplay around here."

"Works for me." He adjusted the stool and climbed up. Her behind wasn't that appealing. From the front she looked human, but from the back it just looked like a horse. But it didn't matter; if she wanted to get laid, he wanted to get laid. It was worth a shot. He unzipped his pants and dropped them. He moved her tail aside and leaned in, trying to make sure he was going to place it in the right spot. With his other hand he was getting himself ready. He felt his way around with his free hand. He reached down and pulled a condom out of his pants. He went to open it.

"You don't need a condom, we're not compatible with humans." She called back.

He shrugged and put the condom down. When he found the spot and was ready, he slipped himself in. He placed his hands on her hips and thrust as hard as he could. *She's so big, I wonder if she can even feel it?*

She moaned and kicked her feet.

I guess she can.

They were not even 5 minutes in when Cane and Chiron busted through the door. "Get your dick out of that horse!" Chiron yelled.

Skyler stopped thrusting and pulled out. "Why, and what are you doing here?"

"Breeding between Sagitarians and humans is illegal." He went over to Skyler and pulled him down from the stool.

"It was just sex, not breeding."

Chiron frowned. "I don't see a condom on that penis. That's when it is called breeding."

"She said we weren't compatible."

Chiron narrowed his eyes at Grettle. He raised his hand and slapped her, "You're going to jail for this, traitor."

Cane grabbed Skyler and pulled him away, "You two are compatible, that's how Lotrians are born, and it's illegal to produce any more of them. Their race are all prisoners of war."

Skyler put his pants back on. "So, am I in trouble?"

Chiron turned to him. "Did you come?"

Skyler shook his head. "No, wasn't long enough,"

"Good, then you're fine." He turned his focus to Cane. "Take Skyler back to the house and I will be with you shortly."

Cane grabbed Skyler and dragged him out of the barn. Cane was silent the entire walk back. When they got in the door, Cane threw Skyler onto the couch. "Tell me now what you were thinking!"

"I didn't know it was a crime to have sex with the natives here, I thought it would be fine."

Cane shook his head. "Part of that is my fault for not telling you, but the rest is your fault for being stupid. Rule number 1: no matter what she says, you're on an alien planet always use a condom. Rule number 2, don't fuck the locals!" Cane's eye flashed and his teeth were bared. He snarled and his fists were clenched with rage.

Skyler had never seen Cane this mad. He was beginning to worry.

Chiron came in. "Cane, calm down, there is some good from all of this."

Both turned to Chiron.

He sat on the cushion on the floor. "She was a member of the Lotrian Society, we have been trying to catch them for years. If you would have come inside her, you her and that baby would have been sentenced to death."

Skyler raised an eyebrow. "Okay, you guys have to explain to me what's going on. I am very confused."

Chiron and Cane shared a glance. Chiron began. "We are warriors, but peaceful ones. And there used to be a race of bipeds that we would fight against, and to make it more challenging we would have competitions: if they won, we got their women, and if they won, we got their women for the day. It soon created a race of tripods. Bipeds could not bear tripods and within a few decades the bipeds died off. Then we had the tripods as our friendly enemies, until one of them fought to be our leader. He thought he was better and started a war. His people lost and we took all the tripods and made them prisoners of war. They can reproduce with each other, but no new ones were to be made. There is an underground society that exists that wants to breed new tripods; that's the Lotrian Society. You encountered them tonight. Therefore, when we joined the Federation, we gave the contract of the tripods to the Federation so they could have freedom. But if new tripods are born, they would not be prisoners of war and this whole uprising could start again. We try to stop all of this."

"So why would others want to start this uprising again? You seem peaceful."

Chiron laughed. "Keep up, boy, and follow along. We're not peaceful, we're warriors who are laid back. We see something, we get it." He shifted his glance over to Cane, "What's that thing you humans have where you ask for permission?"

"*Consent*, Chiron," said Cane with a stern tone. "Something your people should look into it developing."

Chiron laughed. "We take what we want, and if you don't like it, we challenge you to combat, and if you win, we don't take it."

"How do you know for certain it was a set up?" Skyler asked. "Maybe she was just really horny like me."

Cane frowned. "You haven't had sex in 2 days, how horny can you be?"

"Yes, it was a setup. Women don't just come up to you in bars and say, 'hey, let's have sex'," Chiron added.

Skyler raised an eyebrow. "The girls I hang out with do, and I have a very high sex drive and very high testosterone, I need it constantly."

Cane rolled his eye. "Then we're getting you fixed. You could have been in a lot more serious trouble if we didn't come to help you."

"Okay then, what are we going to do about this?" Skyler asked.

Chiron took out of his pouch a few square packages about the side of his palm. "Use these if you want to get freaky with the beasties."

Cane and Skyler both gave Chiron a very strange look.

"Please tell me that you just made that phrase up right now, because I recommend you change it." Cane said.

Chiron raised an eyebrow. "Nope, we say that to all the tourists."

Skyler took the condoms and looked at them. "Well thanks, but um, I'm not this big. These won't fit." He reached into his own pocket and pulled out a human-sized one. "These are the ones we use."

Chiron picked up. "Wow, these are small. Poor human women."

Cane let out a deep sigh. "Let's just drop the subject and get some sleep." He looked at Skyler. "Use your hand if you're that desperate."

They all nodded and went to bed.

Chapter 30

Cane woke Skyler up early in the morning. "Wake up, Skyler, we have to get this auditing report done if we want to stay on schedule."

Skyler was very groggy. "I thought we were staying a few more days?"

"Not after last night. I'm not leaving you here any longer than I must." Cane tossed Skyler's uniform on him. "Get dressed."

Skyler could tell by the tone of Cane's voice he was still upset about last night. He wanted to say something but had a gut feeling that talking about it would just make it worse. He gathered his clothes and put the uniform on.

Cane handed him a horse granola bar and spoke. "Eat, we got to go."

Skyler packed, took a few bites and rushed after Cane to the new building. Today they were going to the basement level. It was the last place to check and for the Sagitarians it was a hard place to get to but it was used for their most secure documents. Skyler wrote down everything Cane said, making sure the report was getting done as swiftly as possible. Skyler stopped when he saw a strange marking on one of the bookcases that Cane had failed to mention. "Cane, why is there a Cass symbol on this shelf?"

Cane came over and placed his hand over the small marking on the side of the case. He picked up a book off the shelf and looked inside. "These aren't books on the Cass. That's odd that it would be here. The Sagitarians have nothing to do with the Cass, and for the most part don't even know they really exist. Are you sure it is a Cass symbol?"

Skyler quickly nodded his head. "I think it means warning or alert in Cass. It is very similar to the symbol for danger in ancient Squall. But what is it doing here? I have seen it a few places in my travels before."

Cane shifted his eye and took the stylus pen out of Skyler's hand and threw it down the aisle of books. There was a small boom and some sparks went off. "Because there was a trap. My Cass is rustier than I thought, but this needs to go for investigation. Skyler, go upstairs and find Chiron, and have him call together every one of the high-ranking officers. We need this looked at."

"Sir, what about you? Is it safe to leave you alone."

"That's what I'm going to find out. Now go."

Skyler didn't hesitate to run out of there. But he did worry about leaving Cane alone to check out potential sabotage. He ran up the stairs and made his way to the main building to Chiron's office. He busted through the door. "Cane's in danger now! He sent me to get you and all high-ranking officers."

Chiron nodded and typed in a code on a keypad. "Get on my back, it will be quicker, biped."

Skyler hopped on Chiron's back before he got up, and they rushed over to the new building.

"In the basement is where I left him. There was a Cass symbol and some small explosion."

BOOM! They just heard another small explosion as they entered the hall.

"*Cane!*" Skyler called out.

Chiron galloped towards the basic elevator and pulled the rope, making it go down. "Lucky humans, you get to use the stairs," he grumbled.

They got down there. Skyler ran towards where he had left Cane. But there was no smoke or debris. Just Cane throwing little pieces of junk he found in his pocket further and further down the halls.

"What is going on Cane, I thought you were in danger?"

Cane turned his head back. "I might be, but I have yet to find a major bomb this is all just rigged with small explosives."

Chiron walked over. "Explosives are banned on this planet, aside from necessary ones for work. Why are these little things going off?"

"I was about to ask you if this was a setup or something?"

Chiron went over and checked the path. "This isn't our work, someone has set this up."

Cane examined the evidence for a moment longer. "Well then, if you didn't, then who?"

"There is corruption going on here, Leon," said Chiron. "I do not have the answers for you today but will have my people investigate this and get back to you as soon as we can."

Cane nodded. "I will await your call."

Chapter 31

Skyler rubbed his head and grabbed his uniform jacket off the floor.

Cane entered the room and handed him a cup of coffee. "Sorry about the long night, good thing you have the next two weeks off."

His eyes were crusty and sore when he rubbed them. He reached for the coffee. "Why do I have two weeks off?" He brushed his hair back.

"Because it's the 15th of December and it's winter holidays." He stood there sipping his coffee.

"You mean I still get those dreaded days off?"

"You know, I thought after all the work you have been doing, I would think you would be looking forward to a few days off."

Skyler drank his coffee. "A day off would be good, but during these holidays the base closes and I have to deal with being homeless or hungry."

"You can go to the cabin you bought and hang out with your friends."

Skyler shook his head. "Not that easy. Kax usually takes the cabin for her family and her Dad doesn't like me. And Michael goes to his Dad's place…"

"Then this would be a good time to go to your mother's, since you promised her."

Skyler clenched his fist and his body tensed. "First you make me drink coffee and then you bring up my mother."

"You said you have nowhere to go."

Skyler let out a long groan. "I guess I will call her."

Skyler went back to his room and grabbed a bag from under his bed and started to throw some clothes into it. There was a knock at his door and before he could turn around, Zarina had entered the room. He smiled when he saw her enter. "Hey there, what's up?"

She came over and kissed him on the lips. "I thought I would catch you before you go and spend two weeks with Kax."

He laughed and held her close. "If she and her family are going to be at the cabin, I won't go there."

She narrowed her eyes. "Then why are you packing?"

He sighed and sat down on the bed. "My mother wants to see me, and I agreed to stay there for two days. Then I will probably come back here."

She sat down next to him. "Want me to go with you?"

He frowned. "My mother is horrible and will call you a whore, and just be mean. I don't think you want to see me fight with her."

She kissed him. "I don't care what she calls me, I will deal with her. I got nowhere to go either. Parents are going away together, and my brother's never coming back to Earth."

"If you are up for the challenge, then come with me. I'm not sure what to expect but I know there will be fighting." He got up and finished packing his bag.

Zarina went over to the dresser and pulled out a few articles of clothing. "Could you add these to your bag?"

Skyler frowned, puzzled. "Why do you have your own drawer?"

"I stay in this room more than you. I have kind of made it my own. It shows how much you use it if you didn't notice I use two drawers." She opened the top drawer and revealed a stash of underwear.

His eyes widened, "Well, I guess I have nothing to complain about, then." He turned his head to cover up the blushing.

She took a lacy emerald green pair out of the drawer and handed them to him. "These can be yours if you want. I know how much you love green."

He held them up and examined them. "I would love to see you wear them. But if I want a pair, I know where to get them."

She leaned in and kissed him.

An hour later, they got up and dressed. Skyler smiled. "Thanks, I needed that."

She kissed him on the lips. "I know you did, and any other time you are feeling tense and stressed, call me and I will make you feel better." She reached her arm around him and rubbed his back.

"You're just so amazing." He found it hard to believe that they had been together for four months. He kissed her. "I told my mother we would be there for dinner. I think we should get going, it's an hour and half from here if traffic is good."

They got to the house around 2 p.m. He pulled up to the driveway, turned the car off and just stopped. He was petrified. There were no good memories left in this place, only pain and more pain lingered.

Zarina put her hand on his leg. "It will be okay, you have me."

He opened the car door stepped out. Zarina grabbed the bag in the back and then followed Skyler into the house.

He walked in through the back porch and then knocked on the door. It was unlocked. "Mother, I'm here."

His mother came around the corner from the living room and was carrying his half-brother. "Oh, Skyler, you came home. I'm so happy to see you."

He put on a fake smile. "It's nice to see you too."

She went over to him and hugged him with one arm while she held her baby in the other. "It's good to have both of my boys in one place."

Skyler had not seen Phineas since his birth just over a year ago. The boy was small but stocky with dark hair and dark eyes. "He looks like Charles," Skyler said out loud.

She stepped back and turned the baby around. "He does, it's so wonderful."

"Funny how both your kids took after their fathers so much."

She frowned and her eyes picked up when she looked over Skyler's shoulder. "Oh, hello there, I didn't notice you. Are you lost?"

Skyler shot her a dirty look. He took the bag from Zarina's hand and held her other.

"No, I came with Skyler. I'm his girlfriend."

Sandy's eyes widened and she took a deep breath. "I hope he told you that I only set the table for four, and there is no guest room."

Skyler rolled his eyes. "She can have my dinner, if that is an issue, and we never had a guest room and that never stopped Charles from visiting."

Charles entered the room at the time. His head turned when he saw Zarina.

Skyler noticed him eyeing her up and down. He shot a glare at Charles and their eyes locked and they stared each other down.

"Honey, we have lots of food," said Charles. "Skyler's girlfriend can stay. She can sleep on the couch and Skyler can have the cot in the attic he loves so much."

She let out a deep sigh. "Fine, she can stay. Just no baby-making in this house."

Skyler pointed to Phineas. "I think it's too late for that."

She glared at him. "The forces offer free vasectomies for officers, in case you didn't know."

He nervously laughed. "Now you don't want grandkids?"

"I don't want bastards and now that I have little Phineas, he can give me good grandchildren." She bounced the baby up and down smiling at him.

Skyler clenched his fist. He felt Zarina's hand on his back. "Mother, I have a bag, can I go put this in the attic?"

She nodded. "Go. I'll have dinner ready in about 15 minutes, so no time for any hanky panky."

"Don't worry, Mother. Cane said you're good at killing the mood." He quickly took his bag and Zarina upstairs to the attic before his mother could reply.

They got up to the attic and Skyler sat down on his cot. He rubbed his head and buried his face. "I should have packed beer, I cannot survive this sober."

Zarina sat down next to Skyler on the cot. "You have me." She put her arm around him and rubbed his back. "You don't need alcohol to deal with your family."

"I know I don't need it, but it really does help." He flexed his muscles to her touch. "Zarina, just a warning. Charles likes you. He is a pervert, my mother has always been blind to this. I will not let you sleep alone while we are in the house. I will bring it up at the table, you are to share the attic with me tonight."

She examined the single military cot they were sitting on. "I don't think there is enough room for both of us."

He pointed behind, "The bay window, you can sleep there. It's big enough to sleep one person or two." He smirked, remembering his youth.

She looked at the window and back at him. "What is so funny?"

"I love that bay window. Before I found my Dad's cot, I used to sleep there under the stars. I lost my virginity there. I was a lot smaller then. If that makes you feel uncomfortable, you can have the cot. Never had sex on this thing."

She rubbed his back a little bit more. "I'll take the window, it doesn't bother me."

He leaned over and gave her a kiss. "You're too good for me."

She kissed him back placing her hand on his leg. He put his hand on her face and kissed her passionately and placed his other hand on her firm breast. He was going to lean her down on the cot when his mother called up the stairs. "Dinner is ready!"

They broke their connection and got up. Before Skyler got to the stairs, Zarina put her hand on his shoulder and gave him a smile he found comforting. "You can do this. Don't let your mother get to you."

He gave her a kiss. "It's not just my mother," he said, and made his way down the dining room.

Sandy had made a spot for Zarina across from Skyler at the table. Charles was at the head, Skyler and Zarina to his side and Sandy at the other end with Phineas. Skyler glared at the fact he had to sit between his mother and stepfather.

Zarina gave him a kind smile.

For dinner Sandy served them roast beef, mashed potatoes, and veggies. Skyler groaned. *Crap, my mom cooked. She can't cook, always hated her food.*

She brought Skyler a glass of water.

He frowned. "I'm an adult. Could I please drink something else?"

"I could get you a glass of milk if you would like?"

He pointed to the beer can in Charles's hand. "I was thinking of a beer, maybe?"

She glared at him. "No, you're an alcoholic and I refuse to enable you. I ordered Charles to drink all the alcohol in the house, that is the last beer in the house."

His mouth watered as he watched Charles chug the last drop. He clenched his fist. *Damn, I'm not going to survive now, I need to numb this pain in my body.*

Zarina placed her foot on Skyler's knee under the table and rubbed it, as if to say he would be okay.

He smiled back at her and took a deep breath. "Water will be fine then, Mother."

Once the food and drinks were served, they began to eat their meal. Charles broke the silence. "Your mother said that you are the Fleet Admiral's apprentice now, how do you have time to keep a girlfriend?"

Skyler was not sure what part of that was the real question, but knew how to reply. "Her name is Zarina Vorkovich she is the daughter of the most recent Minister of Defense."

Charles frowned at Skyler. He turned and grinned at Zarina. "Is that so? I worked with your father a few times, he seems like a nice guy. I have never known Skyler to have an interest in politics."

"Then that is something me and him have in common. We may not have lots of time to see each other, but he makes up for it when we do." She went back to eating her food.

Sandy choked on her food.

Skyler smirked. "Me and Zarina have been together for four months now, and I would say things are going pretty good."

Sandy's eyes picked up. "You two sound like you're getting serious. Should I be expecting any long-term plans between you two?"

Skyler choked this time. "No!" He paused and looked at Zarina for guidance. "I mean it has only been four months, nothing like that has come up. I have been focusing on my schoolwork too much to worry about anything like that." *Shit, first it is a vasectomy and now it is marriage, why don't I have a beer?*

"Skyler is right. We have both agreed to focus on our studies before we talk about any kind of commitment."

Zarina tugged on Phineas's arm to make the baby cry.

Sandy rushed to her son's side, picking him up, cuddling him, trying to get him to calm down.

Skyler pushed his plate away. "I'm tired and full. Me and Zarina are going to bed. It's been a long time since we had a rest from school."

Sandy cradled Phineas in her arms. "Zarina is sleeping on the couch. You can go to bed, but the couch isn't ready."

Skyler stood up. "She will sleep on the bay window."

Zarina stood up and tried to hold Phineas.

Sandy turned the baby away from her, and he continued to cry. "Just get out of my way, I will check on you two later."

Skyler signaled to Zarina to get out of there. They went up the stairs to the second floor. "Thank you for that. I saw you pinch the little rat, but I don't think she did."

"I tried to help. Are we going to the attic?"

Skyler shook his head and went to the room at the end of the hall, "Not yet, were going to go get some beer." He entered the nursery and opened the window on the wall opposite. "They redecorated my room again."

"This was your room?"

Skyler put one foot out the window. "My room, Charles's office and not the baby rat's room. Come on, follow me."

She followed him out onto the roof, and they climbed down the wall with him.

Skyler started on his way down the street.

"Where are we going?" She asked trying to keep up with his fast pacing.

"I told you, we're going to get beer. There is a store up the road. I'm not going to survive the night if I don't have something to help me get through it. We got one more day of this. I don't know how I will survive." He paused and knelt on the ground. "I'm so sorry you must see me like this. My family is horrible."

She knelt on the ground next to him. she placed her arm around him. "Hey, don't feel so bad. I knew it wasn't going to be easy for you to show me your family, but I came to support you."

"Charles is the reason I didn't want you here." He brushed his hair back. "Charles is a pervert, he attacked two of my girlfriends when I was in high school. He promised to drive them home and I found out later what he did. Whatever happens tonight, you must stay with me tonight. Who knows what he will do when I'm not around? You saw what he does in front of me."

"That's why I made Phineas cry so that we could get out of there."

Skyler shook his head and got up. "Come on, let's just get to the liquor store and back before my mother notices we're gone."

They went to the local liquor store. Skyler grabbed a bag and started filling it up with six-packs.

"Don't you think that's a lot?" Zarina asked.

Skyler pulled his head out from the fridge. "You are still underestimating my parents. Do you want anything? How much do you think you can carry?"

Zarina pulls Skyler's shoulder back. "Come on, three is enough."

Skyler looked up at the with puppy eyes.

"Okay, one more because I will help you drink some."

Skyler stood up with his bag and four six-packs. As he walked to the counter, he grabbed an extra bottle of vodka.

Zarina sighed as she watched Skyler paid for everything.

"Hey this ID is real for once," the cashier said.

Skyler laughed, "I had to grow up one day."

"Still not sure of that. Your drinking habits are still the same." The cashier scanned the beer. "Please tell me your mother is at least happy you're visiting?"

"I have no idea what goes through her head." Skyler pulled out his wallet and paid the bill.

Skyler handed Zarina two six-packs while he carried two with the bottle of vodka tucked in his jacket. They headed back to the house.

"How are we going to get this into the house without your mom seeing?" Zarina asked.

Skyler pulled out his keys and unlocked his car. "Leave three in car and we will carry one and the bottle in through the window." When the car was locked up, Skyler started climbing the fence and from there hopped to the roof. He held out his hand. "Come on Zarina, I'll help you up." Once on the roof, Skyler carefully walked up and then hopped in through the window. Skyler looked around. It didn't seem that anyone was in his brother's room. He helped Zarina into the room. "Now we got to be quiet." He took the beer and vodka and slid it under his brother's crib. "We will come back for that."

He took Zarina's hand and began to take her down the hall to the attic. When they got to the attic, Charles was standing there waiting for them. Skyler rolled his eyes. "What kind of lowlife can't go one night without a beer?"

"I don't know what you are talking about, Charles. I just took Zarina out for a walk."

"You went out the window, that's the exit you use when you're sneaking out."

"I didn't want to use the front door and disturb you and Sandy," Skyler snapped.

"I don't believe you." He went over to Zarina and began to place his hands on her.

Zarina slapped Charles and pushed him away. Charles grinned as he rubbed his face. "Feisty one you got there. She doesn't have any alcohol on her, what about you?"

Skyler's eyes filled with rage as Charles reached out to grab Skyler. Skyler stepped back. "Don't touch me, you pervert!"

Charles stepped forward and grabbed Skyler's collar and slapped him. "Don't tell me what to do." He let go and left the attic.

Skyler fell to his knees and tugged on his hair.

Zarina put her hand on his back to comfort him. "Whatever happens here or tonight, don't leave my side."

"I'm sorry."

Chapter 32

Skyler stayed with Zarina in the attic, avoiding his family. In his mind his Mom wanted him here, but that didn't mean he had to spent time with her. The bay window was a lot smaller than Skyler remembered it to be. When Charles was away, he had snuck back to his brother's room and grabbed the beer and vodka he had stashed there and brought it up for him and Zarina to share. When he was a teen, he could get two people to lay down on it; now it only seemed big enough to hold one of them. Zarina sat at the window and Skyler sat on the floor in front of her.

"So, what is going on here? Why are things so bad here?" Zarina asked.

Skyler hesitantly replied, "My dad loved me and my mother didn't, is the short form. But really my parents had marriage issues and when my Dad died my Mom began ignoring me, I guess I took after my Dad too much. Cane was there for me as a kid until my mother couldn't handle him anymore and married Charles. Charles hates my guts and whenever my mother turned her back, he was finding some way to attack me. At the age of 16 while my mother was away Charles beat me bad before throwing me out. Then I went to live with my uncle Justin until I joined the Academy. I couldn't communicate with my mother to tell her the truth, Charles intercepted our messages. She always took his side no matter what. Finally, when I joined the Forces, she started trying to dictate my life again. I told her I was done with her until the baby was born. That's when she started harassing me to come back and be a family. I can't seem to get rid of her even when I spend a year in another galaxy. I just want all of this done with and her to leave me alone. I don't want to live here. I want to be a captain like my Dad. I know the risks and

I don't care; dying in space is better than dying in some dead-end job on Earth. This isn't my home."

Zarina rubbed his shoulders, "I'm sorry, I didn't know life was so rough for you. I thought you were one of us rich kids with annoying families but they stuck together for appearances. I thought maybe you went to private school."

Skyler laughed. "No, my life isn't like that. I went to the small local school here until I moved in with my uncle. He made sure I went to a good school but not fancy. In the summer I did go to England with him and hung out with nobles. but I wasn't one of them. My mother liked keeping me close to home. They all have money but I don't have my own. I live on a trust fund my uncle gave me, but that was to get me until I finished the Academy. I can't write home to anyone and ask for stuff."

"I see," said Zarina, "For me my life is totally different. My mother is Russian and my father is Indian, they are both from rich powerful families. They married for business reasons. My mom spent time with me and my brother and hated having to send us to boarding school. My brother was Mom's favorite but she always spoiled me to be the princess. My dad was always away. My dad wanted my brother to be a diplomat like him and for me to marry one. My brother wanted to help people and travel. He thought this was my mother's idea and so he barred her from seeing him. Caused her to act out and be resentful. My brother did defy our father and became a doctor, and well my mother is still legally married to my Dad; they don't talk. As for me, my Dad still expects me to marry some diplomat's son. I have dated them and fucked them they're annoying and full of themselves. I want something different."

Skyler took a sip of the vodka before handing it to Zarina. "Well, I'm something different."

Zarina laughed. Before she could say anything there was a call from up the stairs. "Skyler, son, I would like to talk to you."

Skyler groaned as he got up. He wanted to take another sip of vodka but knew not to go down to his mother smelling more of alcohol. He kissed Zarina. "Come down with me. Go to the car, go for a walk if my mother won't let you stay in the room while she talks to me. Just don't be in a place where Charles can get you alone."

Zarina sealed the bottle and hid it between two pillows. "Why all these precautions about Charles? I can take care of myself."

Skyler sighed. "I'll explain it to you all later. My mother needs to talk to me now." Skyler made his way down the stairs. His mother was in his brother's room. "What did you want to talk to me about?"

His mother was changing little Phineas. She turned towards Skyler and saw Zarina behind him. "Does she have to be here?"

"Well, she is my girlfriend, why can't she be with me?" Skyler said, holding his ground.

"Skyler, just hand me the baby powder and tell her to leave us alone."

Skyler turned to Zarina, giving her a look for her to leave. Skyler handed his mother the baby powder. "So, what was so important that my girlfriend couldn't be here for it?"

"Whores aren't girlfriends, Skyler. Sorry you never understood that." She finished changing the diaper and picked Phineas up.

"Zarina is the daughter of the Minister of Defense; she isn't a whore. Now what did you want to talk about that was so important?" Skyler said standing impatiently.

She placed Phineas into his crib and kissed him on the forehead. "All those rich brats are whores, Skyler. But follow me to my room. I have something for you."

Skyler followed his mother across the hall. In her room she pulled a book out from under her bed. "Skyler, you mean so much to me. I know we haven't always gotten along." She paused, "I know you have your father's stuff from the attic. When I noticed the stuff was missing your uncle told me you had it. I never complained. Because the stuff is rightfully yours. Skyler, I want you to have this." She handed him the book.

Skyler knew what it was as soon as he held it. "Which one is this?" he began to flip through his father's journal.

"It's the one where you were born. I don't approve of what you are doing with your life, but I feel it is time you had this," Sandy said.

"What about the other journals? The box I have ends just before he met you?" Skyler asked while he flipped through the journal.

His mother, not wanting to answer the question, responded with, "Are you and that girl really going to stay in the attic together?"

Typical mother, never will discuss my father. Skyler closed the book. "Yes, we are, I'm an adult and I can do what I want."

His mother let out a deep sigh and ignored him. "Well then, have a good night. I'll see you in the morning."

In the morning Skyler awoke next to Zarina on the floor of the attic. His back was stiff as he got off the hard wood. Zarina got up and stretched. "Thanks for camping out on the floor with me last night. You didn't have to." Skyler said.

"You looked like you needed the cuddles." She leaned over and kissed Skyler.

"I'll feel much better once we get out of here." Skyler said.

"Where are we going after this?" Zarina asked.

"No idea. I just know I'm not staying here." Skyler said, getting dressed.

"I could call Kax and see if her family is using the cabin. My uncle Justin sold his house out here so that's off the list. If you're coming with me, Michael's is off the list; his place is too small." Skyler took a long pause. "Base is closed but I still have my key to get in or we can go to Cane's."

"Cane's sounds like a good idea. I'm sure he is lonely during this time." Zarina began to get dressed. "Oh, we could just book a hotel for the remaining 2 weeks. I got my dad's expense card."

Skyler thought about it. "That sounds so expensive, and from what I remember Cane's place is so big that it will feel like that. It's only him and his cleaning staff that live there."

"Well then, let's go!" Zarina brushed her hair and gathered her things.

Skyler got dressed and handed her the case of empties. "Put these in your bag so my mother doesn't see them."

They had their bags on their backs when Sandy came up the stairs to see them. "You leaving already? Are you not going to stay for breakfast?"

Skyler groaned, "I'm not really a breakfast person. Where is Charles?"

"Charles is in his office working. He won't be down, so how about you leave your stuff here and pick it up after food?" she asked.

Skyler's tummy started the grumble and he couldn't think of any other excuse. "all right we will stay for breakfast then head out."

They made their way down for breakfast. Skyler tried to stay as quiet as possible. For breakfast it was just oatmeal. Skyler picked at his food, *Typical breakfast, mom still hasn't learnt how to cook.* Skyler wasn't sure of the purpose of why his mother was so insistent of him having breakfast with her. It was not like when he was younger, they had many breakfasts together. This time she wasn't saying much and mainly just fussing over his little brother. Skyler choked down his plain oatmeal avoiding conversation.

"So, son, what are your plans for marriage and kids?" Sandy enquired while she fed Phineas.

Skyler coughed. "Mother, haven't you asked me this question before? I feel you already know the answers."

She cleaned the baby's face, "I have, but I want to hear it again because people change their minds."

Wishing he had a beer or an escape route, Skyler replied, "As I told you before, Mother. I plan to never get married or have kids. And before you ask, no, that does not mean I will live as a sexless hermit."

She sat down at the table and with a serious expression she stared at him. "Skyler, I only ask and bother you about these things because I'm worried you will grow old with nowhere to spend your money and no one take care of you."

"Mother, if I have no one to spend my money on I will have the money to hire someone to take care of me." He pushed his bowl of oatmeal away. "If you care so much about people being alone in their old age, why did you break Leon's heart? Why weren't you there for me when I was a child? Why weren't you by my father's side?" He stood up and pushed his chair in, "Maybe I have just seen what relationships do and how they tear people apart to the point where I don't want anything permanent. We're done talking, I got to go."

Before he and Zarina left the room his mother spat out, "just keep your lovers to one at a time."

Skyler was confused by that statement and continued towards the attic to get his stuff.

Skyler and Zarina made their way up to the attic to collect their things. Skyler was crawling on the floor one last time to make sure he had gotten everything, when there was a knock on the stairs. He groaned thinking it was his mother. "What do you want now?"

As the sound of footsteps came creeping up, Skyler realized it was Charles. "Is that anyway to greet anyone? You made your mother very upset, I hear."

Skyler stood up with his bag in hand. "Charles what are you doing here? If you would like to know we're leaving now. We will be out of your hair in the next few minutes."

Charles set his gaze on Zarina. "I know that, you're not leaving me a lot of time to get to know this lovely lady." Charles moved towards her.

Zarina stepped away from Charles's outstretched hand.

Skyler shoved his bag towards Zarina. "Get out of here now! I'll meet you in the car."

Zarina ran out of the attic as fast as she could.

Charles's eyes filled with rage. "Now why did you have to do something like that?"

Skyler's body tensed as he made a fist. "Charles, you are married to my mother, and Zarina is my girlfriend, not yours."

Charles lunged forward, pinning Skyler to the wall by the throat. "You know our arrangement. You bring a pretty girl over to the house. I get a share of the action."

Skyler struggled with his lack of oxygen to break free. "That was never a thing, you sick bastard. Zarina is my girlfriend, and I will never let you touch any of my girlfriends again!" Skyler punched Charles in the side, trying to break free.

Charles winced and quickly readjusted his grip on Skyler's shoulder, pinning him again, preventing him from running away. With his free hand he grabbed Skyler's hand. He placed Skyler's hand on his own crotch.

Skyler turned his head in disgust, closing his eyes, wishing he wasn't there. Wishing he was dead or just anywhere else.

"See Skyler this is what happens to me when you bring over one of those pretty girls, now how am I going to deal with this? How are you going to fix it?"

Skyler wanted to just die, and be somewhere else, anywhere else. He searched his racing mind for all the things he had learnt over the past couple of years. As Charles leaned in closer, Skyler faced him and headbutted him, then lifted his knee and kicked Charles. Charles was down on the ground, Skyler kicked and stomped on him hard. "Don't you ever fucking touch me again or any of my friends!"

Skyler took one last look at the attic before leaving.

As he left the house, he heard his mother crying in her room. Phineas was sitting in his playpen in the living room. Skyler went over to him and rubbed his head, giving him a kiss, "Sorry you have these two goofballs for parents." Then he rushed off to the car. He pulled the keys out of his pocket and grabbed a case of beer out of the trunk. He then tossed the keys to Zarina. "You drive." He got into the passenger side and rode off.

Chapter 33

Zarina drove a far distance away from the house. She turned off before they hit the urban part of the city. She turned the car off and turned to Skyler. He was curled up into a ball and was drinking can after can of beer. "Skyler, what happened?"

"Zarina, I care about you. I would never let anyone hurt you. I try to not let anyone ever hurt any woman. It was just some old things. Charles never changes. You're not the first girlfriend he has done this to. Those girls I found out later. Just keep driving. I will tell you more. I hate going home and this was just the worst trip possible."

Zarina turned on the car and looked at Skyler. "I'll keep driving, but you have got to tell me where we are going. A hotel or Cane's."

Skyler rubbed his head and sat up. "Food first, then we will go to Cane's. You pick a place, the closer the better."

"Right got it, let's go." She stepped on the gas and drove them off.

Sometime in the afternoon they got to Cane's. There was no one at the door so Skyler and Zarina just walked in with their stuff. The place looked empty when they entered. "Hmm I wonder where they could all be?" Skyler said.

"Are you sure Cane is here?" Zarina asked.

They continued to walk around. "Naw, Cane wouldn't have left his door open. This place is a mansion. He is probably in one of these rooms." Skyler pulled out his communicator and as he dialed Cane's number, he called out, "LEON! Are you there?"

Leon's voice came from around the corner, "Skyler, is that you?"

The voices headed towards each other. "Yes, it's me, where are you? This place is so big!"

Finally, Skyler and Cane found each other. "Skyler, why are you here?" Leon said.

"I was at my mother's for two days and, well, I couldn't stay there another day. I tried." Skyler stared down at his feet. "You said I could come visit any time I wanted to?"

Leon gave Skyler a hug. "Yes, you can, and I am sorry things didn't work out at your mother's. I would have offered you to stay with me sooner, but I thought you would be sick of spending all this time with me." They broke the hug.

"I don't have many options on where to go and with Zarina tagging along, I can't just go to Michael's." Skyler rubbed his neck.

"Well, you two are always welcome here. Now come out to the backyard, there are some people I would like you to meet." Leon patted Skyler on the back.

Skyler was confused by the mention of 'people.' *Does he mean his house keeper's family? Is that who he wants me to meet?* When they walked out to the backyard the barbecue was on and there was a senior gentleman tending the grill. A senior lady was stretched out on the outdoor recliner and a middle-aged man was setting the table.

"Hey Leon, get ready to eat lunch, these steaks are juicy," said the older man.

"Mom, Dad, Martin, I would like you all to meet some people." He patted Skyler on the back, bringing him forward. "This is Skyler Therris and His girlfriend Zarina."

Skyler looked as shocked as the rest of the people. "Mom, Dad? You have family?"

"Of course, Leon has a family. What did you think? That he popped out of thin air or something?" Leon's father put the tongs down and made his way over to Skyler. "The name is Maurice and it is so great to meet you." He shook Skyler's hand.

Leon's mother got up and made her way over to give Skyler a hug. "Oh, Skyler, we have heard so much about you."

Skyler, feeling a bit overwhelmed, took a step back. "Uh, it's nice to meet all of you too. I just never heard of you. This is all a big shock to me. Sorry if I'm a bit on edge."

Zarina went up to the parents and shook their hands. "It is nice to meet all of you. Sorry me and Skyler had a long trip up here, we are not quite ourselves."

"Oh well don't you worry. You seem like such a lovely girl, come on over and sit next to me. We can have some girl talk while the boys bond. My name is Elizabeth by the way."

Skyler turned towards Leon, "Leon can I talk to you alone for a moment?"

Leon turned to his father and said, "Dad, go finish up with the steaks and we will join you at the table in a few moments." Leon walked with Skyler off to the other room.

"You have a family, how come you never talk about them? I thought you were an orphan or something?" Skyler blurted.

"Skyler, calm down, no need to freak out. Everything is fine." Leon pinched the bridge of his nose. "I don't talk about them often because I regret, I can't always see them. As you know I joined the Forces and didn't have time for a personal life. They don't live near me and when I finally have time I see how much has passed. I don't get to talk to them often. It also pains me that my brother didn't join the Forces and he has a wife and two full grown kids. This year is the first in five that I have gotten to see them in person." Leon let out a sigh. "I'm sorry I didn't invite you or tell you about them sooner."

Skyler took a deep breath. "It's fine. I just didn't know. If it is okay that me and Zarina can still stay here, then I won't mind getting along with them."

Cane smiled. "You will love them. I have also told them about you over the years. So, I can assure you that they are thrilled to meet you, and Zarina." Cane gave Skyler a pat on the back. "Come on, and see what it is like to have a real family."

Skyler stretched his legs out on the couch in the living room. Leon picked up Skyler's feet, moving them onto the floor. "No feet on the furniture." Leon then sat down in one of the arm chairs next to his father.

Skyler groaned as Zarina took a seat next to him on the couch. She cuddled up to him.

"So, Skyler, did you enjoy the meal?" Mrs. Cane asked, sitting in the love seat next to the couch.

"Both meals were amazing today. I can't remember the last time I had so much home cooked food. Thank you so much." Skyler said.

Martin came into the room with a couple of beers. He handed one to his father and Skyler. "You sure you don't want a beer, Leon?"

"I prefer not to drink beer, you know that." Leon said.

Skyler offered a sip of his beer to Zarina, but she declined.

"You know, Skyler, if I would have known you were coming, I would have brought the wife. She would have loved to have met you." Martin said while taking a seat next to Zarina.

"It was kind of a surprise; I wasn't planning on coming." Skyler replied.

"So how long have you two been dating." Mrs. Cane asked.

"A couple of months. We don't get to see each other all the time so this holiday time is perfect for us to see each other," Zarina said.

"The Forces can keep you busy. I know how often I see my Leon, even in his early years. But I guess both being cadets you see each other more often." Mrs. Cane enquired.

Skyler had never thought about it. He didn't really have anyone outside of the Forces he wanted to see, but if he had he really wouldn't have much time. "I guess you're right I never thought about it that way. My whole family is in the Forces so I never quite noticed."

"Speaking of that, how is your mother doing?" Mr. Cane asked.

Skyler and Leon both cringed at the mention of her. "Um, she is well. Has another child with her new husband and she's semi-retired. Do all family get togethers involve talking about personal things?"

"Mom, Dad, give Skyler a break. Can't you see he has had a rough time?" Martin said.

"I'm sorry, Skyler. It is just your mother was the longest relationship Leon has ever had and he always talked about you from the day you were born. Leon never had kids, you're the closest thing we have to a grandchild from him and we have not heard about your mother in so long." Mrs. Cane said.

"Bro I'll take that beer you offered me before." Leon said. Martin handed his brother his beer.

Skyler laughed. "Well, my mother is not worth talking that much about. So how about we change subjects? You can ask me anything about my life. Get to know me, just my mother and step-father are off limits."

The elder Canes looked at each other. "I think we can manage that."

When it was time for bed Skyler flopped down, arm stretched, face down. He mumbled something into the quilt.

Zarina began to get undressed. "Skyler, everything will be all right."

Skyler rolled over. "Zarina, the last few days have just been an emotional roller coaster for me. I'm sorry I must drag you into all of this and see this side of me. Therefore, I like my job so much, because I don't have to deal with emotional pains."

She folded her clothes and placed them on the dresser. She got into the bed and cuddled Skyler's motionless body. "Skyler, it's fine, I understand. None of this bothers me. Your life makes more sense to me. I have my own set of baggage that I wish I could drop too. Just because you live in a nice house doesn't mean nice things are going on inside."

He rolled over and hugged her. "How is it that you understand me so well?"

She kissed Skyler. "Let's get these clothes off you and have some rest. Like you said, it has been a long day."

Chapter 34

Skyler was lounging in the billiard room. He lay sprawled out on the couch, drinking a beer, flipping the channels.

Martin entered the room and pulled a beer out of the fridge. "Anything good on?"

"Not really," Skyler mumbled.

Martin put his beer down on the pool table. "Do you play?"

Skyler sat up. "I know how to, but I don't play that much."

"Well, if there is nothing good on TV, come and play a game." Martin grabbed an extra pool cue off the wall for Skyler. "I'll teach you."

Skyler got up from the couch and took the pool cue. "Is it just me, but you seem like the more laid-back version of your brother?"

"That's because I am." He set the balls on the table. "Leon is my little brother. He always tried to be the responsible serious one. I was the one who ran around causing trouble."

Skyler aimed the cue towards one of the balls. "I'm surprised you are here. I mean I didn't know you existed. Leon never talks about his family. I thought I was the only thing he had?"

"You are." Martin took his shot. "I mean, my brother joined the Forces when he was 18 and he is now 60. I haven't seen him much in his career. He joined right around the time I got married to my wife and put his everything into his work. He just had different ambitions. He was the first in our family to join the Forces. Broke our mother's heart when he joined, but she was proud of him."

Skyler struggled with the angle of this one ball. "Speaking of your wife, where is she on this trip? Why didn't she come?"

He came around the table to help Skyler with his aim. "If she knew you were going to be here, she would have. No, she stayed back in Hawaii to enjoy the holidays with the kids. We don't see them often either, now they are adults and moved out. I wanted to see my brother and thought I could see my kids often, but not my brother."

"Wait, your wife knows about me? And you're from Hawaii?" Skyler was confused.

"Yeah, we are all from Hawaii. That's where we grew up, of course, my wife knows about you. Kid, Leon was dating your mother before your father, he loved her. He and your father were closer than I was to him. From the day you were born we heard everything about you. We were sad we never got to meet you. Leon was going to arrange something when your mother accepted his proposal but when she rejected him that was it. Skyler, as far as I'm concerned you are family."

Skyler blushed. He didn't know how to feel. He had never known that there was a family waiting for him just around the corner. "Well, I'm glad to have a family now."

A humph came from the doorway. "Sorry to interrupt your little bonding session but I need to see my apprentice in the meeting room."

Skyler took a large finishing sip of his beer. "It was nice talking to you Martin, but the boss is calling."

Martin patted Skyler on the back. "You have fun, I'll see you at dinner."

Skyler followed behind Leon's lead.

In the office, Cane sat down at the head of a large oak table. "So, Skyler, some urgent business has come up."

Skyler took a seat next to him. "Um, what kind of changes? I thought we were still on holiday. Will we have to leave here?"

Cane shook his head and opened his laptop that was on the desk. "Nothing like that. We just need to be verified on some matters before we go back. Because the first day back we have a meeting to update us on the war. We will probably have to travel to deal with things. They want to have some of the meeting on Squall, but I know of your record so I'm trying to see if they can move things. Then after these negotiations at the end of January, we have the Officers' Ball. This year it is held at the Kremlin in Russia. You may want to inform Zarina about it because I'm assuming she will be your date."

Skyler was confused. "That's all in January, right?"

"Yes, there will be a few things on the side that we will need to take care of but for the most part those are our biggest things." Cane said, typing a few things into the computer.

"Okay then, what do you need to brief me on?" Skyler leaned over trying to read Cane's screen.

Leon pulled up a file. "I have sent this one to your friend Michael already for him to look over. Everything is still in ceasefire but we must figure out the proper transportation of the bodies and how many before the ceasefire is lifted or is satisfactory."

"Wait, I once we return all the Cass bodies then, what? First there is the security in transporting the bodies: which ships and pilots we are sending? And when we do, what is the guarantee that our officers will be returned, and what happens when they are all returned? Will Cass really stop fighting with us, or continue? What will the Squallites say?"

"These are all things that are coming up in the meeting." Leon explained.

"Wait, I thought these things were dealt with?" Skyler asked.

"The meeting we had about this a few months ago was to find out about the demands. Then the government and the king were talking about the cost and the ability to dig up all the bodies and transport them back. They have been able to start doing that in some places, but it takes time, and then we are collecting them while we find ships and pilots that can transport them. It isn't something that can be done overnight and it does cost a lot of money to do this," Cane answered.

"So, the meeting coming up is to discuss all this with the other higher-ups?"

"Yes, because I have to figure out how many of my fleet will be going and such."

"Cool, so that's all the briefing?" Skyler asked.

"For now, yes. I just had to let you know what was going on." Cane closed his laptop. "You can ask Zarina about the Officers' Ball she has been to it before. Also, I want to know, how are you enjoying your time here?"

Skyler smiled. "I love it. Your family is nice to me and caring. I wish I would have known them sooner. I also didn't know you were Hawaiian."

Leon laughed. "Your mother stopped me from making you a part of their lives. But on a lighter note, yes, I am Hawaiian. I grew up there and my family has lived there for generations."

Thinking about all the things he had read and heard about Hawaii in his life, Skyler asked: "I'm guessing that the island is completely different from life here. Do you ever miss it?"

Leon let out a sigh. "There's more than one island, Skyler. Mine was too small for me and I had to spread my wings and fly. I miss things about the islands, like my family and some feelings you can only get at home. But for the most part I don't regret leaving. I regret not making time for the more important things in life. If that makes any sense."

Skyler nodded his head. "Yeah, I can understand that."

Just then there was a knock at the door. "Come in," Leon called.

Zarina was standing there. "Your mother wanted me to tell you that dinner is ready. So, when you two are done your meeting, you can come join us."

Cane stood up in his seat. "Thank you, Zarina, we were just about done. We will be there in just a moment."

Zarina smiled. "Okay, I will tell her."

Chapter 35

Skyler was lying in his bed with Zarina in his arms. "Have you been enjoying your stay here the last few days?"

Zarina kissed him on the cheek. "Leon's family is amazing, I love them. Thank you for bringing me here."

"Well, I only planned to spend the time in a big empty house with Leon, but more people have made it awesome." He held her close. "Hey, Leon told me about this event coming up at the end of the month. He recommended that I invite you but I'm not quite sure what the event is. It's the Officers' Ball and it is being held at the Kremlin this year."

She hugged him tighter and kissed him on the lips. "Oh Skyler, I would love to. The Officers' Ball is amazing! You will love it. It is always held near the end of the year only the highest officials in the world and ambassadors go to it. I guess you get to go this year because you're the Fleet Admiral's apprentice. That is so amazing, we are going to have so much fun."

Skyler rolled on top of her. "I'm so glad, you are going to have to tell me what to do to get ready for it because I have no idea." He began to kiss her body. "I love making you happy."

A voice called from down the hall. "Skyler! Zarina! We're about to watch a movie, would you like to come and join us?"

Skyler sighed and rolled off Zarina. "Do you want to go?" He whispered.

"Yeah, do you?" She asked.

"I would, but I kinda want to just have some time to myself if that's okay? Maybe call a few friends? I'm not used to this much socialization." Skyler requested.

She kissed him and got out of the bed. "Sure, you have some quiet time. Have fun."

Skyler waited for her to leave then got up and went over to his bag and pulled out his tablet. He pressed a few buttons and soon a familiar face popped on the screen.

"Hey Skyler, long time no hear." Paul said.

"Hey Paul, what's new?" Skyler asked.

"Not much, keeping busy with the kids. I should be asking you what's new? You're the one who lives the exciting life, future space captain," Paul said.

"Well, that is for sure. I'm back on Earth and this year I'm the Fleet Admiral's apprentice. Things are going sweet for me."

"Wow, that is awesome. How did you manage that? Great to hear things are looking up for you."

"Yeah, the Fleet Admiral is an old friend of my Dad's, so he's sweet. But hey, speaking of the Academy, I got about two weeks of holidays coming up in January. I was wondering if it would be okay if I stopped by for part of that?"

"Skyler, I will let you in on a little secret, since the second kid, me and Xandria have been having some bumps and you know what? I think seeing you again will be good for both of us."

"Oh man, that sucks. Hey, you need any help, let me know. You guys are my friends, I want to help you." Skyler answered.

"Ever babysat any kids?" Paul laughed.

Skyler laughed, "I could learn, I guess?"

The two boys shared a laugh until they heard a baby cry in the background. "Ah man, the kids are up. I got to go. Thanks for the chat. Call when you're coming over. Stay if you need. There is always a place for you here." Paul said, standing up.

"It was nice talking to you too. Give Xandria my love." Skyler turned the chat off and placed his tablet on the night table. He heard laughing coming from downstairs. They all sounded like they were having fun at the dinner table. He lay there, debating if he should go down and join them. He wasn't that hungry but knew he would wake up starving. But for the first time in a long time, he was alone in his bed. There was nothing to worry about and he was in Cane's house so he was safe. He decided to just lie there and stare up at the ceiling, clearing his mind and slowly drifting off to sleep.

Chapter 36

The winter holidays were over and Skyler was heading back to the base. He had been informed about everything that had happened at the meeting. There was a stalemate until the bodies from Earth could be returned to their home planet for a proper burial. He was excited to go back to work even though he knew there would be a lot of paperwork waiting for him on his way back. he was happy to have had the time with Paul and Xandria. He had missed them, but the path they had chosen was not the path for him. Having a glimpse of the past was a bittersweet experience. When he got back to the base there was no time to drop off his stuff. Cane had sent him a message saying to come right away. So, Skyler left his bags at the front gates, having them sent to his room, and quickly rushed to Cane's office. When he got there, he saw a man who was measuring Cane while he stood in the middle of his office. Zarina was there watching. Skyler frowned. "What's going on?" he asked.

Cane turned around to face him, "Ah, Skyler. You are back. and good timing. I was just getting measured for my dress uniform for the Officers' Ball."

Skyler said, "But we have dress uniforms. Why do we need to be measured?"

"Because the dress uniform for the Officers' Ball or non-working situations is slightly different." Zarina spoke up, "This one cannot be measured by standing in a machine that scans you to fit the best fit. This one has to be hand tailored."

"There are also certain personal touches that have to made into the suit that you get to express when we do it this way. There is a questionnaire on the desk you can fill out," the tailor said.

Skyler grabbed the tablet off the desk and sat down next to Zarina. "All right, but why is Zarina here then?"

"I'm not wearing my uniform for my dress, but I have a dress being made. I picked it out in advance, and now i need to go for another fitting to match yours," Zarina said.

Skyler was still confused by all of this. He hadn't been fitted for a suit since he was 17, when his uncle used to insist that he wore one when they were in England. "So, Zarina and Cane have the same tailor?"

Zarina laughed. "Oh, Skyler you are so new to this. There is only one family that still tailors like this. and there are about five active members in this part of the world. So, all of those under the government's employment go to this family."

"It will be really interesting when we get to Russia because their suits are tailored by a different family and you will get to really see the art," Cane said.

Skyler rolled his eyes. These two were reminding him of his aunt and uncle, who were obsessed with the quality of the suits, "All right, whatever you say."

The tailor put his measuring tape down and wrote down a few things. "All right Leon, you are finished I will have this suit ready for you in the week. Now Skyler, please come up, it is your turn."

Skyler handed him the clipboard and stood on the stool. the tailor looked over the questionnaire. "For place of birth you wrote down 'space?' is there a base or planetoid that you were born on, or something close?"

Skyler shook his head. "No, I was born in the medical bay of the HMSS *Blackstar*. Not close to anything. My father was born on Earth, in Toronto, and my mother was born in New York. Why is this important?"

The tailor wrote a few notes down. "A true space birth is uncommon. I don't think I have done a suit for someone who was born on just a ship. I know more and more kids are being born on ships, but this is new, interesting."

"You might want to note who Skyler's father was. He was Levi Therris. I think you made a suit for him once," Cane added.

The tailor typed in a few things into his tablet. "Levi never liked my suits. That man was such a rebel. Didn't he always end up showing up to all his formal meetings in that red coat?" The tailor began to measure Skyler.

Leon laughed. "We all had those red coats back then. He just wore his every time he had the chance. I remember one time when they discontinued them as part of the uniform, he stitched it on. Your father was the reason they allowed the discontinued uniform policy."

Skyler groaned and let out a big yawn as he returned to work and entered Cane's office.

"You would think with all the holidays you just had that you would be wide awake and refreshed." Cane said, looking up from his tablet.

Skyler slouched down in his chair. "I forgot how uncomfortable the beds here are. I just slept funny is all. We got in late last night."

"Well, we got a long day ahead; we have to get caught up on paperwork from over the holidays and then we have to brief and prepare for the meeting on Squall," Cane said.

"Why do I need to be briefed for a meeting I'm not even allowed at? Or have the Squall elders changed their mind about me?"

Cane chuckled. "No, they have not. They really don't like you. I can't get the meeting moved like predicted, so I'm giving you your two weeks holiday then. You do need to briefed because until the day your Holidays start, you do everything I do. Also, once the meeting is done you will have to continue work as if you know everything. I will be sending you lots of messages during the time of this meeting."

Skyler placed his head on the desk, "I don't think I'm cut out with all this diplomatic work, paperwork is so painful."

"Skyler, you want to be a Captain. A very important job where you are in charge of hundreds of people's lives. It is not all fun and games like your father wrote in his journal. It is a job that has tons of paperwork and it's not fun. Being my apprentice is not just preparing you to have my job one day. It is preparing you for your responsibilities that you will have in the future very quickly. It takes time to be a Captain because you work your way up through the ranks. You want it as soon as you graduate and I don't see that happening but I will do everything in my power to get you closer than anyone else here. I want to help you."

Skyler let out a deep sigh. "I'm sorry Leon. Sometimes I get impatient. I have been taking for granted all the things you have been doing for me. Thank you. For everything. You won't see me talking out of line again. I realized something this past two weeks. That you are the only person I have looking out for me and that cares."

"I'm not the only one. I'm the one with more resources but you have Michael and Kax who care about you deeply and a lovely girlfriend. There may be more you just need to know who and when to ask." Cane tossed a set of keys onto the desk. "Here in case I'm not around one day I want you to know the door is always open for you."

Skyler took the keys off the desk. "What are these? Why are you giving them to me now?"

"They are keys to my house. If I own the place, consider it yours. I was debating about giving them to you, I just didn't know when the right moment was. Now feels right."

Skyler smiled and put the keys in his pocket. "Thank you, Leon, no one has ever done this for me in my life. I will take care of your place."

"Good, I'm glad. Also, we got to get back to work your shift is done at six tonight. I need to use you as much as I can before that."

"What do you mean shift? I finish work when you do?"

"I'm giving you tonight off. It's been too long, go have a night with Michael and Kax. I'm certain they miss you." Cane smirked.

Speechless, Skyler smiled. "Thank you, sir."

Skyler finished work. He tried to call Kax and see how she was doing. There was no answer, so he stopped by her room. He knocked on the door. "Hey Kax, It's Skyler. I was wondering if you wanted to hang out." He said while he knocked on her door.

A lady with a dark complexion, yellow flashing eyes wearing only a large pink towel answered the door. "Kax isn't here right now? Are you her new boyfriend? I thought she said he was older."

Skyler blushed and rubbed his neck, "No, I'm her friend, Skyler, the Fleet Admiral's Apprentice. I had the night off and was going to see how she was doing. But since she is not here and I notice you just had a shower, do you have any plans tonight?"

There was a tap on Skyler's shoulder. "What happened to your girlfriend?"

Skyler turned his head and saw Michael standing behind him. "We're in an open relationship. How have you been?"

"I do have plans tonight, but I will give you my number in case that girlfriend is interested." She quickly went back into the room.

"I'm sure she will love that." Skyler turned to Michael. "So, what are you doing here? where is Kax?"

"Kax had plans but sent me a message to get you. We're meeting her and Rex at the bar." Michael said.

Skyler got the number from the girl then left with Michael, "She is still seeing Rex?"

"She is, they had a bit of a rough patch but they seem to have worked it out." Michael said, walking down the hall.

"Do you like him? Is he good for Kax?"

Michael stopped in the hall. "Skyler, I have no experience with relationships but I will tell you this. It's her life, let her make her own mistakes."

Skyler took a deep breath. "What has she done? I haven't seen you guys in a while. I have been letting her do her."

"Don't say I didn't warn you." Michael continued on his way.

They made there way to the bar. Kax and Rex were sitting down in a booth. Skyler's eyes popped when he saw Kax. "You cut your hair, what is going on?"

Kax's long wavy styled hair was half the length. It was shoulder length and curled out. "You know, 'Hello' would have more casual. But thank you for noticing. It's been a while."

Skyler sat down next to Michael. "It's been too long. I'm sorry I haven't really talked to you. How are things going?"

Kax smiled. "Really good, the winter holidays were just what I needed to get away."

Rex took Kax's hand. "Also, something big happened tonight." He showed everyone the big diamond ring on Kax's hand to her friends.

Skyler's heart stopped. Kax was growing up and moving on without him. She was changing her hair, going on adventures without him, solving her own problems. Now she was engaged. "You're engaged. Wow, I thought you weren't interested in marriage."

Kax hid her hand. "It's not a short engagement. We are planning on getting married after my graduation. But I took Rex up to the cabin this holiday and he got along with my Dad and the family and we just connected more. And with hair I thought it was time for a change. It fits in my helmet better."

Skyler was happy once the beer arrived. "Well, that is great. Me and Zarina spent the holidays together with Leon's family. Did you know he has parents and a brother?"

Kax's jaw dropped. "Wow, Cane has a family. I'm so happy you got to spend time with them on the holidays. You and Zarina are getting close, that's nice."

Michael let out a sigh. "If anyone is interested in my personal life, I may not be in a relationship but my Dad is doing a lot better and is now able to return to full time work. Also, I'm being transferred back to the development department, so Kax, I will be seeing you less at work."

A shocked look crossed Kax's face. "Wow it seems like all of us are doing things separately in our lives. Anyone hear from Perry?"

Skyler could see Kax was upset, probably just as upset as he was. "Perry is doing great in his job, only thing new with him is developing new types of plants. That guy is such a bore, am I right? I don't think Perry will ever change."

Skyler finished off his beer. "Yeah, you know what? This was nice seeing you all again, but I got an early morning. We will make plans to see each other again soon." He left some money down on the table and got up. Outside the bar he leaned against the wall. He tilted his head back and slid down to the ground, holding his knees.

Kax rushed out the door and sat down next to Skyler when she saw him sitting on the ground. "Skyler, what's up?"

"Everything is changing so fast. I go off to do this job and I feel like I have missed so much. I thought I knew you so well, and you have changed. Michael has changed. Everyone is moving on without me. I think I understand what Leon went through, why he never married. Are you really happy with Rex?"

Kax gave Skyler a hug. "Skyler, I still care about you and we are close. This wedding isn't happening for a while, and I just got engaged tonight. Nothing is changing that fast."

"Kax, I hope you are making the right choice, I hope he is a really great guy. I hope he can give you everything you want and more." He played with her hair. "With your hair short you look so mature. Kax you are an amazing woman, anyone would be happy to have you. I think I was expecting something different tonight."

"Skyler, I love and care about you in different ways and me being with Rex isn't going to change that. He is okay with me having all types of friends."

Skyler stood up and dusted himself off. "I don't want you to think this is a date or me trying to change your mind but the next night I get off early, or have the time, want to just hang out like old times?"

"That would be great, Skyler. So, you heading back to your room now?" She asked while getting up.

"Yeah, Zarina will be waiting for me. She kind of lives with me."

"You two getting serious? I think I was the last girl you lived with."

Skyler laughed. "I'm rarely at my place so she is more like a roommate. Things are getting there though. We have a trip to Russia at the end of the month and things might be going somewhere with her. But nothing that happens between me and her ever changes how I feel about you."

"Same," she said, looking back through the door. "I should head back, I told them I was going to the bathroom. I look forward to our next date."

Chapter 37

"Leon, can I have the night off again tonight? Like last night?" Skyler asked while organizing stacks of paper for Cane.

Cane looked up from his computer and said, "Why two nights in a row? What happened last night?"

Skyler let out a long sigh. "Last night wasn't so great and I just wanted to take Kax out again. That's all."

Cane narrowed his brow. "Well, if that is the only reason, then we will see what we can get done in the time we have. There is still work to get done, I can't let you go early every night."

"Okay, when are we going to be briefed about the meeting on Squall?"

"This weekend. I have a meeting set up with Michael. Instead of telling you everything now, it is best to do it when Michael is here. Answer both your questions at the same time," Cane said.

"All right, I guess that works for me. It would be nice to work with Michael again."

The evening came and Cane was nice enough to let Skyler have an early night again. Skyler knew exactly what he was going to do. His plan was to take Kax out on a date well a friend date and show her the time of her life making her wish she was with him and not Rex. It was his plan to win Kax over.

He stopped by Kax's room; she was there this time. "Hey Kax I got the night off again, want to go out?"

"Skyler, I'm with Rex, remember? I mean I will hang out with you but it's not a date."

Skyler laughed, "I know, I didn't mean it like that. I mean just go out and have fun. I thought maybe we could take a trip into the city. I know some fun places we could go, what do you think?"

"Does Zarina know that you are taking me out?" Kax asked.

"It's not a date, and yes, I tell her everything, she is fine with us hanging out. So, what do you say? Want to go get a movie or go play minigolf?"

Kax laughed and smiled. "We can go play minigolf."

Skyler grinned. "Good, then let's get going."

They drove off into the city in Skyler's green convertible. "So Kax, tell me, how have things been? What's the update on life? Has Tom gotten married yet?"

"Tom's wedding is set for this summer. Things are going well. Whatever you said to your mother worked. Thank you, it has made work a lot easier. She still gives me dirty looks but me and Michael can live with that."

Kax mentioning his mother brought back all the bad memories from this past winter holidays. "The visit to her place this winter was not nice at all. Let's just say it is something I never want to do again and I am glad you appreciate it."

Kax knew the look that came over Skyler's face and knew better than to ask about the things that had happened. "Well thank you. So, you mentioned Cane has a brother? Is he in the Forces?"

"No, he lives in Hawaii with the rest of Cane's family. After I left my mother's, I took Cane up on his invitation and stayed with him for the rest of the holidays. His brother Martin is very nice. He is married and has two kids older than me. Cane's parents are nice too. He had this whole other family before he joined the Forces but to him space was his dream."

"I had no idea there was anything more to him outside of the Forces. That is fascinating."

"So, what is new in your life?" Skyler asked.

"Well, I'm getting used to my job. It is nice having Rex there at work. I miss working with Michael, but I'm glad he got transferred he wasn't happy. But I am thinking of transferring off Earth soon. Rex is thinking of moving to Catillion and I plan on marrying him, so why not? My family is there."

The memories of the year before came back. "Whose idea was it to move? I thought you have issues with training on your homeworld and weren't going back. You wanted to come to Earth?" Skyler asked.

"I do,but it will be hard to live a galaxy from your husband. I'll make it work," Kax said.

All this talk about Rex was bothering Skyler. The point of this date was to not talk about relationships. "If the love of my life had to live in another galaxy for a few years because it was a better career move then I would do it. I would trust them and find a way to make it work."

"What about Clyde? I thought you broke up with him because you were leaving the Galaxy?" Kax asked.

"What me and Clyde had was temporary. We both knew that. I'm certain if I were to ever go back, we would pick things up. But we both had different career paths." Skyler stepped on the gas.

Kax was silent for a moment. "Skyler, aren't you driving a bit fast?"

"Were almost there, I thought I would try and get us there before the hour it's cheaper." Skyler pulled the car into a parking lot. "Here we are, and just so you know this place is all ages, so I won't be drinking tonight. This is all about you and me being friends and playing some mini golf."

"You are giving up a night of drinking just for me?" Kax asked, surprised.

"Kax, I would do anything for you as long as you don't make me regret it." He locked up the car and went with her into the building.

They were on their last round of mini golf. Kax was winning and Skyler was getting frustrated. "Okay, Kax, how about this? Whoever gets this next hole gets bragging rights?"

Kax was setting up her swing. "All right, but you only get to brag about getting the last hole."

"You're mean. I thought you said you never did this before?" Skyler said, watching Kax's ball getting close to the hole.

Kax did a little shake. "I guess I am just a natural at this. Come on, Skyler, you can't be good at everything."

Skyler swung and missed the ball. "Ugh. That swing doesn't count." On the second swing he hit the ball but it was no closer than Kax's.

Kax walked over to her ball. "It's just a game. I'll buy you a snack or something after if it will make you feel better."

Skyler groaned. "I don't want a snack. I just you to swing and finish this game so we can head back."

"Are you really not having fun?" Kax asked. She took another swing at the ball, hitting it back the hole.

"I'm enjoying my time with you. It is just frustrating I can't seem to get any of these balls in holes." Skyler gripped his club tightly.

Kax put down her putter and walked over to Skyler. She put her arms around him and grabbed the club. "I don't know if I was doing it right, but here. Let me try and show you what I was doing."

The two swung the club together and Skyler managed to get the ball in the hole. He was so excited he turned around and gave Kax a big hug. He held her tight. "Thank you Kax. You're amazing."

"It was just luck." She gave Skyler a kiss on the cheek. Then she backed off. "I'm sorry, I was just excited." Feeling guilty she turned away from Skyler.

Skyler placed his hand on her shoulder and turned her back towards him. "Hey don't worry, I won't tell. Thanks for help though."

Kax stared back at Skyler and smiled.

"Come on I'll get you some ice cream and we can head back to base," Skyler said, making his way towards the exit and food stands.

"Skyler, why are you being so nice to me?" Kax asked.

Skyler gave Kax a gentle smile. "Because you are my best friend, and I care about you. Life has gotten busy for both of us, and I feel that I have been neglecting you. I wanted to take you out and just have a fun outing like we used to."

"Thank you, Skyler, for a wonderful night." Kax gave Skyler a hug.

Chapter 38

Skyler returned to Cane's office. When he got there Michael was sitting in the chair he normally sat in.

"Hey Michael, what are you doing here so early and we are he here?" Skyler asked.

Cane looked up from his desk. "Skyler, remember we need to brief for the meeting next week. I trust you had a good night."

Skyler nodded his head and sat down in the seat next to Michael. "I did. There are a few things I wanted to talk to you about concerning Kax."

Michael spoke up. "Is Kax all right?"

Skyler looked at Cane. "Is it okay if I bring them up now? I have no problem talking in front of Michael."

Cane looked at the time on his computer. "We can talk about them now because the meeting with Michael hasn't started yet, so we have a bit of time. What is on your mind?"

Skyler took a deep breath. "Kax didn't get a good job placement and she feels that the placement is being biased towards her. She wants to be a deep space pilot but was rejected from the placements for the summer. She has the qualifications to be more than a junkyard pilot but is stuck as one."

Cane typed in a few things on his computer. "Well, this is part of the problem. She has the training like you said but her grades and average are low after the issues of last year. She has a mark on her file. I'm not sure who she has applied to but when they look at the eligible candidates, they take the best they can. This red mark on the file doesn't disqualify her but, a polite way to put it, makes her complicated."

"But that is not fair, it wasn't her fault." Skyler said.

"I know it isn't. I will work on taking this off, so that it doesn't look there is an issue. Her grades are low because as much as the incident wasn't her fault, she still didn't get the highest mark on her exam and so it brought her average down. I will see what I can do about cleaning this up. I can't get her into any special programs that is her job and responsibility. I can only make sure that the file looks like it is just one of a cadet with her list of qualifications and average. That should help."

Michael looked at Skyler. "Wait, Kax isn't happy with her job posting? I thought she liked it. I mean we hate having to work with your mother, but that's a small part. And she and Rex are getting along."

Skyler sighed. "All I know is what she told me last night and she is not happy."

Cane turned to Michael. "Speaking of job placements, Michael, if everything goes well with the meeting next week, I want you to know you will not be working at your engineering post for the next while. You will be doing a bit of diplomatic duties. When this is over, I want to give you the job placement of an instructor. you will be a junior instructor but with your advanced knowledge you can assist Commodore Ipinik with the new recruits."

Michael thought the about the offer for a second. "We will see how things go in the next four months. But thank you for the offer."

"Michael, this is a great job. You should take it," Skyler said.

Michael turned his head to Skyler. "I didn't say no, I said that I would discuss it later. Skyler, it is not that simple all right?"

Cane typed in a few things in on his computer. "He is right, Skyler. And thank you, Michael. We will be in touch about it. But right now, we need to start the briefing. As you all know, Skyler will not be accompanying us to the meeting on Squall. He will be given all the info on it, he just can't set foot on the planet, but nonetheless is still involved. The Squallites have requested you, Michael, because you are the one who has initiated these events."

"Are they mad at Michael for taking the Worm Orb too?" Skyler cut in.

Cane shook his head. "No, they are not. They just blame you for everything. The meeting is to discuss what Earth and the Squallites are going to do during this ceasefire. Earth's plans are to listen to the demands and see what Earth can do to stop this war and all the potential future wars. Does this make sense to everyone?"

Skyler and Michael nodded. "Do we know what the Cass want yet? Like what if they want something ridiculous that we cannot deliver?"

"We don't know exactly, but it is my belief that the Cass government is not giving up ridiculous demands. Earth can fulfill the request."

Skyler shrugged. "All right cool, is that it then or is there anything else?"

"Skyler, by now you should know your work is never over. Now I got to give Michael all the info on how the meeting is set to go. Also go through what he plans to say and find out all the background info he can give us."

"So why do I have to stay if this all has to do with Michael?"

"Because you are my apprentice and you will know what I know and do as I do. Also, when I send you the info and tell you about the meeting I just want to tell you about what happened in the meeting, not inform you on everything. So, if everyone is ready, let's begin."

Kax was in her room brushing her hair getting it ready for tonight. She went out with Skyler the night before as friends and tonight was her date night with Rex. She put down her brush when she got a ping on her tablet. She read the email. It was a letter from the piloting base on Mars. She was accepted for a piloting exercise there for the summer. It wasn't deep space but it was a better job than what she had been doing. She was excited and was about to write back and say that she accepted the offer when Rex knocked on the door.

"Hey Rex, I was just finishing getting ready. If you don't mind waiting." Kax said.

"You don't need to get all gussied up for what we're doing tonight," Rex said, sitting down on her bed.

"I wasn't, I was just brushing my hair when I got an email. I'm going to be going to Mars!"

rex frowned, "Mars? With who? When?"

"This summer. I just got offered a summer job being a pilot at the Mars base. Isn't this great!"

Rex frowned. "But what is wrong with the job you have now? What about me? I can't leave my job and go to Mars."

Kax's smile faded and she put the tablet down. "Rex, I don't like my job. I want to be a deep space pilot and this is my first step. This one is only for four months. I will be back. I can come see you on weekends or something and we can chat online. You won't even notice that I am gone."

"Oh, I will notice. Kax, you're my fiancé, you can't just leave me to go to some other planet. We got to stick together. It is bad enough you still want to be with other guys while you're with me."

Kax frowned. "What are you talking about? Michael and Skyler are just friends. Nothing happens between us. And Rex, I'm not abandoning you. This is a better job and I will get paid more."

"Oh, don't make me sound stupid. I see the way Skyler looks at you. What did you two do last night? You can get a different job but there are many here on Earth you would be good at."

"Rex, what is with you? I have never seen you act like this? Trust me, you're the only guy I'm with. I'm not abandoning you."

Rex got up and took Kax's hand. He held it up and showed her the ring. "If you care for me in any way, you will not hit accept on that job. We will find you another one is that understood? I am a reasonable guy. I will not force you to be with me only, but when you don't you come back to me. You don't have to tell me the details about what you and Skyler did, but you are going to make it up to me." He grinned and moved his eyes down.

Kax was scared. She had no idea Rex was like this. She was going to have to figure out how to get out of there. She liked Rex, he was always kind to her on her dates, he never acted like this with her. She really wanted to be a real pilot. She wasn't unfaithful to him; Skyler was just a friend.

Rex put his hand on her lower back. "Come on, babe, let's come over here to the bed and you can start by making it up to me and rewarding me for being such a good fiancé."

She sat down on the bed and followed his guidance, trying to figure a way out of this. She tried to get up again. He held her back down. "Kax, don't worry, everything can wait except me."

Where can I go? What can I do? who can I see? This isn't Rex. This isn't the Rex I know. In a panic she pushed Rex off her. "I got to go. Sorry Rex." She went to reach for her tablet to take with her. He grabbed her arm. "No, you don't. If you can fuck Skyler, you can fuck me."

she kicked him, making him release her hand. She ran out of the room, leaving everything she had behind. *I'll get in it in the morning.* She had nowhere to go. She could go to the bathroom but what would that do? He would find her there. Michael was living at the cabin and she had no ride. she didn't know what room her old roommate Ona was in. She had no choice but to run to Skyler's room. It might make things worse, but she knew Skyler would protect her and make sure everything was all right. She ran the out the building into the officer's barracks. She found Skyler's room and banged on the door. Zarina answered. "Kax, what are you doing here?" she asked.

Kax had tears running down her face. "Is Skyler here? can I come in? It's urgent."

Zarina stepped aside. "Please come in. Skyler is not here but you can talk to me about everything, I'm here to help."

Kax sat down on the nearby couch. There were tears running down her eyes.

"What is the matter? What happened to you?"

"It was Rex. I never seen him this way. All I wanted to do was be taken seriously and not treated like a whore. I don't understand. He has never acted like this before," Kax said.

Zarina got up and grabbed the box of tissues next to Skyler's bed and handed it to Kax. "Tell me everything. You can trust me and maybe we can find a way to fix this."

Kax told her everything that had happened and what led up to it.

"Wow, that is quite a story. I am glad you found me and not Skyler. How do I put this? you got to dump Rex. No man should be treating you like that. You go wherever your career will take; don't be held down because someone said no." Zarina said.

Kax blew her nose. "All I ever wanted to be was a deep space pilot and find a guy who understands me. Why does it seem like every relationship is going well until Skyler shows up in the picture? He is just a friend, they don't worry about Michael."

Zarina put her arm around Kax. "Because Skyler is in love with you. Michael isn't a threat to them. If anything, Skyler is a good way of finding out what their true colors look like. The right guy will understand. Also, is Rex a pilot too, or is he an engineer?"

"Rex is a pilot too. He also does the junkyard patrols."

"Well, there is your other problem. He is older than you, is stuck in his job and doesn't have anyone. I can see how you two got along but I bet you anything that because you have a chance to go higher in your career it threatened him. He probably believes you that you and Skyler didn't do anything, but he is going to use it to knock you down. Honestly I think you need to break up with him."

Kax stared at the ring on her finger. "But he is a nice guy. He is someone serious and I enjoy his company."

Zarina raised an eyebrow at Kax. "Really? After what he did to you tonight, you really want to get back with him? Or is it that you don't want Skyler to defend you and get involved?"

Kax looked down at her ring. "I just can't imagine how one night could ruin everything."

Zarina rubbed Kax's back. "Look, I won't tell Skyler if you don't want me to. But you can't stay with Rex. You are going to write back and accept that job. You know it is the right thing and it is one step closer to your goal. Rex has got to go."

Kax took a deep breath and wiggled the ring off her finger. "You're right, thank you."

"I have another question, since we are on the topic of relationships. Do you love Skyler?" Zarina asked. "I won't get jealous."

After what Kax had been through she wondered how Zarina would react, but she was willing to trust her once again. "I'm not sure. I like him a lot and he is always there for me. He is a sweet guy. But he is looking for someone to take care of and protect. He wants to feel on top. I don't need a man like that. I want to find me first. I want to be independent and on my own and find my footing first."

Zarina smiled at Kax's words. "That sounds like a Skyler thing. But just so you know, he admires your strength. He wants to be on top just as you want to be taken seriously. Deep inside he is fighting his issues and himself to be the one who has everything figured out and be a strong leader. You and Michael are the two who keep him together."

Kax was unsure how to respond and just smiled in reply. "Oh my gosh, my stuff! Rex has all my stuff! I left him in my room. I need my uniform and tablet. What am I going to do? If he is still there, he might wreck it or leave the door unlocked!"

Zarina looked at the time on her watch. "You stay here. Skyler won't be back for a bit. tell me your room number and I will deal with Rex. He will not be able to mess with me. I will get your stuff." Zarina got up and handed Kax her communicator. "If something is wrong you can contact my watch with this number." She showed her on the tablet. "If I need you, I will call you from my watch." Zarina handed Kax the remote. "Here is the remote. Watch anything you like on the screen. I'll be back in a bit everything will be fine."

Kax smiled hesitantly as Zarina left. As Zarina had said everything was fine, Zarina got Kax her stuff and came back to the room. Kax's nerves were still shaking from everything so Zarina joined her in watching videos. They watched videos into the night and fell asleep on couch watching together.

It was around midnight when Skyler got back to the room. He was tired and just wanted to go to bed. He flopped down on the bed and began to take his clothes off. He dropped the uniform jacket on the floor when he noticed Zarina and Kax on the couch resting. He wondered what events had happened tonight to lead to this. He saw Kax's ring on the table. He knew it was best to leave them alone and let them rest. He continued getting ready for bed and grabbed a pair of shorts out of the drawer and wore them. He got into his bed and slept.

By 6 in the morning, Skyler didn;t feel like he had gotten enough sleep, but it didn't matter. He had to get to work anyway. The alarm woke up Kax and Zarina. He thought about what he would say to them and then went with. "You two sleep well."

Kax stretched. "Yeah, me and Zarina were just having a girl's night is all. I like her."

Skyler smiled. "That's great. Well, you can both keep sleeping or not. I got to get back to Cane's. Zarina, I do need to talk to you about my upcoming holidays next week. I have two weeks off."

Zarina stretched as she got off the couch as well. "Can't help you. My unit is going to the moon for two weeks on a mission and I can't take anyone extra with me. You got two weeks to yourself. But I will be back in time for the Officers' Ball. I will gladly go with you then."

Skyler walked over and gave Zarina a kiss. "Well, that sounds good to me. I look forward to the Ball with you."

"Hey Skyler, it was nice seeing you again but I should get going." Kax said.

Zarina picked up Kax's ring off the table and followed her out.

Skyler was unsure what happened last night, but he did know that if they wanted him to know, they would have told him.

Chapter 39

Skyler kissed Zarina when he woke up in the morning. "Morning, sweetie."

She snuggled in between his arms. "Morning," she mumbled.

They laid there for a moment enjoying each other until the alarm went off. Zarina got up and started getting dressed. "Are you sure you can't spend my two weeks' holidays with me?"

Zarina leaned back over the bed and kissed Skyler. "Nope, but hey, you're free to spend it with whoever you want. We will have fun on the next trip."

Skyler didn't quite understand it. He was finally going to get two weeks of holiday to himself, but he wanted to spend it with Zarina. It was odd having a girlfriend who lived with you. He got up out of the bed and began getting dressed. "Yeah, when you get back you will have the Officers' Ball that will be fun. You enjoy your trip to Mars and I have one more day working for Cane and then I will start my two weeks."

Zarina was finished getting dressed. She turned to Skyler. "Two weeks won't be long, have all the fun you can. And hopefully we get back early and then we can have some fun for your last two days."

They kissed as she left the room. Skyler did have to be at Cane's but not for another hour. He knew it was early, but Paul was expecting his phone call. He sat down at his desk and called Paul on the holo-phone. Paul answered. "Hey buddy, right on time."

"Hey Paul, sorry I'm calling you so early. I hope I didn't wake you."

"Skyler, when you have kids you always wake up this early, that's why I said to call. So, what's the plan?" Paul asked.

Skyler checked his notes quickly. "Well, I get off from work today, so what I am thinking is I finish today, then I start driving tomorrow morning when I wake up."

"You do know you can just fly up here or get a teleport, it would be a lot quicker." Paul suggested.

"Yeah, but what about my car, buddy? Who is going to drive me from the transportation depot to your place?" Skyler said.

Paul raised an eyebrow. "Really dude, you didn't think we would be willing to drive you? Look, unless you have something to do on the way up here, I suggest you get a ticket and contact us with the time. One of us will be there to pick you up."

Skyler smiled. "Thanks buddy, I will do that. Can't wait to see you." A baby crying in the background could be heard.

"Sorry buddy, that's my cue. See you tomorrow." The line was cut.

Skyler used his computer to book a ticket. He sent the info to Paul and then headed to work with Cane.

Before Zarina left on her trip, she stopped by the hangar to check on Kax. She had forgotten that Kax and Rex worked together and was just curious how that was going and what their relationship status was now. *I hope she dumped him,* Zarina thought to herself. She had never gotten confirmation about the breakup.

She made her way to the hangar.

Zarina stopped by the front desk. She saw the aging brunette at the desk with the soft features and small nose. *Of course, Skyler's mother is the only one working here.* Zarina paused to gather her thoughts. *You know what, maybe she won't care.*

Maybe she thinks me and Skyler have broken up. She went over to the desk. "Hello, has Petty Officer Tillion checked in yet?" Zarina asked, hoping Sandy didn't recognize her.

"Do all you whores hang out together?" Sandy asked.

I guess she does remember me. Zarina smiled. "This is a work matter, Commodore Roux. I just need to know."

Sandy glared and pointed to the door. "She's in there, and I have no idea what your intentions with my son are but you better not break his heart."

Zarina stopped for a moment to think about her words before walking in. *Did Sandy really care about Skyler? Or was Skyler falling in love with her and Sandy knew it?* Zarina didn't want to think about that and continued her way into the hangar. When she got in, she saw Kax and Rex hugging by one of the ships. *What is going on?* Zarina thought. She waited until Kax and Rex were separated then she went over to Kax. "Hey Kax, how are things going?"

Kax smiled. "Very good, me and Rex got back together. He just apologized to me and he has agreed to support me no matter where my career takes me."

Zarina thought this was odd, "Kax, is there somewhere we can talk in private?"

Kax signaled her to follow her to the ship. They got in and Zarina sat next to her. "Kax, why did you go back with him? I don't understand."

Kax took a deep breath. "We're not really together. The first day back was hard and so was the day after. He just wanted to talk and fight. I didn't want to deal with him at all. I tried to get a transfer, but I am under contract at this posting for a few more months. So, I figured I would pretend to be his girlfriend. I hate his guts and he is not getting close to me. That hug was just being polite, but I'm doing this just to keep him calm."

Zarina looked concerned. "Kax, this isn't right. No one should have to deal and go through this. Please, can we put in a complaint and a report and get you away from him?"

Kax shook her head. "Zarina, I like you. I think everything you have done for me is great. But I can handle myself. I have had so many issues with this work placement that it is just going to look worse and worse. All I want to do is get my training and contract over with as painless as possible. Is that too much to ask?"

Zarina shook her head. "I get it. So, it doesn't bother you to be around him?"

Kax shuddered. "Oh no, it bothers me. I hate his guts. But if I say anything it will just make things worse. I'm staying at the cabin with Michael and I plan to ignore his calls and hopefully he will get the idea and leave me alone. If he tries anything again, I will go after him. Right now, I'm in this placement for three more months. I can handle that."

Zarina was hesitant but knew there was no way that she could force Kax to change her mind. "Well, if you need the help, don't hesitate to contact me. I am here for you."

Kax gave Zarina a hug. "This is my way of dealing with things. Thank you."

Zarina got out of the cockpit and made her way to join her class and unit for her trip.

Skyler was working on his paperwork with Cane, speeding through things. Cane looked over some of Skyler's papers. "Hey, slow down there, you forgot to sign these last ones. What's the rush?" Cane asked.

Skyler put the papers down and then looked up at Cane. "Sorry, I am just looking forward to my holidays."

Cane raised an eyebrow. "Really? Do you have any plans? I mean the last few years I have seen you; you normally don't care for holidays."

Skyler nodded his head, "You are right. And most of the time that is true for me. But I have recently reconnected with some good friends from high school and I am going to visit them for most of the two weeks. I'm just excited to see them."

Cane smiled. "That's great to hear. They are on Earth, right? Because as much as these are your holidays, I need you to be on Earth for diplomatic reasons."

"Oh yeah, they are up in Thunder Bay, I'm going to be flying up there."

Cane frowned. "This is going to sound like an odd question, but have you ever left the mega city in your life? Like, I mean, not to go to other planets, but to go to other locations on Earth?"

Skyler thought about all the places he had ever traveled. He grew up in Rochester and went to Toronto a bunch of times. Michael lived in London and Kax was from Pennsylvania. He once went to New York for a weekend. Then he remembered the two summers in England. "Yes, I spent two summers in England with my uncle when I was sixteen and seventeen. Why do you ask?"

"Because I know for a fact that you have UGF citizenship. you don't have Earth citizenship or American/Canadian citizenship so I was worried you didn't have your passport. Thunder Bay is outside the mega city. You are free to roam here because of the UGF base. And You can go to the other bases on Earth but outside of that, you need to have your passport."

Skyler hadn't thought about this for a long time. "Um, is there a way to get these things overnight? I don't remember where mine is. I haven't seen it since I joined the Forces."

Cane sighed. "Glad I mentioned it now. Call your uncle on your lunch break. I will check your file, in case you used it for your ID when you joined. Skyler, these are important documents you can't lose."

Skyler put down his tablet and called his uncle.

Justin soon answered. "Hey Skyler, what's up? Long time no hear. How is Leon doing?"

"Not much. Cane is fine and I'm about to go on my two weeks' holiday. And I realized I need my passport for travel. Do you happen to know where I left it? It has been years since I last used it."

Justin paused and thought about it for a moment. "You caught me at the right time. I am at my desk. If I have it or something that important of yours, I will have put it in the safe. Give me a minute."

Skyler put his communicator down while his uncle searched. "He's looking for it," Skyler said to Cane.

"I don't have it on file," Cane whispered back.

Justin came back a few moments later. "Found it!" He called into the phone.

"Really? That is great. Can you transport that to me? My flight is early in the morning." Skyler said.

"I can't do that. Official government documents have encoding that can't be reproduced so they must be in hand. Where are you traveling to, and where are you now?"

"I'm flying to Thunder Bay to visit Paul and Xandria, remember them? Right now I'm on base."

"I will have a driver deliver it to you at the base." Justin said. "I am so glad you are still in contact with them. Send them my best wishes."

"I will, thank you uncle, you are the best."

"Skyler, I have always wanted the best for you and I'm so happy you are Cane's apprentice. One more thing before you go, are you going to the Officers' Ball in Russia at the end of the month?"

Skyler smiled. "Yes, I am, are you going?"

"Well, it is always an event that me and Elaine could attend, but if you are going it would be nice to see you again."

Skyler smiled. "It will be great to see you then. Thanks again."

"Take care, my little star." the phone disconnected.

Cane smiled. "I'm glad you have a good connection with your uncle."

"Yeah, we have always had a bond. He was just always busy."

"Well, I'm glad he is there for you. But we got to get back to work if you want to enjoy your holidays."

Skyler stuck his tongue out. "No problem."

The hours went by, Skyler was tired and could barely keep his eyes open. Skyler put down his tablet. "Cane, are we almost done?"

Cane smiled. "Yes. I was just seeing how much we could get done, two weeks without doing this stuff is going to make this pile worse."

"Why do all these reports come to you? Aren't there commodores who work on these things? I saw many other people's names on all these files."

Cane tidied up the physical papers and the piles of secure tablets. "They do go through them. I just must acknowledge I have seen everything in the fleet. So, I'm the last step before they get filed and put into the archives. Why do you think I have so much power? If I see something and I don't like how it was handled I could audit it. This is also how I'm able to help your friends. Instead of having one of the lower ranking officers deal with it, I do it for them. These never end. And as much as we don't use paper for most things nowadays, we need a hard copy for certain documents for them to be legal. Make sense?"

Skyler nodded. "Yeah, this job sucks."

"After your holidays there will be more traveling. These files never get done. It is great to have someone to help with things."

Skyler looked at the clock. "It is almost midnight, can I go now?"

Cane nodded his head. "Yes, I need to finish up a few things, but mine and Michael's ship leaves at 2:30 a.m. so I got to get ready for that. I will sleep on the way to Squall. What about you?"

"My flight is at six so I got time for a nap. I packed a few days ago."

"Good, then you are dismissed, and don't forget your passport."

Skyler pointed to his tablet. "Yeah, I got a notification that there was a package waiting for me at the front gates. I will pick it up on my way out."

Skyler left the office and made his way back to his room. He was tired and excited all at the same time. He couldn't wait to see his old friends and enjoy a time away from work. As he walked back, he saw Kax in the hall. He went up to her. "Hey Kax, how are you doing?"

Kax let out a long sigh. "Stressed, I hate work and I can't wait for it to be over."

"Does this have something to do with why you were at my place?" He asked.

"Yeah. The short of it is I broke up with Rex and he doesn't want to break up so I'm pretending to be with him and staying at the cabin. I'm just keeping up this act until the summer or he gets the hint."

Skyler offered Kax a hug. "Hey, I'm sorry. Please take it easy. I'm sorry about you and Rex."

Kax accepted the hug. "Hey, don't you worry about me. I can handle him. I just hate how I keep falling for crappy guys."

Skyler broke the hug and placed his hands on Kax's shoulders. "I love and care for you. I can't tell you to stop what you are doing or tell you to do something different. But what I want you to start doing from now on is think about yourself and what you want first. You come first. Then the rest of the world, understand? I have only ever wanted you to be happy."

Kax gave Skyler a kiss on the cheek. "Thank you, Skyler."

"Hey Kax, do you need a car for the next two weeks during my holidays?"

"Well, Michael did lend me his bike. But if you're not using it. But what is the catch?" Kax asked.

"I need a ride to the airport in the morning. My flight is at six."

Kax looked at the time on her communicator. "Yeah, you know what, I can do that. I will be a little late for my job but I'm not worried. I want to do this. The only thing is I'm here early because Michael's flight was at two and Michael was giving me his bike. I figured I would just go to the bar for a few hours."

"If you want, Zarina is gone, you could crash at my place. I'm going to just sleep and it is stocked with beer. It would be cheaper." Skyler offered.

"I could get in a couple of beers then sober up to drive you. Sure, why not? Does the TV bother you when you sleep?"

Skyler shrugged. "Not sure, but I'm so tired I don't think it will bother me."

Chapter 40

Skyler's bags were packed and he was in his car. Kax was sober and was driving to the airport. He had only been there a few times in his life and was curious to see what it would be like. "Hey Kax, I really want to thank you for doing this."

Kax smiled and pulled up to the drop-off at the airport. "No problem, you are my friend. Also, who are you going to visit? If you don't mind sharing."

Skyler got his bags out of the car. "Paul and Xandria. She is my ex from high school, the one who got pregnant I mentioned before. They invited me up to Thunder Bay to visit them. I'll get you a souvenir if you want."

Kax shook her head. "You don't have to. Well, I hope you have a great holiday. Let me know when you are back, I will pick you up then too, okay?"

Skyler gave Kax a hug. "Thanks, see you soon."

Skyler made his way through the airport and checked in his bags. He had one suitcase and then his carry-on bag. He handed his suitcase in with no issue. When he got to the security checkpoint, he got stopped. "Sir, is this your bag?" The green humanoid alien asked.

Skyler nodded. "Yeah, what is the problem?"

"You can't bring a case of beer on with onto the airplane. It needs to be checked and locked up."

"But I'm not going to drink it on the plane, I just need to make sure it comes with me," Skyler said.

The security guard opened the bag to reveal a suitcase full of beer and bottles of alcohol. "You need to stand over in that line to bring your items over to someone who can properly have these transported and make sure you are within the legal limits."

Skyler rolled his eyes. "You have got to be kidding me."

Skyler took his bag with him as he walked through the other lineup.

the other security officer looked over his bag. "Sir, this is too much alcohol to take over the border."

"Really? Too much to transport? I can buy this stuff on the other side. I just have it now. Why can't I take the rest with me?"

The security officer typed in a few things on the computer. "What is your citizenship?"

Skyler handed her his passport. "Federation citizenship. Does that make a difference?"

She nodded. "It does. Because we can send this in the lock up free of cost. And your limit is increased because you are an officer. I will say this is for work purposes." She typed in a few more things then handed him a paper slip. "When you get off the plane, hand this to the desk at the baggage claim and it will be ready for you."

Skyler smiled and took the slip. "Thank you. I appreciate that."

Skyler soon was on the plane and ready to have a nap. It was going to be a few hours and he was still tired from that long day with Cane.

When he got off the plane and had his bags, he went over to the passenger pick up and searched for Paul.

in a red minivan his friend Paul pulled up.

Skyler waved and smiled at his friend. He gave Paul a hug and handed him his bags. "Hey buddy, nice to see you!"

"Dude, it has been too long. I really missed you."

Skyler stood there staring at his friend with his dark bowl cut hair. He was slightly taller than Skyler and a slim build. He had a rough beard. He was wearing a plaid dress shirt and slacks. "Wow, look at you. You look so mature and old."

Paul laughed. "Skyler, I'm married with kids. I don't have a need to wear the tight shirts and leather pants anymore. Also, I'm on my way to work. What is going to happen is I will drop you off at the house. Xandria is there. The kids will be at school and then I will head to work. you, Xandria and little Scott will be the only ones in the house."

"How many kids do you have now?" Skyler asked.

"Three, Logan, Bobby and Scott. Logan and Bobby are old enough to go to school now and Scott is about a year old. "Paul said while driving the car.

"Three kids? How can you handle that at our age? Is it easy or something?" Skyler asked.

Paul laughed. "Not easy, but that is part of the reason we are up here. Xandria's family got me a job so we have the income and they are around to help her with the kids. It isn't the life I planned for myself, but hey, I got everything under control. But no more kids for a while. We have agreed to stop at three."

Skyler laughed nervously, "Man, I can still barely imagine having one kid. I have come close a few times, but I don't think I'm father material. I want to be a single captain who stays available for the ladies."

"And guys," Paul said and placed his hand on Skyler's knee.

"And guys." Skyler stared into Paul's eyes. "I'm still getting used to that. It is weird. My sex life was always touch and go. I never really sat down and thought about it. But looking back on my life it makes sense."

Paul pulled up in front of the house. "I understand, Skyler. Sexuality isn't always something that is clear for us."

"It's great to see you again and thanks for the ride. It will be a nice vacation."

Paul put the car in Park and leaned over and gave Skyler a kiss on the lips. "I'm glad you came to visit. I'll be off work around six."

Skyler put on his flirtatious smile. "I will be waiting for you."

Skyler got out of the car and grabbed his two bags out of the van and made his way to the front door. He rang the doorbell. Xandria quickly answered the door. She stood there with her long black hair. Her body was more curvaceous than he remembered, but her large light brown eyes were still as gorgeous as ever.

"Skyler, it is nice to see you again." Xandria said, holding the door open.

Skyler grinned. "It is nice to see you again too."

Xandria gave Skyler a big hug. "Come in, we have the house to ourselves."

Skyler picked up his bags and made his way in. "Paul said Scott was still here?"

Xandria helped Skyler with his bags and put them in the hallway away from the path. "He was, but I called my aunt to take care of him. Told her we had a guest and to give you time to get settled in before bombarding you with kids."

"Well, isn't that sweet." Skyler looked around, "Can I sit down or have a drink?"

Xandria came towards Skyler and played with his hair. "Not before I give you a tour and show you where you will be sleeping."

Skyler grinned. "Well then, please, let the tour commence."

She took Skyler's hand and took him upstairs. "Up here we have the bathroom, hall closet with all the towels and stuff. The kids' rooms are on the other side." She took him back down the stairs. "On the main floor we have the kitchen with the replicator so don't worry about cooking. The bedroom is right over here and this is a walk-in closet we did up as a nursery. And this door." She took him to a locked painted blue door. "This is where we take our guests." She took him down to the basement.

In the basement there was a lovely plush carpet and long leather couch, a TV and a mini bar. Hooks and apparatuses attached to the walls and ceiling.

Skyler looked around. "Well, I see you and Paul haven't stopped being active. My guess is this room is for adults only?"

"It is, the kids don't know about it. We have told them it is for storage and stuff." Xandria sighed. "But me and Paul don't have many guests down here anymore. Honestly since little Scott was born we have been in kind of a slump. I'm glad you came."

Skyler offered Xandria a hug, which she accepted. "Hey, don't you worry. I'm here now and I will do my best to help you two out. I still care and owe you guys one."

She kissed Skyler's lips, "Oh, you owe me more than one." She took Skyler to the long leather couch and pushed him down. Skyler quickly started taking his clothes off before she sat down on him. He began to kiss and caress her body. "I missed you," Skyler said.

"I did too," she answered.

Skyler and Xandria were on the couch laying in each other's arms. "That brought back a lot of old memories."

She played with his chest. "You have gotten better, I'm impressed. It was great doing this again after all this time."

"So, am I sleeping down here? I didn't see a guest room." Skyler inquired.

"No, you are sharing the bed with me and Paul upstairs, and don't worry the kids won't freak out, me and Paul have told them you're Mommy and Daddy's friend. You're not the first friend who we have had stay over."

"Well, that is good to hear." Skyler kissed Xandria. "This was long overdue. I'm so sorry I fell out of touch."

She played with Skyler's hair. "Skyler, you went down your own path and so did we. I don't blame you at all for any of that. I'm just glad now we have gotten back together."

Skyler took a deep breath and enjoyed being in the arms of his old high school flame. "I'm glad you are still here."

He dozed off for what he thought was only a moment, then he heard the slam of a door. Xandria was sitting up and getting dressed. "The kids are home, get dressed."

Skyler quickly put on his clothes and went up the stairs with Xandria. She locked the door behind them.

The two boys were running around the living room. Xandria rushed to the kitchen and pulled out a plate of sandwiches and poured some drinks. She handed the plate to Skyler. "Take these to the boys." Skyler stepped out with the plate while Xandria brought out the cups. "Logan and Bobby please sit down, we have a guest."

Skyler froze when he saw Logan. He hadn't seen him since his birth and the boy had grown tall. But the shocking part was his blonde hair. He had his mothers' dark brown eyes, but as far as he knew no one in their families had blond hair. He put the plate down and sat down on the couch. The town boys sat on either side of Skyler. Xandria put the glasses down on the table and sat in the chair.

"Hey kids, this is your Uncle Skyler. He is visiting us from the space academy." Xandria said.

The kids grabbed their sandwiches with their mouths full and started asking questions. "Are you going to be a captain and fly a spaceship around!" Logan asked.

"Yeah, are you going to shoot people too and fight in wars!" asked Bobby.

Skyler laughed. The kids reminded him of how he was when he was a kid and all the questions he asked his Dad. "Well, I'm going to be a captain but pilots fly the ship. I tell them where to go. And I have a bit of combat experience."

The kids listened to him in amazement. "Wow, cool. Did you bring us anything?"

Skyler got up. "I sure did." He went over to his large suitcase and opened it up. He pulled out a toy spaceship and action figures for the kids. "Here you go."

"Wow, cool thanks! Do you want to see our other toys?"

Xandria stood up. "You didn't have to get them anything. "It would be rude not to. I got you and Paul something too. It's in the other bag."

Xandria gave Skyler a kiss before the boys dragged him up the stairs.

The boys showed Skyler all their toys and their rooms. Skyler thought he was going to be trapped, then they heard the door again. The kids dropped their stuff and ran down the stairs. "Daddy's home!"

Skyler made his way back down stairs. Paul was there giving the kids a hug and Xandria kissed him too.

"Hey Paul, how did work go?"

Paul rubbed his neck. "Long but I'm glad to be back home."

Xandria checked her phone messages. "Aunt Jeanette called, she is going to be dropping Scott off after supper."

"You had Jeanette watch the baby?" Paul asked.

"It was just easier." Xandria said.

The kids full of energy running around playing.

Paul called the boys over. "Hey I know Skyler is here and he is new and exciting. But could you boys give Mommy and Daddy some privacy while we get dinner ready? You can go and play with your toys."

The boys nodded and ran upstairs.

Paul flopped down on the couch, exhausted. "So Skyler, what do you think?"

"It's a nice place. I really like the basement."

Paul laughed. "Well, I see someone waited no time to give you a tour."

"Honey, you can have him tonight." Xandria said.

Skyler laughed, "I'm here for the two weeks, there will be plenty of time to have fun."

"Yeah, you're right. How are things being the Fleet Admiral's apprentice? And how is your girlfriend during this time?"

"Zarina is on Mars and I assume is having a great time. We have texted to make sure that we are safe but no big conversations. I don't know how much I will hear from her in the next little bit. But what I am curious about is Logan, you two never mentioned how much he looks like me?"

Paul and Xandria stared at each other for a second. "You think he looks like you?" Xandria said.

Paul pulled out his phone out of his pocket and flipped through his photos. "You might not have met them, but here are Xandria's cousins and aunt. The blond comes from my side."

Skyler took the phone to examine the photos carefully. And without a doubt Logan looked more like Paul's side of the family than him.

"Hey I'm sorry I didn't realize that. I guess I'm still nervous after all these years."

"Skyler, you were there for the tests and saw the results. We wouldn't lie to you about something this big. But it is a nice reminder of you."

"When he gets older, you will see how much he looks like my family. He is already growing into his big family nose and high cheek bones. He's just at the age when all kids look like anyone," Xandria said. She got up out of the chair. "I'm going to start replicating dinner, any special requests Skyler?"

Skyler shrugged. "Not really. Replicated food all tastes the same to me."

"You boys have fun getting caught up. I will call you if I need you."

Paul tugged on Skyler's T-shirt from where he was sitting, indicating Skyler to come closer. Skyler laid down on Paul on the couch. Paul gave Skyler a kiss and rubbed his hand through Skyler's hair. "I'm so glad you came to visit. You have no idea how much I have wanted to do things with you."

Skyler kissed Paul back, rubbing his body. "We're going to have fun, aren't we?"

Paul slapped Skyler's ass. "You bet we will."

They continued to make out until dinner was called.

Skyler woke up from the bed in the middle of the night. He did his best to not wake up Paul and Xandria. He went to the kitchen to get a drink when he noticed a light flashing on his communicator. He quickly stepped out to the back porch and took the call. "Hello, Skyler speaking."

"Hey sweetie, how are you doing?" Zarina said.

Skyler was happy to hear her voice. "Hey, how are you doing? Enjoying Mars?"

"Well, it is kind of boring but I have been paired up with this hot alien and we have been having some fun. How about you?"

Skyler smiled. "I got here today, and I have been having a great time. They make a great family. Have you ever thought about having a family?"

The phone was silent for a moment. "Um, I hope you are not asking if I want to start one. I don't think I am ready for that. Do you want one?"

Skyler let out a deep breath. "I didn't mean right now or with me. It is just this could have been my life. That is what bothers me. Logan was almost my kid, but he was Paul's. I don't want a family, but it feels like everyone around me is having kids and families and I'm still on my own. I'm the only Therris."

"Skyler, you have a different type of family, one that you make. The one that you make. Kax, Michael and Cane are very close to you. Soon, in a few years you will be employed on a ship and the crew will be your family. You will have one soon. But you are not alone. You don't need to have kids to solve that problem."

Skyler took a sip from his drink. "I guess that is one way to look at it. I just hope that day comes sooner. There are days when I feel so alone."

"Skyler, I can't help you with this from here. Talk to your friends about it to see if they can help. when I get back, I will check in with you on these feelings."

"Thanks, Zarina. You're great. I should be heading back to bed. Thanks for calling."

"No problem, I will see you soon."

Skyler put the communicator away in his pocket. He sat down and took a sip of his drink. He sat there reflecting on his life.

Paul opened the screen door. "Hey buddy. I heard part of your call. Mind if I join you?"

"Sure, come join me."

"Skyler, you know me and Xandria see you as family. You are a close friend and we went through so much together. I could never forget you. Skyler, what has been going on with you in your life? What happened to the spunky teen I knew?"

"Honestly Paul, I think I have been doing it for too long. That's all. I think I lived my crazy life to cover up the loneliness I felt inside. You know I don't have a family. I was living with my uncle who wasn't really there when you met me."

"Skyler, I remember how lost you were when I met you. To be fair, I was too. I have no idea how we would have turned out if it wasn't for Xandria. She kept us distracted or something."

Skyler laughed. "Yeah, she got me to calm down a little bit and kept me busy. My uncle even liked her."

"Your uncle liked us a lot. Did you know he bought us this house? He also put a savings fund away for little Logan. He wanted to make sure we had a good start in life and was a great help. Honestly Skyler, we couldn't have received a better support system. That's why I feel so guilty now that we are having marriage issues. It is like we have money; we have relatives and friends to help us out. But I don't know what to do. It gets so hard some days. I'm getting tired. I'm 23 and I shouldn't be getting old at my age. But I feel we have less and less time. Xandria is getting a temper and a short fuse. I don't know, man. Life has just become so hard."

Skyler rubbed Paul's shoulder. "When was the last time you had a holiday? Maybe you need to get away, reset things and sleep. I know for me this past year I have never worked this hard. And just a year of working 12 hour shifts. I need more time off than I get. I have a great girlfriend who renews me with energy, but sometimes that isn't enough."

"I don't know if it is a holiday, but then I don't know. I have never had one. Me and Xandria never had a honeymoon. This is the farthest I have ever traveled from home. I love it up here. But that's it. I didn't go anywhere else. What you see here is what my life has been like for my entire adult life. I never went to college. I didn't go to Mars. I have only ever gone to work and had more kids. You have gotten all that. You have left the galaxy and gone places many people still haven't gone to. You are friends with extraterrestrials. I tell you this, the alien population isn't that big up here. I don't know if I have lived or I'm in some kind of purgatory."

Skyler finished his beer. "Paul, you have done things I could never do and you manage your time so well. Maybe one of the reasons I don't want to get married or have a family is because I have no idea how I would take care of another human being. I can't even take care of myself. We both chose different paths. And I'm sorry if I get to have all the fun. I should have been Logan's father and you could have been free to walk away."

Paul raised an eyebrow at Skyler. "Skyler, my life has nothing to do with Logan. You know I wouldn't."

"I guess you are right," Skyler said. "I just always wish I had the resources to do what you did. You were ready to be a father and take on this life. I'm still not, even if I try to pretend I am."

"Skyler, if you had gotten Xandria pregnant, I would have still been her life, because you were going to the Space Academy and nothing was stopping you. I would have been the one raising him. Nothing would have changed. I probably would have knocked her up in the next year or so after. The past isn't the issue. What the issue is, I don't know what else there is to life. We have kept an open marriage and have a few people who come over from time to time. But I feel so outdated living here. I want to go out and know what I am missing. It isn't something that can be found here. Maybe it is, but I don't know what is outside my fishbowl."

Skyler gave Paul a hug. "You need a vacation. Everything you are describing is the definition of a vacation. I will help you book a trip and you can go for a short period of time and then come back to your regular life. You need to rest and see that there is more to life than what can be found here. I'll help you. this is what I am here for."

Paul kissed Skyler. "Thank you, buddy. That means a lot to me."

Skyler looked at his watch. "Do you want to go back to sleep, or is it too close to your shift?"

Paul looked at his watch and groaned. "I guess I'm staying up. Not worth me sleeping now. I will get the kids' lunches ready."

"Do you want any help?" Skyler asked, standing up.

"No, you go back to bed and rest. Thanks a lot buddy, you are a good friend."

"You helped me out a lot too."

Chapter 41

"Why do all these locations have to be off planet? Isn't there some place on Earth that would be just as interesting?" Xandria asked.

"Hey, it doesn't matter where you go. We can look on Earth," Skyler said, flipping through the site.

"Xandria, I want to leave the planet," Paul added. "I'm not sure how many of these we will have in our lives. So, one thing I want to do in my life is leave the planet. It doesn't have to be far. It could be the moon."

"I'm not sure. I like being grounded. It bugs me, the idea of space travel," she said.

"You don't have to travel together. I mean we could try and get you two different vacations. If you would prefer that," Skyler suggested.

The two of them stared at each other. Paul then added, "there will be a holiday no matter what, but I think where and who's going will have to be decided later. That is going to take some time."

Skyler nodded his head. "I get it. That doesn't bother me, name whatever one you want when ready and I pay for it. It is my gift to you."

"You're paying? Skyler, are you sure about that?" Xandria asked.

Skyler nodded his head. "Yes, I am. I have the money and it is my job to help you out. We are a team."

Xandria got up and shook her head. "This is too much for me right now. I have to think about things."

Paul was going to get up and say something, and Skyler placed his hand on his shoulder. "Paul, give her time. She needs to think. First holidays are hard. The first time I left Earth I was freaking out. I totally understand."

"Yeah, I hope you are right."

Skyler gave Paul a kiss. "Everything will be all right." Paul began to kiss Skyler passionately. Then Skyler's communicator started to vibrate. The ID flashed Cane's name. "One moment, I got to take this call in the basement if that's okay. It's work."

"Go ahead, take all the time you need."

Skyler made his way down to the basement and set up his tablet for the call. "Hey Cane, what's up?"

"Skyler, I need to know if you will be around tomorrow."

Skyler nodded. "Yeah, why tomorrow?"

"Tomorrow is the meeting and I need you to be around for afterwards to know about everything that happened in the meeting."

Skyler nodded. "Yeah, I can be around for the day, no problem."

"Good, how are you enjoying your holidays?"

Skyler smiled. "They have been good. It is really nice up here."

"I'm glad. Michael has been really good to work with."

"Is there anything I will need for tomorrow?" Skyler asked.

"No, just yourself, anything else I will have emailed and sent to you," Cane said.

"Okay cool, thanks for the call."

"No problem, see you tomorrow, Skyler."

Skyler ended the call. While he was down there and had some privacy he decided to call Zarina, but she did not answer so he left her a message. He then had an idea to call his uncle. Justin answered the phone. "Hey Skyler, how are you doing? Enjoying your trip?"

Skyler smiled. "Yeah, it is going great."

"How are Logan and the other two doing?" he asked.

"You know about the other kids? They are fine. Uncle, how close have you been to Paul and Xandria?"

Justin hesitated for a moment. "I kept an eye on them. You were very close to them and they could use the support from time to time. I haven't given them money in years but Xandria sends me photos of the kids and a general message every so often."

Skyler let out a sigh. *Really, they kept in touch with my uncle but didn't contact me. Why?* "I had no idea. Either way, everyone is doing great. I was really calling because I may need your help."

"Go on, you know I will do anything for you." Justin said.

"Paul wants to travel. Xandria is a little nervous about it. But I'm trying to help them get a vacation deal or a place to go. They never had a honeymoon and I think since Scott has been born they have been in kind of a rut."

"I can help with that. If they want to go to England, they can stay at your aunt's place. Anywhere else I can cover the cost. Same with you. If you want to do that, you can ask me." Justin paused. "Speaking of expensive things, for the Officers' Ball, will you be needing a suit?"

Skyler scratched his head. "Why would I need a suit? I have my dress uniform to wear."

Justin laughed. "You won't want to wear that the entire weekend. Sometimes that will be needed but you should have a suit. I'll send you info on how to do a digital measuring and then if you can find out what kind of dress Zarina will be wearing so I have the tailor match her."

Skyler laughed nervously. "Uncle, you know how I hate suits, do I really have to?"

Justin laughed. "Yes, you do. It is a handy thing to have. There will be many times in your life you will need one. Your dress uniform won't always be the one outfit."

Skyler groaned. "Fine, I will find out what I need. Anything else?"

"Skyler, you were the one who called me," Justin laughed. "I know formal wear isn't your thing. But you will thank me for it one day. I will let you go though. I'm sure you want to get back to having fun."

Skyler brushed his hair back. "Ya, thanks for everything, Uncle. I will be in touch."

The call ended; Skyler sent a message to Zarina asking about the dress before he went back upstairs. He looked around and he didn't see or hear anyone. "Hello?" Skyler called out.

"I'm in the kitchen, Skyler," Xandria called out.

Skyler went over and saw Xandria drinking a can of beer Skyler had brought while sitting alone at the table. "Where are Paul and the kids?"

"He took them for a walk. I told him I needed time to think," she said, sipping her beer.

"Think about what? Is everything okay?" Skyler said, grabbing another beer from the fridge before sitting down.

"About traveling." She let out a long sigh. "I don't know if I can do it."

"What do you mean? I can cover it and you have a babysitter. What is the issue?"

She groaned, running her hand through her hair. "I'm afraid of space travel. Terrified. I have never done it. Traveling from here to Rochester is the farthest I have ever traveled, and I have only done that three times in my life. I have no idea what the rest of the world is like. I have never had a need or a desire to travel. I know you can find me a location that is full of things and activities I would be interested in, but I can't see myself leaving the area."

Skyler took a sip of his beer and listened. "Does Paul know? Is there a problem with him traveling on his own? I can't always get holidays but I could try and vacation with him if you want."

Xandria stared at Skyler. "Paul doesn't know. But he can't travel alone because my fear goes deeper than me. It goes to him too. The same things I'm worried about traveling myself are the same things I'm worried about with him and you. Skyler, I'm sorry I have been distant these past few years. I love you, but I did not want you to call me up and tell me about all your space adventures. It would have freaked me out. I don't know how to tell Paul, or deal with it."

Skyler moved his seat over and put his arm around Xandria. "I'm sorry, I didn't know." In that moment he realized why Xandria had been writing to his uncle all these years and not him. It was her way of keeping contact with Skyler, but not through him. "How far are you willing to travel? Paul wants to go somewhere. Maybe you should start your trips off small. You could go on a trip to Toronto or

New York, those are both near where you have been. My uncle is okay with you using his place in England if you want to go farther. They have things for people who are afraid of space travel. And maybe you just don't want to because you never have. I don't think it is fair to Paul, but if nothing is going to work then we have to find a solution for Paul."

She sighed. "Maybe you're right, it bothers me so much that I am denying Paul from traveling. I have no idea how to think about others. Dammit, me and Paul work so well because he just does everything I say. I am so happy both of you put up with me."

Skyler laughed. "Paul stays with you because he loves you. Not because you're bossy. I mean that might be what attracted me to you in the first place, but you and Paul have something strong and genuine. No one is making you travel, you just have to decide on how this is going to work."

She took a deep breath. "How long does it take to get to the moon from here?"

Skyler pulled out his tablet and looked it up. "About three hours, give or take how long it takes you to get to a transport station. Why do you ask?"

"Because the moon is close enough that I hear there are lots of shuttles to it. So, if I freak out we can catch the next one, but it would be the least amount of time in space."

"This is progress. Is it the travel or the actual going? Because they can give you something to knock you out." Skyler suggested.

"That would freak me out a bit more, not knowing how I got somewhere. I am going to listen to you and try this. I want to try and do this for Paul. I probably will enjoy it."

He patted her on the back. "You will enjoy it. I have no doubt. We will work on things. you don't have to travel today but someday."

She gave Skyler a kiss. "Thanks for being there."

Chapter 42

Skyler was all set up in the basement waiting for Cane's call. Had a notepad to write down anything he thought of while he talked to Cane. He also had the call on record. Everything was set up and ready to go. Skyler checked the time Cane was running late and he hoped that everything was going all right. Just as he was about to send a message to Cane and find out, he got the call. Cane and Michael looked tired on the call, while Skyler was happy to see them. "Hey guys, what is up?"

Cane and Michael shared a look. "The Squallites and the Cassiopeians really do hate you now," Michael said.

Skyler raised an eyebrow. "Because of the Worm Orb?"

Michael nodded. "Oh yeah, you came up a bit."

Cane interjected. "To be fair, Earth is not mad at you, and you are still protected. Nothing has changed, but when the Cass started talking to the Squallites, they brought it up to ask the status of it and, well..."

Michael sighed. "There is a bigger story behind that orb. I do not know the language well enough to get the whole thing, but I believe they did it on purpose. My Ancient Squall is decent, but this was a different dialect. What we do know is that it appears that this mess looks like Earth's fault. I know that the gift has been handed to the Squallites for giving safe passage and Earth said no. We are looking into the records to see if we can figure these things out, but the Cass blame Earth for something. We are not sure how much of it we caused."

Skyler nodded his head. "Okay, good to know, but does this mean I'm banned from the Cass planet too?"

Cane shook his head. "No. It is not part of Federation space, so you would need a special visa to get in. You're not banned, but it is highly recommended by everyone you never go there. Me and your father never even went there."

"Okay, I understand, off limits," Skyler acknowledged.

"We got good news, though," Michael spoke up.

"Oh yeah? What is that?" Skyler perked up.

"We have a ceasefire on the road to peace. It is official now that Earth is going to be returning all the bodies of the Cassiopeians to their homeworld for a proper burial at the cost of the Earth Government," Cane said.

"The king approved the spending of that?" Skyler asked.

"We had a feeling a few months ago this would be the case, and numbers have been run and it will probably be cheaper than having a full-on war with them. The Squallites will help the returning of the bodies, but mainly they will be keeping an eye on things." Cane answered.

"So, we don't have peace yet. They will not declare peace until every part of the deal has been upheld." Michael said.

Skyler made two fists and cheered. "All right, so we have a ceasefire, this is great. What is the next step?"

"We can celebrate tonight, but there is lots of work to do." Cane said. "When your holidays are over and the Officers' Ball is done, we will have to start checking on the ships and the work the people have been doing to return the bodies. There are others involved, but since the Forces is responsible for all of the Earth's ships and transports it will be our job to oversee how many ships we can spare and how many pilots we have. Lots of paperwork, but also a lot of field work."

Skyler rolled his head back. "Yeah! more paperwork."

"It never ends," Cane said.

Chapter 43

Morning of the end of the week came. Skyler was getting used to waking up with baby Scott crying and the kids getting ready for school. For some reason this didn't bother him as much as he thought it would. He was about to join everyone for breakfast when he got a call. It was Zarina. He laid in bed and answered the call.

"Hey Zarina, how have you been doing? Have you been getting my messages?" Skyler asked. He had the video part of the phone on, but not the holo part so he could still see Zarina.

"I have been busy. This trip was not a vacation. But the good news is I had a great roommate," she spoke.

Skyler raised an eyebrow. "Really, who are they?"

She moved the phone camera over to reveal a familiar amphibious alien and Skyler recognized him. "Oh hey, I know that guy! He is the one me and Cane recruited at the beginning of the year on the planet Skwoampan."

Zarina was surprised. "Oh really?" She waved to him.

Groakie came over. "Hello,"' he said into the phone.

"Hey, how are you enjoying the academy?" Skyler asked.

"Yes, space and life outside are very fascinating to me. I am really enjoying it. Is Zarina your partner? I'm still not sure on how Earth relationships work."

Skyler laughed and held up his hand. "No, she is a girlfriend but we are not committed. There are many relationship styles, and I'm not an expert, so you're free to do whatever you want with her consent. I'm not committed to anyone. How are you adjusting?"

"I see, well, thank you for informing me." He paused. "I am adjusting well. Life is strange here but I enjoy it."

"I'm glad to—"

Zarina cut him off. "Skyler, I'm sorry, but we got to get going. It was nice talking to you but class is going to start soon and we have got to get going."

Skyler nodded. "Understood, take care!"

Their phone call ended. Skyler got up out of the bed and got dressed and headed out to have breakfast with the rest of the family.

Skyler left the bedroom and went out across the small hallway to the kitchen. The kids were sitting down to eat and Paul and Xandria were finishing up setting the table. "Hey Skyler, you are just in time. Take a seat." Paul said. Skyler took a seat next to logan. Logan stared up at Skyler with his big bright blue eyes. He just stared at him. Skyler turned his focus on Logan. "Is there something I can help you with?"

Logan just blinked his eyes. "Are you really my uncle?"

Skyler was taken aback and thought of the question for a moment. "Well, of course I am. You dad isn't my brother but he is like a brother to me. We are very close. I was there for you when you were born and the entire time your mother was pregnant."

"Were you there when I was born?" Bobby asked.

Skyler shook his head. "No, sorry, I was in space at the time. But I heard about your birth."

The two boys looked at each other. "Do you like action figures?"

Skyler wasn't sure much about these toys, but they were what he bought the kids when he asked Paul what he wanted. He figured he had enough knowledge to respond. "Why yes I do."

The two boys high-fived and smiled. "Yeah, okay you're cool." Logan said.

"Okay now kids, settle down." Xandria placed some of the bowls of food on the table and sat down. "Kids, we have some big news for you."

Skyler frowned as he watched Paul take a seat next to Xandria. "What's going on?"

Xandria held Paul's hand. "After our conversation, Skyler I talked to Paul and we have decided to go on a family trip to the moon in the summer."

Skyler's jaw dropped. "Really? But what about your thing, can you do it?"

"Paul looked into it and there are classes I can take. But I am more than certain that I can do this," Xandria said.

The kids were super excited. "The moon, really! That's awesome!" Logan said.

"There is an amusement park on the moon called Astroland and it seems like a great first trip to take the family." Paul added.

Skyler smiled. "I am super happy for you guys, this sounds amazing. My offer to help still stands."

"I know." Paul began to eat his food.

"Are you going to be coming with us uncle, Skyler?" Logan asked.

Skyler shook his head and finished his bite of food. "No, it will just be you guys. I will be going on a different space adventure."

Logan was sad. "Aw darn. What space adventure are you going on? Is it cool?"

Skyler wasn't sure at the moment where he would be in the summer, but he knew he was Cane's apprentice until September. "It will be cool. Flying around in a spaceship and seeing the stars. It will be just as cool as you going to the moon."

"Cool," Logan said.

Chapter 44

Skyler's holidays and trip were over and he was back in his room relaxing on the bed. His suitcase was on the floor and he was feeling a bit jetlagged. He kicked off his boots and began to drift off to sleep. His door opened and Zarina came rushing into the room and gave him a giant hug.

He jerked awake. "Zarina, what are you doing here?" He brushed his hair back. "I mean, don't you have class?"

Zarina showed him her watch. "It's 7 p.m., and the classes are done, cutie. You must have slept longer than you thought."

Confused, Skyler double checked the clock, "Huh, I guess I did, I thought I only closed my eyes for a second." Skyler smiled and gave Zarina a kiss. "I don't have to work until the morning. Is there something you would like to do to welcome me back?"

She kissed him. "I would love to, but..." She pointed towards the door. "You do have to work. Michael is waiting to see you and you do have work tonight."

Skyler lifted his head and saw Michael and waved, "This is so not fair. All I ever do anymore is work."

Zarina kissed him as he stood up. "Well, when you get back from your meeting, then you can try on your suit. It arrived while you were gone."

Skyler groaned as he got out of bed. "Ugh, I guess my vacation is over." He put on his boots and went up to Michael. "So, we are having this meeting with Cane."

"Actually," Michael said, "I was hoping that we could have the meeting here. Cane is not needed, but Zarina would have to leave."

Skyler looked over his shoulder at Zarina. She was sitting on the bed—with her eyes wide and pointing to herself. "You want me to leave?"

Michael nodded, "Yes, only for the meeting. You may return after. Is this going to be an issue, do you not have your own room?"

Zarina got off the bed and walked over towards the boys. "I technically have a room. I haven't been there in a while. I guess I could see how my roommate is doing. Do you know how long the meeting will be?"

"It will be as long as it needs to be," Michael answered.

Zarina rolled her eyes and kissed Skyler on the lips. "Call me when it is done, okay sweetie?"

Skyler waved. "Will do."

When Zarina was gone, Michael stepped further into the room and sat down at the kitchen table. He placed his tablet down and typed in a few things. "So, remember the meeting we had on Squall?"

Skyler walked over to the mini fridge and grabbed a beer. "Ya, I remember it was only a week ago, and I was briefed on it after. Why do we need to go over it now?" He stuck his head into the fridge more. "Zarina has some fruit juice in here. Do you want that or just water?"

Michael leaned over in Skyler's direction. "You have a kettle. If you would not mind, I would like a glass of orange tea."

Skyler spun around looking for the kettle, "Huh? I guess I do have one, didn't know that." He opened the cupboards, "I don't have any tea bags but I can offer you a cup of hot water?"

Michael reached into his own pocket and pulled out a tea bag. "I came prepared, so put the kettle on and I will do the rest."

Once the kettle was filled and on, Skyler came over with his beer and casually sat next to Michael. "Okay, so what is the big news?"

"We have worked out a deal with the Cass and it is going to take a lot of work. Cane wanted me to go over with you on what side you want to be on with this."

Skyler raised an eyebrow, "What deal, and what do you mean 'side'? I'm on the side of peace."

Michael typed a few things into his tablet and showed Skyler while he got up and made his tea.

"They are moving bodies? They are going to dig up the ones from the past and more of them. I thought we knew this?" Skyler scanned through the brief.

"Yes, but Cane is overseeing the part of the organizing of the transport of the ships. But you want to be a captain, and there is a need for leaders who will be making sure their crews are following protocol and treating the bodies with the respect they need." Michael took a sip of his tea. "Or you could work hands-on with Cane, filling the demands of the ships and crews that are needed to haul all this cargo."

Skyler rubbed his head. "Ugh. Both sound like a pain. I thought I was just Cane's apprentice?"

"You are, but that is for the next few months, not years, and this is going to take two to three years to complete with proper management. That's why you have the choice to go higher and continue with Cane later." Michael explained.

"What job are you taking in all of this?"

"I don't have a placement yet. Right now, I am doing diplomatic stuff. But it would be nice to get a job assisting in making sure the bodies are transported with respect."

Skyler thought about it for a few minutes, thinking to himself. *If I get a captaining job, it is what I want, but I know nothing about Cass traditions. What if I screw up? But I could work on filling spots and jobs. More office work, but hmm...* "I think the administration one would be better. We have Cass captains that would probably be better qualified. Also, I might be able to get you and Kax better jobs."

Michael nodded. "That is good thinking. Smart, really."

Skyler shrugged, "Hey I'm going to be captain one day, but I got to do it right. Because what if I don't get hired again? Also, I feel these jobs are just temporary."

"That is true." Michael sipped his tea, "So how was your trip?"

Skyler smiled. "Great trip. I hadn't seen Paul and Xandria in years, it was so fun to just hang out."

"I'm glad that you had fun. I have no friends from my school days. I was always teased and picked on for being different. There weren't many Squallite kids but when I got older, they got taller and even they thought I was weird for being short." Michael finished his tea.

"Really, not even a girlfriend? Someone had to have been your friend?" Skyler pondered.

Michael shook his head. "Nope. There were a few people who were friendly for a couple of years, but no long-term friends. And when it comes to relationships, hanging out with you was the first time I was exposed to any of the dating scene. It never came up even if someone was interested. I just kept to myself in school. I wanted to be homeschooled, but my Dad thought it was best for me to get the interactions." He got up and put the kettle on again.

Skyler knew that another cup of tea meant Michael would be staying longer. The meeting was done and Zarina was waiting for him, but he could tell Michael had missed him and wanted to have a night to spend with a friend. "So, Michael, if we are done with this meeting, want to hang out and watch a movie or play a game or something?"

"What about Zarina?" Michael asked, putting in another tea bag.

Skyler shrugged. "She has gone two weeks without seeing me, she can go another day, and like you said, she has her own room. It's been so long since we have just hung out as buds."

Michael smiled. "Yeah, a movie sounds nice."

Chapter 45

Skyler entered Cane's office. Cane looked up from his desk. "Oh, good Skyler, you're here right on time."

Skyler smiled. "Well, I was well rested."

"Good to hear, did you have time to talk to Michael last night?"

"I did, and I want to do the administration part of the job with you," Skyler answered.

Cane raised an eyebrow, "Wouldn't you prefer a captain job, though?"

Skyler sat down in his chair, "I would, but I feel it would be temporary, and I do not feel I would be the right person for the job."

"That may be true. But I thought it would be best to give you first pick of the jobs." Cane said. "You are making a very responsible choice."

"That might be so, but I also want to make sure Kax and Michael get the jobs they want," Skyler pointed out.

Cane laughed. "It's really nice when I hear you thinking about your friends first. I was already thinking of assigning Kax as one of the pilots; we promised her a transfer. Michael will be a little harder to place because he is still needed in the diplomatic stuff and I cannot assign him to a ship and then call him for a meeting. But we will figure something out."

Skyler smiled. "This sounds great. So where are we on the roster today?"

Cane pulled up his calendar. "So right now we have some old paperwork to finish filling then we have a meeting at eleven with the other admirals talking about the new assignments. Then we have a small break for lunch before we have another meeting with the local politicians to make sure they are on the level. That meeting I can't see us talking much, it's mostly just us being there. If all goes well, we can be done on time tonight so you can get your suit looked at because we are leaving this weekend for that."

Skyler let out a sigh. "All right, full day. Let's get started."

Zarina opened Skyler's door in the morning, to only find Michael resting on the couch. She went over to Michael and loudly said, "So your meeting went all night?"

Michael opened his eyes. "Most of the night, yes. And what time is it?"

"It's almost noon. I was expecting Skyler to call me. Where is he now?" Zarina demanded.

Michael got up. "Dang it, my shift starts at one I got to get ready." Michael got up off the couch and put on his cadet jacket.

Zarina just stood there staring at Michael.

Michael grabbed his belt. "What, did I do something wrong?"

"I missed Skyler and I wanted to see him!" She pouted.

Michael rolled his eyes. "So, you get him all the time. You practically live with him. I do not. Sorry I took away some of your private Skyler time but you two are going to spend the week together soon." He pointed to the suit.

Zarina sighed, "I guess you are right. Skyler is just in such high demand nowadays that it is hard to get time with him."

Michael nodded, washing out his tea cup from last night. "Skyler and I have lived together on and off for the past four years. This is the first time we have not, and it feels a bit weird not seeing him around. He used to drive me nuts, but I have just gotten used to him."

"I'm sorry for overreacting, I guess I just was a bit jealous." She went over and gave Michael a hug.

Michael tensed up from the hug. "Please do not touch me. I am not used to that."

Zarina let go. "Oh, I'm sorry…"

Michael waved his hand. "Do not worry, I am just not used to it but I appreciate it. Also, I feel like in time Skyler will make time to see all of his friends."

Chapter 46

Skyler was off work and heading to go see Zarina with his suit to get that taken care of. As he was walking down the hall, he saw Kax leaving the hangar alone. He waved to her and went over to see her. "Hey Kax, nice to see you. How are you doing?"

Kax rubbed her forehead. "How do you think? I cannot wait for this job placement to be over, and I never see Rex or your mother again."

Skyler laughed, "Hey, how do you think I feel, I wish I never had to see my mother again."

She smiled. "Oh Skyler, I'm so sorry."

"Which way are you heading? I got to go pick up my suit and I shouldn't be late." Skyler said.

"I will walk your way; Rex is getting off soon and I don't want to see him outside of work. He keeps talking about the engagement and I'm avoiding plans." Kax started following Skyler.

"So, you and Rex are a done deal now?"

Kax nodded, "Yeah, I didn't want to admit it for a bit, but no way I'm going farther with that man. Are you and Zarina still a thing?"

Skyler nodded, "Yup, I think we have a good thing going."

"She seems nice, out of your girlfriends I think she is a good fit."

Skyler grinned and stopped. He snapped his fingers. "Oh, before I forget, I got good news for you!"

Kax gave Skyler her full attention. "Really, what kind of good news?"

"We struck a deal to end the war. I don't know how public the info is yet. But Earth will be transporting all the bodies of the dead Cass on Earth to their home planet. It will take about two to three years to get these bodies moved, they are predicting." Skyler grinned, proud of himself. "I have been given the job for assigning crews to transport the bodies. We are going to need more than we have to get this done ASAP—"

"Get on with it, this sounds exciting," Kax blurted out.

Skyler chuckled. "Okay, okay let me finish. I will be one of the people in charge of assigning the new crews. And the first thing I asked Cane about was transferring you, and he said yes."

Her face was bright, covered in a big smile. "Really, that would be amazing! Thank you so much!" She jumped up and gave Skyler a big hug.

He hugged her back, "Shh, don't go bragging. I don't want people thinking I can do this for everyone. But I knew you had requested a transfer and this just felt like the right one."

She calmed down. "I would have been happy with anything, but this is just great. Do you know a time frame when this will happen?"

They were almost at Skyler's room, "Just had a meeting about it today, and I think the assignments will be happening in the next month but the job will not start till about the end of the semester. We are trying to rush this as soon as we can because it is expensive but important for peace."

"Thank you, Skyler, this means a lot to me." She leaned in to give him a kiss when Skyler put his hand up to stop her.

"We are at my room. I got to go in." Skyler placed his hand on her shoulder, "Kax, I really like you but I did this because it was in my power to help you, not because I'm interested in you. I want you to live a long, happy and fulfilling life."

Startled by Skyler's words, she nodded. "Thanks again, Skyler. I will let you continue on with your day." She waved to him as she left.

When she was gone Skyler turned around and opened the door. Inside his room, Zarina was standing there, his suit was laid out on the bed, and the tailor was sitting at the kitchen table.   "Good, you are here, let's get started." Zarina took her dress bag off the bed and went over to the bathroom to get changed.

Skyler stood there dumbstruck. "I knew this was happening right after work. I didn't think it would be right now."

The tailor smiled. "I'm sorry, I was just told to be here I didn't know I would be rushing you."

Skyler shook his head. "No problem, I am used to a busy schedule." He made his way over to the bed. "Um, Zarina is in the bathroom. Would you mind turning around so I could get changed?"

"No problem." The tailor turned round.

Skyler got dressed and by the time he was finished putting on his suit, Zarina walked out of the bathroom fully dressed. For the first time Skyler saw her dress and it was an emerald green mermaid cut, with a sweetheart bust made from a silk crepe fabric, with bead embroidery on one breast going down with the flow of the wrapped fabric around the curves of the body. Skyler stood there in amazement looking at her. "Wow, you look amazing!"

She did a hair toss and smiled. "It will look better when my hair, nails and jewelry are put all together but thank you. You look great in your suit."

Skyler walked over to the mirror and examined himself. His suit was an emerald green that matched Zarina's dress. There was a hint of another color thread woven into the fabric that had a brighter green glow to it, but only flickered in the light. No lapels, just a zipper but it had the mandarin collar like his uniform. The trim was color-shifting purple and blue. The epaulets had shooting star designs on them, in the color sifting design that matched the design on the cuffs of the sleeves. The whole thing fit like a glove. The pants were the same fabric, only embellishments were stripes of the same color shift down the leg. The lining of the jacket was made of a fabric that could only be described as a cosmic holographic swirl design. Skyler stood there, awestruck on the lovely craftsmanship of the suit.

"What do you think?" the tailor asked.

"It is the loveliest piece of clothing I have ever owned. But it wasn't the type of suit I was thinking of." Skyler commented.

"Well, I was informed you were not a fan of ties and vests, so I was looking for suits that looked more like your uniform. Giving it a modern feel but a traditional military look. Since you have a legacy in an ancient Earth and now space tradition."

Skyler was more amazed by the design. "I love it, thank you so much." A feeling of pride came over him wearing it. "Whatever was paid for this suit, it wasn't enough."

"I assure you, it was enough." The tailor stood up and went over to Skyler and pinched a few parts of the suit. "Making sure the adjustments are correct."

"I think it is fine the way it is," Skyler said.

"There is always room for improvement," the tailor said.

The tailor examined the two of their outfits and jotted down a few notes. "Okay, I think you two can take them off. I will do the adjustments and they will see you when you get to the Kremlin."

Skyler smiled, unzipping the jacket. "I'm really impressed with the work, thank you. It's a suit I actually like."

"Thank you for the compliments."

After the tailor left Zarina went over to Skyler and kissed him. "You looked so handsome in that suit I cannot wait to take it off you this weekend."

Skyler leaned in and kissed Zarina, "I missed you so much."

She kissed him back. "I have been wanting some alone time with you, you know that, right?"

"Oh, I know, I have been wanting some time with you too."

"Well then, I think I know what we need to do."

Skyler put his hand up. "I would, but I have just changed my clothes three times and I'm tired from work. Can I have a nap first? And in my clothes, I don't feel like getting changed again."

She pouted. "This is completely unfair, but fine. Nap first, but you owe me."

He held her close and gave her a big kiss. "I plan to make it up to you, and so much more. This weekend."

She gave him a hug before they both went off to bed.

Chapter 47

It was the day before the trip and Skyler was excited and anxious. He had never traveled so much in his life; it was still new to him. He had also never traveled around the planet. The farthest he had ever traveled outside of the mega city was to England with his uncle. Russia was a totally different story. He got to Cane's office and there was a suitcase in the office. "What's with the suitcase?"

"After work tonight we are heading to the Kremlin. They are six hours ahead," Cane said.

"Wait, so we got to be there for the morning, not leave in the morning. I was going to have drinks with Michael and Kax tonight," Skyler whined.

"Sorry, you will have to cancel. I can give you lunch off for one hour since this seems to be unexpected," Cane said.

Skyler slumped in his chair. "Why do we have to go so early when the ball isn't until the night?"

"The ball is three nights and we have meetings to go to. The ball is the party after the work," Cane said.

Skyler sighed. "Okay, I guess, if I must. Ugh, this is sounding like a glorified business trip."

"It is," Cane said. "Now let's get to work."

Chapter 48

Skyler slept most of the trip to the Kremlin. He was looking forward to the party but not the business part. He knew he was making the right choice but he didn't like the endless hours of paperwork.

Cane woke him up when he arrived. "We're at Vnukovo. Grab your stuff, we have a meeting soon."

Skyler brushed his hair back after waking up. He grabbed his bag and headed out. As they walked to the car Skyler questioned, "Why are we so far from the Kremlin? Why isn't there a direct way to fly right there?"

They got into the car. "Our base is modern and transportation is built inside. But Moscow is a very old city that was already long established before the United Galactic Forces. There are ways to fly in but it would be easier to go by car. Besides, you have never been here enjoying the view."

Skyler stared out the window of the car on the way there. Most of the drive from Vnukovo to the Kremlin was flat and full of trees—not a rest stop for miles. The landscape was almost uniform. Skyler was amazed that every time he left the mega city the world was full of trees. The landscape of the world was impressing him, leaving him with a sense of awe. It was completely different from the world of neon and chrome he was used to. The closer they got to the Kremlin, Skyler began to see the city—it was also very clean and uniform. While the architecture was uniform and clean and so old compared to what he was used to, they were still the same historical buildings. As they approached and entered the Red Square the massive red brick wall was more than Skyler could have ever imagined. They pulled up to a building, the clean white and gold uniform archways glowing in the sunlight. The building looked like it went on forever, and the arches made it look longer than it was.

Skyler and Cane stepped out of the car. Skyler stared up at the architecture and the scenery around him. Cane elbowed Skyler to pay attention as they were greeted at the steps by the current leader of Russia, Nikolai Petrovich Myshkin. He greeted them with a serious smile, holding out his hand to Cane and Skyler.

"Leon, it is nice to see you again. Who is this young man with you? I have never met him before." He examined Skyler with his eyes.

Cane kept a very serious tone with him. "It's good to see you again too, Myshkin."

Skyler came back to reality and answered, "I'm Skyler Therris, Cane's apprentice. It's nice to meet you. This place you have here is really cool."

Myshkin appeared humoured by Skyler, "Yes, it is very nice. Come with me. Ivan will assist you with your needs." He turned around and followed him into the building.

"Wow," was all Skyler could say when they entered the halls of white and gold. "This place is amazing."

Cane elbowed Skyler again. "Yes, it is, but please stay serious, we are here on business."

The glistening sparkle of clean antique walls were full of intricate detail and design from a far past. Skyler tried to stay focused but this place was more lovely than any that he had ever seen before in his life. Giant chandeliers lit the entire building. Ivan tapped Skyler on the shoulder, "If you think the walls and ceiling are nice you should look at the floor."

Skyler, out of his daze, looked down at the floor to see a perfectly polished carved stone floor that felt like it was never the same twice. The whole experience was ethereal for Skyler. They soon reached the room where their meeting was. The room was painted red and with some pillars of white and a large rectangular perfectly polished boardroom table in the middle. Myshkin sat at the head of the long table. Next to him was Ivan, behind him two security guards. Cane and Skyler took their chairs close to him and soon other high officials from around the world appeared at this meeting.

From the briefing that Skyler had gotten from Cane, this meeting was just about Russia's continuing contributions to the United Galactic Forces. The meeting was pretty much routine and done every year, followed by the Officers' Ball. Skyler was more interested in the beauty of the room than what the people were actually saying. He did manage to pick up bits and pieces about what they were talking about. Things like where the ball should be held next year, how many ships would each country contribute to the war, how many officers would be traded with each base. Nothing was really changed to the system that they already had. This was a meeting where Skyler was glad there was something lovely to look at because it was not a meeting where he could contribute anything, it was mainly about him observing and seeing firsthand the system he could look up and read in a book. Thankfully the meeting wasn't long, mostly formal and so Skyler was able to go quickly. Cane and Skyler were escorted to their rooms. They had two different rooms right next to each other. Once they were settled into the rooms, Skyler lay on his bed and couldn't stop staring at the—

There was a knock at the door. Cane entered. "Hey Cane, isn't this place amazing? Every inch. I didn't realize a place could exist like this on Earth."

Cane let out a sigh, "Skyler, I know this place is lovely and new for you, but could you try to pay attention just a little bit more?"

Skyler put his head down, "I'm sorry, Cane, it is just so hard to. I have been to palaces before, and nothing compares to this place."

"I know, Skyler, but that is how they get you. This place is as lovely as it is deadly. Watch your step. You have been so distracted. Can you tell me who besides me and Myshkin was at the meeting?"

Skyler paused to think about it for a moment. In his memories he knew there were other people, but he couldn't name a face. He shook his head. "No sir."

"This is how badly you were distracted, you sat next to Fleet Admiral Davis the entire meeting." Cane snapped.

Skyler's eyes widened. "I didn't realize. I'm so sorry."

Cane sat in one of the chairs in the sitting area of the room. "Skyler, I care about you, but you have got to stop being so easily distracted." Cane looked at his watch. "Look, there is time for a short rest before the ball. I suggest you take this time to enjoy everything and watch your step. Also, did you eat at the meeting? There was food."

Skyler's tummy grumbled. "There was food. Damn, I missed it."

Cane stood up and showed Skyler an intercom on his wall. "If there is anything that you need, any hour of the night, press this button and request it. Also, when it comes to food, ask for anything. The chefs will have it prepared."

"Okay, now this is the coolest feature in the building." Skyler and Cane both shared a laugh.

Chapter 49

A knock at the door woke Skyler from his nap. He got up out of the bed and opened the door—Zarina was standing there with her bags. "Zarina, you're here!"

"Yup, and I made arrangements and we are sharing a room," She said, moving in.

Skyler wrapped his arms around her, giving her a deep kiss. "I expect nothing less from you. Also, this place is so big that if we weren't staying in the same room, I don't know how we would find each other."

"You liking the place?" Zarina went over and sat down on the bed.

Skyler came over and sat next to her. "I'm loving this place. Most lovely place I have ever been."

"Well then I will have to show you my top 3 places to bang here." She placed her hand on Skyler's leg.

He raised an eyebrow. "Top three? How many times have you been here?"

"I have been here a few times but really there are only two great spots, but we got three days so maybe we will find a new favorite spot." She leaned in and kissed Skyler.

"Sounds very fun." Skyler kissed her deeply back, pushing her down onto the bed.

"Where do you think you are going?" Zarina said, sitting up in the bed with a blanket around her.

"I'm getting dressed, the party is starting soon," Skyler said, going over his suit bag.

Zarina rolled her eyes. "Suck-ups go to those parties on time. We don't have to show up on time, it will make a statement."

Skyler began putting on his suit. "Cane will notice that I am not there, and do you really want to brag to everyone we were late? Your father is at this party."

"Skyler, I have been to many of these parties. Same people. And the fact that my father is there makes me want to be there even less. Have you not been to parties like this in the past?"

Skyler took a long break to think. "I guess you have a point. I went to a few of these back in the two summers I stayed with my uncle and they do get repetitive seeing the same people. But I have never been to a party like this. This place is beautiful and I don't know the people here."

Zarina sighed and got out of bed. "Fine, we will go. I know most of them and it's the same snobs and pervs every year. But if this is what you really want to do."

Skyler went over to her side. "If you don't want to come you don't have to. But I'm here for a reason, and I'm going to do my best to enjoy it."

She got up out of the bed and went over to her dress, "No, you're right. I should get ready and join you."

Once they were finished getting dressed, Zarina showed Skyler the way to the ballroom. The lighting of the large crystal chandeliers made the room like it was made entirely out of gold. The floor was polished, giving it a mirror reflection, creating the illusion that the room appeared endless.

There was an open bar and tables of food. With Zarina on his arm, he looked around the room looking for Cane. Once spotted him, he nudged Zarina, "There is Cane, do you want to come with me or do you want to part?"

"I will come with you. If it gets boring, I will leave." She answered.

Skyler smiled and nodded to her and as they got closer to Cane Skyler noticed his uncle talking to him. He tensed up. Zarina held him tighter. They went over.

"There is a favourite nephew. I must say that is a lovely suit," Justin turned to Cane, "Angelo did a really good job with the suit."

"Thank you, Uncle," Skyler said, "Uncle, by the way, have you met my girlfriend Zarina?"

Justin held out his hand, "It is very lovely to meet you. I have heard so much about you."

Zarina took it. "it is nice to meet you too. Thank you for taking care of Skyler all these years, he talks highly of you."

"Well, someone had to." Justin replied.

Cane cut in. "Me and Justin were just discussing your progress and future career, Skyler."

Skyler grabbed a drink from a passing server, "You are? Well, I hope that means I'm doing good. I wouldn't want to disappoint."

"You are doing very well according to Cane." Justin commented. "Cane thinks you have a future in the political side of the Forces."

Skyler's eyes widened and Zarina squeezed his hand. "I have been doing that well?"

"I guess all those years of late nights and little sleep have prepared you for this." Cane joked. They all chuckled at the comment.

Nikolai came over with Ivan, laughing along with the joke. "Lovely joke, it is nice to see you again Leon. Has it really been a year?"

"It has. You've already met my new apprentice Skyler Therris." Cane pointed his hand toward Skyler.

Skyler shook Nikolai's hand again. "It's an honour, sir."

"The honour is all mine. I'm also courteous to see how your mind thinks this coming weekend. It's always good to have fresh minds on topics." Nikolai smiled, "it is rare Leon takes an apprentice, so this year is going to be a treat."

Zarina lightly nudged Skyler to indicate it was time to go, but Skyler continued to talk to the group, and before Skyler could turn his head, she was gone.

The conversation continued to a table where the Cane, Nikolai and Ivan sat down at a table where the drinks kept coming. Every so often, Skyler looked for Zarina, but not long enough to find her.

Zarina was nearby keeping an eye on Skyler. When she saw the alcohol on the table subtly change from champagne to tall glasses of vodka, she knew it was time to act. She went over to the table and slid in next to Skyler. "Skyler, we have been here for hours and I haven't had a dance."

Nikolai laughed. "It is best not keeping a lady waiting. Go have a dance and we can continue our conversation after."

Skyler got up and took Zarina's hand, "Sorry, guys, but I can't keep a lady waiting."

Zarina quickly took him away. "Skyler, how much have you had to drink?"

Skyler looked up at the ceiling trying to count, "I'm not sure, maybe six glasses of champagne. Why you asking you never minded my drinking before."

They began to dance on the floor, "You had six glasses, and now you think it is a good idea to switch to vodka? Skyler, I don't mind you drinking and I know you can hold your alcohol but please listen to me, be extra cautious when it comes to Nikolai. When he pulls out the heavy stuff, he is trying to get something from you. He is not to be trusted. Now let's dance and continue the party without him."

Skyler danced with Zarina. "How do you know so much? You realize I am working with him this weekend. It's kind of rude not to accept his drinks."

"You're not being rude, you are dancing with me and keeping your girlfriend happy. I just want you to talk to him when you are a little more sober," she said while letting him lead. "I have been to these parties most of my life. I know most of the people here. Now is there anyone else here you would like to talk to?"

Skyler looked around. "I'm not sure, who is here?"

"Well in that case, how about we go to bed and you can talk to them tomorrow? Everyone will be here again."

Right as soon as she thought that she had Skyler convinced, Nikolai danced over toward them with his wife. "I'm sorry to interrupt you two lovebirds, but there are some pressing issues I must discuss with Skyler tonight before tomorrow."

Before Zarina could cut in, Nikolai had switched dance partners and now she was dancing with Nikolai's wife. She tried to wiggle away to get to Skyler, but the woman held onto her. "He will be fine, Niko just wants to talk to him."

"What's his game? What does he want Skyler for?" She demanded.

"You seem tired, princess, you should rest. Skyler will be fine."

"I'll do what I want, when I want, thank you." She broke away. She looked around the ballroom trying to find Skyler, he was nowhere to be seen. She didn't see Cane either but she did see Justin. She rushed over to Justin. "Justin, I'm looking for Skyler. Did you see where he went?"

He shook his head, "no idea, is something wrong? You look worried."

She let out a long sigh, "Nikolai came by and wanted to talk to Skyler alone and I don't know which way they went."

"Oh, I see," Justin wrinkled his mouth. "I don't know what to say, but I would say leave them be for the night. There has to be a reason. I wouldn't worry too much, Skyler is a big boy. He knows how to handle himself."

"Yeah, I guess you are right," Zarina said before going to sit down at the nearest table.

Chapter 50

It was late into the night when Skyler returned to the room. Zarina was woken up by the sound of him stumbling. "Where have you been? what time is it?"

Skyler took off his clothes and stumbled into the bed. "Lots of things happened, lots of talking, lots of other things, it's late, let's talk in the morning."

"Do you want to mess around before bed?" Zarina asked, leaning in and kissing him.

"In the morning, I'm too tired right now. But I will make it up to—"
Skyler fell asleep.

In the morning, Skyler was awoken by the alarm. Zarina was already dressed in her day clothes. Skyler sat up and looked around the room, "What's going on? What happened?"

"You came back at like 5 a.m. drunk out of your mind and passed out." She drank her tea, and continued her breakfast.

"Are you upset with me or something?" He got up out of bed and went over to the table where there was a full breakfast laid out. "Where did this food come from?"

"The food was delivered while you were sleeping." She took a bite of her toast, "Yes, I am annoyed because you didn't listen to me. Do you remember anything that happened last night?"

Skyler shook his head while he poured himself a screwdriver. "I don't remember much, there was a bunch of talking and then things got fun—" he paused and went to take a sip from his drink.

Zarina took his drink away from him and handed him a cup of tea, "No more alcohol for you. And what do you mean fun? You said that last night, but no details."

Skyler tried to grab his drink back, "I think I might have slept with Nikolai. Is that possible? I mean he is not...right? He's married."

Zarina let out a long sigh. "Watch yourself, Skyler. I'm certain that is exactly what happened. Talk to Cane about it. I'm sure he will fill you in more. But Skyler, let's hope that is all that happened. Watch yourself here. You're nowhere near home and the rules are different. Please understand that."

Skyler sat down and grabbed a plate of waffles, dousing them in syrup, "All right, I will be more cautious tonight. Sorry I was a jerk last night."

Zarina took Skyler's hand and handed him a hangover pill, "I have been through this so many times. I love you and I want to take care of you."

Skyler took the pill and smiled back at her, "For you I will try to be more responsible."

There was a knock at the door. "Skyler, it's Cane open up, we need to get ready for our meeting."

Skyler jumped up and grabbed his pants and put them on and went to the door. "Hey Cane, I just woke up. Can I finish my breakfast before the meeting?"

Cane checked his watch. "We have a little bit of time, if you don't mind me briefing you about our meeting?"

Skyler went over and finished putting on his uniform and then went back to the table. "I don't have an issue, take a seat next to Zarina."

Cane took the seat and looked over at Zarina. "So what are your plans for the day?"

She shrugged, "Nothing planned so far, I might head to the library and check in on things or go out and see the city. You two won't be done until the ball tonight, right?"

Cane nodded, helping himself to a cup of tea. "That is right. As much as these are fancy parties, it really is more of a working retreat for us high ranks."

"Oh, don't I know it." Zarina finished off her toast. "One of the main reasons I have grown tired of these events."

Cane laughed, "Zarina, I was going to them long before you were born. If anyone should be tired of them it is me. But your point is valid. The good thing is these parties have an entertainment aspect to them."

Skyler finished off his breakfast and got his uniform on. "Okay, I'm ready for the meetings to start!"

Cane laughed as he stood up from his seat, "Don't sound that excited, it isn't that exciting."

Nikolai and Ivan were at the meeting. They sat across from Skyler and Cane at the long table. Skyler felt nervous being around Nikolai since the memories from last night were still foggy. In his mind he knew something was off, but what he thought he remembered he wasn't sure was true.

Skyler looked up at the projector to see that this meeting was about the trading of units in the Forces. Skyer leaned over and whispered to Cane, "I thought all these meetings had to do with the war?"

Cane shook his head, "In some ways yes, but no, they are a meeting of all the powers to discuss trade and international and intergalactic matters. We do this once a year to see if there is anything that needs change."

Skyler sat back looking at everyone around the table. He saw so many leaders he did not recognize and only some that he had seen on the news. Skyler was one of the youngest, if not the youngest at the table.

Nikolai was the first to speak at the meeting, "I want the number of exchange and transfer officers increased from twenty thousand to thirty thousand—"

Cane cut in, "You asked for this increase last year and it was denied, why are you asking again? What are you offering back? There is a war going on."

Nikolai shot back a glare, "I just want more officers to have the chance to learn and fight on the Russian side when it comes to the war and for training."

"When we fight this war with the Cassiopeians we fight as Earth, not nationalities," one of the other leaders commented. "Cane is right. Before the numbers of exchange, there needs to be a larger war contribution. Now is not the time to exchange units, but to increase the exchange of resources."

"Well, what if there are more officers who want the experience and to transfer?" Nikolai mentioned.

"I came prepared for this because I knew you would bring this issue up again. In the last five years we have had only fifteen thousand apply for the program; the rest of the units we sent were just to meet the minimums. We just don't have the demand. If the demand ever increases, I will let you know, but many of the transfers are staying in the Russian forces. Now if you are trying to transfer more of your forces out, then maybe some of the other leaders will want yours, but I feel there are more important issues than exchange numbers right now."

"Cane is right, we need to talk about resources, not units. We have the numbers and as many as we are going to get for a while, so let's move on with the conversation." Another leader spoke up.

"What I feel is the biggest issue this year is getting organized on returning the bodies to the Cass and getting a system set up," Skyler said.

Another leader spoke up, "We already had a meeting about that and the leaders voted on agreeing to this."

"They agreed that we as a planet would return the bodies," Skyler commented, "but haven't been able to find any stats on any other powers working on returning the bodies. The only thing I can find is that a couple of leaders have sent the bodies to the United Galactic Forces."

"You do know that the United Galactic Forces are the ones with the ships, that's why they are being sent there," another said.

"Not only the ships, the Russians and the Chinese have their ships too. And the bodies that have been sent to UGF are new ones," Skyler pointed out.

"What is your point, boy?" someone said.

"All Cass bodies have to be returned, not just the new ones. I feel that to save time and money we need all nations to be working equally. And using all our resources because the sooner we get this done, the sooner we get long-term peace and we can start moving forward faster."

"Nice statement, but not all the leaders have enough staff or the right staff for the job." Nikolai mentioned, "what do you plan to do about that? We send them to the UGF because you have all the resources and the manpower."

"The only reason UGF has more workers is because of the multiple bases but when you divide up the numbers per base, we have the same as anyone else. Now if any of the leaders require more trained people because they cannot recruit their own, I think the numbers of trade could be increased temporarily." Skyler finished his point.

The table turned their eyes toward Cane. "Do you agree with your apprentice's words, Fleet Admiral?"

Cane took a deep breath in. "I do. If we want peace then we need to work together and want peace together. The Cassiopaeans have an issue with all of humanity, not just a certain group."

"All right then," said the moderator at the head of the table. "Let's use the keypads in front of you and place your vote to see if this is something that we should be working towards."

They all placed their vote and within a couple of minutes they had the results. The moderator revealed the results for all to see: 80% of the votes were in favour of working together.

"With the majority of the votes in agreement, the motion is passed and we can move on to how we plan to work out how each one can help and begin working on arrangements."

The meeting and plans went on for hours. Skyler was happy that peace was on the way and more were working together, but it was tiring. He wanted to get out of there and get some food, but progress was coming along. Hours into it and he was starting to doze off in the meeting with just sitting there listening, because his part was over. The meeting was finally called to a close. Cane nudged Skyler when the meeting was over, "Come on, it is time to go."

Skyler stretched as he got up out of his seat and followed Cane to the boardroom. Cane checked his watch, "Well, Skyler, if you want to have a rest and food before the party, there is time."

Skyler nodded. "Leon, how do you manage to stay awake through these long meetings?"

"Practice, and a good night's sleep which I know you don't get many of," Cane pointed out.

"You did very well today in the meeting, Skyler. Me and Nikolai were quite impressed with your ideas. Have you ever considered a career in politics?" Ivan interjected.

Startled, Skyler looked at the Russian leader who was standing behind him. "Uh, I never thought of it before. I'm just Cane's apprentice for the year."

"Is that so? Well then, I cannot wait to see you at the party tonight."

"You speaking about the party last night, what happened? I'm having a hard time remembering," Skyler inquired.

Nikolai let out a deep laugh, "You drank too much and I had my men return you to your room. That is all. I'm impressed how well you can hold your liquor, you drank a lot."

Skyler was not satisfied with that answer, but was more determined to stay a little more sober tonight. "I see."

"Well, if that is all then I will see both of you tonight." Nikolai winked at Cane and Skyler before turning and running away.

When they were out of sight, Cane signaled with his hands for Skyler to follow him. Cane took Skyler down the hall heading towards Skyler's room, not talking along the way, just walking at a quicker pace.

They got back to Skyler's room where Cane quickly checked the room to see if it had been bugged again. Once he was done, he sharply turned to face Skyler and said, "what were you thinking!?"

Skyler raised his shoulders. "What did I do?"

"Skyler, I know you like to drink but you can't do that around Nikolai. Drink less, take your time." Cane said.

"But the drinks were free and they kept giving them to me." Skyler responded defensively.

Cane slapped his forehead, "That is exactly when you don't drink. When you're with friends you drink all you want, but here you are not with friends, you have got to watch yourself."

Skyler let out a long sigh. "I know I screwed up. I'm also not sure what happened last night. What can I do?"

Cane took a seat, "I have a plan."

Chapter 51

The second night of the party was here. Skyler was more prepared for Nikolai's plans then he was the night before. Zarina was on his arm while he walked into the ballroom. Skyler spotted Ivan in the distance, and ignored him and took Zarina out onto the dance floor for a waltz.

"You know Zarina, you look so lovely in that dress," Skyler said

"Thank you, I'm actually impressed with how well our outfits turned out. I'm having a wonderful time with you."

Skyler looked deep into her eyes. "Me too. I know we had a plan tonight but seeing you in this light, would you like to just skip the party after this dance? We made our appearance, and I do not see Nikolai around anywhere."

She leaned in and gave him a kiss. "Maybe after this next song, right now let's just enjoy these moments."

They danced for a few moments before breaking and walking to the side of the dance floor. They were going to leave the room when Justin came over to them. "Skyler, how are you doing tonight?"

"Uncle, thought you were just here for the one night?" Skyler asked.

"Me and Melanie decided to say an extra night. It worked out since Zarina and Melanie went shopping during the day." Justin commented.

Skyler raised an eyebrow at Zarina, "Is that what you did all day?"

Zarina smiled, "yes I did and your aunt is a lovely lady."

"Well, I'm glad that you to had fun." Skyler turned his focus back to his uncle. "I would love to talk, but me and Zarina were just about to head out."

Justin placed his hand on Skyler's shoulder. "Ah, young love. Well, it was nice seeing you again. Also, I know you are busy but please stay in touch when you can."

"I will do my best, thanks." Skyler patted his uncle on the back.

Skyler and Zarina bumped into Cane at the doorway. "Where are you two going?" Cane asked. "What about our plan?"

"Nikolai is not here so we were going to step out for a bit," Skyler responded.

"Really, he is not here?" Cane scanned the room, "That's unlike him. Okay, just be cautious out there."

Skyler nodded back to Cane and then took off down the hall. When he and Zarina were away from the ballroom, they kissed and fondled each other in the hall. "Do you want to just go back to the room?"

Zarina smirked, "No, I have a better spot that we can go, follow me." She took Skyler's hand and ran with him down the hall. After a few moments and a couple of turns Zarina took them to a room that looked like a boardroom.

"Oh, this room is nice, want to get on the table or under?" Skyler said, undoing his jacket.

Zarina giggled, "Not here, almost there." She went over to the wall and tapped on a panel and a hidden door opened up. She used her finger to signal to Skyler to follow. He followed her into the passage. In the passage there was one tube light that lit up the hall. Brick walls decorated with paintings of former Russian leaders, ones that were no longer shown on the public walls for they were things no one wanted to look at anymore, these going back centuries. Skyler slowed down to look at the paintings. Some of them were familiar to him and others were mysteries.

"Are you coming?" Zarina called to him.

Skyler looked away, "Yeah sure, why are all these paintings here? Some of these are neat and really old."

"Because many of the past leaders of the Russia are not well liked, but it's not my decision. But come on, we can look at artwork later."

Skyler took one last glance and the paintings before running back towards Zarina. At the end of the hall there was an alcove with a sectional couch. Zarina sat down on the couch. Skyler looked at the walls and the alcove. "What is this place? Seems weird to have a couch here."

Zarina shrugged, "I do not know who set it up like this, but my ex who showed this place called it the hall of reflection. These paintings from here are receding down the hall. With the current leader being here above the couch."

Skyler took a minute to feel the power and the weight and history of the hall. "Wow, this place is amazing, thank you for taking me here."

Zarina pulled Skyler down and kissed him. "Stay focused."

Skyler kissed her back and took off his jacket, "That would be my pleasure."

After they were done, Skyler sat up and began to put his clothes back on, when they heard talking through the walls. Skyler looked around. "Where is that coming from?"

Zarina pointed to a nearby door, "I think through that door. It sounds like Nikolai."

Skyler finished getting dressed and listened to the door. "He is talking to someone. Be quiet and come over here and listen with me."

Zarina got dressed and listened to the door and turned on the recorder on her arm band.

"The plan is going well," said Nikolai's voice. "I will soon have the boy on our side. Once on our side we can get into what he knows and hack the United Galactic Forces. I was close last night, but the boy is useless when he is drunk."

Zarina and Skyler stared at each other in shock and continued to listen.

"Also, with the new plan to return the bodies to the Cass, I want the orders to gather them and hold onto them. We can use these bodies as leverage and maybe negotiate for some land. We can colonize the Cass homeworld and make them Russian allies."

"Who is he talking to?" Skyler asked.

Zarina listened a bit closer, "I'm not sure. Who would the Russians be working with?"

Skyler listened to try and hear the voice of the person on the other side, but it was someone whose voice he didn't recognize. "No idea, but Cane might just know."

As the call ended, he heard Nikolai say, 'Supazarkania.' They heard footsteps come towards the door. Skyler and Zarina stood up and ran back towards the other door. When they got back to the main hallway Skyler stopped to catch his breath, "what was that?"

"I have no idea, but it wasn't good." Zarina said.

"I wonder if I go back to the room, can I get a history on who he called?"

"Don't go back, he will know we are listening. I will go back and check later," Zarina responded.

Skyler took a deep breath to process what he had just heard. "What do you think he meant by that word Supazarkania? Is that a Russian word? I have never heard it before."

Zarina shook her head, "It was not Russian, and I have no idea what that word was. Maybe Cane will know?"

"Let's head back to the ballroom and find Cane," Skyler said.

They tried not to make it look like they were rushing back. They went straight to Cane, avoiding all others. "Cane, do you have a moment to step aside?"

Cane paused talking to one of the other leaders and turned to Skyler. "Skyler, is this something that can wait?"

Zarina cut in, No, it's not."

Cane faced the leader again. "I'm sorry to interrupt, but I will need to cut our conversation short."

She nodded, "Not a problem, until next time." She bowed her head and left them.

Cane's focus was on Skyler and Zarina, "What is so important?"

"It's Nikolai. He is up to something we didn't think of. Can we go back to the room?" Skyler requested.

Cane nodded and followed them out of the ballroom. On the way back to the room Nikolai and Ivan greeted them in the hall. "Ah Cane and Therris, surprise to see you in the hall. Are you not enjoying the party?"

"The party is lovely, but official business takes us away. We will be no longer than needed," Cane responded.

Nikolai stared down at Skyler, "Is there any chance that I could borrow Therris for a moment."

Without saying anything, Skyler used his facial expressions to signal 'no' to Cane.

Cane shook his head. "Not right now, official business first. I will be sure to send Therris your way once we're done."

"I will be expecting him later," Nikolai grinned.

Skyler was nervous around him; Cane cut the conversation and went back to the room with Skyler and Zarina.

Once in the room, Cane looked at the two pale faces of Zarina and Skyler, "What is going on with you two?"

"Nikolai is working with someone to conquer the Cass," Skyler blurted out.

Cane frowned and looked at Zarina. "What is he trying to say?"

"We overheard Nikolai talking to someone we didn't see on a screen. Who but Nikolai wants to hold the Cass bodies hostage to negotiate for some of their planet?"

Cane took a seat at the dining table. He rubbed his forehead and shook it in confusion, "how could he do that? Who would agree to support them?"

"We didn't see, but I heard him use the word 'Supazarkania'—"

Cane cut Skyler off. "Supazarkania, he really said that?"

Skyler nodded, "Yeah what does it mean? Is it Russian?"

Cane shook his head, "No, it's not Russian, it's an old greeting used by the Senoch, but I didn't think they were still around. If they are still around, this changes many things."

Skyler scratched his head, "What are you talking about? Who are the Senoch?"

Cane buried his head in his hands for a moment then spoke, "Back in the first space war not the first Cass space war, this one is long before my time. There was a race of aliens known as the Senoch. They were said to be a very old race, and our technology was primitive back then so understanding them was difficult. I thought it was said that they all were wiped out during the war, but I have never met one in my life; there are only photos of them that remain. There are none on Earth."

"If they no longer exist, then how do you know their language?" Zarina asked.

"Because in Xenolinguistics they teach you about all of the alien languages of the past. We don't have recordings of them talking, but from what we believe, 'Supazarkania' means 'glory to the Empire' and they uses it commonly. But much more I don't know. I have no idea why they would be talking to the Russians or how they survived."

"Right, but what about the part of Russia using the bodies as leverage?" Zarina asked.

Cane took a deep breath. "I will talk to the other leaders and see if we can get something written in the agreement that we are not allowed to conquer or ask for anything else in exchange. If Russia doesn't agree, they can be removed from the United Galactic Forces. The ability to go to space is a united effort, not individual. Thank you for bringing this to my attention."

"So, what do we do till then?" Skyler asked.

Cane took a long moment to pause. "Nothing, now that I'm aware that there is some corruption, I will take care of it. You two act normal, like you never heard anything. Also, Skyler, you are not needed at the meeting in the morning tomorrow. You can do what you want. I would send you back early, but I figure you would want the time off. I only have one short meeting in the morning, so you can sleep in or something until four when our flight leaves."

Skyler looked over at Zarina. "Anything you would like to do tomorrow?"

She shrugged, "I think I can find something for us to do."

"Now that it is settled, let's head back to the party so it doesn't appear too suspicious that we are gone this long."

Chapter 52

Skyler woke up in his bed next to Zarina. He examined his surroundings and was relieved nothing happened to him in the night. He lay stretched out in the bed enjoying the peace. After a moment he rolled over and looked at the time on his tablet. It was 11 a.m. He nudged Zarina, but she was still sleeping. He got up and grabbed a beer from the fridge and made himself a quick sandwich. Since Zarina was asleep, he pulled out his tablet and began to call his friends one by one. Kax was the first to answer the phone. "Hey Kax, how are you doing?"

"Skyler, why are you calling me at 4 a.m.?"

Skyler laughed and scratched his head, "I'm sorry I didn't realize that it was so late. It is morning here."

"Well, I was up anyway, been busy with the new flight schedule they gave me. But the good thing is I have a better job posting."

"I'm so glad that you have a better job and are enjoying it. How are you dealing with Rex?" Skyler asked?

"I have gotten rid of Rex. I made a new friend. Their name is Orn and they gave me the courage to get rid of him forever." Kax said.

"They? What gender is your friend?" Skyler asked.

"They are an offworlder, from the Semple Colonies on Ceres. There's a non-binary culture, and Orn is awesome." Kax said.

"Interesting, well I'm glad that you have a new friend. Maybe when I get back, we can all find time to hang out sometime," Skyler said.

"I think that would be a good idea. I have missed hanging out with you," Kax replied.

"A return to some normalcy would be really nice for a change," Skyler said.

Skyler heard Zarina getting up. "How about when I get back, the first opening in time I have you, me and Michael and your new friend all will hang out? I promise."

Kax smiled. "Sounds like a plan."

They waved goodbye as the call was disconnected.

Zarina called from the bed, "How is Kax doing?"

Skyler turned around in his seat. "She is doing great. She has a new friend who she wants me to meet."

"I'm glad to hear that." Zarina got out of the bed. "Do you need time to pack?"

Skyler stood up and held up his bag. "Already packed."

Zarina started to get dressed. "All right then let's eat breakfast and get ready to go."

At the loading dock for the trip back home, Skyler gave Zarina one last hug before they headed to their own compartments for the trip. When he was about to follow Cane into the cabin, a Russian guard came up to him and tapped him on the shoulder. He jerked around and looked at the muscular 6'5" tall Russian guard and stared at him, dumbfounded.

"Mr. Therris, you are going to have to come with me, I cannot permit you to board this plane."

Cane stepped out. "What seems to be the matter here?"

The large man already had his hand on Skyler"s wrist. "Sir, please step back but I have direct orders from President Myshkin himself to take this boy into custody, don't get in my way."

"What did I do?" Skyler tried to free his wrist.

"My orders were to detain you." the man said.

"I knew leaving would be too easy." Cane grumbled to himself. He checked his watch before making a call directly to Nikolai. While they all waited for Nikolai to answer the call, he appeared on the loading dock in front of them, with the phone buzzing in his pocket. Cane hung up and glared at him. "What are you doing?"

"I am only protecting my country and I cannot allow this boy to leave," Nikolai said.

"What did I do?" Skyler asked.

"It appears that Skyler is in possession of Russian documents that cannot leave the country and his visa is expired. I cannot allow him to leave the country without further investigation." Nikolai said.

The security guard grabbed Skyler's bag and pulled out a thin red book with a heavily armed spacecraft on the cover. Skyler's eyes widened. "You planted that, anyone who knows me, knows I don't even read for leisure." Skyler pulled his Visa out of his pocket. "My visa cannot be expired, I just got it a month ago."

Nikolai took the visa from Skyler and placed it in his pocket. "What visa?"

"What do you want from Skyler?" Cane glared. "What are you trying to gain from keeping us here?"

Nikolai waved his hand, "Oh, you Leon can go. Skyler is the one who has to stay. I'm only doing what is best for the country. I cannot let every criminal just walk out of here."

"Look, I might be a lot of things but a criminal I'm not," Skyler shouted.

Nikolai moved closer to Skyler and stared him down. "Here I make the laws and you are whatever I say you are. You are not leaving this country unless I say so, and criminals like you would make a great addition to our Army."

Right then Skyler knew what this was about. It wasn't about what he had overheard and there was still a chance that Nikolai knew nothing about this. It was about the first night when he was asked to leave UGF and join the Russians. As much as Skyler's memory from that night was fuzzy, he was certain that he would not have agreed to join, because for him Cane was like a father and he would never betray him. "I'm sorry, but regardless of what you do to me I'm not joining. I made a contract with the United Galactic Forces and with Fleet Admiral Cane and I cannot just switch. Please let me go."

"You want me to just let you go?" Nikolai pondered for a moment, "You do know that the Russian Federation can further your career beyond anything that you had ever imagined?"

Skyler kept a firm stare. "No, money and power doesn't interest me. What interests me is something that you cannot offer or provide."

Nikolai took a long time staring back at Skyler. Then on the PA system they all heard, 'Last Call! Please board now!'

Cane cleared his throat. "I can't imagine what you want with this intern," he said. "Sometimes I don't even know what I want with him. But I am one of three Fleet Admirals of the United Galactic Forces, and ceasefire or not, we are in an active war. If that shuttle leaves and we are not on it—me *and* my apprentice—the entire planet we defend will want to know why. I don't think the Russian Federation needs that kind of trouble, and I know you don't."

Nikolai let out a sigh. "You have some powerful friends," he said to Skyler. "You may go. But watch yourself next time you ever want to enter Russia. You will not always be traveling in good company."

Cane went with Skyler into the cabin with no further ado. Once they were on the shuttle and were further along on the trip Skyler asked, "So is Russia now added to my list of places I'm not allowed to go to?"

Cane shook his head. "Not at all. Nikolai did the same thing to me on my first visit. Might even have been the same book. Under UGF, he cannot ban you from the country for special events. Leisure is the only time he has some control. When we get back though, please prepare for some intense work."

Chapter 53

Skyler awoke to the sound of his communicator ringing. He rolled over in the bed and grabbed it before it fully woke him up. "Hello?" He answered.

"Hey Skyler, I haven't heard from you in a month. I just wanted to know if everything is okay and you still wanted to hang out?"

Skyler sat up and scratched his head. "Kax, is that you? What time is it?"

"It's noon, I assumed you would be up. Is everything okay?" she asked.

Skyler looked at the time on his communicator. "Yeah—thing is fine. This was just my first day off in the last month that I guess my body needed the sleep. But I'm up now. I actually have the weekend off to make up for the lack of holidays I have been getting, so if you, Michael and your friend want to hang out, we can anytime."

"Tonight sounds great. I too need a day out to just be me again. The main reason I was calling."

"Well, if you ever need someone to show you a good time you know who to call." Skyler smirked.

"You're funny Skyler. I will see you tonight, usual place?"

"Is there any other bar on campus?" Skyler joked.

"I guess not, but I will call Michael and tell him the plan. See you later."

"Ya, see you then." Skyler ended the call and searched around the room. There was no sign of Zarina anywhere. *She must be out.* He got out of bed and reached into the fridge and grabbed out a beer.

It was the first time in a long time that he had a holiday. He wasn't quite sure what to do with his time. He sat back in his chair was busy checking his emails when Zarina entered the room.

"Hey sweetie, what's up? Want some beer?" He held up his beer to offer to her.

"Don't you have anything for breakfast besides beer?"

He shrugged. "It's a wheat beer."

She had a package of papers in her hand and sat down at the table across from him. "No, I don't want any beer, and we need to talk."

Skyler crinkled his face in confusion, "Okay, talk about what?"

She sighed and put the papers down, "Skyler, I'm pregnant."

He almost fell back in his chair, and with eyes wide he responded with, "What? How can this be?"

She sighed, "Don't worry, it probably isn't yours and I have known for a while but I was waiting to figure out what I was going to do."

"Wait, what do you mean that you knew for a while?"

"I had a feeling in January and was waiting for confirmation. That is why I do not think it is yours," she spoke.

"Okay I have been through this before, I'm not sure if you have but you kind of know, if the test and doctor say you are. I'm confused?"

She let out another sigh, "Not if the baby isn't human. I think the baby is Skwoampan. remember that guy I hooked up with during my trip to the moon? Because the tests were not clear on yes or no, and now that it has been about fourteen weeks things are starting to be clearer."

Skyler sat and pondered for a moment. "So, what did the doctor say? Is the baby green or not?"

"Well, that's the thing, the ultrasound doesn't show skin colour, and at first the baby was small and it was more like a definite Skwoampan, but now it is picking up in size. If this baby is a hybrid, then it could pick up any number of traits from either side. The reason I still doubt that it could be yours is if I count back the days, it seems to be during the weeks we were apart." She sat there looking down at her folded hands at the table.

Skyler took a look at the paperwork and ultrasound photos, "Have you told Groakie about this? And what would you like me to do with this information?"

"I was going to tell him tonight, now that I'm certain I'm pregnant. If you want to break up, that's fine, I understand, this isn't your responsibility."

Skyler shook his head. "This is my responsibility, you are my girlfriend and I'm committed to you and there is a slim chance that it is mine. I have been through this before, and I'm okay taking care of someone else's kids. As long as you are my girlfriend, I don't mind whatever shape our relationship and family need to take."

Her eyes widened, "Really you don't have to. I'm shocked that you are not mad."

"I was unwanted as a child. My Dad wanted me but after his death my mother had no interest in me. Due to the way I was treated, I refuse to let anyone else go through that. I don't care if I'm the father or not. I have been through this before so I have some experience."

"Really?" She raised her eyebrows, "Why would you raise someone else's kid? Why would you want to take responsibility for a child that is not yours?"

Skyler tapped his hands on the table. "Okay, I will start at the beginning. I do not want kids of my own, and do not care for them. But I do not want unwanted uncared-for children in the world. In high school me and my friend Paul were seeing a girl, Xandria, who got pregnant. I had no means of my own to take care of a child, but there was a chance it was mine. Why I helped her was because I cared about her, and wasn't going to be a jerk and leave her alone. If it was mine or something happened to Paul, I would have done whatever I could to not let her suffer alone. I do not know why, I just feel the need to be there. Maybe because almost every man in my family has done that for me, like Cane and my Uncle Justin. Also, I care about you and I would hate to find out that Groakie doesn't want to have anything to do with you, and on top of that deal with a break up. You are still my girlfriend, and while this situation isn't ideal, it is still my duty to take care of you. Does that make things clearer?"

Zarina stared at Skyler dumbfounded. "Wow, that's a lot. I never expected that. You always seem like the kind of guy who bangs them and leaves them."

"Oh, I am, but I go looking for the people who want that sort of thing. Also, like I said, I don't want kids, so why do I want a commitment?"

"That's understandable." Zarina sat there silently for a moment.

Skyler spoke up, "So when you tell Groakie about this tonight do you want me to be there or is this something you want to do on your own?"

Zarina paused to think about it, "I will tell him on my own. You go out and have fun with your friends."

"All right, but if you need me at all, please do not hesitate to contact me at any time in the night. Also, if you will still have me, you are welcome here and with me anytime." Skyler reached out and held her hand.

A tear came to Zarina's eyes. "Thank you Skyler, never in my wildest imagination could I have thought of someone as kind as you."

The night came and Skyler was keeping the booth warm while he waited for Michael and Kax to arrive. Michael showed up first, he got his drink at the bar and sat down next to Skyler, "Started drinking without me?" he joked.

Skyler fiddled with his glass. "Just the one, I don't want to get too drunk tonight, I might be needed later."

Michael frowned. "I thought you had the weekend off? Is Cane working you this hard?"

Skyler took a sip of his beer and shook his head. "No, Cane will not be calling, I might get a call from Zarina. I want to stay clear headed for her."

Michael raised an eyebrow, "What is up with her?"

Skyler saw Kax and her friend enter the bar. He waved them over and called out, "Over here!" He spoke to Michael, "I'll tell you all about it in a bit."

Kax and her friend came over. "Everyone, I would like to introduce you to Orn, we're in the CBD program together."

"You're kidding," Michael said.

"Cass Body Delivery," she clarified.

Michael held out his hand and shook Orn's hand. "Michael, and it is nice to formally meet you."

Skyler leaned over the table and shook hands. "Glad to meet you too, I'm sure Kax has told you all about me."

Orn spoke in a deep voice, "Kax did. Well, Kax has told me about both of you. I'm glad to finally meet you two."

Skyler smiled, "So Orn, where are you originally from?"

"Ceres, but I'm not an alien," they spoke. "My family came from Earth."

"But where on Earth? I'm from the Rochester area." Skyler asked.

"Oh, more specifically, Utah," Orn answered.

"Cool and like Kax you wanted to be a pilot too?"

"What's with all the questions? Yes, I'm in the pilot program, but I'm hoping to stay more on the ground crew and be air traffic personnel. I'm better with numbers than I am with navigating," they replied.

"Sorry, I didn't mean to offend, I just have never met you. I'm curious." Skyler responded.

"That makes sense, I was just wondering."

"Well, are there any questions that you wish to ask me?" Skyler asked.

"Skyler, stop flirting. I don't think Orn is interested," Kax butted in.

"What? I wasn't flirting," Skyler said.

"Kax, it is fine, he is just being friendly," Orn mentioned.

"Kax, while flirting is in my nature, I assure you I'm in no mood to flirt tonight. Also Orn is your new interesting friend. I know very little about them," Skyler said.

"I'm sorry Skyler, I misunderstood." Kax responded.

"Ya, that is all right nine times out of ten you would have been correct," Skyler said.

Michael butted into the conversation, "Is something up with you and Zarina? I noticed that she is not here and you're not your normal self."

,Skyler took the finishing sip of his beer. "Ya, it does have to do with her. She's pregnant and there is a 50/50 chance that it could be mine. She told me this morning."

Kax's jaw dropped, "What do you mean, could be you? Skyler, you're going to be a father?"

Skyler waved his hand down to signal her to be quiet. "Shhh, don't want the whole bar to know. We don't know if it's mine, she is talking to the other guy tonight and I'm waiting for her to call and tell me how it went. No need to freak out about it right now, and I will keep you all up to date. But for just right now, we are hanging out having fun like the old days."

Michael raised his glass, "You're right, let us have fun like the old times."

They all raised their glasses and said cheers.

Chapter 54

Late into the night, Skyler was more tired than he was drunk. He stayed out until the bar closed with his friends. Michael carried him home because he was too tired to walk straight. There was never a phone call from Zarina, and Skyler wondered if there would ever be a phone call. Michael helped Skyler into the bed.

"Skyler, I know you didn't want to let on if anything was wrong, but are you okay?"

Skyler flopped his head back into the pillow. "I don't know. Last time this happened I didn't know what to do. I went with what was the right thing, but I know nothing about babies or what an adult family needs. I live in a one-room barrack. How do you fit a baby in here?" Skyler covered his face.

Michael was looking for a nearby place to sit. "I get that, I wouldn't know where to start either. I'm sorry that this wasn't planned."

Skyler patted on the bed, "You can sit on the other side, I don't mind, no one is here."

Michael sat next to Skyler. "I know it is not my place, but if you need any help let me know."

"Michael, you're such a good friend, and I have no idea why. I'm often a jerk to you." Skyler said.

Michael let out a sigh, "Because maybe before I met you my life was boring and there was not much fun to live. I had little direction and meaning. In the short time that I have known you, I have gained a new sense of purpose in my life. You and Kax are my first two real friends ever." Michael looked over at Skyler who was fast asleep. "Knew it," Michael whispered to himself before he himself fell into a meditative trance.

In the morning Skyler woke up and checked his phone. There was no word from Zarina. He sat up and looked around the room, she wasn't there either. But he was startled to find Michael next to him. He shook Michael, "Hey buddy, get up. What are you doing here?"

Michael opened his eyes. "Hey, sorry buddy. I drifted off after you fell asleep. You weren't your usual drunk, but you were also tired so I helped you back to the room. We talked a bit before you fell asleep."

Skyler stretched and got up out of the bed. "Ya, I remember a little bit about that. Okay cool, so any word from Zarina?"

Michael shook his head. "I have not seen her."

Skyler checked his communicator again. "No messages, I hope that everything is okay with her."

Michael got up out of the bed, "I am going to assume that everything went well. If she is not here, I would assume that things are well and that she did not need you."

Skyler sighed, "Ya, I guess you are right."

Michael helped himself to a glass of water. "I would not worry. When she is ready, she will talk to you."

"Ya, I guess you're right."

"Since I am here, do you want me to make breakfast and stick around?" Michael offered, opening the fridge.

Skyler shrugged. "Sure, why not, you're here and we're both hungry."

Michael pulled a few ingredients out of the fridge, "I'm glad that Zarina keeps the fridge stocked."

Skyler got up and dressed, "What makes you think that I didn't get those groceries?"

Michael smirked, "I have lived with you, I know your grocery habits." He went on to make some pancakes. While they were sitting down and enjoying their food, Zarina opened the door.

"Michael, what are you doing here?" she asked.

Skyler answered, "Michael stayed the night and we were just having breakfast. How did things go?"

"Michael stayed the night?" She raised an eyebrow. "All right." she shrugged and sat down at the table with them. "I think I'm getting married," she said.

Skyler's jaw dropped, "Married wait, what about us? Are we breaking up?"

She grabbed a plate and a pancake. "I didn't say yes, but he went on about something about tradition and things, I didn't really pay attention too well. I think if the baby is his I have to go back to Skwoampan and have a ceremony or something about ancient slime goo." She began eating her pancakes.

Skyler pushed his plate away, "You didn't answer me, are we breaking up?"

She took in a deep breath and rubbed her forehead. "I don't know, Skyler! I am just as confused and upset by this as you are. I guess if it is his, then we are done. But right now, I have no way of proving it, when I do that answer will be quite clear."

Michael got up and started to get ready to leave the room.

Skyler stood up. "Well, prove it, because I will not be strung along."

"Skyer, you're free to do whatever or whoever you want. I never asked you to be a part of this."

"Dammit Zarina, I love you and would do anything for you. If only you understood that." He headed towards the door with Michael. "Contact me when you do, you don't have to move out."

Skyler left with Michael down the hall. He grabbed his hair and pulled tight, letting out a frustrated shout. "Argh! Why does she do this to me? Dammit, I love her and she just makes this baby thing, pushing me aside."

"You know when I got up, I was not saying follow, I just wanted to give you two space." Michael said.

"I know what you're doing, but it was a good cue for me to leave too." Skyler stopped at the end of the hall and hit his head against the concrete. "I loved her, Michael, and now I have to break up with her for something I didn't do?"

"Do not get me wrong, Skyler, but if I remember correctly, you are the one who said at the beginning it was casual and that you two were having fun. I thought you never wanted a wife or a child?"

"I don't want those things and it was casual back in September, but it's almost March and things have changed between us. I was actually beginning to let her in. We fit and worked so well." He let out a sigh. "Well I at least I thought we did."

Michael went over and put his hand on Skyler's back. "Come on, let us go get a few drinks and clear our minds. If you want you can stay with me and Kax."

Chapter 55

"Skyler, you're here early this morning. Enjoy your weekend off?" Cane said, unlocking his office.

Skyler yawned and followed Cane in. "I had a horrible weekend, I'm here early because Kax gave me a ride in. I'm staying back at the cabin."

"You know you're supposed to be staying on base because you're on call, right?" Cane turned on the light and sat down at his desk. "Did something happen?"

"Ya, Zarina got pregnant and is convinced that it is not mine and the other guy wants to marry her. So, it looks like I'm out of the picture," Skyler said, slumping into his seat.

Cane's jaw dropped when he heard the news. "Zarina's pregnant? Has she told her family? Who is the other guy?"

"Remember that green alien guy we picked up at the beginning of the year? He is the father. I have no idea if she has told anyone else. She told me first, apparently. She says she is trying to figure things out. I told her I would be there for her but she is just pushing me aside and with the other guy taking charge, I don't think that there is room for me. So, I'm single again, but I love her."

Cane pulled out a bottle of brandy and put it on the table, "I know it is early in the morning, but I think you need this. Your mother did the same thing to me, and I remember how I felt."

"I have been drinking most of the weekend. I'm going to try and be sober today, thank you. But wait, how? My parents were married when they had me." Skyler fiddled with his empty glass.

"You're right, she wasn't pregnant but I was dating her and she was dating your dad at the same time. I didn't know that was the other guy, and finally she said she was marrying him. And she did it again to me with Charles. I went away on a three-month tour and she married Charles while I was gone." Cane poured himself a drink.

Skyler rubbed his hand through his hair. "That's what happened? you got to be kidding me. I never knew it was that bad."

"Yup," he said and took a drink.

"So, what should I do about Zarina?" Skyler asked.

Cane leaned back in his chair. "Dump her and don't look back. I know that sounds harsh and you do like her, but you don't want her to string you along and continue to play with your heart when she doesn't want you."

Skyler slumped lower into his seat. "Great."

Chapter 56

Skyler was tired after the ride he got back to base. Cane had kept him on tight hours, but now that he was getting rides from Kax and Michael, he was restricted to their schedule on top of things. But he wasn't ready to go back to his room and face Zarina. He wasn't even sure if she was in the room. He left Michael in the parking garage, wanting to take a nap, but he didn't have the time. He was near Cane's office when he spotted Zarina outside the office. He tried to move away so that she did not see him, but it was too late. She must have been waiting for him. She saw him and rushed over to him. "Skyler, please. I want to talk to you."

Skyler tried to rush away from her, but his movements were slow from fatigue. "Zarina, what do you want?"

"Skyler, I'm sorry. I have been going through a confusing time and I still want to try and make things work."

Skyler stopped dead in his tracks. His eyes widened and he was fully alert. "What did you say? How can we be together? It's not mine and you're going to be with him?"

She tried to put her hand on his shoulder, but he shuddered away. "I haven't committed to Groakie yet and there is still a chance that the baby is yours. The ultrasound was inconclusive. Skyler, I feel so bad for what I did to you and I want to make it up to you."

Skyler remembered what Cane told him and his past experience. "I'll meet you for dinner tonight and we will talk then. but I need to get to work." He brushed her aside and went to the office.

Skyler didn't want to go to Cane's or work today after that. He knew if he told Cane about what happened he would self-medicate with alcohol, and while Skyler enjoyed drinking, he really needed to talk this out and drink after. He went to the door and checked down the hall to make sure that Zarina was gone. She was. He went to place his hand on the door and then pulled it away. He couldn't turn the knob. He ran, took a few steps away from the door before pulling out his communicator. He first called Michael. "Hey Michael, have you signed into work today?"

He could hear Michael groaning on the other line. "Skyler, I just checked in, what do you need?"

"I just ran into Zarina in the hall and I don't feel like facing the world right now," Skyler replied.

"Skyler, you're my best friend and I do care about you, but I don't think I can help you this time. I know nothing about women and relationships."

Skyler let out a deep sigh. "Ya, it was worth a try. Thanks, I will see you later."

"Thank you for calling, but I really don't know what to recommend."

"It's okay buddy, thanks." Skyler turned off the communicator. He needed a break but still didn't feel like facing Cane. He took a long moment with his hand on the doorknob of Cane's office, before removing his hand. He walked away from the door and down the hall. He kept on walking. He sent a message to Cane on his phone saying that he was unwell and couldn't make it in today.

Skyler went to the bar alone. He sat on a stool and drank his beer. His phone went off a few times but he couldn't bring himself to look, answer, or check his messages. He needed this time alone to think. By the time he was starting his third beer, a person came and sat down next to him.

"Hey, what are you doing here so early in the day?" The voice asked him.

Skyler lifted his head, "Orn, what are you doing here? Aren't you in the same pilot program as Kax?"

Orn waved to order a drink. "I am, but we have different shifts. I'm glad that I ran into you here."

"Oh, why is that?" Skyler asked.

"Because I kind of like, you know, wanted to have some one-on-one time to get to know you at some point," they spoke.

"Oh?" Skyler raised an eyebrow, "I thought that you were with Kax? And I'm afraid that I'm not that great of company today."

They put their hand on Skyler's back, "I'm only friends with Kax, not in a relationship or anything like that, and might I ask what is wrong?"

Skyler took a sip from his beer. "My girlfriend wants to meet and talk about her being pregnant with a baby that is probably not my baby and what this means for us going forward tonight."

"Wow that is heavy, I guess you care about her if you are worried so much," Orn said.

"I do, we were open and I remember talking to her about this guy but I don't think that this guy wants me around if the kid is his. I'm not a family person, but I will do what is right. I also don't do girlfriends and I think I started to care about her." He took a large sip of his beer.

"Wow, that is not what I was expecting to hear. Have you thought that maybe it is time to move on?" They placed their hand on Skyler's knee.

"I have, but there is still the chance that the kid is mine, so I can't walk away until that is dealt with, and oh so many things. I want to move past this and know which way things are going. It's just bringing up so many feelings."

"Have you thought of trying to move on? If you cannot get a DNA test right now, then why not wait until it can be confirmed before caring?"

"Because I care about Zarina and I thought for a moment maybe we could have a future. But maybe you are right, that I shouldn't worry and should move on."

They looked at Skyler. "I'm not trying to take advantage of you, but I like you and I didn't know that you would be in this situation."

"I understand, I don't know if Kax told you that I used to date her sister. I don't want to upset her if we were to hook up. But if you two are just friends..."

"You seem like you need a distraction and a way to clear your head. I won't tell Kax if you don't, and we won't have to worry about her. I assure you me and Kax are just friends."

Skyler took the last sip of his beer and stood up. "If you got a room, I could let off some steam and clear my mind."

"I got a place, but what happened to yours?" They stood up and walked with Skyler to the door.

"Zarina is living there. I don't know if she has moved out yet."

"Got it. I will stop asking questions."

Once In Orn's room, Orn kissed Skyler and pushed him onto the bed. Skyler took off his jacket and shirt. "Okay so we're jumping right into this, all right."

They got on the bed and kissed Skyler, "am I going too fast?"

"No, I think we are going at the right pace. I'm doing this and using this as my therapy and clearing my head," Skyler said, rubbing his hands over Orn's body.

Orn reached down and undid Skyler's belt. "Good, I'm glad. Then let's get started."

Chapter 57

Skyler waited in his room for Zarina to show up. He was pacing, planning out what he was going to say to her. He cared a lot for her and maybe even loved her, but there were still things that needed to be discussed.

The door opened and Zarina stepped in. "Hey Skyler, long time no see."

Skyler sat down at the table and looked directly at her. "Is the baby mine?"

She sat down at the table, "Wow, straight to the point. Short answer, I still don't know."

Skyler rolled his eyes, "Well then, we need to find out ASAP. I was looking up things and they can do a test very early on."

"Skyler, they cannot test an alien baby that early for paternity." She quickly covered her mouth.

"So, it isn't mine! Because I'm not an alien and you're not an alien and if this baby has alien DNA, then it is not mine." Skyler raised his voice. "We didn't even need to test for paternity. It sounds like we just needed to test for flippers."

"Skyler, I'm sorry, please don't hate me, I really like you, but I'm so confused."

Skyler took a deep breath. "I like you too, and I'm disappointed about how things are going. Did you know that I was planning at the end of the year to branch into a more diplomatic role in the Forces so that I could give you more of the life that you are used to? Zarina besides Kax, you are the only woman I have ever thought about settling down with, and the only woman I have lived with."

Tears began to roll down her face, "I know Skyler, and that's why I did it. That's why I took risks, I don't want to live the diplomatic life. I dated you because you were different, and fun. Skyler, I never wanted to break your heart, but I want you to follow your heart and be a captain. I want you to continue on your path and not to change because of me."

"Why didn't you tell me that? If you want, I won't continue and just be a captain, and you can be my captain's girl."

"Skyler, I don't want that either. I want out of the Forces and this lifestyle. I want my own destiny. I thought with dating you I would find that, but I didn't. I discovered that early on in the relationship, but I saw you needed someone so I stayed for a song as I could. I didn't think this would end this way, and I didn't expect to get pregnant. I wish I could be with you longer."

Skyler tugged on his hair. "I don't understand you. You played with my heart when you had no interest in being with me, and go and get pregnant by some other man in order to break up with me? A simple 'let's break up' would have sufficed."

"No, Skyler," she sobbed. "It's not like that. I have my own set of baggage and when I saw yours, I thought I could help. I liked you. Pregnancy was never a part of this plan. I never wanted to hurt you."

Skyler let out a long sigh, "I believe you, but what is next for you if this is the end?"

"Groakie wants to get married and take me back to his swamp planet and have more kids." She wiped the tears from her face, "All things I don't want to do in life and I'm trying to negotiate, but I guess I'm going to be trying this out for the next little bit."

"Your whole life has been bouncing from one place to another, hasn't it?" Skyler asked.

She paused for a moment, then answered, "Yeah, I think you're right. Maybe then this is fate pointing me in a new direction. To be fair this swamp planet is as far from the Forces that I can get, maybe I will fit into this life. If not, I'll bounce around again."

Skyler went over to Zarina and put his arm around her in a hug, "I wish you all the best and hope you find what you are looking for. I think it's going to be a while before I find it myself."

She looked up at Skyler with her large sad eyes, "Oh Skyler, you are much closer than me at finding it."

He gave her a kiss on the forehead. "I hope you're right."

Chapter 58

The next morning, Skyler went to Cane's office and received the reaction that he was expecting. Cane opened the door glaring at him and shot out, "Where were you yesterday?"

Skyler let out a big sigh, not making eye contact. "Zarina and I broke up," he mumbled.

Cane stepped aside letting Skyler in. "Oh, I see."

Skyler slumped down in his chair, "Not when I canceled, but we had made a plan to talk about it, and well, I just needed to be alone if that makes sense."

"It does, and I won't write you up for it." Cane made his way back to his chair.

Skyler lifted his head, staring at Cane, "I don't want to be a diplomat. I want to be a captain and that only."

"What makes you think you want to be a captain?" Cane leaned forward.

"This entire year, I have been learning how to be a diplomat and going to all these formal events. That's not me," Skyler said.

Cane let out a laugh. "Your Dad was the same way he passed up many promotions. But he still had to do a lot of the things we have done this year. I'm not teaching you to be a diplomat, this is just part of the training. But you did sign up for the full seven-year program and you only chose command training. You need to either have another division or be put to work for your next year."

"My plan was to graduate as a captain not to do small jobs, and work my way up. I figured if I stayed in school longer, I would gain that experience."

Cane chuckled. "Okay I see the plan I will do my best in getting you a few more beneficial skills in the hopes, but you will still not be a captain at graduation since that doesn't happen."

"I'll find a way, and I will be the best you have ever seen." Skyler leaned back in his chair with a large grin.

Chapter 59

Getting closer to the end of the school year Skyler was aching to finish his apprenticeship with Cane. He only had to do it till the end of August and it was now the middle of April. He could not wait to end. Cane had been giving more work, but his schedule was a bit lighter now that Zarina was gone, giving him more time to see Michael and Kax. Saturday night was here and he was going to party like the old times. He met up with Michael and Kax at the bar. He went down to the campus bar, and sitting there next to Kax was Orn. Skyler sat down next to Michael and groaned.

"I thought that you would be enjoying the time off Skyler?" Kax asked.

"Oh, I am, I'm just tired from all of it. But give me a beer or two and I will be back to normal." He grinned.

Kax put her arm around Orn and sat a little closer to each other.

Skyler raised an eyebrow. "When did this happen?" He pointed and shook his finger between the two.

"Skyler, we have been together for the last couple of months. I thought you knew that?" Kax said.

Skyler shook his head. "Right, I completely forgot sorry, too much work."

Michael spoke up, "I have news."

All eyes were on Michael. "You're the modest one, so this must be big news, then," Skyler said.

"I have a summer job at the Chinese base developing some new computer tech for the ships," Michael mentioned.

"What about your Dad, how is he doing?" Kax asked.

"He is doing better, and hoping to return to work someday. I found a good full-time nurse for him. But where I will be located is not far from the transporters so I will be able to pop back and forth when needed," Michael said.

"Do you know what type of computer program you will be working on?" Skyler asked.

"Something that will be of an interest to Kax. It is a new interface for the navigation systems on the ships to make it easier to navigate through the portals." Michael said.

"Wow, that sounds like a pretty important job." Kax said.

"I hope so. It is a large team and I am not quite sure what part of it I will be working on. But I am excited about this."

"That's great, Michael. I have a few more months with Cane. My contract is for the full year, so I will finish in time for September." Skyler mentioned.

"I'm still trying to get a different piloting job," said Kax. "I don't mind the one I have, but I would like to get a job on a deep space ship. The issue is that with the war going on, there aren't many exploration missions going on."

"So, it looks like I will be the last one still in school," Skyler said.

"Well technically I haven't graduated," Kax said, "and I'm just getting my hours in, but you are the youngest of us Skyler. Also, you want a very specific job. Don't worry, Skyler. I am sure that we will still find the time to all see each other."

Skyler finished off his beer, "I'm sure we will find a way to meet up, has anyone heard from Perry lately?"

"Yeah, he contacted me once to ask about how he could get some plants transported, but that was it." Kax said. "Have you not heard from him, is that why you're asking?"

Skyler shook his head, "No, I just haven't talked to him a little while. I wanted to know if anyone had any updates is all."

"I think he and Stellik are getting more serious," Michael commented. "The only reason I know is because a few weeks ago he called me and asked for Squallite dating advice."

Skyler laughed. "You are giving dating advice?"

Michael chuckled along, "I agree, and I don't think I was very helpful but it was nice to hear from him again."

"I'm glad that he is doing well is all," Skyler said.

They drank into the night and got caught up on the last few months and reconnected like the old friends they were. Skyler waited until they were getting ready to go, before he picked up a mate for the night.

Chapter 60

Skyler returned to Cane's office on Monday after a long relaxing weekend. He stepped into the office and saw Michael sitting at Cane's desk. "Michael, what are you doing here, and before me?"

Cane laughed. "I invited Michael here to talk about his summer position."

Skyler took his seat next to Michael. "What about it?"

Michael spoke. "We are trying to figure out if there is a way to hurry up my role in negotiations so that I will not need to interrupt my work this summer. Because it turns out my job is going to be long hours and more demanding than I thought when I signed up."

"Oh no, will you still be getting the holidays you need to look after your Dad?" Skyler asked.

"I will probably be away more than I would like, but I will figure it out." Michael said.

Skyler leaned forward in his seat. "Okay then, how can we help Michael out?"

"Well, I have arranged a meeting with the other higher-ups to talk and make sure our plan is working for now. And what the updates are. Then we can see if we need to meet again over the next few months. I think that we should be fine but it is good to have an update. Also, over the summer I'm sure some of the high-ranking officers will be away doing other jobs," Cane said. "But it is good to check and see how Michael's career is going as well and I think he is on a promising path."

"Thank you, sir." Michael said.

Cane typed in a few things on the computer. "I just got the first of the emails back, Admiral Judson will be away and not able to make most of the summer so if we do any meetings it would need to be remote. Well, that is good to know. I expect that the rest of the emails will be in by the end of the day."

"I'm sorry, Cane, but I thought that we had figured out that everything was fine and dealt with, it was only a matter of doing it now?" Skyler asked.

"You're right, but progress meetings are important to make sure that everything is going according to plan and schedule," Cane said.

The computer made a couple of more BINGs. Cane quickly scanned some of the emails. "Well that was faster than I thought I would get a response. But it looks like many would prefer distance, or are going to be busy. So, Michael, I think you will be fine." Cane typed in a few things. "Michael, I think you're good to go back to work. I will send you out with a note that I had made you late for your work. Thank you for coming by, keep me up to date on how the project this summer goes."

Michael stood up and lightly bowed to Cane. "Thank you for everything. I will see myself out."

"See you later, buddy." Skyler said.

"See you later, Skyler." Michael said then made his way out the door.

Skyler turned back around in his chair to face Cane. "So what is on the agenda this week?"

Cane finished typing things on the computer. "Well, that I need to talk to you about. It is then end of the main school year so we will start getting busy. This week we have got to make a three-day trip to Catillion to check on the pilot program and how the ships are doing. You will be able to see Perry because I also have to do my annual inspection on Fogg. Then we need to run back for the fall graduation. And the we got a few more trips after that. Not certain on some of the trips I'm trying to work out with Judson and Davis who gets what assignments, but I recommend keeping your passport handy."

"So, there won't be many free weekends for me, will there?" Skyler asked.

"Not on Earth, but there may be some free time on the trips. I thought you would be excited to see Perry," Cane said.

"Oh, I am. That will be great to see him. And as much as I like travelling, I'm just getting tired of all of this. I don't think this diplomatic life is for me," Skyler said.

Cane took a deep breath. "I knew this day would come. Skyler, I know this year was going to be hard for you and it is not really your thing. But we are almost done and then in the fall you can go back to a regular class schedule…"

"I know and we have been over this. I just want you to know that the diplomatic life is not for me. I think that is what is making this year a lot harder," Skyler said.

"That may be so, I haven't had many apprentices and you have encouraged me to take a couple of more, because I enjoy the company more than I thought I would. But is there anything that you would like me to do for you?"

"I don't have any requests, I'm just tired and don't want to be a diplomat is all," Skyler said.

"Before you leave this program, you will have the tools you need to be a diplomat or not, whatever your choice may be. Another good thing is your rank will go up greatly because of this, because almost no one will have the experience that you are getting here, and this is not commonly a program that a cadet takes. Commonly this is for officers who are trying for promotions and not cadets, but the rules are only for command division officers," Cane explained.

"I know, Cane, and I appreciate everything that you have done for me. I will probably notice the effects of this after I'm out back on my own. I really do appreciate this opportunity," Skyler said.

"I'm glad to hear. But if we are all good then we should be getting back to work. We have a lot to set up for," Cane said, typing in a few things into his computer.

Chapter 61

Once Skyler was done work, he quickly made his way back to his room. He had been so tired from working overtime for the week that he had forgotten to send a message to Perry to tell him that he was coming. Skyler sat down at his desk and attempted to call Perry. There was no answer. He tried a couple of times, no answer. He double checked the time to make sure he wasn't calling too late before he called Dr. Fogg directly.

Dr. Fogg answered the phone, "Skyler, why are you calling so much, can you not get the message that Perry and I are in the middle of some very important plant stuff? I would have ignored your call too, but part of my probation I have to answer all calls, just be glad you didn't interfere with the growing of one of my plants."

"I'm so sorry, Dr. Fogg, but I was trying to get in touch with Perry because I will be there tomorrow and I wanted to see him," Skyler said.

"We know. Cane already sent us a message me and Perry are working on finishing the plants for tomorrow so that you can have time to see him. But if I were you, I would just send an email to Perry next time would be a better option." Dr. Fogg said.

"Sorry sir. I will leave you be." Skyler said.

"You will." Dr. Fogg cut the call.

Skyler went over and laid down on his bed and thought about all the people that he needed to contact before he left. He thought about Kax and seeing if she needed anything, and Kandice to see if she needed anything and then Clyde came into his mind. Clyde had meant something to him over the summer, and in a way still did, but so much had changed over the last couple of months that he wasn't sure where to begin and how to talk. He was still getting over what Zarina had done to him; he wasn't sure he wanted to open up to another past relationship. He called Kax first and left a message for her, letting her know the update. Then he called Kandice. Kandice was more of a good friend now to him than a past lover. She was the sister of the woman he loved, and someone he felt he could open up to. He went back to his desk and called Kandice.

She answered. "Hey Skyler, long time no see. Calling for some long-distance fun?"

His face lit up with a large smile, "While I love that idea, I am calling because I'm coming into town for a couple of days and wanted to know if there was anything that you wanted?"

"Well, you are already coming. I wouldn't mind seeing you." She winked.

Skyler laughed. "I never get tired of hearing your voice but I'm not coming for that kind of trip."

"I know, our relationship has changed, and we don't do that anymore, it is just fun to flirt." She grinned. "So are you planning on contacting Clyde when you're in town? I feel he would like to see you."

"That was one of the reasons I called you because I know that you see him more than anyone else I know," Skyler said.

"That is true, we are good friends, but why are you not contacting him yourself? What is wrong? Did something happen between you? He hasn't said anything."

"Nothing happened between us, it is all me. I have been busy since I got back with all the things with Cane; so, we haven't really talked to each other, but then shortly after that you know I met Zarina, right?" Skyler said.

"Yeah, I remember Zarina, you two still together? I haven't heard much about her, but not much from you either."

"Well, we broke up, long story short she got pregnant—"

"You dumped her because you knocked her up? That's low and rude dude—"

"If you let me finish, it wasn't mine and we agreed it was best to split and, well, it was quite recently, and while I have been able to hook up those weren't people who meant anything to me. Clyde meant something to me like you, but that was me 8 months ago. I have changed and been through stuff. It won't be a long visit and I don't want to be a downer the entire time if you understand."

"I get that, but I think knowing this it would be good for you to see him then. He would understand. He's pretty understanding and grounded. That is one thing I love about older men." She smiled cutely at Skyler, "I think you two will have a great time together."

Skyler smiled, "Thank you, I will call him now and talk to him. Do you still need me to pick up for you here on Earth?"

She paused for a moment, "Not right now, I'm planning on coming back to Earth soon. I'm thinking of moving there, at least for a few months."

"Sounds cool, I will keep in touch till next time." Skyler and Kandice waved to each other before ending the call.

Skyler sat in silence thinking about things for a moment. It had been a long time since he had called Clyde or even sent him a quick message on updating him.

"Hey Skyler, how are you doing?" Clyde answered the call not wearing a shirt.

"Hey, comfy day at home?" Skyler asked.

"Yeah, a friend came down and he is staying here. But what have you been up to?"

"Oh, I was going to let you know that I was going to be in town for the next couple of days. I hope I am not interfering?" Skyler asked with a sinking feeling.

"Oh, Skyler, I would love to see you. Don't worry about my guest, if you want you can meet him. But it's been so long I would love to spend time with you." Clyde said.

"Thanks, I wasn't worried about him, I would understand if you were serious. The only thing that I am not sure about is what kind of mood I will be in."

"What is going on? Busy?" Clyde asked.

"I just got out of a big relationship with a girl who got pregnant by some other guy and I have been a bit down and still to fully back so I'm not sure how much I will be in the mood to do." Skyler looked down at his desk, looking at all the things that were there.

"Wow, that is rough. Well, hey I would like to see you no matter what you are in the mood for. You're a friend, Skyler, no matter what shape that takes." Clyde kindly smiled at him.

"Thanks buddy. I will let you know when I am in town, so watch for the texts." Skyler smiled.

"Will do. It's late over there so I will let you sleep," Clyde said. "We can spend your visit catching up."

"Sounds good to me, see you soon." The two waved at each other before cutting the call. After the call Skyler proceeded to remove the rest of his clothes and grab a beer from the fridge. He laid down on the bed and all he could think of was Zarina. She would sleep next to him in this bed. Even though she had moved out she never left this place. Skyler continued to drink and tried to distract himself from thoughts of Zarina so he could sleep.

Chapter 62

"Skyler, we are almost at Dr. Fogg's greenhouse. I need to talk to him privately for a couple of hours so I need you to take perry out for a bit. Fogg is unaware of this so don't worry about the plants. Because Fogg's stuff is all legal stuff, it is only for the eyes and ears of the parties involved in the case. Perry will have his time but it is earlier today, so your job is to take him out," Cane said.

Skyler was looking out the window daydreaming, remembering the last time he was here all the memories of staying on Catillion for the last year.

"Skyler, are you listening to me? This information is important." Cane asked.

Skyler looked away from the window. "I'm listening. It will be nice to see Perry again. I have a few friends I would like to see during the trip."

"You will have a bit of time. This is mostly a legal matter but there will be a small amount of work so you will have more free time, stay nearby but you can do whatever until called to work." Cane explained.

"I got it, and if you don't mind, I will probably be staying at Clyde's when I am there," Skyler mentioned.

Cane took a moment to think about who Clyde was, then responded, "All right. I will keep that in mind." Cane continued to brief Skyler about the mission but Skyler was only half paying attention.

They landed the ship and quickly made their way to the greenhouse. They entered the greenhouse and Perry was pruning some plants. Cane waved to Perry and knocked on Dr. Fogg's door before entering. Skyler went over to Perry, "Hey buddy, long time no see. I think I'm supposed to take you out."

Perry snickered, "Only if you're paying. But it is great to see you again." He put down his clippers and gave Skyler a hug. "I missed you, dude."

Skyler hugged him back. Then the voice of Dr. Fogg came over the intercom. "Time for you two to leave."

Skyler and Perry broke the hug and made their way out. Perry locked the door of the greenhouse before leaving. "So have you eaten? Because I could," Perry said.

Skyler walked with Perry down the hall, "I could eat. But tell me more about how you are doing?"

They walked down the hall to the campus bar. "Been busy. Still dating Stellik, been too busy to worry about anything. I have stayed in touch with Kandice. She is a good friend to talk to, sad she is moving to Earth but I don't have time to really hang out with people."

"Yeah, Cane has had me so busy this year. I am lucky if I get the weekend off, but it sounds like I have had more free time than you this year." Skyler said as they made it down the hall to the cafeteria.

"That may be true, but I have gotten to go on many trips this year. They might have been simple like go here and there picking up a pack of seed or a plant and bringing it back. If Fogg lets me, I will show you some of the new plants we have. The greenhouse has grown so much." Perry got in line for the cafeteria food.

"It's weird. When we were roommates I couldn't stand your plant talk, but after this time apart I missed it." Skyler grabbed a tray off the rack and continued walking through the line with Perry.

"Thanks buddy, that means a lot to me." Perry walked through and placed a few food items on his tray. Once they had gotten their food, they sat down at the table together. "So how long do you think we need to stay out?"

"You tired of me already?" Skyler laughed and checked his communicator for messages. "I think we are out until Dr. Fogg calls you back. Do you think that you will continue doing this for the next year?"

Perry finished his bite of food. "Yeah, I love working here. If they let me stay it is a great gig."

"Well, I'm glad that you have found your thing and are enjoying it." Skyler said, finishing his sandwich.

"Well, you know how much I love plants." Perry cleared his tray. "My guess is that you don't have anything planned. Want to go do something like make our way to the city and hang out like old times?"

"If we have a ride, that would be great." Skyler said, clearing his tray.

"Oh yeah, we do. I have a car—well, a van. Well, it is a Forces van, but I have access to it for anything I need. It is mostly for making plant pickups and drop offs with the plants but I can still use it."

"Sounds like an awful boring van, but if it gets us there let's go out."

Chapter 63

It was close to eleven o'clock at night. Skyler was tired but he got a ride from Perry to Clyde's place. He buzzed into the tall building and then took the elevation tube up to the suite. He knocked on the condo door and Clyde quickly answered.

"Hey Skyler, long time no see." As soon as Clyde finished his sentence Skyler reached forward and gave him a large kiss and pushed him into the room.

Clyde took the hint and took them up the stairs and up to the bedroom.

A while later after Skyler had a small nap he woke up to a wide-awake Clyde in the bed.

"Ah, you're awake. How are you doing, sleepy head? I must say I wasn't expecting that so fast." Clyde said.

Skyler sat up in the bed. "This was not the plan. I guess I missed you more than I thought I did. I didn't plan to nap either, but I had a long day hanging out with Perry."

"Hey, no worries, like I told you in our call, whatever you feel comfortable with, I'm not going to pressure you to do anything you don't want to. But I did miss you too," Clyde said, putting his arm around Skyler. "I should let you know that Shane is still here and downstairs. He is staying a couple of more days, if that bothers you, we can figure out some kind of arrangement. I told him a little about the situation and he is flexible and understanding."

Skyler brushed his hair back with his hands, "Oh man, Shane is still here? I didn't think of that. He probably thinks I'm so rude taking you away like that."

Clyde laughed and rubbed Skyler's shoulder, "He was out when you showed up, and when you were sleeping sent me a message he was back. If you want to go and talk to him, we can go downstairs and meet him. He also is in the Forces, you two have that in common."

Skyler stretched and adjusted himself more. "Why not? It would be interesting." Skyler and Clyde got out of the bed and dressed themselves and made their way downstairs.

Shane was sitting at the kitchen island enjoying a snack. Skyler saw the furry black northern Catillion. For being a northern Catillion, he was slimmer than Clyde, who was more muscular. He had more patches of fur and darker skin. He turned around in his seat and it was clear that the hair on his head was cut short and he had amber cat eyes.

As Skyler and Clyde walked down the hall they waved to Shane. "Hey Shane, we're up and this is Skyler." Clyde introduced them.

Skyler waved to Shane. "Hey, I'm Skyler, and it's nice to meet you. Clyde tells me that you are in the Forces?"

He got off his stool and shook Skyler's hand, "Yes, I am in the medical department. Well, the medical sciences. My job is to study medical practices from other worlds and figure out which ones are suitable for adding to the practices of the Forces doctors, and if there is anything that can be cross-used. Who knows what medical technology can and cannot help a species from another planet? But enough about my work, tell me about you. I could go on about my work all day."

Skyler laughed. "It's okay, I used to have a roommate who was a botanist. I know how passionate people can be about things. My goal is to be a captain. Running and managing a ship is my dream and going on adventures to new places."

"Clyde mentioned that. Your father was a captain, if I am correct?" He mentioned.

"He was, and taught me a lot about it from his journals," Skyler said proudly.

"Well, that is great. If you ever get a job posting for a galaxy class ship, look me up, because most of my time is spent in a lab and not really working hands-on with clients and I really enjoy that. I'm a people person and I like trying out and practicing techniques rather than running experiments."

"I will keep that in mind. I still have some time before I graduate," Skyler said.

Clyde cut in, "I see, Shane, you have a snack, but Skyler, do you want anything? If you want, we can all sit down and chat on the couch or something." He made his way to the fridge.

Skyler went over the couch, "Ya. if you have stuff for a ham sandwich or something like that."

"Got it." Clyde began making sandwiches.

Shane stood up and took his empty plate over to the dish clearer and ran it under and then placed his plate away in the cupboard. When done, he went and sat next to Skyler on the couch. A short time later, Clyde came over with the sandwiches. Shane looked between Skyler and Clyde, "Since it is late, before we get too tired, what is the sleeping arrangement going to look like?"

"I think I might have another busy day tomorrow, but Clyde has a big enough bed I don't mind if we all share," Skyler said.

Clyde raised an eyebrow. "Skyler, are you sure? I do have an automatic pull out that is no effort or pull out. We don't have to all share a bed if you're not comfortable."

Skyler grabbed a sandwich and shook his head. "no, I have no issue."

Shane stayed up with them a bit more and they talked into the night. Finally, he said, "I have to go to bed, you two can stay up if you want."

Clyde looked over at Skyler, "I know you had a nap, but..."

Skyler let out a yawn, "Ya, I could sleep."

The three men got up and went upstairs to the bedroom, shared a bed and slept peacefully in the night.

Shane left early in the morning for work. Skyler got up and made a couple of calls to Cane and Perry. Today was Perry's day in the hearings so he was going to be busy until the evening. Skyler made himself a sandwich and sat at the island. Clyde got up and joined Skyler downstairs. "Nothing planned today?" He asked Skyler.

Skyler put his sandwich down, "I will go out and see Perry in the evening. But not on that day."

Clyde sat down next to Skyler, "cool, so we can hang out for the day, I was wondering when we were going to get some alone time to just talk."

Skyler frowned. "Oh is there something you wanted to talk about?"

"Yeah, I wanted to talk about you. What's going on? When we talked before your visit you weren't sure you were ready to open up again and were nervous about seeing me and then you jump into bed with me? No complaints, I just want to know what is going on in your head?"

Skyler put his sandwich down and took a deep breath, "Well, that's the thing. I'm not quite sure. I didn't think I was ready, but then when I saw you so many old and unfinished feelings came back and I missed you. But my head has been all screwed up since Zarina. I don't do relationships well, not committed ones, and I wasn't ready to end this one. I was ready to make it more serious and she did this. It's not like she cheated because we agreed, but she..."

"Betrayal is the word you're looking for. You agreed to be with other people but not start a family with them. You feel betrayed, even if it was an accident." He placed his hand on Skyler's shoulder. "It's okay to be hurt and upset."

"Ya, I just don't know what to do. There is a part of me who was excited to settle down and have a family and maybe a more political desk job in the Forces." Skyler stared down at his sandwich.

"Stop right there. Now you are getting off track. What happened to the Skyler who is going to be a captain? Who wanted to explore space and never settle down and just be a free spirit?"

"I can have a family and still be a captain. I will take them with me."

"Okay, but you don't have a job yet, and if the wife you take is in the forces, who knows if she will be posted to the same ship? I might not be in the Forces but I have known a lot who are. Skyler, you're 23 and don't even know where you are going in your career and you want to add a family to the mix? I'm not saying don't do it, but I think she was dragging you away from your goal. Skyler, I know this sounds harsh but in the next couple of years you are going to define your career. It is not the time to pick up a family."

Skyler got off his stool and went over to the couch and sat with his feet on the couch, "I have had this happen before to me. This is the second time in my life I have been so close to having a family with a woman that I cared about. It is not from being reckless, it is from being the one who is careful. I have lost two people I have cared for. Xandria it was fine. I was in high school and it didn't make sense back then, but now I'm older and a bit more ready."

Clyde got up and sat next to Skyler on the couch, "So you don't want kids, but you want a family?"

Skyler let out a deep sigh, "you're right, I don't want this responsibility, but I will do the right thing and I'm trying. I also care about these people. I don't know what to do. I don't have any skills in the dating world. The women usually told me what to do. My whole life women have told me what to do from my mother, to my first girlfriend, and even Zarina."

Clyde gave Skyler a hug, "That's the breakthrough we were looking for. I'm not going to tell you what to do, but what I am going to tell you is do what you want to do and not listen to anyone. Which is kind of funny since I'm the one telling you not to listen to anyone but yourself. But Skyler, you need to be you. It isn't bad to ask for help when you are confused. Skyler, I care about you and you are a close friend."

Skyler cuddled up to Clyde. "the worst part is I think I loved her and I got too attached to her."

"She really did a number on you. Skyler, it's going to take some time but I think she might have had too much of a hold on you. Maybe she realized it too. You need to take some time and remember who you are. Refocus on your goals to be a captain and win Kax's heart."

Skyler laughed, "Ya, I like Kax but I don't know if we will ever end up together. She was engaged this year, and seems to be certain that nothing is going to happen between us. But she is a good friend and we still talk often. So, I guess I buried myself with Zarina because I needed to break myself away from Kax."

"I really should get my training to be a certified counsellor." Clyde mumbled to himself. "Skyler, I am so glad that we are getting to the bottom of things, but I think you really need to take the time and see a real therapist. There should be a few in the Forces for people."

Skyler sat up and paused to think for a moment. "Therapy? I never thought about that. I have never really known anyone who has done therapy. I will talk to Cane about booking me up with one. Because I always just latched onto other people to solve my issues."

"I think that would be a good idea, also if you're in therapy you cannot be in a relationship with them, so even though Zarina was helping you, she was too physically attached."

"How do you know so much about this, Clyde?" Skyler asked.

"Skyler, I'm a social worker here, remember? I am a general family counsellor. Mostly I visit families who have issues and assess them, finding what type of help they need."

"I'm sorry, I guess I never paid attention to your job." Skyler rubbed his neck.

"It's fine, we never really talk about our personal lives. But I think Kandice hooked us up to help each other, not just for fun."

Chapter 64

The trip was almost over. Skyler was hanging out with Perry one last time before he had to meet Cane at the shuttle. Skyler was sitting in the cafeteria picking at his food.

"Is there something wrong Skyler? you don't seem like yourself." Perry asked.

Skyler let out a deep sigh. "Do you like your job? Being an apprentice?"

"I love it and think it is the greatest thing ever. Why do you ask?"

"How is it that you love being an apprentice and I cannot stand it?" Skyler asked.

"Well, one thing is that I love working with plants and I would enjoy just about any job with plants because it is my passion. I'm not certain about a lot of your work, but I do know you want to be a captain and you like to be in charge. So following orders in a department that you're not really a fan of is probably a lot harder," Perry said.

Skyler took a small bite of his food, "Ya, I got a few months left and I do not think that I am going to make it. I enjoy having personal time with Cane but this job is not for me."

"Well, maybe some things will happen and it will get better." Perry gave Skyler a small smile. "I wish I could help you more."

"Well, I will say one thing, these past three days have helped me a lot."

On the shuttle home, Skyler was trying to rest by laying down on the couch spread out. Cane came over and sat on the couch across from him. "So, how was your visit?"

Skyler rolled to turn towards Cane. "It was a good trip. I needed it, but there is something that I need to talk to you about."

"Oh, what would that be?"

"I think I am in need of a mental break; I made a mistake with dating Zarina and maybe taking this job. And I need some professional help," Skyler said.

Cane leaned back and rubbed his hand through his hair. "I knew this would happen. As you know, you are under contract so I cannot let you go, but I can get you a counsellor and see what they recommend for you. I'm not good with relationships so I cannot give you advice on it, but it is looking to me like this one has made it harder for you. I don't think this work is too hard, I think it may be a bit advanced. I will do my best to try and find you a program suited to your desired work. I'm sorry it didn't work out between you and Zarina, and I think talking to someone will help. I think I would have been better off if I had talked to someone earlier in my life. I would probably not be so screwed up. Now for me I'm too far gone, many of the things that I have issues with I cannot talk about. I don't want you to end up like me, I want better for you."

Skyler sat up. "What kind of things can you not talk about? I mean what does that even mean?"

Cane took a deep breath then lifted his eyepatch. Instead of a hole for where an eye should be, there was a large scar and it was covered over with pink and white scar tissue. "Did you ever read in your Dad's journals about my eye?"

Skyler stared in shock, never having seen the eye. "Not really. I know it was his decision to give up your eye, and that it was the only choice."

"It was, sort of. We were trapped on a planetoid that we didn't know was occupied by the Cass. It was back in the days when the High Emperor traveled more and he was there. We interpreted a ceremony which we had no way of knowing and they captured us. We saw rituals that outsiders were not supposed to see they were going to kill us. The High Emperor came over and talked to us and gave your father an option, that was to let us die or to take my eye for some reason. Your father let them take my eye. I don't understand why but they took me to a room, held me down and the High Emperor used his long claws and ripped my eye out. I don't know what the full purpose was, but I know that I have nightmares. I thought for a long time they were due to trauma, but I would see things I had never seen—and if you remember the meeting, we had the High Emperor asked me if I still had nightmares. They did something to me and know it. And he kept the eye and, I don't know why, but I will tell you I have seen things so unpleasant. I wear the eyepatch to cover the scar, but what I see and what I saw that day I cannot talk about and I don't know if I will ever recover. It sounds like a jerk move of your Dad to just give them permission without my consent but it saved the crew's life, so I would rather everyone live then have both eyes. I will deal with it." He put the eye patch back down.

"Wow, that's insane. I had no idea. Do you know why they did it?"

"Only thing I can think of is they wanted me to see something, but I don't understand how. I'm still being light on the details of what I see, and that is only one of the many things I cannot talk about." Cane let out a sigh. "I will put in an order for you to get some mental health care for when we get back to Earth. It is always good to get some care now and then."

Chapter 65

A month had passed since they had come back to Earth. Skyler was finishing up his counselling session before he returned to Cane's office. He got back to Cane's office and sat down. Cane was typing away at his computer and looked up. "So how did today's session go?"

"Well, I will say that it is nice to talk to someone about a lot of things. It was only the second session, but I'm enjoying it." Skyler said, pulling out his tablet.

"Good to hear, is there anything that she suggests that you should work on?" Cane asked.

"Ya, I was going to talk about that. She thinks I need to take some time off and get away from the Forces for the summer."

Cane sighed, "She knows that type of program you are in, right? And that it isn't so simple?"

Skyler rubbed his hair back. "Ya, she does, and that's why she thinks it is more important that I get away for a bit."

Cane typed in a few things. "I figured that something would like that would come up and be unavoidable. So, I have made some arrangements for the summer schedule to be adjusted and to go on a retreat for most of the summer. You will still be working, but the environment will be better suited to helping your mental health. It also might be good for mine as well."

Skyler raised an eyebrow, "What about our original schedule?"

"Since I don't think anything major will be happening around the summer based on the location of some of the other officers, I traded a couple of jobs with Fleet Admiral Judson so we should be able to get away. Also, I looked into if you did for some reason really need to break your contract, you could take a leave and it would put things on pause and you would finish your hours when you returned. There is no way out, but it can be put on pause."

Skyler took a moment to think about things. "I don't want to throw my program off for the fall, so I need to get these hours and now."

"All right, in that case we will finish up today's work and you will have the weekend off and we will travel Monday to the retreat." Cane said.

"Monday, that is soon. All right I will make that work."

Skyler was finished work for the day and was heading out to go hang with Michael and Kax before his big trip. He was walking down the hall when he saw a triggering face. A largely pregnant Zarina was walking towards him. He scanned around, trying to find a way to hide from her but it was no use, she got to him before he could turn out of the hall.

"Skyler, I need to talk to you." she abruptly said.

Skyler groaned, "All right, what do you want from me?"

She handed him a card. "That's the date I'm scheduled to give birth. Because it is an alien baby, they need to induce. I thought maybe you would like to be there."

Skyler's heart filled with rage, then he paused and thought about how she worded it. She wasn't asking him, she was requesting him to be at her side. He wasn't going to say anything negative to her. He took the card and replied, "Thanks for the card, I will see what I can do." And without ending the conversation he turned and walked away.

As he turned, Zarina said, "I'm leaving at the end of the month and won't be around, I wish you all the best." He turned and walked away, not knowing if she said anything else. He checked the time on his watch, to see if he had time to make it to his room before he was supposed to meet his friends. There was a small window, but he could use the time to get changed and decompress. He rushed back to his room and flopped down on the bed, trying to get Zarina out of his mind—trying to break free of the hold on him. He lay there with his face in his pillow, screaming in frustration, when he heard his communicator ringing. He got off the bed and went over to the computer. It was a call from Paul. He accepted the call and sat down in his chair.

"Hey Skyler, how are you doing?" Paul said in a cheerful voice.

Skyler tried to put on a smile, "It has been rough since I saw you. Zarina and I broke up and she is pregnant with someone else's child and well since then I have been in a bad headspace, but I am getting therapy though."

"Wow that sounds like a lot, dude. I was calling you to tell you good news." Paul paused, "Do you still want me to tell you?"

"Ya, please tell me. I need some good news in my life, as long as you don't mind me getting changed while you talk, I'm supposed to be going out soon." Skyler got up out of the chair.

"You have nothing I haven't seen, so go ahead." Paul said. "As for my good news, I just got back from the moon. The therapy you suggested worked and the trip was great. I really enjoyed it. Thank you so much, it was the holiday me and Xandria needed."

Skyler took off his shirt and put on a casual black shirt. "That is so great, I am so happy for you two. I'm glad it worked out."

"Also, we think Xandria is pregnant with kid number four." Paul smiled.

Skyler's eyes widened, "Four? Seriously? Why so many in such a short time?"

"I will admit that four is a lot to have in six years, but we wanted to have all our kids right away and then they can grow up together and be out of the house sooner." Paul smiled.

Skyler laughed, "Okay, well, hey, that is the life you chose, and I'm happy for you. Question: why do you think it didn't bother me in high school when Xandria got pregnant and it does now with Zarina?"

Paul shrugged. "Not sure, but I can assume that it has to do when we were in high school, we were both kind of goofing around and it was nothing serious. I didn't get serious with Xandria until Logan was born. You and Zarina were in a relationship and were taking things a lot more serious, and you were a little more open to settling down. Back in high school you did the right thing, but you were still not that attached. I'm sorry it didn't work out."

Skyler quickly changed his pants. "That makes a lot of sense. Also, Xandria was dating us. She persuaded us and kind of chose which one she wanted. Zarina persuades me but I insisted on the relationship. I guess I'm not ready for a serious relationship."

"Skyler, don't say that, I think you just have different priorities, but don't give up, you will find the right person one day but no need to rush."

Skyler adjusted his belt and fixed his hair. "I'll keep that in mind. Thank you. I wish you all the best, and if you ever want to go on another trip, let me know. I can help pitch in."

"Dude, you have done too much for us as it is, no need to do more. But if you ever want to visit, the door is always open."

"You have no idea how much you do for me." Skyler checked the clock. "Thank you for calling but I need to get going."

"Yeah, you go have fun. You put me in a good mood and I hope that I cheered you up and you can go out and have a good time out," Paul said.

Skyler leaned over the computer, "You did and thank you. Have a great day." They waved to each other before Skyler cut the call. Now that he was in a better mood, he was ready to go out with Michael and Kax.

He made his way to the campus pub. When he got there Michael and Kax were already sitting down. He went over and sat down next to Michael.

"Hey Skyler, what took you so long? You are normally the first one here," Kax asked jokingly.

Skyler waved to the waitress to bring him over a beer. "As I was getting changed, I got a phone call so I had to answer, but all is well and I'm here now. So let the good times roll."

The friends drank into the night later than any of them should have stayed out. Skyler noticed his watch and saw the time. "Gosh, it is getting late and I haven't even told you about my summer plans. Or heard if Kax has any official ones."

Kax let out a sigh, "Well, I got a job posting for the summer and I will be with the CBD program all summer, but it is not the posting that I wanted. I was up for a six-month placement on a galaxy class ship, but instead I got the four-month placement on a cargo ship. So, on one hand I get real ship experience, but on the other it's a cargo ship so back and forth. It is better than nothing, but still not my dream job."

"Give it time, Kax you will find the right job. And I was wondering where Orn was, I thought maybe you two had broken up or something?" Skyler mentioned.

"Not broken up, but I'm not sure how serious we are. I think this might be a relationship that will run its course, because we are more friends than anything."

Skyler debated about telling Kax about the night he spent with Orn, but Michael cut in, "So what is your big news, Skyler?"

Skyler regained focus and smiled, "I'm going to Droftebon for the summer. Cane has figured that I have been working too hard so we are going on a stress releasing retreat and I can still complete my contract."

Michael raised an eyebrow, "You are going to Droftebon for the summer? Really, I thought you were not the therapy type. What happened to drinking and sleeping your problems away?"

Kax laughed. "Sorry for laughing, but Michael does have a point."

Skyler leaned back, acting all cool, not letting on the real reason for the therapy. "Those things are staying and I think it is great. This is only because I have been working too hard. It's good to get away."

"Well, I'm happy for you and I'm glad that you are getting some help. I think it is a smart move, and we could all use a little bit of therapy. I think it is the only way any officer could stay sane," Kax said.

"Well, thank you, Kax, do I get a reward for self-improvement?" Skyler winked at Kax.

Kax laughed, "Okay, some things are going to take longer to fix with you than others. The answer is no."

Skyler laughed, "Aw well, better luck next time."

Michael let out a yawn, "As much as this was great, it is late and if I am going to get any rest before work, me and Kax have to take off now."

Kax checked the time on her communicator, "He is right. Let's try and meet one more time before we go away for the summer."

They all stood up out of the booth and hugged. "Let's try," Skyler said.

Chapter 66

The time was here. It was hours before Skyler and Cane were to head to Drofte-bon for the summer. He was packing his bag, excited to say goodbye to his barrack and not having to worry about coming back. This room had too many memories of Zarina and he didn't want to deal with them anymore. He knew that today was the day she was also supposed to go into labour. He had the time and he knew he could have gone if he wanted to, but he was done with her. If he was ever going to get over her, he had to cut the communication and move on with his life. There would be more people in his life, and some would be painful, and some would be happy, but all it meant was that Zarina wasn't for him. He was uncertain where his life was going, but the one thing that he was certain of was that his life was going forward and this was just the first step into the next chapter of his life.

Books by Kay Hawkins

www.ingramcontent.com/pod-product-compliance
Lightning Source LLC
Chambersburg PA
CBHW020216260626
47156CB00002B/411